LAND
RITES

ALSO BY ANDY MASLEN

Detective Ford:

Shallow Ground

DI Stella Cole:

Hit and Run
Hit Back Harder
Hit and Done
Let the Bones Be Charred
Weep, Willow, Weep
A Beautiful Breed of Evil

Gabriel Wolfe Thrillers:

Trigger Point
Reversal of Fortune
Blind Impact
Condor
First Casualty
Fury
Rattlesnake
Minefield
No Further
Torpedo
Three Kingdoms
Ivory Nation
Crooked Shadow

Other Fiction:

Blood Loss – A Vampire Story

LAND RITES

A DETECTIVE FORD THRILLER

ANDY MASLEN

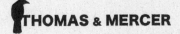

Text copyright © 2021 by Andy Maslen

Published by Thomas & Mercer, Seattle

www.apub.com

Amazon, the Amazon logo, and Thomas & Mercer are trademarks of Amazon.com, Inc., or its affiliates.

ISBN-13: 9781542021005
ISBN-10: 1542021006

Cover design by Dominic Forbes

Printed in the United States of America

To my family – Jo, Rory and Jacob

'If it is not right do not do it; if it is not true
do not say it.'

Marcus Aurelius, *Meditations*

CHAPTER ONE

Polly Evans gasped for breath, unwilling to believe what lay at her feet.

Sparks fizzled in her peripheral vision and tremors broke out all over her body.

Five minutes earlier, she'd been enjoying a walk through the countryside with her border terrier, Murphy. They'd stopped in a tussocky meadow at the edge of a shallow section of the meandering River Ebble.

Mid-drink, Murphy had raised his dripping muzzle, splashed through the water to the muddy bank opposite and raced towards a white-blossomed hawthorn hedge.

By the time Polly had reached the yelping little dog, he'd disappeared into a gaping hole in the reddish earth big enough to fall into.

Polly had got down on her knees. She could see Murphy's bunched rear end as he struggled to retrieve something. He'd reversed out and dropped his trophy before her on the grass, tail wagging, pink tongue lolling.

Mustering all the self-control she'd acquired in her thirty-year career as an inner-city biology teacher, she took out her phone and called the police.

To calm herself as she stared at the object Murphy had retrieved, she began naming its parts. *Ulnar artery, flexor muscle of wrist, fibrous sheath of finger* . . .

CHAPTER TWO

As Eric Clapton played 'Three O'Clock Blues' on the Discovery's stereo, Ford glanced at the satnav. The dog-walker's location was less than a mile away. Control had called him twenty minutes earlier.

He slowed to pass a young woman pushing a bicycle up the steep hill. She smiled and waved. He smiled back and accelerated away from her.

He saw a lay-by on the other side of the road, just before a hump-backed bridge. A gate beside it stood open. Someone must have asked the farmer to unlock it. He eased the Discovery through the gate and into the field beyond. The grass rippled in four-foot-wide undulations, the troughs containing six inches of water.

In the distance, he could see a forensics tent. A white van marked 'Wiltshire Forensics Service' sat off to one side, its rear doors open. White-suited CSIs moved between tent, van and a spot a little further towards the centre of the field, also protected by a tent. Uniforms were present, too. They'd erected a blue and white tape cordon. The Discovery rolled and heaved its way across the field, splashing through the drainage ruts.

Ford's stomach churned as he drove closer to the crime scene. Ever since he'd left his wife to drown on a sea-level rock shelf on their last climb together, he'd experienced nausea at every murder scene he'd investigated.

The rational part of him knew he'd done the right thing. But the emotional Ford, the Ford who lay awake at night, endlessly rerunning those last, precious few moments with Lou, saw things differently. It leaned across a judge's bench. Pointed an accusing finger. Screamed *YOU KILLED HER!* Loaded guilt on to his chest until he sat bolt upright at 3 a.m., gasping for breath.

Pushing the memories, and the nausea, down, he parked next to the CSI van. He gave the uniformed loggist on the cordon his collar number and slid under the tape she held up for him. The uniforms had set up an inner cordon. The white plastic tent occupied its centre, sides sucking in and bellying out in the breeze as if breathing. It backed on to a hedge of white-flowered hawthorn, through which brambles and ivy twined.

Out of the wind's rough caress, the temperature rose. Standing just inside the doorway, Ford loosened his tie. The CSIs had erected the tent over a hole that opened out at the foot of the hedge. It was enormous. Easily big enough for a man to fall into. Around the edge, earth had been piled up. He looked closer. Sitting atop the soil he saw a few fragments of eggshell and a tiny white bone.

'It's a badger sett, sir,' a male CSI said. 'The lady who found the hand said her dog pulled it out of here.'

Ford left the tent and went over to a couple of uniforms standing with a woman in late middle age holding a scruffy little terrier on a lead. They'd managed to procure a cup of coffee for her, which she drank in small sips, her eyes darting every which way from over its rim.

He introduced himself, then said, 'I understand you found the hand.'

'Murphy did, really,' she said. 'We were down at the stream back there. Suddenly, Murphy zoomed across the stream and ran off to the hedge there.' She pointed at the tent. 'He was tugging at

3

something. Then he just pulled and it came out and it was' – she shuddered – 'a hand. Well, most of one, anyway.'

'And when you were walking Murphy, did you see anyone else?'

She sipped the coffee then shook her head. 'No. Not a soul. Sometimes I do. This route is popular with dog-walkers. I mean, the countryside's so beautiful, isn't it? But no. Not today.'

Her tone suggested she wasn't avoiding responsibility or trying to please. She knew what she'd seen and what she hadn't, and was unafraid to state it plainly.

'I'd like you to make a formal statement. One of these officers can take it from you,' he said. 'We could do it here, or at home if that would be more comfortable for you.'

Polly opted to do it at home. Leaving her with a uniform, Ford walked towards the knot of CSIs. He saw a familiar face, or its top half, above a surgical mask. China-blue eyes met his own. Dr Hannah Fellowes, the deputy chief forensics officer.

Hannah would take him to view the body part: confronting him once more with the physical reality of violent death. And it would start. The whole unpleasantly satisfying process of entering the mind of a murderer and feeling that sense of connection that existed between all who'd taken another life.

In her first week at Bourne Hill station, Hannah had pushed him on why he hadn't moved past Lou's death. He'd avoided giving a straight answer. But sometimes he caught her looking at him, head cocked to one side, as if studying for clues. He hated that feeling of scrutiny, even though he respected her as a colleague and enjoyed their blossoming friendship.

He joined her and said, 'Morning, Hannah.'

'Good morning, Henry. Guess what?'

'What?'

She pulled her mask down and smiled, curving two dimples into her cheeks. 'I have a nickname.'

'Really? Congratulations. Am I permitted to know what it is?'

She frowned. 'Of course! Otherwise you wouldn't be able to use it. It's Wix. Which is short for Wikipedia. Because I know a lot about a great many subjects,' she added.

Ford smiled. Among the quirks that had spurred his affection was Hannah's fascination with nicknames. When still new at Bourne Hill, she'd learned that his – Henry – came from the founder of the car company. In response, she'd researched an array of facts, from sales of the Ford Mondeo to the date the company had been founded.

He'd thought her Asperger's might make her shy or stand-offish, but Hannah was the opposite. She was good company. No-filter company, but good, nonetheless.

'What have we got?'

'Come with me and I'll show you,' she said, resettling her mask.

He followed her. Breathing deeply. Aware of all that was to come.

CHAPTER THREE

Ruth Long didn't consider herself an anxious woman. In general she was content to let life unfold at its own pace. Plenty of time to react to the present, without worrying over a future that might never happen. But when her husband, Owen, hadn't returned from his planned two-day trip after three days, which turned into five once she checked her diary, she felt the flutterings in her belly that used to accompany her performances with the Royal Ballet.

She put on some shoes and left the house, not bothering to double-lock the door, and hurried towards the police station on Tolpuddle Street.

The young uniformed officer on the front desk looked up and smiled. She noticed a spot on his chin, which was largely devoid of stubble, and wondered if they'd lowered the minimum age.

'Yes, madam?' he said in a pleasant, helpful tone.

On the walk to the station, she'd had time to marshal her thoughts. She'd rehearsed a short statement she felt would deliver the most information in the fewest words. She cleared her throat and straightened her back.

'My husband is missing. He's seventy, vulnerable, and I think he may have been hurt. I haven't heard from him in five days, and that has never happened before.'

The officer nodded. 'When and where did you last see him?'

'Don't you want to take notes?' she asked.

'Let's just talk through the basics first,' he said with a smile she felt was bordering on patronising.

She bit back the urge to tell him he should be taking her more seriously. 'He left five days ago. From our house on Cloudesley Street.'

'And he's seventy?'

'Yes,' she said, unable to tamp down her fear, which was making her irritable. 'As I just said.'

Now he did reach for a notebook. Somehow the action bothered her more than his little smile a moment ago. She felt her pulse racing.

'What's his name, please?'

'Owen Long.'

'When exactly did he leave your house?'

'On Wednesday, April the twenty-eighth. Just before nine a.m.'

'On foot? In a car?'

'In the car. A Toyota Prius. It's more environmentally friendly,' she added, immediately wondering whether he cared.

Ruth felt a lump in her throat. Sharp-edged, like a flint. She swallowed, felt tears, hard as gravel, trapped beneath her eyelids. She became aware of voices behind her. Tutting. She turned to see a young couple eyeing her suspiciously as though she were there to commit a crime instead of report a missing person.

With a smile, the young officer directed her to a row of plastic chairs. 'I'll get someone to come and talk to you. Get a few more details about Owen.'

Sniffing, not trusting herself to speak, she moved away from the counter and took one of the chairs. It was hard under her behind and she shuffled around, trying to get comfortable. Five minutes later, a fortyish man in a grey suit emerged from a door and came over to her.

'Mrs Long?' She nodded. 'I'm Detective Constable Wallace. Do you want to come with me?'

He led her through the door and into a small room furnished with a blue two-seater sofa and a matching armchair. He took the armchair and opened a laptop, which he balanced precariously on his knees.

Over the next fifteen minutes, he asked Ruth a series of detailed questions relating to Owen's physical appearance, the car and anywhere she thought he might have gone in it. He entered each answer into the laptop, prodding the keys with two fingers. She wanted to scream at him to learn to type.

He closed the laptop and looked her in the eye. 'I've created a record for Owen in the National Crime Agency's missing persons database,' he said. 'That means every police force in the country now has access to Owen's description. If something crops up, they'll notify me and I'll get straight on the phone to you.'

'But what are you actually going to *do*?' she asked, alarmed at how shaky her voice sounded in the airless little room.

'At this point, there's not a great deal we *can* do,' he said apologetically. Then he smiled. 'Look, in the vast majority of cases like this, they do come home again, safe and sound. Try not to worry. He's probably just letting off some steam.'

'But he's seventy! He's hardly likely to have gone off on some jaunt, is he? He used to be a vicar!'

She was aware how pathetic she sounded, but she didn't care. Maybe younger men did occasionally feel the need to slip away for a few days to let off steam, or whatever they did nowadays. But Owen? No. No. *Nonononono.* She fished a tissue out of her sleeve and dabbed her eyes.

'Let's not panic. Give Owen a few more days. Then if he's not back, call me and we'll have a think about what to do next.' He handed her a card.

Somehow, she found herself back on the pavement again, having listened to the detective's stream of reassurances as he steered her out of the police station. And why was he only a detective constable? Surely they'd give the job to somebody more senior?

She returned home and poured herself a large glass of wine. Noticed the kitchen clock said half past eleven. Didn't care. Drained it. Poured another.

CHAPTER FOUR

Ford followed Hannah across the field towards the smaller of the two tents. It had its own mini-cordon of fluttering police tape. He lifted it for her and they both ducked under.

A hand, severed at the wrist, lay on the grass. Flies crawled over the pale, mottled skin and ragged flesh. He squatted and pointed at it. 'What do you make of that, then?'

'There's clear evidence of animal interference.' She pulled out a ballpoint pen and indicated the grooves and gouges in the flesh. 'See? Toothmarks.'

'From the badgers.'

'I think so. Rats are a second possibility. Badgers are omnivores, and although their usual diet includes earthworms, beetles and birds' eggs, they will eat flesh if it presents itself. Though I don't suppose many have tasted human.' She adopted a formal tone like an old-fashioned newsreader. *Flesh-eating badgers are roaming Salisbury.'*

She turned and looked at him. The crinkles fanning out from the corners of her eyes suggested a smile behind the mask. Hannah possessed a sense of humour just off-kilter enough for her to join the black comedy club that included medics, emergency workers and the armed forces.

Ford pointed to the protruding bones. 'Did they do that as well?'

'I can't say at this point. But to the naked eye, they do appear to have been gnawed.'

'You'll be at the post-mortem?'

'Yes, I will.'

Ford straightened. Sighed. 'I have to go. I'll see you later, Wix.'

'Bye, Henry,' she said, and he heard the pleasure in her voice at his use of her nickname.

He went to find the crime scene manager. Experienced in matters rural, the DS from General CID had dressed for the job in green wellies and a thornproof jacket.

'Morning, sir,' the DS said.

'Morning, Harry. We need to check if there are more remains down there,' Ford said, pointing at the tented badger sett. 'Any bright ideas?'

'I had a word with the farmer. Chap by the name of Ball. He's bringing a tractor with a digger attachment on the back. Said he'd be about half an hour.'

Ford nodded his appreciation. 'God knows how long it would have taken if we'd gone through channels.'

Harry grinned. 'Quicker to do it by hand, sir.'

Ball arrived with his tractor. All work stopped as the assorted coppers, CSIs and a couple of dog-walkers kept behind the outer perimeter watched him manoeuvre the machine into position. The CSIs dismantled the tent, dragging the assemblage of poles and flapping fabric out of harm's way.

'Natural England'd have a field day if they saw us doing this,' Harry said.

'Let's hope they don't find out then, eh?'

They watched as the farmer laboriously scraped away the red earth from the entrance to the sett and began digging down. The

11

growl of the tractor's diesel engine rose and fell as the scoop bit into the earth. Five minutes later, Hannah shouted. An arm, missing its hand and smeared with mud, tumbled from the clawed scoop.

The CSIs laid out an unzipped black body bag on the grass, and piece by piece they began assembling the filth-encrusted remains into a disarticulated corpse . . . missing its head.

Ford looked at the sad array of body parts. Here and there he saw traces of discoloration on the skin. He looked closer, holding his breath, and realised what they were.

He called over to Hannah. When she arrived he pointed at one of the arms. 'I think those are tattoos. Do you think you could get them cleaned up? We could show some photos around today, see if anybody recognises them.'

She nodded. 'I've got water in the van.'

It wasn't much, but it was a start. Maybe he'd get lucky and the golden hour might actually last sixty minutes for once. He watched as Hannah squirted water over an arm and began gently swabbing the skin with a sponge. As she revealed the tattoo, of a futuristic, black and grey machine gun with a winged skull on the barrel, Ford's mind whirled. He'd seen it before. Where the hell was it?

He closed his eyes. Heard a cocky young guy with a thick Wiltshire accent giving him lip as he snapped a pair of cuffs over his wrists: *When my brothers hear about this, you're going to be in so much trouble, copper, you'll wish you never even saw me.*

Muscular arms flexing in their restraints. And the same tattoo.

Ford opened his eyes. There couldn't be two like that in Salisbury.

He was looking down at the right arm of Tommy Bolter, youngest of three brothers who were the nearest the city had to an organised crime group. The distance was still great, but they had ambition, which was always a dangerous quality.

As well as Tommy, Ford had once arrested the older two: Jason John, aka JJ; and Ryan, aka Rye. That case had been dismissed after a key witness failed to attend court. Nobbled, was the shared opinion of the cops who'd worked so hard to get the brothers before a judge.

He had to get out in front of this one fast, because JJ and Rye wouldn't sit quietly and play the role of what the media liked to call 'grieving relatives who just want to be left in peace to mourn'.

Ford heard the tractor's engine rise in tone and turned to see the scoop angling down to take another huge bite out of the earth. Running back, he waved his arm at Ball. Having caught the farmer's attention, he signalled with a slicing motion across his throat for him to kill the chuntering engine. He climbed up to the cab.

'We need the head intact,' he said. 'I'm worried you'll damage it.'

Ball shrugged. 'Either that or I'll just end up pushing the damned thing further in. You'd be surprised how far back those setts go. I nearly lost one of my dogs down one a year or two back.'

The story gave Ford an idea. A deeply unpleasant idea. An idea it would be wrong to foist on anyone he outranked. He sighed and climbed down. He retrieved a torch from his murder bag and climbed into a Noddy suit, booties and gloves.

DC Julie 'Jools' Harper, his bagwoman, had just arrived.

'What are you doing, guv?' she asked him as he returned from the Discovery.

'I think I know who the dead man is, but I need to be sure.'

'Who is it?'

'I'm ninety-nine per cent sure it's Tommy Bolter.'

Jools bit her lip. 'Jesus! Let's hope the one per cent comes up trumps, then.'

'We need the last piece of the puzzle. Unless we're facing someone who collects human heads, I'm betting it's still down there.'

Her face contorted as nose, mouth and eyes all scrunched up into varying twists of disgust.

'You're not—'

'I'm afraid I am. No other option unless we want to risk Farmer Giles over there turning it into a meat bowling ball or smashing it altogether.'

'What do you mean, no other option?' she asked, hands on hips. 'We could send a cadaver dog down. Or get ground-penetrating radar over it. Or even find a caver to take a look for us first.'

Ford nodded. 'We could do any or all of those. And they'd be safer. But what if it rains, Jools? Have you seen the forecast? The sett could flood and the head could be washed to God knows where,' he said, warming to his theme. 'Or another animal could take it and drag it too deep to recover. I'll put my risk assessment in the policy book, but I'm going. It's wide enough to get into. I'll be fine.'

'I still think it's too dangerous, guv. And you'd be breaking about a dozen health and safety rules. What if it caves in on you?'

'I agree. It *is* dangerous. But if we go on the College of Policing website and look up protocols under "B", I don't think we're going to find "Badger".' Ford made a concession. 'How about this? Get a rope, say thirty feet, and tie it round my ankle. That's as far as I'll go. If it goes taut, you can give it a tug and I'll come out. OK?'

'I'm not happy, but yes, I suppose that could work. And Wix'll be pleased.'

Jools went off to get some rope. She brought it back and accompanied him as far as the now-ravaged sett. The digger had turned the opening into a deeply grooved trench, at the bottom of which the black mouth, three feet across, waited to swallow Ford whole. Jools tied the rope around Ford's right ankle.

'Wait!' she said sharply, as Ford kneeled at the sett's gaping mouth. He looked over his shoulder at her. 'What if there's a badger down there? Don't they have really sharp teeth? Or claws?'

The thought had occurred to him at the same moment. He derived no comfort from it. 'Thanks for that. I'm hoping the torch will scare them off. Otherwise, if you hear me scream, pull me out!'

He went for a *braver than I sound* grin. Jools's frown made him sure he hadn't pulled it off. He was tempted to abandon his plan and join her in the reverence for the rulebook she'd brought with her from a stint in the military police. He looked over her shoulder and saw he'd attracted an audience. A dozen or so CSIs. Uniforms and detectives. The dog-walkers. Ball with a grandstand view from his tractor seat. That decided it. He was going.

Hannah proffered a large evidence bag. He folded it up and stuffed it into the hip pocket of his Noddy suit. He took a deep breath and slithered down the sett's sloping sides.

With his head and shoulders in the shaft, he aimed the torch at the roof, hoping badgers had a natural equivalent of pit props. Tangled, hairy roots dangled from the earth like the long straggly whiskers of a tramp's beard. Were they binding the soil? He hoped so.

He shuffled along on his elbows, concentrating on breathing evenly. He pulled himself forward another six inches and kept swinging the torch beam from side to side, searching for his prize. The earth smelled old, as if he were descending not just in space but also in time. Riding on the bass notes of iron and loam he detected a sweeter smell, tinged with putrescence. Decaying flesh. Here and there he saw dark smears.

Something white flashed at him a few yards further on. Trying to ignore the sense of a crushing weight above him, and the way the narrowing walls were scraping at his shoulders, he swung the torch up, down, left, right and – *Ohmigod* – saw it. Him.

He came face to face with a battered, bloody but still recognisably human head. Was it Tommy Bolter? It looked a little like him. But the eyes were milky and clouded, upturned in their sockets so only half the irises were visible. The skin, a sickly blend of greenish-brown and purple, had begun to sag and slip. Something – the badgers, he assumed – had taken a few bites out of the cheeks, leaving bone shining through. Blood and earth matted the hair. The stink made his eyes water. His guts churned and he had to exert himself not to throw up.

His fingertips were tingling and he found he couldn't breathe. He heaved air into his lungs, sucking in small particles of dirt that produced a bout of coughing. He fought down a sudden wave of panic as sweat broke out all over his skin. How ridiculous to die down here in a senseless act of bravado.

He took in a breath and held it. He squeezed his eyes shut. His son's face swam into view.

Sam was sixteen, on the cusp of manhood and taking more of an interest in Ford's work. Ford thought he knew why. By connecting with his father's work, Sam could make sense of death. A solved case meant a death explained. He'd asked about his mother's death, too. Asking for explanations. Details. And, above all, reasons.

But how could Ford give him reasons, when he hardly dared examine them himself? Sam wanted to understand why his mother had died. He'd never cope if his father died, too. It was why Ford kept things back from him. No, give it its proper name. He lied to him.

He found thinking about Sam allowed his panic to recede. He offered up a heartfelt prayer to the saints of his own personal pantheon.

Dear Saint Ella, Saint B.B., Saint Rosetta and Saint Buddy. Saints Jimi, Eric, Jeff and Peter. Please let me get out of this hole, and I promise I'll try to open up to Sam a bit more. Amen, brothers and sisters.

And he heard them answer, a bluesy chorus:

'*You ain't gonna die down here, Ford.*

You ain't gonna die down here.
Now, get your ass in gear and pull yourself together,
'cause you ain't gonna die down here.'

He counted down from ten and, when he reached 'one', he opened his eyes. He could breathe normally. The panic was gone.

He reached back for the evidence bag, but his arm wouldn't go past his ribcage: the passage was too narrow. He groaned, dropping his head until his nose touched the cool, dank earthen floor of the tunnel. Idiot! He should have had the bag in his hand before getting wedged in tighter than a cork in a bottle.

The head lay just an arm's length away. He hadn't come all this way to leave it. Flinching, he extended his right hand and curled his fingers into the matted hair. He tugged lightly. The hair came away from the scalp. Wincing, he tried again. This time he hooked his fingers under the jawbone and clamped it with his thumb.

And then, already feeling Hannah's disapproval as she saw her prime exhibit mishandled by the lead investigator, he shuffled backwards, dragging the head and trying to avoid that milky stare.

The light level increased. So did the space around him. He heard voices. Someone grabbed his ankles.

'Don't pull me!' he shouted. 'I've got it.'

A few more awkward elbow pushes and he could finally bring his knees into play and free himself. He stood, the head swinging at his hip.

The watchers burst into applause. He told himself it was genuine, but every copper he'd ever met possessed a fine sense of irony. Add in the state of him and the clapping took on a satirical edge.

A CSI bustled over, a plastic evidence bag already held wide. Grateful to be free of his burden, he placed the head inside. Jools joined him and brushed some crumbs of dirt from his forehead before crouching to untie the rope from his ankle.

'You look like shit, guv,' she said.

'I love you, too, Jools. Come on, let's get back to Bourne Hill. I'm in need of soap and hot water.'

He walked back to where Hannah was photographing the tattoos. On the left shoulder, a red rose wrapped in barbed wire and pierced by a serrated dagger dripping blood. And on the right pectoral, a large-breasted, naked woman reclining on a motorbike, above script reading 'I love to ride!'

Sighing, Ford left her to it. He peeled off his forensic gear and threw it all into the back of the Discovery. Freshening up would have to wait. He wanted to brief his boss, Detective Superintendent Sandra 'Sandy' Monroe, aka the Python, as soon as they got back.

Driving away, he asked Jools to call Dr Georgina Eustace, the forensic pathologist at Salisbury District Hospital, and put her on speaker.

'You've got a body coming in this morning,' he said. 'In bits. I know who it is. Can you get him prepped for a viewing before you do the post-mortem?'

'When?'

'A few hours?'

'That's not really long enough, but it's quiet today. Who is it?'

'Tommy Bolter.'

There was a three-second pause.

'Ah. I see. I'll put Pete on it. I'll tell him to do his best work.'

Jools looked at Ford as he ended the call. 'This is going to be a shit-show, isn't it?'

He nodded, thinking that they had ringside seats. The worst in the house.

As he cruised past the hospital's main entrance with its fund-raising thermometer graphic, the cathedral's spire appeared on the horizon. Wherever you were in the city or the surrounding country-side, you'd either have a clear view of it or be within minutes of one.

When he and Lou had moved down ten years earlier, that soaring monument to man's desire to connect with the eternal had taken their breath away; literally, on the day they took part in a sponsored climb to the top of the spire and looked out over half the county.

He'd wanted to bury her in the Cathedral Close, but apparently for that you needed a special dispensation from the bishop. Instead, she rested in a country churchyard where he could visit her undisturbed by tourists snapping selfies with their backs to the cathedral and its wonders. Probably for the best. Her graveside didn't bring out his most rational side.

CHAPTER FIVE

Gripping two mugs of coffee, Ford walked into Sandy's office. She looked up at him and puffed her cheeks out. Her normally sleek ash-blonde hair stuck out at angles as if she'd recently been pulling at it. Then he saw the spreadsheet on her screen and understood why. Faced with budget forecasting, Sandy liked to list increasingly painful physical procedures she'd rather undergo.

'Henry,' she said, accepting the proffered mug and taking a sip. 'Please tell me you're bringing me good news.' Then she wrinkled her nose. 'What's that smell?'

'My news. Not sure it's good, though.'

Ford sat in the leather chair across the desk from his boss. Blew across the surface of his own coffee before taking a sip. 'I've just watched a digger pull pieces of Tommy Bolter out of a badger sett. That's the stink.'

She regarded him steadily. 'You're sure it's Tommy?'

'I need a positive ID, but I'm certain it's him.'

'Jesus! I knew Tommy when he was just nicking other kids' lunch money in junior school,' Sandy said with a grimace. 'What a waste of a life.'

'And before you hear it from anyone else, I had to go down the hole to get his head myself. Couldn't reach my evidence bag, so—'

She frowned. 'You're not about to confess to contaminating evidence, are you?'

'I had no choice. If you want the whole gory tale, I dragged it out by the jawbone.'

Sandy barked out a single laugh. He didn't hear any mirth in it.

'Sorry, Henry. It's bad, I know that. It's just you have no idea what a relief it is to be discussing actual crime instead of budgets and' – she peered at her screen – 'multimodal performance metrics, whatever the hell they are.'

'I think it means, are we catching enough criminals?'

'Well, go and catch this one, then. Give me a green tick to put in the bloody column.'

Back in his own office, he spread out the crime scene photos on his desk.

The way the body had been cut up was interesting. These were not the random hackings of a disordered mind. No trial-and-error cutting, looking for joints. No raking away at solid bone with a chainsaw. No practice cuts. No stab wounds. The dismemberment was – he hesitated to use the word 'clinical' – *professional*.

He decided on a quick briefing with the team to get them going. Because what he really needed to do urgently was get out to see JJ and Rye Bolter.

Ten minutes later, he stood to address his assembled officers in the big meeting room in Major Crimes. They'd started calling it the 'sugar cube' after the Powers That Be had sent in decorators to paint the whole room white. Presumably drawing on a different budget to the one that consumed so much of Sandy's time.

'This morning, a member of the public out walking her dog found a human hand down a badger sett. We recovered the rest of the body. It's a white male—'

'IC1,' DC Olly Cable murmured, already scribbling in his leather-covered notebook.

'Well done, Fast-Track,' Mick Tanner said, to grins from a couple of the older CID detectives and most of the uniforms.

Olly scowled at Mick. Ford had observed growing friction between the two men: Olly, the young ambitious graduate, and Mick, the long-serving DS and one-time rival for the job that was now Ford's.

'As I said, white male, chopped into bits,' Ford said. 'This isn't confirmed yet, but I think it's Tommy Bolter.'

A ripple of murmurs swept through the room. Only Olly looked confused.

'Sorry, who's Tommy Bolter?' he asked.

Ford frowned with irritation. OK, Olly was a recent transfer, but he ought to have got himself up to speed by now.

'Tell him, someone,' Ford said.

Mick turned in his chair to address Olly. 'Tommy, JJ and Rye Bolter are a bunch of wannabe Goodfellas. Or were, in Tommy's case. Grew up watching too many Martin Scorsese films on stolen DVD players. They think they're the crime lords of our fair city,' he said, looking around the room and earning a few nods. 'Drugs, nicking high-end agricultural machinery, sheep rustling, a bit of this, that and the other. Mum and Dad Bolter built the family firm on a scrap metal business. All dodgy, of course.

'Since they died of drugs and alcohol abuse, JJ has ruled the roost. He's ruthless and he's made enough cash to employ a decent lawyer if we ever feel his collar. Rye's the muscle. Borderline psychopath. And, until he recently took up caving, Tommy was the office junior, learning the ropes and chasing crumbs from JJ's table.'

'Thanks, Mick,' Ford said. 'Now, it *appears* to be a homicide. But until Doc Eustace tells us otherwise, there's a slim chance it could just be a natural-causes-slash-accidental-death with a particularly grisly aftermath.'

'Really, guv?' Olly asked. 'You don't dispose of a body like that if they just died of natural causes, do you?'

'Why not?'

'Well, for a start, there's no need, is there? You just call the undertaker. Or the police. And second, it's so brutal. Who chops up a body and stuffs it down a badger sett unless they want to conceal a crime?'

'I don't know. But,' Ford added, as murmurs of the same basic flavour as Olly's assertion broke out, 'either way, I'm launching a murder enquiry. We found hardly any blood at the scene, so I'm thinking the killer did it somewhere else and took the pieces there in an off-roader of some kind.'

'You want me to, er, *head* off and check all local 4x4 owners, guv?' Mick asked, his face a mask of innocent enquiry.

Ford ignored the provocation. Caught Jools's eye. 'Please.'

Mick nodded. 'Sure. I don't mind *noggin* on a few doors.'

A couple of people sniggered. Ford didn't like it. Black humour was one thing, but he'd just dragged a decapitated head out of the ground by its jaw.

'OK, that's enough!' he snapped. 'Save it. Love him or loathe him, Tommy Bolter's been murdered and chopped into bits. The clock's already ticking, so let's focus on finding whoever killed him, yes?'

The murmur of agreement pacified him a little. But he was still dreading his impending visit to the Bolter place.

'I was thinking, guv—' Mick said.

'Makes a change,' Jools interrupted.

Ford shot his bagwoman a grateful glance.

Mick pointed at the photos of the body parts. 'Whoever did that knew what they were doing.' He looked around for support. A few heads dipped in agreement. 'Not necessarily at the medical level, but maybe a butcher or a slaughterman? Somebody who knows how to cut joints cleanly, anyway.'

Ford nodded. People could say what they liked about Mick, and plenty did, but his copper's instincts were honed by years of dogged police work. And he knew all the local villains – 'nominals', in the parlance. Hell, he'd been at school with half of them. Including, as he often boasted, JJ and Rye Bolter.

'Start putting a list together of all the butchers and abattoir workers round about. Say within a five-mile radius of Salisbury.'

'Butchers aren't the only people who know how to cut up bodies,' Jools said. 'What about surgeons? Pathologists, even?'

'You think Doc Eustace has been moonlighting?' Mick asked with a grin.

'Ha ha. But I'm right, aren't I, guv?' Jools said.

'It *could* be a medical professional, but it could just as easily be a painter and decorator. In my experience, I'd say all you really need is a sharp tool and sufficient willpower,' Ford said. 'We'll keep it under consideration, but this isn't screaming surgeon at me.'

'Search, guv?'

Ford turned to face DS Jan Derwent. As his qualified POLSA – police search advisor – she was unbeatable. She'd find a needle used as a murder weapon in a field full of haystacks.

'As soon as possible. I'll see how many uniforms I can scare up to join the team.'

'You want me to do the death knock, guv?' Jools asked.

He shook his head. No way was he sending a DC, even an ex-military cop like Jools, to deliver the worst possible news to men like JJ and Rye Bolter.

'Thanks, but it's got to be me.'

Ford ended the meeting with a request to be kept informed of every new development as it happened.

Before he left to see the surviving Bolter brothers, he went to have a wash. The Noddy suit had done its job of protecting him from the filth down the sett, but still he felt the stink of death on his skin. Drying his hands, he thought back to the day the older two Bolters had emerged from the Crown Court free men.

From arrest to acquittal had taken three months. JJ had sauntered over to him, smirking. He'd leaned in close and muttered in Ford's ear, well below the volume anyone else would catch. 'You're lucky you only got your nose rubbed in it by our brief, Ford,' he'd said. 'The last cop to cross me walks with a stick now.'

Ford returned to his office and pulled the blinds. He called Pete.

'How are you getting on with Tommy?'

Pete sniffed. 'I've patched his face up, but the rest's going to take me a while given what they did to the body. Can you hold off for a couple more hours?'

Ford checked his watch. 'Yeah, I can manage that. How's he looking?'

'Pretty rough, to be honest. It was a bit of a rush job. Best I could do in the time, but it should be fine through the window. I was just sticking the photos in the family folder when you called.'

'Thanks, mate. I'll see you in a bit.'

Ford filled in the time he'd promised Pete updating the murder book and reading all the initial reports. When it was time to go, he changed into the spare black suit he kept in his office. If only they made body armour that would fit underneath it.

CHAPTER SIX

Ford turned off the Coombe Road on to Old Shaston Drove. The road predated the modern city of Salisbury by a few hundred years. In Saxon times, herders had driven their beasts from pasture to market along the simple rutted track. Over the centuries, it had grown and widened, eventually acquiring a patchy coat of tarmac. It ran in a sinuous curve from deep in the Wiltshire countryside towards the city centre, with its market and famous cathedral.

As he drove away from the city, the quiet country lane assumed a grittier character that would have nervous hikers turning back. Negotiating the increasingly challenging surface, dodging potholes, lumps of scrap metal and fly-tipped garbage, Ford swore, cursing the attitudes of people who'd take so little care of their own road.

The satnav directed him to turn right into a caravan park, and announced that he'd reached his destination. He looked around at the rundown static vans and rusted-out cars. Surely the Bolters didn't live here? He'd spoken to a DS in General CID and formed the impression they were doing well for themselves, albeit on the proceeds of crime. He'd never had cause to visit them at home, but the DS had told him, with a wry smile, that they lived 'on the park'.

He pulled up on an area of hard standing between two of the slab-sided dwellings, and climbed out. Sunlight glinted off a pile of broken glass. He saw nobody around to ask where he might find the Bolters.

A caravan door opened with a rattle. Out stepped a skinny young girl who didn't look old enough to vote, carrying a grizzling baby on her hip.

She turned in his direction, and squinted. 'You police?'

He nodded, smiling. 'Is it that obvious?'

'What do you want?'

'I'm looking for the Bolters. Have they got a van here?'

She laughed, a hard-edged cackle that set the baby wailing. Casually she retrieved a dummy from the back pocket of her skin-tight jeans and plugged it into the round red O of the baby's mouth.

'That's a joke, right?'

'Do you know where they live?' he asked.

She jerked her chin at a narrow concrete lane between the two static homes. 'Down there.'

She turned away from him and wandered off, jiggling the baby and pulling a packet of cigarettes from her other jeans pocket.

'Thanks,' he called after her.

She flapped a hand in the air. Ford chose to interpret the gesture as 'you're welcome' and not 'whatever'.

He drove between the caravans and followed the winding road-way for a couple of hundred yards, passing broken-down toy prams and pedal cars, piles of scaffolding poles, discarded white goods, stained mattresses, and rolls of soggy-looking carpet from which sprouted leggy weeds bearing acid-yellow flowers.

The wall came as a surprise.

Eight foot tall, topped with razor wire and constructed from unmarked red and sand-coloured brick, it loomed over him as he drew up to a pair of wide wooden gates overlooked by security cameras. At the gates, he got out, pushed the button on the aluminium intercom box and placed his ear to the speaker grille.

It buzzed and clicked. 'Yes?'

'This is DI Ford, Wiltshire Police. I'm here to see JJ or Rye Bolter.'

'Step back. I want to get a look at you.'

Ford thought he recognised JJ's voice. He did as he was asked and looked into the lens of the left-hand camera.

The intercom crackled again. 'What do you want, Ford? Come to try and fit me up again?'

Ford ignored the provocation. 'It's personal, JJ. Can you let me through, please?'

His pulse had picked up as JJ began speaking, and he was aware of a runnel of sweat trickling between his shoulder blades. His only consolation was that he'd refused Jools's offer.

'What do you mean, *personal*? You've got nothing personal on us. Piss off!'

Ford felt a tap on his right shin. A scruffy little dog was nosing against his trousers. It went to cock its leg and he pushed it away with his foot.

'It's about Tommy,' Ford said, desperate not to have to deliver the news via a squawk box. 'It's important. Can you let me in, please?'

Five seconds of silence passed. The mutt returned to his leg and began whining. Ford squatted to scratch it behind the ears. The latch above his head clacked and the solid wood gates swung inward on silent hinges.

'Got to go,' he said to the dog.

As he drove through, Ford whistled. Facing him from behind a landscaped lawn was a long, low, white-painted bungalow. Roofed with terracotta barrel tiles, it looked as though it belonged on the Costa del Sol rather than in the Wiltshire countryside. He imagined the Bolters would refer to it as a 'hacienda'.

He retrieved a tie from the glovebox and slipped the loop with its ready-made knot over his head. Tightened and adjusted it. Settled his suit jacket down on his shoulders, which he squared before marching up to a limed oak front door with a square of rippled glass in its upper half.

He rapped on the window. Stood back. Waited.

A shadow materialised behind the glass. The door opened wide to reveal JJ Bolter, his black hair gelled back from his forehead revealing dark brown deep-set eyes, a long straight nose and a sensuous mouth. His strong-smelling aftershave wafted towards Ford, making him wrinkle his nose.

JJ stared down at Ford.

'Nice suit,' he said. 'Where d'you get that, then? Oxfam?'

'M&S.'

JJ puffed out a dismissive breath. 'Yeah, that's about your level.' He ran the lapel of his navy linen jacket through thumb and forefinger. 'Versace.' He pointed down at his shoes, black alligator-skin loafers with oversized gold snaffle bits across the insteps. 'Gucci.'

Ford felt his shoulders tensing inside his suit jacket, which was uncomfortably hot. 'JJ, please. I—'

'Yeah, yeah. All right. Don't get your knickers in a twist. What's this about Tommy, then?'

'Can I come in, please?'

'Not without a warrant, you can't.'

Ford tried again. 'It really would be better if we could do this inside.'

JJ folded his arms across his chest, completely blocking the doorway. 'I haven't seen him for a few days, if that's what you're asking.'

Dreading the bigger man's reaction, Ford tried to ease his way into what he knew would be the most difficult moment of his day so far. 'JJ, we found a body. I'm sorry, but it's looking like it might be Tommy. From the tattoos. We need someone to make a formal ID. One way or the other,' he added.

JJ pulled his head back, frowning. Then he did something that surprised Ford. He laughed. Loudly. 'Loads of people have tats, you muppet.' He shook his head. 'You must be really bored over at Bourne Hill if you came all the way out here to tell me that.'

'I recognised one. Can you come to the mortuary with me, please, JJ? Just take a look. And I want you to prepare yourself.'

Still shaking his head, JJ retreated into the depths of the house. 'Wait there. I'm going to get Rye.'

While he waited, Ford wandered over to a double garage built on to the side of the house to form a shallow L. In the shade, he saw a black Mercedes estate, a sporty AMG model, parked beside a couple of Japanese motorbikes in white, lime green and purple.

JJ called to him from the front door. 'We'll follow you. I'm not going anywhere in that shitheap you came in.'

Ford turned to see that JJ had been joined by his younger brother. Where JJ was well over six foot and looked gym-fit, Rye was shorter by a head and built like a barrel. His forehead bulged oddly above pale blue eyes buried in puffy cheeks.

Grateful that he wouldn't have to drive JJ and Rye back from the mortuary, Ford nodded. He didn't know which he feared more – showing them the preliminary photos or the actual body.

Once they arrived at the hospital, JJ cracked jokes as the trio walked from the car park. In the mortuary, Ford ushered JJ and Rye into the family room, officially called the Chapel of Rest. No outside sound penetrated the softly lit space. Ford gestured at the sofa, but neither man sat.

JJ had stopped joking. Ford knew why. Coppers didn't bring you to a mortuary for a laugh. JJ knew he was about to be shown a body and asked whether it belonged to Tommy. Amusement had been replaced by hope. And fear.

Rye had sunk into a silence so total it felt like it exerted its own gravity. Now he, JJ and Ford stood in an awkward triangle. A black vinyl folder lay on a low table in one corner of the room.

Ford fetched it. 'I'm going to show you a photo first. If it's not him, tell me and we can get out of here. If you think it's him, just nod or say yes and then we'll go next door and see him' – horrified, Ford realised he was about to say 'in the flesh' – 'for real. I want you to prepare yourselves. It's not pretty. Ready?' he asked.

Dumb question. Who was ever ready to see a photo of a corpse that could be their dead brother?

JJ nodded.

Ford opened the cover. As JJ stared at the ravaged face, Ford saw a vein begin to pulse in his left temple. His broad chest heaved in and out and the whistling breath through his pinched nostrils broke the silence.

Rye crowded in next to him and looked down. He gasped. 'No! Tommy!'

He backed away and flopped on to the sofa, staring dead-eyed at the curtained viewing window.

'Is it him?' Ford asked quietly.

JJ nodded. Lifted the cover of the folder with his index finger and closed it with a small slap as it hit the plastic sleeve containing the photo.

Pete had entered the room. He stood ready to the left of the curtains, his hand on the pull cord. He raised his eyebrows at Ford in a mute question. *Now?*

But JJ forestalled the answer. 'Not through that,' he said. 'I want to *see* him.'

Ford shook his head. He'd been dreading this moment. 'I don't think that's such a great idea. You know why.'

JJ whirled round and grabbed Ford's lapels. Stuck his face, contorted now into a mask of fury, into Ford's. 'Yes, I *do* know why.

Now, either you take me to him or I'm going to go through you and Lurch over there and see him anyway.' A beat. 'Your choice.'

Ford took hold of JJ's thick wrists and pulled them out and down. Jesus, the guy was strong! 'Come on, then.'

Pulse bumping in his throat, Ford signalled with a shake of his head that Pete could go. He followed him out into the corridor with JJ close behind him. Turned right through the next door. Took JJ into the room where Tommy's corpse waited.

The family room smelled of lavender. Pete had told him once that it had a calming effect. Hadn't bloody worked on JJ, had it? The body room – its informal name – didn't smell of lavender. Instead, a mixture of pine disinfectant and the sharp, sappy, broken-branch smell of formalin swirled in the air. And beneath both, the whiff of decay. Well advanced in Tommy's case, but never pleasant, even with fresh ones.

Ford led JJ to the table. Pete had draped the corpse in a sheet of a soft dusty blue. No doubt this colour had also been chosen by the hospital authorities for its so-called calming properties. Ford had his doubts.

He turned to JJ. 'You sure you want to do this?'

JJ nodded. A stiff jerk of his head. He turned his gaze to Ford. A deep, unfathomable hatred burned in those dark brown irises. At that moment Ford knew he'd be under additional, unwelcome pressure to solve this one fast. God help the man who'd slaughtered JJ Bolter's kid brother. And then a most unpolicemanlike thought chased the other away. *He shouldn't have killed him and cut him into bits, then, should he?*

Ford took the edge of the sheet at the top end of the table and drew it down slowly to reveal Tommy's face. JJ hissed in a breath.

Beside him, Ford couldn't take his eyes off Tommy. Pete had done an amazing job of patching up the badger bites, or whatever the hell they were. But the cheeks had the uneven look of car body panels loaded with filler. And the skin colour was wrong. Under the foundation and powder, that horrible greenish-brown shade still showed through.

Only an idiot would say he looked peaceful. Something had happened to the skin. It didn't look properly joined to the muscles beneath. Wrong, somehow.

Ford knew the source of the problem. Whatever gave the skin its elasticity – collagen, presumably – had broken down. That's why Tommy's face looked the way it did.

No, not Tommy. He was staring at a joke-shop 'Tommy' horror mask.

With a sharp tug, JJ whisked off the sheet and flung it into a corner. The scream he emitted raised the hairs on the back of Ford's neck.

Ford knew Pete had put Tommy back together. But he hadn't followed the thought through to its real-world conclusion. Now he knew. Now he could see. And so could JJ.

At the wrists, shoulders, neck, waist, groin, knees and ankles, lines of ugly black spiders marched across the green-purple skin. Crude knotted Xs of thick surgical thread with nasty little wounds trying to burst open beneath them. And the genitals. Jesus Christ! Ford looked away, tried to pull JJ with him by the shoulder.

JJ wrenched himself free and staggered into the table. Which Ford could now identify as a standard hospital gurney. Pete had locked the wheels; good practice normally. But it meant it couldn't move when JJ went into it. Or not along the carpet, at any rate. Instead, it toppled over, throwing Tommy Bolter's mortal remains to the floor.

Pete rushed in. He was too late. Howling, JJ picked up the gurney and flung it at the viewing window. It shattered, showering him, Ford and Pete with shards of glass.

JJ barged Ford aside and ran out. Through the jagged-edged aperture Ford watched, in shock, as JJ grabbed Rye by his elbow and dragged him to his feet, then out the door.

The mess at the mortuary would mean even more form-filling than was usual at the start of a murder investigation. Ford tried to see the positives in the whole sorry situation. They had an ID. And, given who it was, they could start on victimology straight away.

After a decent interval, he returned to the Bolter place and sat down with JJ. The meeting did not go well.

CHAPTER SEVEN

Ford sat opposite JJ in a room furnished with a long boardroom table and eight chrome-framed office chairs upholstered in white leather. Through a picture window that gave on to the garden at the rear of the house, he could see Rye pacing up and down. He was lighting a cigarette from the butt of another. In one meaty paw he clutched a bottle of golden liquid, which he brought to his lips every ten seconds or so.

Dry-eyed and staring at Ford as if he was the person responsible for dismembering Tommy, JJ worried him more than Rye. Rye was a bruiser who enjoyed inflicting pain for its own sake. But JJ was the cunning, ruthless brother who'd built on his parents' business and turned it into something more akin to a big-city crime gang. He was concealing his grief so effectively, all that was left was this emotionless exterior.

'Who killed Tommy?' he asked.

'That's what I'm going to find out. You can help me. I need to know if Tommy had any enemies.' As he said it, he was aware of how lame it sounded.

JJ confirmed his opinion. 'You do know who you're dealing with, don't you?'

'Of course I do.'

'Well, then.'

'Fine. Has Tommy had any run-ins with anyone recently? Anything serious enough to have caused' – he paused – 'all this?'

JJ shrugged. 'Not that I know of. He was our baby brother, but he wasn't a kid anymore. He did what he wanted. He had plenty of places to bed down if he didn't want to sleep here. Girls loved Tommy.'

He clenched his fist on the polished tabletop as he spoke these words, and sniffed loudly. For a moment, Ford thought he was about to burst into tears. He found himself wondering if he'd brought a packet of tissues with him.

The bang as JJ slammed his fist down startled Ford. JJ leaned across the table and pointed a thick finger between his eyes like a pistol. His eyes were cold, and his face had paled so that blue veins were clearly visible at his temples.

'Somebody,' he ground out, 'some *bastard* murdered my little brother. Murdered him and then cut him up and chucked him down a hole like he was rubbish. I want him found and I want him punished.'

'And I do, too. I promise you we'll do all we can to—'

'No!' JJ shouted. 'Not good enough. Don't give me all that bullshit. I've got a funeral to organise. I reckon it'll take a week to get it sorted. You've got till then to find the fucker who killed Tommy.'

Ford had a terrible suspicion he knew where this was going, but he forced himself to continue. 'We'll do our best, JJ. But murder investigations don't always run to plan. They can take longer than—'

'I said a week. After that, we'll do it our way. We'll find out who did it. And we'll punish them. And that's a promise I *will* keep,' JJ said. 'As for you, your cosy little career will be over. You built it on that dodgy arrest of me and Rye just after you pitched up down here. Don't think I've forgotten.'

36

'You were covered in the victim's blood. I'd hardly call that dodgy.'

JJ waved his hand as if dismissing a servant. 'Old news. Give me your card. I want your number.'

There didn't seem any point staying after that. Ford was used to working under pressure, but it was usually the reasonably good-natured pressure from Sandy. Or the interfering but easy-to-ignore bleating from Martin Peterson, Wiltshire's busybody police and crime commissioner.

A threat from JJ Bolter belonged to a completely different place. A place where industrial-strength cable ties stood in for Quik-Cuffs, iron bars for extendible batons, shuttered outbuildings for interview suites, and, from time to time, deserted woodland for sentencing hearings.

He pushed the thought down. He could cope with it. He had to. He had no choice.

Ford left the station at seven feeling frustrated with the lack of early progress. In the lift, he texted Sam to say he'd cook as soon as he got home.

He got behind the wheel of his Discovery. His phone pinged. Sam's reply couldn't have been any shorter.

K

He sighed. Sam had been going through a stroppy phase. He texted again.

How about pizza out instead?

cool where

Italian place on New Canal?

Ye

I'll pick you up in 5.

K

◆ ◆ ◆

As they ate their huge thin-crust pizzas, slice by slice, Ford looked across the table at Sam. He saw, as always, echoes of Lou's face beneath that mop of dark curls. Not in the eyes: Sam's were brown. But the expression.

Sam's lanky frame hadn't filled out yet, but Ford had noticed a broadening of his shoulders recently. The man beginning to emerge from the boy.

Ford asked his standard question. He used it as a way in, more than a genuine enquiry. 'How was school today?'

Sam swallowed his mouthful then took a gulp of water. What would he get, Ford wondered, the 'OK' or the thumbs-up?

'We had a careers talk today.'

'Yeah?'

'Mrs Chantry asked if anyone had any ideas about what they wanted to do.'

'And did they?'

Sam groaned. 'Darius Finney said he wanted to be a hedge fund manager, 'cause he wants a Lambo by his thirtieth birthday. He's such a posh twat.'

'What did Mrs Chantry say to that?'

'Once we'd all stopped laughing, you mean? She said in that case he should definitely do maths and economics for A level. And psychology, 'cause he'd meet a lot of psychopaths.'

Ford raised his eyebrows. 'She sounds kind of cool.'

Sam nodded as he bit off the corner of a new slice. 'She is,' he mumbled around the pizza. 'I volunteered too.'

'What did you say?'

'I told her I wanted to do something I loved.' He paused. 'Like my dad does.'

Ford felt tears prickle behind his eyes and had to fight down the urge to round the table and hug his son.

He swallowed and nodded. 'Thanks, mate. I caught another case today.'

'Murder?' Sam asked, the slice of pizza stopping halfway to his mouth.

'Usual rules, yes?'

In a sing-song voice, Sam said, 'Don't repeat anything. Don't post anything. On pain of no Wi-Fi. So?'

Ford looked around. The nearest diners were far enough away that he could keep his voice low and not worry about being overheard. 'Looks like it. A dead body in thirteen pieces stuffed down a badger sett.'

Sam frowned and looked up at the ceiling for a second, then back at Ford. 'D'you think thirteen means something?'

Ford shook his head. 'Head, hands, feet, arms, lower legs, thighs and two chunks of the torso. Just the logical number.'

'It would have made it easier to take the body and dump it down the hole, wouldn't it?'

Ford nodded. He remembered the promise he'd made to himself when he'd been squeezed into a black funk in the badger sett. That he'd let Sam into his world a little more. A world that clearly didn't frighten him. Here was his chance.

'Much easier. Say a grown man weighs twelve stone. As a dead weight, that takes a lot of muscle to carry, or even to drag.'

'How much does just a leg weigh?'

Ford rubbed the stubble on his chin. 'Hannah would know. I haven't got a clue.'

'She likes to be called Wix now,' Sam said. 'I'll text her.'

Ford watched in amazement as Sam pulled out his phone. He hadn't realised they'd swapped numbers or that they were on nickname terms.

Sam's thumbs danced over the screen. A few moments later he smiled, tapped in a final few words and put the phone down. 'A leg is roughly ten per cent of your body weight. For a twelve-stone man, that's sixteen point eight pounds.'

'Which is typical Wix, but also interesting. So, over a stone.'

'Yeah, but you could still carry one.'

'Agreed.'

'Why dump it down a badger sett?' Sam asked.

'When you've committed a murder there are two big things you have to do pretty much as soon as you can. One, dispose of the murder weapon. Two, dispose of the body,' Ford said.

'Yep. I've seen *CSI*, Dad. I just watched the whole of the first season on Netflix.'

'So, you just killed a guy. Now you need to get rid of the evidence. And the body is the biggest piece.'

'Not if you've chopped it up, it isn't.'

'Thank you for that. Which just goes to show that teenagers have the same black sense of humour as coppers.'

'If you think that's bad, you should come to Chequers with me one day and hang around at break.'

Ford shook his head. 'Not sure I could cope with that much testosterone in one place.'

Sam smiled. 'Why not bury it properly? Dig a hole?'

'People with bodies to bury are often in a hurry. And, to be honest, buried bodies have a habit of popping up again,' Ford said. 'Farmers plough fields. Forestry people plant new trees. Disturbing the earth enough to bury a body makes a big visual change to the ground. It's noticeable. Maybe not straight away, but grass can grow differently, or the ground can subside.'

'Do you know who he was?'

Ford sighed. 'Yes. And right now that's my biggest problem.'

'Who is it?'

Ford hesitated. But Sam would hear about it on social media or on the radio. 'A guy called Tommy Bolter. Part of a bad family who live up towards the racecourse.'

Sam just shrugged. 'OK.'

Ford felt relief that at least the Bolters hadn't touched Sam. Their world and his didn't intersect at any point. He prayed it would always stay that way.

Sam's phone buzzed. He looked at Ford pleadingly. They had a strict rule at home: no phones at the table. But Sam's friends were important to him and Ford felt he could relax the rule today. He nodded and smiled. 'Go on then.'

While Sam engaged in a long series of messages on whichever social media app he and his mates currently favoured, Ford reached behind him and picked a magazine off the windowsill: one of the local glossies, *Salisbury Life*. All the local shops and cafes had them lying around, on counters, tables, racks by the door. The cover featured a photo of a goldfinch.

He flicked through and came to another bird photo. 'Lords and Lapwings', the headline blared. The article profiled one of the local landowners, Lord Baverstock. In it, he expressed a passion for birdwatching. He'd taken the front cover image himself.

'I'm playing *Mortal Kombat* with Josh later,' Sam said. 'Can we go now? I don't want any pudding.'

At home, the house Ford and Lou had named Windgather –
after the place where they'd first started climbing – Ford and Sam
went their separate ways: Sam to do biology homework, Ford for
a twenty-minute music break playing his guitar before returning
to the day's paperwork. Because it all started in earnest tomorrow.

Upstairs in the small bedroom Ford had converted to a home
office cum music room, he flipped the catches on a battered brown
leather case and lifted the lid. There lay his prized 1962 Fender
Stratocaster. The red paint was showing its age, but wasn't everyone?
Lou had given it to him as a wedding present.

While he waited for the valves in the amp to warm up, he
strummed a few chords with the guitar settled across his knee. He
thought back to Sam's questions. The boy had the makings of a
detective, though Ford knew better than to even think of suggesting
career choices. Instead, he ran through the lines of enquiry – LOEs
– coalescing in his copper's brain.

Witnesses. A second dog-walker? Earlier on the scene than
Polly Evans. Someone who saw the body being dumped. It would
have been the middle of the night, though. Had to be. Who'd
risk something like that in broad daylight? OK, so an insomniac
dog-walker.

The tinny sounds emanating from the unamplified strings
deepened and rounded out as the amp kicked in. He played a few
old B.B. King blues licks, enjoying the pressure on his fingertips as
he bent and released the thin steel strings.

How about motives? Not always the most fruitful LOE. As JJ
had said, he *did* know who Tommy was. Narrowing down the pool
of potential aggressors meant acknowledging its sheer size in the
first place. Forensics could be the best route forward for now. And
the search. He turned his attention to the nature of the cover-up.

People killed each other all the time. Sad but true. But they
often panicked afterwards. They'd leave the body in full view. Run

away, tracking perfect bloody footprints that led right back to the crime scene. Tell people. Even boast about it in the pub or, bafflingly, online.

But not this guy. And Ford knew he was looking for a man. He'd taken Tommy somewhere quiet. And he'd butchered him. Calmly, efficiently. Rendering a human body into more manageable pieces.

He played the introduction to 'Cold Weather Blues' by Muddy Waters. 'Cold' just about summed it up. What kind of man would have the mental strength, as well as the physical, to dismember a human body?

'You're a cold-blooded bastard,' he said to the empty room as he ended the song. 'And I'm going to find you.'

CHAPTER EIGHT

Grateful that the autopsy was taking place in the morning and not after lunch, Ford looked around the forensic post-mortem suite. He'd taken up position at the head end of the stainless-steel dissection table. Georgina Eustace stood opposite him. They'd known each other for ten years. During that time, they'd become good friends. She'd supported him when Lou died; he'd helped her through her divorce. They'd even shared a drunken kiss at Sandy's New Year's Eve party the previous year. Nothing had come of it, but she did allow him to call her George at work. Everyone else stuck to Dr Eustace, or Doc.

As well as Ford and George, the brightly lit space had room for Pete the mortician, who also drummed in Ford's band; a photographer; the coroner's officer; and Hannah, Jools and Olly.

Today, a teal cap obscured George's silver bob. A hinged transparent visor took the shimmer out of her vivid blue eyes. Mask, gown, white rubberised apron, wellingtons and two pairs of rubber gloves completed her professional garb. She looked at Ford, and he nodded.

'Right,' she said briskly, ceasing her humming along to the Mozart playing softly in the background. 'Let's begin, shall we?'

She pulled the sheet back from the pieced-together body to a few stifled gasps.

Ford turned his gaze to the body. He felt no disgust. No horror. Instead, a profound sense of curiosity. Reassembled by Pete, Tommy was asking him questions. *Who killed me? Why did they kill me?*

George turned to Pete, who was waiting patiently. 'PM40, please.'

He handed her a long-handled scalpel fitted with a large blade, curved on its cutting edge. Using it as a pointer, she gestured to the left side of the head.

'Look at this.'

Ford noticed the way Olly and Jools were trying to follow George's instruction without looking at the grotesque parody of a human face.

'There is a great deal of clotted blood in the acoustic meatus,' George said, touching the scalpel tip to the ear hole. 'The tragus and concha have suffered some form of trauma,' she added, gesturing this time to the ridges on the left and right of the opening.

'What could have caused them?' Jools asked.

In the slender area of exposed skin between her cap and mask, Ford saw George's eyes widen. 'I should have thought just about anything, DC Harper. A cricket stump whacked in with a mallet. A tent peg. A butcher's steel. Something with a circular cross section, rather than a blade.'

Ford leaned towards Olly as George went back to her description for the digital recorder. 'Keep your eyes and ears open. You can learn a lot in the mortuary, and Doc Eustace is a good teacher,' he whispered.

He stopped, aware that people were looking at him.

'Something you need to share with the group, *DI* Ford?' George asked him pointedly, her scalpel poised over the corpse's face.

Sniggers.

'Sorry, *Doctor* Eustace.'

'Hmm,' she sniffed, though he saw her eyes twinkling above her mask. 'Please note the extreme exophthalmos, or proptosis. Bulging eyes, in layperson's terms.' The scalpel tip hovered over the left eyeball.

Ford noticed Jools wince. Not Hannah, though. She leaned forward, watching avidly.

'This could be caused by a thyroid problem,' George said. 'However, I notice petechial haemorrhaging on the sclera. See? These scarlet marks on the whites?'

'Aren't they usually caused by choking, Doctor? Could that be the cause of death?' Olly asked.

'Usually, yes. A point for you, DC Cable. But in this specific instance, I think not.' She held out her right hand, palm upwards. 'Magnifier, please.'

Pete handed her a large plastic magnifying glass, which she placed close to the right eye. She straightened and handed it back.

'As I observed with my own, less *insulted* eyes, the petechiae are streaks, not the usual blossom shapes we would expect with asphyxia. And the poor man's corneas are abraded. Something caused the internal pressure in the skull to rise dramatically, forcing out the eyeballs.'

Ford saw it. The damage to the ear. The blood clots. The rise in internal pressure. Someone had shot Tommy through the ear. Instead of exiting his skull, the bullet had ricocheted off the bone and stayed inside. He felt sure it was somewhere in the grotesque array of body parts before him.

'I think he was shot,' he said.

'That's a possibility. Let's find out, shall we?' George said. 'Stryker saw, please, Pete.'

As she brought the whining power tool's oscillating blade down on to the skull, releasing a wisp of foul-smelling smoke, Ford peered at the entry wound. He saw no stippling or powder burns, which ruled out anything up close like an execution-style murder.

He pictured himself as the shooter. *I'm taking a long-range shot because I don't want to risk being seen. I'm using a rifle. A good one, accurate. That means I'm a good shot. I'm confident I can kill Tommy from a distance.*

Pete placed a shallow stainless-steel kidney bowl by the opened skull. George scooped out the brain tissue and deposited it in the bowl in a series of soft plops. She started probing with the scalpel and the tips of her fingers.

Ford watched, but his mind was elsewhere. The shooter probably had their own place. But if they shared a house, they'd have a workshop, basement or outbuilding where they could cut up a body without being disturbed. They owned at least one firearm, almost certainly a rifle. And they were a decent shot. He made a mental note to look at local gun clubs and their membership lists.

'It's not here,' George said, pushing the kidney bowl away from her and wiping her smeared fingers on her apron. 'But don't despair. I once recovered a pistol round from a woman's spleen. She, too, had been killed with a shot to the head.'

'Best guess?' Ford asked.

'The torso. It could be lodged in the viscera, muscle tissue or even wedged between two bones.'

'We're going to leave you to it,' Ford said. 'Can you let me know as soon as you find it?'

'Me too, please?' Hannah said. 'I'll come and collect it. We can start running ballistics analysis on it. I'll alert the lab.'

◆　◆　◆

Later that morning, at the briefing in the sugar cube, Ford learned from Mick that forty-three people fitted the profile he'd drawn up for workers in the meat trade. All were based within five miles of Salisbury. All held either a Level 2 Certificate or Diploma in Professional Butchery, or had done an apprenticeship. That included retail, wholesale and abattoir staff. Of the forty-three, eleven either lived at home or in a shared flat, so he'd downgraded them for lack of somewhere private to do the cutting.

After the briefing, Ford checked his emails. George had sent hi-res photos of the properly cleaned-up tattoos. As he looked them over, he pictured another: a knotted heart of blue and yellow climbing ropes, 'L4E' below in a rugged typeface. Lou had come back from town one sunny Saturday afternoon and proudly showed him her cling-filmed left shoulder.

'It's for us!' she'd said. 'Roped together for eternity.'

Oh, Lou. If only you knew.

CHAPTER NINE

The raft of documents piled up on Ford's desk clogged his brain. He couldn't get a handle on the investigation from behind a desk. He stood abruptly, knocking his policy book against his half-full mug.

He saved the mug but the resulting jerk slopped cold coffee over an untidy sheaf of canvass reports. Figuring they'd dry if he just spread them out, he left his office, took a right and walked along the corridor to the stairwell. Five minutes later he pushed through the door to Forensics.

Hannah was at her desk, peering at a website.

'Hi, got a minute?' he asked as he approached.

She snatched at her mouse and clicked to close the browser. Then she swivelled to face him. 'Henry! Hi. You're here. In Forensics. Why?'

He observed the pallor of her cheeks, which were normally a healthy pink. The way her eyes kept darting to her monitor.

'Are you all right? You seem on edge.'

Beyond her left shoulder he could see an open document. Nothing beyond the four-word title was legible at this distance. His stomach lurched.

Rock-climbing risk assessment.

What the hell? Was she investigating the accident? He'd opened up to her a while back about Lou dying at Pen-y-Holt sea stack.

Now it looked as though, in her obsessive way, she'd got her teeth into it as another puzzle to pick away at. Had he made a mistake? Hannah was a woman who, having thought of something to say, never stopped to think whether she *should*. A woman developing a friendship with Sam. This was unwelcome news.

'I'm fine,' Hannah said. 'Just, you know . . .' She tugged on her long plait of blonde hair. 'Work!' She rolled her eyes, clicking her mouse to close the document.

She'd managed a simulation of professional boredom combined with overwork. A *bad* simulation.

'Fancy a trip?' he asked her, filing his discovery away for now.

'Where to?'

'The site of the body dump. I can't get a feel for the murder cooped up in here.'

'Isn't Jools or one of the others free?'

That was odd. Hannah never turned down requests like this one. Since her first day, she'd enjoyed and even volunteered to take on additional duties that fell way beyond the remit of a CSI. Even the deputy chief.

'They're all busy. I could go on my own if you're in the middle of something?' *Like sticking your nose in where it's definitely not wanted.*

She shook her head. Now she did offer a smile. Genuine, too.

'I'll come. Help ya woik de angles,' she croaked in a cod New York accent Ford suspected nobody had used since the 1940s. Was she trying to deflect attention from the document he'd glimpsed on her screen?

'Come on, then.'

◆　◆　◆

Inside the cordon again, they walked over to the partially excavated sett and stood shoulder to shoulder at its rim.

Ford looked down at the disturbed earth. 'Have you—'

'Taken a soil sample? Yes, several. We're analysing them right now. It'll give us an index reference when you arrest a suspect.'

He turned to her. 'Your confidence is welcome. Thanks.'

'You'll get your man, Henry. Like the Mounties. They're the—'

Now Ford finished *her* sentence. 'Royal Canadian Mounted Police. Did they consult you, too?'

'They did, as a matter of fact.'

'Serial killer?'

'The Wapawekka Strangler. He killed eight college students and dumped their bodies in the lake of that name.'

'Did you catch him?'

'Mm-hmm. Epithelial cells on a rope fragment in his garage.'

'So what do you think about this one?' he asked her.

She compressed her lips and frowned. Ford waited.

'I think,' she said after at least a minute had elapsed, 'we are not looking at a domestic killing.'

'Agreed. The MO is way off.'

'And I also don't think we're dealing with a lust-rage murder.'

'Care to explain?'

'I saw no evidence of sexual injuries as the body parts were being brought out.'

'And the killer had done the opposite of posing his victim.'

'Exactly. He went to some trouble to hide the evidence.'

'Serial?'

'It's possible. But for Salisbury, statistically unlikely.'

Ford stared down into the sett's gaping maw. Pictured himself lugging heavy pieces of flesh from a tractor trailer of some kind and dropping them into the black depths.

'If he'd been serious about stopping us finding the body, he could have burned it, smashed up the bones and ploughed them under,' Ford said. 'Or run it through a wood chipper and fed the slurry to pigs. Plenty of ways you could do it in the countryside. Every farm for miles around would offer at least one of those methods.'

'*Not* a farmer, then?'

'But he knows the area. Look around you.' Ford swept his arm in an arc that took in the fluttering crime scene tape, the uniforms on guard, a CSI van, and a dozen uniforms on their hands and knees conducting a fingertip search. 'You can't see a house, a road, even a power line. It's the middle of nowhere.'

'Polly Evans found it, though,' Hannah countered.

Ford nodded. 'True. And she said she often saw other dog-walkers.'

'I don't think it's feasible to use dog ownership as a suspect identification criterion.'

'That takes me back to the point about knowing the area. That sett's huge. I've seen others, but they're much smaller. You could get a hand down one but not the rest. He knew about it.'

'Who would have that sort of detailed local knowledge?'

Ford scratched at his stubble. He'd forgotten to shave. Again. 'The dog-walkers. The farmer.' He looked over at the shallow chalk stream. 'That's not deep enough for anglers.'

'Birdwatchers?' Hannah asked, pointing up as a charm of goldfinches twittered overhead.

'I'm not seeing a demented twitcher as our killer.' He paused. The goldfinches had reminded him of the magazine in the pizza place he and Sam had eaten in the previous night. And the article about Lord Baverstock.

'Henry?'

The vision dissipated. Ford blinked.

Hannah pulled her mouth to one side in a quirked smile. 'You went far away.'

'Sorry. I was thinking. What if Mr Ball's a tenant farmer? Then somebody else owns the land. And if they did, they might know about the sett, mightn't they?'

'I suppose so. I don't know very much about lords and ladies.'

An admission of ignorance from Hannah was so rare, even in their limited acquaintance, that Ford couldn't help himself.

'I'll make a note of that,' he said. 'Our deputy chief CSI has a gap in her knowledge base.'

Even as he said it, he knew he'd blundered again. Hannah's face fell.

'I'm sorry. There aren't any in the US, and before that I was at university. I should do some background reading.'

Ford reached out and laid a gentle hand on her arm. Smiled. 'It's fine, honestly. You know more than anyone else in the department – hell, the whole station – put together. I was just twitting you. I shouldn't have.'

He let his hand fall. Not wanting her to misread the signal.

'Landowner. Farmer. Dog-walker. Birdwatcher,' Hannah said. 'Or it could be a random stranger scouting a body-dump site.'

Ford had to agree. But he desperately wanted it not to be. 'It could be. But he'd be more likely to dump it somewhere familiar. That would mean he lived close by, and there are no houses for miles around.'

'When Dr Eustace gets me the bullet, we'll have something concrete to go on. Well, metallic.'

Hannah's abrupt change of topic didn't surprise Ford. He knew she preferred science to instinct. Evidence to inspiration. Data to daydreaming. Which was fine. She was an investigator. It was what she did. But in the absence of investigative factors, all activity ceased. Or didn't even begin.

And that was where a case needed a detective. Someone who could close their eyes and paint a crime scene into being. Someone who could imagine, with a greater or lesser degree of success, the thoughts running through a killer's mind in the moments before, during and after a murder. Since Lou, Ford had experienced not merely a greater degree of success, but a one-to-one match. He knew what killers felt.

On the drive back to Bourne Hill, Ford waited for a long straight stretch of road. He flicked a quick glance at Hannah. Inhaled.

'What were you working on when I came to find you?' he asked, striving to keep his tone light.

'Working on?'

'Yes. On your PC. Fingerprints? Blood spatter?' He paused. 'Report-writing? I saw you'd typed something about mountaineering risks. Was Tommy a climber, then?'

If Hannah picked up on the irony, she didn't show it. She hesitated before answering – something of a tell from a self-professed and highly qualified expert in the psychology of lying. 'It's for a friend. He's interested in mountaineering but he's worried about the risks.'

Ford nodded. 'Kind of you. To do some research for him.'

'Thank you.'

He drove on in silence all the way back to Bourne Hill. Maybe she was telling the truth. He suspected she didn't really know how to lie. So, had his own guilt been riding him when he'd seen the title on her PC screen?

He hoped so. He had enough to think about without trying to fend off Hannah if she started asking questions about the accident.

Like JJ's threat.

A week was plenty of time when you were investigating a domestic where the husband was sitting in the flat drenched in blood and weeping into his lager. But this one was different. This screamed *complex*.

◆ ◆ ◆

Olly came to see him as soon as he reached Major Crimes.

'I contacted Tommy's network provider. His phone stopped pinging on Saturday – the one just gone, May the first. The last tower it shook hands with was a few miles south of Coombe Bissett.'

That particular landscape contained nothing but farm animals, and not very many of them. No significant settlements until you reached Blandford Forum. What was he doing? Who had tracked him there? And who owned the land?

Ford thanked Olly, registered the smile the young DC tried to hide, and continued his walkaround. Mick's voice – raised and angry – broke the silence. He caught Ford's eye and dropped his voice, though Ford could make out every hissed word.

'Yeah, I know that, but I . . . That's why I want you to . . . OK, I'm sorry! I would *like* you to at least *talk* about it before you . . . You can't—' Mick scowled at the phone, breathing heavily. Obviously the other party had hung up on him.

Ford waited for Mick to look at him again. It took a while.

'Everything all right?' he asked.

Mick pocketed the phone, his face red; whether from anger or embarrassment, Ford couldn't tell.

'It's nothing. Kirsty's just bending my ear as usual. Women, eh. Can't live with 'em . . .' Mick went for a shrug and a comedy eye-roll.

Ford continued towards his office. The door was open. Odd. He always closed it when he left. Entering, he had to suppress a scowl of his own.

Martin Peterson, police and crime commissioner for Wiltshire, sat behind Ford's desk. Was leaning back in Ford's chair. Leafing through Ford's paperwork. About which Ford now found he cared a great deal.

Peterson looked up. His smile revealed gleaming teeth. To Ford they looked veneered.

'Hope you don't mind,' Peterson said. 'Someone told me I could wait in here.'

Ford doubted that. On a scale of one to ten as to how much people disliked the PCC, Ford rated himself a nine. Most of his team would rate themselves a ten. Or above.

He rounded the desk, forcing Peterson to vacate the chair. 'What can I do for you, Mr Peterson?'

'No need for all the formality. I am here as your colleague. Your friend, if you'll let me. Call me Martin. Do you know,' he said, frowning, 'I don't think you've ever told me *your* first name.'

Ford sat in the chair and shuffled the papers into a pile. He said nothing.

Clearing his throat, Peterson touched the knot of his fuchsia-pink tie. 'I hear you're investigating another murder,' he said.

Ford nodded. 'It's what we do in Major Crimes.'

'Yes, well, I want you to know I'll be taking an active interest in the case.'

'May I ask why?'

'Oh, come now. No need to be so defensive. A gruesome murder. Body parts' – he shuddered – 'disposed of in a hole in the ground—'

'A sett.'

'Fine, a set of body parts—'

'No. They were dumped down a sett. You know . . . where badgers live?'

There. A flicker of irritation on Peterson's smooth-cheeked face let Ford know he'd got to him. He'd pricked that bubble of fake affability.

'I don't, actually, care whether they were dumped down a badger sett or in the cathedral font,' Peterson said. 'The point is, it's a highly unusual situation and I want to see it resolved quickly. As I told you before, the city needs publicity of this kind like a hole in the head.'

'Funnily enough, that's exactly what the corpse had.'

Paling, Peterson stood and extended his hand, which Ford shook briefly. 'I expect to be kept posted. Cheers, now!'

'Prick,' Ford muttered as the door closed behind Peterson's suited frame.

His PC bleeped to announce the arrival of an email. His heart rate picked up when he saw the sender: George.

She'd found the bullet. Although she cautioned against taking her word as gospel, it appeared to be a .308 calibre ballistic tip, a typical deer-hunting round. After bouncing around in Tommy's skull, it had travelled south and lodged in his liver. For time of death, the copper's friend and pathologist's major irritant, she'd estimated two to five days. Whoever cut him up had used a large-bladed knife and a hacksaw.

Thanking whichever stars had aligned to bring George to Salisbury, he called one of his contacts, the news editor of the *Salisbury Journal*.

'Hello, Inspector, what can I do for you?'

'You might have heard there's been a nasty murder. Tommy Bolter?'

'I did hear something, yes. We put a little piece on the website ahead of the next issue.'

'We need people to come forward if they saw him in the days or hours before his death. Even if they didn't know him, they might recognise him,' Ford said. 'He had some distinctive tattoos. If I sent you some photos, could you print them and ask your readers to contact us?'

'Of course. You're in luck. We're going to press this evening. Can you give me some more details?'

Ford spent ten minutes running through the details of the case, securing a promise to have the story in the following day's paper. Then he went to find Jools.

'We've got the bullet. It's a .308 ballistic tip.'

'Wix told me. It just arrived from the hospital.'

'I want you to start canvassing local gun shops, starting with Berret & Sartain in the city centre. We need lists of customers who bought that type of ammunition.'

'On it.'

Ford wanted to know who owned the land where they'd found the body. He'd asked Olly to look at the Land Registry database, but in the meantime he figured that in a small place like Salisbury, locals often had the answers he needed. Some additional background might be helpful, too.

Twenty minutes later, he wandered into a pub on a road running along one side of Ball's farm. He asked the barmaid which of her regulars knew the local area best.

'You'll be wanting Old Dan. Eighty-nine and he's been drinking in here every day since he were sixteen. He's there, love, by the fruit machine.'

Ford looked over and saw the man in question, large of belly, wild of hair, sitting beside a flashing, dinging, bleeping fruit machine. Ford wondered how he could stand the noise. He made his way over and introduced himself.

Old Dan shook Ford's proffered hand, simultaneously using his left to raise his pint glass to his lips and drain the remaining beer.

He replaced it on the thickly varnished tabletop with a meaningful look.

'Get you another?' Ford asked.

Old Dan grinned, revealing a great deal of pink gum and three or four yellowing teeth. 'Summer Lightning. And some cheese and onion crisps. Please,' he added, the grin widening further.

Ford wondered how the man was going to manage crisps with such limited dentition. Smiling, he returned to the bar.

With beer for Old Dan and a lime and soda for himself, Ford raised his glass and they clinked rims. Old Dan stuffed a handful of crisps into his mouth, gummed them enthusiastically, then took a long pull on his drink.

'Well, then,' he said finally, leaning back in his chair and stroking the blue jumper that stretched over his belly. 'What *exactly* is it you want to know?'

'Who owns the land around here?'

Old Dan's bushy white eyebrows crawled upwards. 'That all? Thought it'd be something a bit more difficult. You'd be wanting that Lord Baverstock. He owns all the farmland hereabouts.'

Interesting. Ford made a note. In the space of a single answer, Old Dan had drawn a line from the criminal underclass through the ranks of middle-class farmers to the aristocracy.

'What's he like, then, this Lord Baverstock?' he asked, dropping easily into Old Dan's country way of speaking.

Before answering, Old Dan drank some more beer.

'Well,' he said. 'That's a good question, isn't it? His dad was what you might call old-fashioned. Never 'ad much time for the likes of me. Or you, come to that. But the new lord, now, he's more of a man of the people. Or wants to be, leastways.'

Ford smiled encouragingly. 'How do you mean?'

'Oh, you know, gives you a nice "good morning" if you see him out on his horse. Treats his staff well. My grand-niece works up at

Alverchalke Manor. She's a maid but they calls her a *housekeeping assistant*.' Old Dan uttered the job description as if it were a foreign phrase.

'What else?' Ford prompted.

Old Dan drank some more beer. Ford wondered how much he'd had before they started speaking. But the man held it well, that was the point. He was lucid, once you penetrated his thick Wiltshire accent, and delivered his answers confidently.

'Ex-army, like a lot of 'em. Brave man, too. Got the Queen's Gallantry Medal. And I can tell you, they don't give those out for collecting the tops off Cornflakes packets.' Old Dan threw his head back and laughed at his own joke, revealing the toothless cavern of his mouth. He rubbed at his chin and, as his sleeve slipped, Ford saw the edge of an old indigo tattoo.

In that moment, Ford saw a different side to Old Dan. He followed his instinct. 'Were you in uniform?' he asked.

Old Dan put his drink down. 'I were eighteen when I signed up. The Glosters – that's the Royal Gloucestershire Regiment. I were in Korea, Aden, Kenya, Cyprus, Swaziland: all over.'

'So does Lord Baverstock like old soldiers, then? Is that why he says hello to you?'

Old Dan rubbed his chin again. 'I suppose he must do. His gamekeeper's been in the forces, too, Lily says. She's my grand-niece. The *housekeeping assistant*,' he added, presumably in case Ford had forgotten.

Old Dan excused himself, levered himself out of his chair and headed, none too steadily, towards the toilets.

Ford reflected on what Old Dan had told him and how it fitted with what he already knew.

Someone had shot a local gangster with a high-powered rifle round and dismembered the body, acts requiring a cool head. Both the landowner on whose estate the body had been found and his gamekeeper had military experience.

The stats said the murderer was most likely known to the victim. Ford's instinct was to look higher up the social ladder.

Feeling he'd got what he needed, Ford thanked Old Dan when he returned to the table, bought him a fresh pint and left the pub to make a call from his car. On the way out, he spotted a copy of *Salisbury Life* with Lord Baverstock's photo of a goldfinch on its cover. He picked it up and tucked it under his arm.

A quick Google search revealed that Lord Baverstock, officially the Viscount Baverstock, lived with his family on the Alverchalke estate in the Chalke Valley. The valley comprised unspoilt pastoral land following the River Ebble for eleven miles, from Salisbury towards Shaftesbury in neighbouring Dorset.

Ford called Alverchalke Manor.

'Alverchalke,' a woman's voice announced in the crisp upperclass tones Ford associated with period TV dramas.

'This is Detective Inspector Ford, Wiltshire Police. May I speak to Lord Baverstock, please?'

'I'm afraid he's out with the dogs at the moment. I'm Lady Baverstock. May I help, Inspector?'

'I'm sure you can. A man was murdered on land that I believe you and your husband own. I'd like to come out for a chat, if that's OK.'

'Oh, how dreadful! And of course you must come. Whatever we can do to help. When were you thinking?'

Ford checked his watch. 'It's two now. Could we say three thirty?'

'Of course. I'll call my husband. Make sure he's back by the time you arrive.'

Something about aristocrats made Ford uncomfortable. He'd been to charity fundraisers at the Guildhall with Lou, as well as the occasional mayoral dinner and regional police functions as a representative of Bourne Hill. At all of them, titled people swanned around as if they owned the place. Which, Ford reflected ruefully, they probably did.

Inverted snobbery? That's what Lou used to say, teasing him afterwards in bed. 'My working-class hero,' she'd say, laughing and pulling him close.

He knew the problem. They gave off a vibe that said, *We're untouchable, beyond your reach, masters – and mistresses – of the universe. Leave well alone or you'll be sorry.*

Wanting a second pair of eyes and ears for this particular interview, he headed to Bourne Hill to collect Hannah. On the way there, his phone rang: the *Journal's* news editor.

'Inspector, it's Emily Latimer. We're running the story tomorrow, but we can't use one of the images.'

'Oh?'

'The nudie one breaches our family-friendly editorial policy. Sorry.'

He smiled. 'That's OK. The other three were pretty distinctive.'

Ten minutes later, with Hannah sitting beside him, he turned the Discovery towards Alverchalke.

CHAPTER TEN

Gravel popped and crunched beneath the Discovery's tyres as Ford pulled up in front of the grand house at the centre of the Alverchalke estate. A patchwork of sandstone and flint diamonds and sections of chequered red and black bricks, it had been modified, or repaired, multiple times over the years. At the front left-hand corner, a circular tower rose above four sets of three octagonal brick chimneys, giving the whole edifice a lopsided look. An ancient wisteria climbed over the first storey, flooding the leaded windows with a waterfall of pendulous purple flowers that emitted a sweetish, spicy scent.

He contrasted the house with the Bolters' gaudy ranch-style home. They were affluent, too, in their way, but had nowhere near the wealth that oozed from between the stones of Alverchalke Manor.

Ford stretched his neck in the too-tight shirt collar he'd buttoned on the way over. He looked down at his M&S suit trousers. Noticed a small coffee stain near the left knee. Was JJ right? Should he upgrade his wardrobe?

Yes, because cleaning blood, shit and vomit off a designer suit would be a really useful way to spend his time.

With Hannah beside him, he marched up to the oak door and yanked a wrought-iron bell pull connected to a wire that ran through a hole in the stonework. From somewhere deep inside the house he heard the tinkling of a bell.

While they waited, Ford caught the sound of hoofbeats. From around the tower, a huge black horse, its coat flecked with foamy sweat, trotted towards them. A young woman sat astride it. She nodded down at them. No riding helmet, Ford noticed. In her early thirties, he judged, and built along substantial lines.

Cream jodhpurs emphasised muscular thighs. The sleeves of a royal-blue T-shirt did the same for her broad shoulders and upper arms. Blonde hair held back by a black velvet Alice band revealed a high domed forehead. Her tanned face bore a friendly smile.

Ford walked towards her, intending to introduce himself. He reached into his pocket for his ID and held it out in front of him.

Something in his movement must have spooked the horse. It shimmied sideways, tossing its head. Then, without warning, it reared up in front of him, whinnying loudly.

He stepped back hurriedly, out of range of its hooves. The young woman shifted her weight and rode out the storm before the horse's forefeet came down with a double clop on the gravel.

Leaning forward, she stroked its neck and whispered something into its pricked-up ear. Whatever she said did the trick. The wild-eyed animal that had looked ready to trample Ford into the dirt a few seconds earlier now appeared as docile as a riding-school hack.

'Sorry about that,' she said, looking down at Ford. 'Woodstock's normally pretty friendly around strangers. Can I help you?'

'We're here to see Lord and Lady Baverstock,' Hannah said. 'Are you their daughter?'

'That's me.' She dismounted and led the horse over to them, where it stood snorting and shaking its silky mane. She held out her hand. 'Lucy. But everyone calls me Loopy.'

'Do you live here?' Ford asked.

'Yah. The old ancestral seat's big enough for the whole fam. Mummy, Daddy, me and Stodge.'

'Stodge?' Ford asked, imagining a silky-coated golden retriever.

'Yah. Stodgy Stephen. He's my brother. What are you, anyway? Bankers?'

'Police,' Ford said. 'Detective Inspector Ford.'

She frowned. 'Police?'

'Yes,' Hannah said. 'Although technically I'm police staff, which means I'm not warranted. I'm Dr Hannah Fellowes, deputy head of forensics.'

Ford caught the flash of confusion that clouded Lucy's high forehead then disappeared. Hannah's detail-obsessed mind could catch people unawares. It was a useful, if unconscious, trait.

'Oh, yah, of course. How do you do?'

'We're investigating a murder,' Hannah said.

Lucy flinched. 'Murder? Oh God, how absolutely awful!'

'The body of a young man was found on the land of one of your tenant farmers,' Ford said. 'His name was Tommy Bolter. Did you ever meet him?'

Lucy looked at him for a couple of seconds, then turned away and nuzzled the horse's cheek. 'Tommy Bolter, Woody. Did we ever meet him?' She turned back to Ford and Hannah. 'He says no. Soz.'

Hannah pointed at the horse. 'You're using a Western saddle. Why is that?'

Ford looked. The bucket-shaped saddle had a horn at the front and a lot more padding than those used by the mounted cops he'd worked with.

Lucy smiled at Hannah. 'He can be a handful, as you've just seen. I like the extra security.'

A young woman opened the door dressed in a forest-green uniform of skirt and jacket over a white blouse. Sensible low heels on her feet and dark tights despite the warm spring weather. Ford wondered if she was Old Dan's grand-niece.

'OK, well, have fun with the old folks,' Lucy said. She clicked her tongue. 'Come on, Woodstock, let's get you rubbed down.'

She led the horse away, its soft nickers audible all the way to the far end of the house.

Ford turned to the woman who'd opened the door and showed her his ID. 'Detective Inspector Ford and Dr Hannah Fellowes. We're here to see Lord and Lady Baverstock,' he said.

The maid – what had Dan called her, *housekeeping assistant?* – or whatever rich people called the servant they paid to admit visitors, smiled. The expression dissipated the severe impression created by the sober uniform. 'They're expecting you. Please follow me.'

She led them into a wood-panelled room, large enough to house a grand piano as well as a seating group of two tan leather Chesterfield sofas and several armchairs covered in yellow and grey chrysanthemum-patterned chintz.

Tall windows gave on to a landscape so artful Ford wondered whether it had been designed by human hands rather than Mother Nature's: a winding river, sparkling in the middle distance, beyond which a forest of deep-green trees rolled away to the horizon. To one side, a ruined classical temple. Closer to the house, an ornamental pond with a two-tiered fountain playing on to its water-lilied surface.

'Inspector Ford?' A woman's voice.

He turned, smiling – going for the genial look he'd seen Mick use on people he unironically referred to as his 'betters'.

The woman in her late sixties who had just entered the room wore a creased navy sweatshirt over faded jeans. Below tousled, honey-coloured hair, the suggestion of a smile lingered on an intelligent face. She shook hands with Ford. Her skin felt rough and dry against his.

Hannah pumped Lady Baverstock's hand in what Ford had come to think of as her 'signature shake' and introduced herself.

'Thank you for seeing us at such short notice, Lady Baverstock,' Ford said.

She took one of the armchairs and motioned for them to sit. 'Do take a sofa. And please call me Coco. Lady Baverstock makes me sound like some ghastly old bat out of an Austen novel.'

'My colleagues call me Wix,' Hannah said. 'It's short for Wikipedia.'

Lady Baverstock smiled. 'Are you something of a brainbox, then?'

Hannah nodded. 'Yes. I've always been clever. Cleverer than most people, in fact. Some people find it off-putting, but in my work it's actually very useful.'

'I'm sure it is, my dear.'

'We met your daughter outside with a very big black horse named Woodstock. Is that after Edward of Woodstock, the Black Prince?'

Lady Baverstock's social smile widened into the real thing. 'Well, technically she's my stepdaughter, but nonetheless, how very clever of you! Now I can see why your colleagues awarded you such a brilliant nickname.'

Hannah beamed. Ford marvelled at the easy charm the upper class could deploy. *Must learn it at their posh private schools* was his conclusion.

Lady Baverstock's features assumed a serious expression. 'You said a man was murdered? Do you have his name?'

'Tommy Bolter. Did you know him?'

She sighed. 'It's probably better you wait for Bumble. He's just cleaning up.'

Ford frowned. 'Bumble?'

'My husband. It's his old boarding school nickname. Like the bee? He used to hum when concentrating. I think it even stuck when he went into the army.'

'I sometimes talk to myself to help me concentrate,' Hannah said.

While Lady Baverstock engaged Hannah in small talk, Ford's phone buzzed. A text from JJ.

Find my brother's killer. I meant what I said.

Fighting down the brief surge of adrenaline that elevated his heartbeat, he pocketed his phone just as Lord Baverstock walked in. Tall and, like his wife, dressed casually, he sported a crumpled denim shirt and mustard-coloured cords over boat shoes with knotted laces. Old-fashioned glasses with heavy black frames magnified a questioning gaze. He ran a hand through damp hair: short and dark brown, with a little grey at the temples.

'Inspector Ford, isn't it? And you've brought a colleague. Excellent. Two heads better than one, eh?'

Ford and Hannah got up to greet him. Hannah advanced and deployed her signature shake.

'I'm pleased to meet you, sir,' she said.

'Oh, please. Didn't my wife tell you to call me Bumble?'

'She did, yes.'

'Well, then! Can't have you both calling her Coco and me "sir" or "Your Lordship" or whatever, can we?'

Lord Baverstock took the armchair beside his wife's and motioned for Ford and Hannah to sit.

Ford decided to press on with his reason for coming. 'As I told your wife—'

'Coco,' she interrupted.

'—Coco, a man was murdered, and then dismembered. He's been formally identified as Tommy Bolter. The body parts were put down a badger sett on land farmed by Mark Ball. I believe he's one of your tenants?'

'That's right. I should tell you, Inspector,' Lord Baverstock said, 'I did actually know Bolter.'

Ford maintained a bland expression. People like Tommy Bolter didn't exactly move in the same social circles as Salisbury's landed gentry.

'How?' he asked.

'Our gamekeeper caught him poaching a couple of times,' he said, wrinkling the bridge of his bulbous nose. 'Nothing serious, just a couple of trout and a rabbit or two, but it's the principle of the thing. He brought Bolter up to the house once to see me.'

'What happened?' Hannah asked.

'I gave him a bloody good talking-to. He reminded me of some of the young lads under my command. Did Coco tell you I was in the army?'

Ford nodded. 'Out of interest, what regiment?'

'Grenadier Guards. Bit of a family tradition,' he added with a smile.

'Quite a long one, by the looks of it,' Ford said, pointing at a painting on the wall. It depicted an extravagantly bewhiskered man in a bright scarlet jacket festooned with gold braid and brass buttons. A sabre gleamed at his hip.

Lord Baverstock glanced over his shoulder, then turned back to Ford. 'That is my great-great-great-great-grandfather. They called him Butcher Baverstock. Pretty ferocious-looking fellow, wouldn't you say?'

'You were telling us about your conversation with Bolter?'

'He put me in mind of some of the boys I took out to Afghanistan. Plucky as hell, but they hadn't had all the advantages. Or if they had, they didn't make use of them,' he said.

'Rough diamonds?'

Lord Baverstock nodded. 'A bit wild, some of them. One always felt they'd have ended up in prison if one hadn't got them first, d'you see?'

Ford did see. He'd met his fair share of young men who'd reached a fork in the road and chosen the wrong path. 'How did he respond?' he asked.

'Oh, lots of forelock-tugging and "yes, my lord; no, my lord". Joe escorted him off the estate and he behaved himself until the urge took him and he tried his luck again.'

'Did Joe catch him that time, too?'

Lord Baverstock snorted. 'Yes. It was two weeks ago. Bolter gave poor old Joe a bloody nose. He would have made a fine regimental boxer if I'd had him early enough.'

Ford jotted down: 'Gamekeeper – Joe – fight with TB'. Maybe he'd have something to tell JJ after all. Gamekeepers knew how to shoot. They had to. It was part of the job. And according to Old Dan, the gamekeeper was ex-army. So presumably he was a good shot with a rifle and not just someone content to blast away with a shotgun.

Would coming off second best in a fight be motive for murder? Of course it would! He'd seen men murdered for less. He looked at the two unassuming aristocrats in front of him. He saw open faces. Direct gazes. Not challenging, but enquiring. The sorts of expressions worn by people with nothing to hide.

A uniformed maid arrived with a tray of tea things. She discreetly offered and poured cups for all four people in the room, then retreated on silent feet. Ford wondered how she'd known to bring it in. Perhaps the upper classes had prearranged signals for that sort of thing.

As he was pondering the puzzles of aristocratic hospitality, the door swung open again. A young man stood there in jodhpurs and a sky-blue T-shirt emblazoned with the words 'Rockbourne Polo Club' clinging to his torso. His blonde hair flopped over one eye. To Ford, it looked studied rather than casual, as if he'd arranged it in a mirror.

'You've got company, Pa,' he said, while staring at Ford.

Lord Baverstock turned to him. 'They're police, Stephen. Come and say hello.'

The man now revealed as the Baverstocks' son advanced on Ford, hand outstretched. After the introductions, he fell back into an overstuffed chair and slung a booted foot over one arm.

'What's all this about, then?'

'We're investigating a murder,' Hannah said.

'Awesome! Can I stay and listen in while you interrogate Pa and Coco?' He turned to Lord Baverstock and winked. 'Going to go "no comment", are you?'

Hannah wrinkled her nose. 'We're not interrogating them. We just came to ask a few questions.'

'Whatevs. Don't mind me. I'll just sit here and absorb the atmos.'

'Darling! Be serious. This poor man, Tommy Bolter, has been found murdered on Mark Ball's land,' Lady Baverstock said. 'Or found there, at any rate. In pieces, may I add. I hardly think this is a time for levity.'

Stephen's eyes widened. 'Tommy bloody Bolter? Good riddance! Chap was always stealing from us, wasn't he, Pa?'

Lord Baverstock frowned. 'Yes. But that doesn't mean he deserved to be murdered, does it?'

Stephen's grin vanished, and Ford watched him effortfully rearranging his features into something more serious, though the resulting expression looked stagy. 'Yah. No, of course. Dreadful business.' He stood. 'Think I won't stay after all. I'll go and give Loopy a hand with the horses.'

Ford took another sip of tea and looked past Lord and Lady Baverstock to the paintings on the wall behind them. Landscapes, mostly, some obviously of their own estate. Animal pictures featuring sad-eyed greyhounds, statuesque horses and the occasional pile of dead game. And more military portraits.

One painting caught his eye. A younger version of Lord Baverstock stood beside an attractive woman holding the lead of a shaggy grey wolfhound. Flame-haired and dark-eyed, she looked nothing like Lady Baverstock.

'A lovely portrait,' he said, pointing.

They swivelled in their seats. 'That's Bumble and Sasha,' Lady Baverstock said, with a small smile. 'She was a true beauty, don't you think?'

'Yes,' Ford answered, picking up on the past tense. A dead daughter?

'My first wife,' Lord Baverstock said. 'Stodge and Loopy's mother.'

'Ah,' Ford said.

'She died. Motor neurone disease.'

'I'm sorry for your loss,' Ford said, instantly regretting the trite phrase that they'd all started using nowadays. 'It's a terrible illness,' he added, trying for a more personal touch.

'Indeed,' said Lord Baverstock, his eyes dropping to his lap.

Ford realised he'd opened a painful wound. There was nothing else he wanted to ask right now. Time to go.

'I'd like to speak to your gamekeeper.' He handed Lady Baverstock one of his cards. 'Please could you ask him to call me?'

Once they were outside again, Ford saw Stephen peering in through the driver's window of the Discovery. A couple of dead rabbits swung from his right hand.

'Hope you don't mind,' he said as Ford and Hannah approached. 'I just love Discos. What year's yours?'

'It's a 2002.'

Stephen nodded his appreciation. 'Nice.'

Ford pointed at the rabbits. 'Been shooting?'

'Joe bagged them this morning with a .22. I was just going to dress them. You a sportsman, Inspector?'

'I used to go shooting with my grandad sometimes,' Ford said. 'Rabbits, mostly, like those. My mum made them into pies.'

Stephen smiled and held one out to Ford. 'Here, have one.'

Ford accepted the rabbit. He looked down into its glazed-over eyes. Then at the small bullet hole in its flank. *Hardly any blood.*

He made a brief stop at home, and asked Hannah to wait in the Discovery. In the garage, he put the rabbit in a carrier bag then placed it in the chest freezer.

As they drove back to Bourne Hill, his thoughts turned to the gamekeeper bested by Tommy Bolter. Was it just a punch-up, of the sort that occurred outside dozens of pubs across the city on Friday and Saturday nights? Or something worse?

What was the game Sam played with Josh? *Mortal Kombat?* If you pitted a local gangster, even a junior one, against an ex-soldier, there'd be a hell of a lot of pride resting on the outcome. Losing the fight would be losing face. Maybe it had turned mortal after all.

CHAPTER ELEVEN

The next morning, once Sam had left the house to meet up with Josh before school, Ford drove away from Salisbury, heading out into the Chalke Valley. Twelve minutes later he arrived in a small village called Broad Chalke. He turned off High Road on to The Causeway and parked in the small gravelled space behind All Saints' Church.

He locked the doors and walked through the gap in the hedge. Her grave was on the outer fringe of the churchyard. The stone, a simple rectangle of rough red granite, stood in the dappled shade cast by an old apple tree.

He kneeled before it and, as he always did, read the inscription.

LOUISA KATHRYN FORD
BELOVED WIFE AND MOTHER
'THE MOUNTAINS QUAKE BEFORE HIM AND THE HILLS MELT AWAY.'

At the time, Lou's parents and Ford's mum had been against the quote. After all that had happened, they said, how could he think of even *mentioning* the word 'mountain', let alone carving it into her gravestone?

What could he say? That he wanted to be reminded, always, of what he had done? That he wanted to be forced to remember he had killed her? That he needed the granite to be scarred as deeply as his soul?

Of course not. Instead he had said Lou loved the mountains. Always had. That love was bigger and more powerful than a mere million tons of rock. That, in the end, he and Lou would be reunited, free to climb together without fear.

They'd relented. They'd had to. And now here he was, kneeling at her feet, striving to feel the forgiveness they'd all assured him she would have bestowed on him in an instant. It was an accident. A tragic accident. Nothing more.

He looked up into the branches of the apple tree, thick with blossom, the petals white and fringed with pink. Two sparrows hopped about in its leafy embrace, twittering crossly at each other as they scrapped for the best spot from which to sing. As one flew off and the victor began cheeping loudly from its victory perch, he stood and looked around. The graveyard was empty.

'I wish you were still here,' he said. 'Sam's such a big lad now. You'd have loved the way he's turning out. He's fearless. Just like you.'

Then he turned and walked back to the Discovery, brushing the wet from his cheeks. He reached the station at 8.30 a.m.

Ford's phone rang five minutes later. Unknown caller.

'My name's Joe Hibberd. You wanted to speak to me?'

The man's accent wasn't local. Somewhere in London.

'I did. Could you come into Bourne Hill police station?'

'Why?'

'I'm investigating a murder and I have a few questions for you.'

'But I've got a rearing field full of pheasant chicks. It's a twenty-four-seven job.'

'So's mine, Mr Hibberd.'

He heard Hibberd sigh. Waited him out. Nothing like a copper's silence to push people out of their comfort zone. So what Hibberd said next surprised him.

75

'I can't. Sorry. If you want to speak to me, you'll have to come up to the field.'

Ford found himself listening to the hiss and faint crackles on the line. He thought he could hear cheeping in the background. What to do? Far too early to start throwing his weight around.

'Where are you?'

'I'll text you my GPS.'

Twenty minutes later, Ford turned off the track. Two minutes elapsed while he opened, drove through and closed a five-bar gate. Then he was bumbling across an expanse of lumpy grassland dotted with bushes thick with creamy-white blossom. He switched off the satnav, because in the distance he could see a man who appeared to be shooting. He stopped a hundred yards back.

Outside the Discovery, he smiled as the sun warmed his face. Up here, the wind was keener than it had been in the city centre, and it brought the pungent, farmyard smell of muck-spreading up from the south.

He walked upwind towards the man who was stood side-on to Ford, a long gun to his shoulder. It emitted a sharp crack. Hibberd took the rifle from his shoulder and walked away. Not wanting to engage in a slow-speed walking chase through the Wiltshire coun-tryside, Ford called out.

'Mr Hibberd! Wait!'

Hibberd turned and began walking back, the rifle swinging by his side. He arrived a minute later. Dressed in a forest-green polo shirt, jeans and heavy work boots, he was in his late thirties: solidly built, with short dark hair and tattoos on both exposed forearms. He had the weathered skin of a man whose job kept him outside year round.

'You Ford, then?'

Ford showed his ID. He looked at the rifle. 'Nice little gun.'

Hibberd looked down as though he'd never seen it before. 'This? Yeah, it's all right, I suppose. Just got a bunny before you showed up. For the pot.'

'Do you want to go and pick it up? Be a shame to waste the meat.'

Hibberd shook his head. 'Nah. Don't worry. I'll get it later. Or shoot another one if a kite gets it.'

Ford thought of the rabbit in his freezer and that two might make a decent pie. 'Can I have it, then?'

Hibberd's face flushed alarmingly and he moved to block Ford's way. 'No! Leave it! Jesus, why does every townie always think they can come out here and have whatever they like? I should never have agreed to meet you.'

Ford held his hands up. 'It's fine, I'll leave it. I'm sorry.'

Hibberd sighed and rolled his head on his neck. 'What did you want to see me about?'

Ford smiled, intending the expression to be taken as reassurance. He stored Hibberd's extreme reaction away for later consideration. Sweat had beaded on the gamekeeper's forehead and the bridge of his nose. His deep-set eyes darted left and right as if searching for an escape route. And he was biting his lower lip.

'Thanks for agreeing to talk to me, Mr Hibberd,' he said. 'Or can I call you Joe?'

'Joe's fine. Let's get it over with. I need to get back to the chicks. I was just taking a little break.' His lip-chewing had pulled loose a sliver of skin and produced a bead of blood.

'Busy job being a gamekeeper, I should imagine.'

'Yeah, it's not a job for slackers. Shoots to organise, dogs to train, vermin control,' he said. 'Even working with you lot trying to stop those bloody bastards badger-digging and hare-coursing.'

'Ever come across a bloody bastard called Tommy Bolter?'

Hibberd's reaction to Ford's question developed in several discrete steps. His Adam's apple bobbed twice in his neck. He rubbed his chin fiercely. He bit his lip again, then sucked it into his mouth. 'Is that what this is about?'

'He was found dead on land owned by your boss. According to Lord Baverstock, you had a bit of a scrap with him a couple of weeks back. He gave you a nosebleed.'

Hibberd shrugged. 'Lucky punch.'

'Did you hit him back?'

'Of course I did! But it was just a fight. Nothing more.'

'You didn't feel he'd humiliated you in front of your employer?'

'No! People like Bolter are just vermin. Foxes bite, poachers throw punches. That's if they're not pulling a knife. No difference.'

'So you weren't tempted to control this particular vermin, then? Shoot him in the head, for example?'

Hibberd smiled, shaking his own – intact – head. 'No point, is there? Put one down, there's two more to take his place. Plus, I wouldn't fancy getting on the wrong side of that family, know what I mean?'

Ford did. He'd crossed that line years back. 'If I were to give you some dates, would you be able to tell me your whereabouts?'

Hibberd touched the back of his hand to his lip and inspected the red dots stippling the skin. He looked at Ford. 'Don't need you to do that. I can tell you now. Working.'

'All day, every day?'

'Pretty much. If I'm not working, I'm asleep.'

'Can anyone confirm that?'

'Bess and Molly.'

'Can I talk to them?'

Hibberd shrugged. 'I don't know. Can you speak collie? They're over there somewhere,' he added, pointing off towards a small patch of woodland.

Ford decided it was time to rein in the uncooperative game-keeper. 'You know, Joe, it's looking like you were one of the last people to see Tommy Bolter alive,' he said quietly. 'You were involved in a fight with him a week or so before he died. You obviously know your way around guns. You work for the family on whose land his body was found. Save the jokes for the pub, yes?'

Hibberd folded his arms. 'Fine. But if you're looking at people who've had fights with Tommy Bolter, that puts me at the end of a long queue.'

'They don't all have guns, though, do they?'

'I wouldn't be so sure about that. Half the people who live in the countryside have them.'

'Fair point. And please don't think I'm trying to pin anything on you. I'm just trying to get to the truth.'

'If it's the truth you're after, you should talk to the lowlifes Bolter used to hang around with,' Hibberd said. 'They're all into drugs, thieving, fly-tipping. Anything they can make a bit of money from without doing honest work.'

'Anyone in particular?'

'No idea. I didn't exactly ask him to show me his Facebook friends.'

Ford heard barking. He looked over towards the woods. Two black and white border collies were racing towards them. Ten feet out, they dropped to their bellies and began creeping along, their eyes not leaving his.

'Easy, now,' Hibberd crooned. 'Inspector Ford's a friend, girls. Friend!'

As if they understood him perfectly, the two dogs stood and trotted up to Ford. He offered the back of his hand for them to sniff. Apparently satisfied he presented no threat to their master, they went to nuzzle Hibberd's free hand for a second or two, then, with joyous yelps, streaked back towards the woodland.

Hibberd watched them go, smiling. 'Best two dogs I've ever had,' he said. 'They're like family to me. Better than kids.'

Ford looked at the dogs, then back at Hibberd. 'Do you own a gun?'

'Of course I do! I'm a gamekeeper.'

'What guns, specifically?'

'A .22 like this one and a Browning Phoenix 12 gauge. Check your database. My certificate's all in order.'

'I will. You said "like this one",' Ford said, pointing at the rifle. 'That not yours, then?'

'Mine's in for a repair. This belongs to His Lordship. I use it from time to time. He doesn't mind as long as I put it back after I've finished with it.'

'One last question. Do you look after Lord Baverstock's guns as well as your own?'

'Not just his. The whole family's.'

'What calibre weapons do they own?'

'What calibre?'

'Yes. You know, it means—'

'I know what it means,' Hibberd snapped. 'Shotguns in 12 and 20 gauge. Couple of four-tens from when the children were little. A few more .22 vermin guns like this one,' he said, holding up the rifle. 'His Lordship's got a Sako .243 rifle and an old Springfield Arms .30-06. Off the top of my head I couldn't tell you all of them.'

'Any .308s?'

'No. Why?'

'Just curious.'

Ford wrapped up the interview with a polite request that Hibberd make himself available if Ford needed to talk to him again.

He drove away thinking about the family who lived at Alverchalke Manor. Stephen in particular. The man had practically crowed over Tommy's murder. Could he have been involved? His father had shut him down pretty effectively. Was that a sign of anxiety that he was about to incriminate himself?

And what of Lord Baverstock himself? Another military man. And the employer of a gamekeeper who'd come off worst in a scrap with Tommy. Guns and grievances made terrible bedfellows. This family had both in abundance.

CHAPTER TWELVE

Jools and Hannah were the only customers in Berret & Sartain Gunsmiths. The shop smelled pleasantly of leather, wet dog and gun oil. Jools spent a few minutes looking at the racks of shotguns and rifles while they waited for a member of staff to appear.

'Can I help you, ladies?'

Jools turned to see a guy in his mid-twenties, wearing a buttercup-yellow bow tie above a patterned waistcoat. His close-set eyes were magnified behind thick-lensed horn-rimmed glasses. He wore his hair in a style she associated with the 1940s matinee idols her gran used to love watching before dementia claimed her.

She approached the scratched glass-topped counter and showed him her ID. Hannah stood beside her, the bagged bullet secure inside a rucksack over her shoulder. She'd confirmed George's hunch about the calibre the previous day in her preliminary analysis.

'We're investigating a murder,' Jools said. 'The victim was shot with a .308 expanding bullet. We think it was a ballistic tip. If we showed it to you, could you tell us anything about it?'

'I'll try,' he said, pushing his glasses higher up his nose.

Hannah brought out the small red-taped evidence bag containing the bullet and laid it on the counter.

'Please, only hold the bag by the taped end,' she said hurriedly as he reached for it. 'Don't put any pressure at all on the bullet itself.'

He did as she asked, holding the bag close to his eyes.

'Definitely a ballistic tip,' he pronounced. 'Hollow points have regular petals. These are ragged and uneven in size.'

'Exactly! It's because hollow points are pre-grooved,' Hannah said to him excitedly. 'The copper jackets split predictably. Ballistic tips split randomly once the plastic point breaks off in the tissue.'

Jools liked Hannah's company, but she'd seen how eagerly she dived down informational rabbit holes. Or badger setts. What was worse – the shop guy was cut from the same cloth. They were talking eagerly about how bullets split open on impact, spin rates, calibres, propellant types and other firearms esoterica she didn't have time for.

She jumped in, wanting to drag them back to the salient point. 'We just need to know if you've sold ammunition of this type to anyone recently.'

The man pulled his mouth to one side. 'How recently?'

It was a good question. Jools stopped to think. Yes, how far back did they need to go?

'How much of that type of ammunition do customers usually buy in one go?' Hannah asked.

Jools looked at her with admiration. God, the woman had a way of seeing different angles.

The young man smiled. 'A hundred rounds at a time. On average.'

'And how long would that last them?' Hannah asked.

'That's impossible to say. It depends how many times they pull the trigger. And on whether they're using them for hunting or target-shooting.'

'A guesstimate?' Jools asked.

'If you were at a club, you could easily get through a hundred in a day. If you were hunting, on the other hand . . .' He looked up at the ceiling for a couple of seconds, then back at Jools. 'If you only came across a couple of deer, that might just be two rounds if they were clean, one-shot kills.'

'Better go back a year, then,' Jools said.

She looked around. The shop didn't exactly feel like it was at the cutting edge of technology. A plaque above the door referred to the company's founding in 1755. It didn't look as if it had changed much in the interim. Her heart sank as she pictured waist-high stacks of cardboard boxes, each holding neatly piled white cylinders of till receipts.

'It'll take me a while to pull all the names and addresses together for you,' he said. 'I could email you, if you like?'

'Perfect! Here,' Jools said, handing him a card. 'One last thing. Do you have a list of local gun clubs?'

He nodded and handed her a pre-printed sheet from a pile in a literature rack.

Outside, Jools's vision dimmed. Had someone just turned the lights out? She looked up. The sky, so blue it hurt when she and Hannah had entered the gun shop, had taken on the colour of lead.

She and Hannah ran for the car as rain pelted the streets.

Four miles south of the city, Tom Adlam stared out of the window in frustration. He, his wife and their two grown-up sons farmed 560 acres in the Chalke Valley. They raised chestnut and cream Simmental cows and grew wheat, rape and barley.

This was the afternoon he'd set aside to move the Simmentals over to the new grazing. Trouble was, rain made them impossible to handle. He'd have to leave it till the morning.

The rain continued for the rest of the afternoon and into the evening. Adlam filled his time fixing a spring harrow in one of the barns.

The rain filled the soakaways at the rear of the farmhouse until they overflowed. It flooded the bottom of the garden and created an impromptu pond in the centre of the lawn. It ran in rippling sheets down the track from Fisher's Lane to the farm gate, creating vast puddles around the tractor and combine harvester. It swelled the chalk streams that crossed his land until the meandering watercourses burst their banks and turned the fields into mirrors reflecting the sky.

In the centre of the farm, the River Ebble snaked across a tussocky meadow. Swollen by tens of thousands of gallons of highly alkaline rainwater that slid straight off the sun-baked fields into the river valley, it swirled through an ancient brick and stone sluice gate into a deep drainage pond, then out through a second, narrower gate and on, through the rest of their land, before heedlessly crossing the property line into the neighbouring farm.

The inflowing torrent carried a bulky object into the pond, where it sank to the silty bottom. Six feet long, it rolled over and over before jamming in the narrow gap of the outflow sluice.

Vegetable matter and dead branches washed downstream caught on its various protrusions. They wove themselves into an untidy yet solid mass that grew in height as more items snagged on it. The topmost pieces of debris lay just a few feet below the roiling surface.

The unabating water, having had its exit from the pond curtailed so severely, looked for an alternative. It found it to left and right, rising over the banks and flowing away through the grassy hillocks all the way to the single-track road leading from the farm back towards Salisbury, where Ford was meeting JJ Bolter in a dingy pub in one of the city's less salubrious quarters, between the railway station and the Churchfields industrial estate.

◆ ◆ ◆

Ford had entered The Gundog five minutes earlier. The early-evening drinkers paid him no attention as he bought a Coke and took it to a table in a corner where he could watch the door.

The pub smelled of spilled beer and, even though smoking had been banned inside for years, stale smoke. The moulded tin ceiling had once been painted cream. Now it bore a greasy-looking coat of brownish gunk that he imagined must be the exhaled nicotine of thousands upon thousands of cigarettes.

The door swung inwards, admitting a wedge of grey light into the gloom. JJ strode in, a trench coat flapping open to reveal Burberry's tan, red, white and black check. He scanned the room, saw Ford, then carried on to the bar. He returned a few minutes later with a tumbler of whisky clinking with ice.

He folded himself into the chair facing Ford and took a pull on his drink.

'What's that? Rum and Coke?' he asked, pointing at Ford's glass.

'Just Coke.'

JJ snorted derisively. 'God, you've really got no style, have you? Chain-store suits and bloody Cokey-Coley. Want me to buy you a bag of crisps to go with it?'

'What did you want to see me about, JJ?'

JJ leaned forward. He fixed Ford with a cold, hard stare. 'I've just been up to the coroner's office. Cagey old fart wouldn't give me a straight answer before the inquest. But he *suggested*' – JJ made mocking air quotes – 'that he won't release Tommy's body to us, on account of you lot haven't caught his murderer yet. Which means I can't organise his funeral.'

Ford felt a wave of relief wash through him. JJ had summoned him to tell him he was backing off. 'I understand, and I'm sorry. But it's standard practice.'

JJ shook his head, then took another mouthful of whisky. 'You're missing the point. We're having a wake first, and the funeral whenever we get him back. The wake's in six days. You've got till then to arrest someone.'

Ford shook his head. 'This is pointless. It's not how murder investigations work. You can't just impose arbitrary deadlines.'

JJ stared at Ford, then spoke quietly. 'Don't tell me what I can and can't do. You're dealing with the Bolters now. If I say you've got six days, that's how long you've got.'

'And if we haven't caught him by then?'

'You'd better start looking behind you if you're out at night. Maybe check under your car in the mornings. Who knows? Maybe I'll have a word with your boss,' he said with a slight lift of the corners of his mouth. 'Tell Detective Superintendent Monroe her golden boy's on the take. I bet that would put a spoke in your wheel, now, wouldn't it?'

Ford stood, briefly taller than the man he'd started to think of as his nemesis. He looked down at him. 'Do what you like. I'm a clean cop.'

He left the pub and reached the Discovery without looking back. Though his thumping heart told him the cost.

Ford locked the door and pulled away. Six days. It wasn't impossible, he told himself. Nothing was impossible.

CHAPTER THIRTEEN

At 6.45 a.m. the following day, Tom Adlam wiped up his egg yolk with the last corner of fried bread and checked the big clock on the wall. He peered out of the kitchen window.

'Thank heavens that rain's finished,' he said to his wife. 'I wanted to move the cows on to the new grazing yesterday. But I can get to it this morning.'

Tom took his quad bike, enjoying the smell of rain-soaked earth as he powered north-west from the farmhouse towards what the family called River Field. The Simmentals would be ready for a change of scene, he reckoned. Ushering the forty beasts from trampled mud studded with the last of the stubble turnips to a meadow thick with grass would be one of the easiest jobs in the month.

He gunned the engine, loving the surge of power from the Yamaha's punchy little engine as he crested the final incline and looked down at River Field. Which reflected the cloud-streaked sky across half its area.

'Oh, bugger!' he said, with feeling.

Seeing him coming, and lowing in anticipation, the Simmentals ambled across to the gate between their field and the flooded meadow beyond, their curly-haired heads nodding. He shook his head. Daft things would have to wait, now, wouldn't they? Something must've blocked the sluice. Washed downriver by the storm, most likely.

Flicking open the throttle and churning up muddy ruts in the field, he powered back home. There, he swapped the quad for a tractor, slung a grappling hook and a coil of rope on to the floor of the cab, and arrived back at River Field thirty minutes later.

With an audience of curious cows, he tied the rope on to the tow bar then carried the coil and grapple over to the pond, splashing through the floodwater. He peered down into the murk. Saw merely his own reflection looking back out at him and the outline of a thick mass of twigs and branches.

He swung the grapple a couple of times and slung it out into the pond. Then he dragged it back towards the sluice gate. He tugged on the rope, jerking the grapple up and down, hoping to hook whatever lay at the bottom of the blockage. Feeling it snag on something, he increased the tension and noted with satisfaction the way the rope gave, then resisted.

Looking over his shoulder, he eased the big John Deere forward, letting the rope tauten. The rope snapped tight, shaking a spray of water droplets into the air, where they caught the sunlight and refracted briefly into a rainbow.

Little by little, the pond gave up its treasure. Twenty yards from the sluice gate, Tom stopped as he saw the rope begin to stretch. He put the tractor into neutral, climbed down and walked back to the sluice. He really hoped he wouldn't look down and see one of his neighbour's sheep.

As he leaned down to hook the vegetation away with his hands, he realised it wasn't a sheep. Someone must have dumped a scarecrow into the Ebble. City kids, most likely. He scowled. *Or pikeys, having a laugh at my expense.*

The oddly humanoid figure had long, twiggy arms and a crudely shaped head. But as the water in the pond rushed through the newly cleared sluice and the level dropped, his opinion lurched sideways. Not humanoid. *Human.* Twisting in the turbid, outflowing water, the naked, vegetation-wrapped body rolled over.

◆ ◆ ◆

Before Ford had taken a second sip of his coffee, his phone rang.

'Control, sir. Farmer just called in. Says he's got a dead body in a drainage pond. On a grappling hook.'

'Where?'

'Roseveare Farm, sir. Between Coombe Bissett and Rockbourne. I'll send you the details.'

Ford picked up his murder bag. He knew Roseveare Farm. And Tommy's body had been found not a mile away. Had Ford believed in coincidences, he might have written off the proximity of the two bodies as just that. But he didn't. As he got behind the wheel of the Discovery, he was already wondering not if but *how* the two deaths were linked.

He arrived at the crime scene to see a middle-aged man in waders and mud-spattered overalls leaning against the fat rear tyre of a bright green tractor. A rope ran in a straight, cobalt-blue line from the rear of the tractor to the edge of a pool of water.

He climbed out and saw to his disappointment that the Discovery's blue paintwork, which he'd recently washed, was now coated in claggy, greyish-white mud. A marked Skoda Yeti trundled over the grass to join him.

The call from Control had been clear about what to expect at the end of the rope. He joined the farmer, having first paused to take a look at the body. The corpse bore the telltale signs of a body that had been submerged in water for more than a couple of days. The face was swollen but he saw no sign of the white jelly-like froth around the mouth that typically indicated drowning. That was interesting. If not drowned, then dumped?

'Can you tell me what happened?' Ford asked the farmer.

'I came up to move the cows in. But when I got here, the field was under six inches of water. So I figured something had blocked the sluice gate. I put a grapple in, and that' – he jerked his chin over at the pond – 'came up on the end of it.'

Adlam's conciseness impressed Ford. The body had sunk. Had it been weighted down? That suggested foul play. Foul play suggested murder. And murder suggested Tommy Bolter. Again.

'Have you seen anyone acting suspiciously on your farm in recent weeks?'

Adlam shook his head. 'Nobody. We get dog-walkers, of course. And the odd hiker with their maps and those daft poles they all use, but no. Just the usual.'

Ford looked around. 'Where's the nearest road?'

Adlam turned and pointed past the front of the tractor. 'Fisher's Lane. It's pretty quiet. You think they came that way?'

'I don't know. We'll get a search team to take a look.' Ford paused. 'Tell me, Mr Adlam, do you own your farm?'

Adlam snorted. 'Yeah, apart from what the bank does.'

Ford smiled. 'You're not a tenant, then?'

Adlam shook his head. 'The farm's been in my family for three hundred and seven years.'

'How about your neighbours?'

'That way, you've got the Baildons,' he said, gesturing past Ford's right shoulder. 'They own theirs outright. All the rest are tenants of Lord Baverstock.'

'Thanks.'

Another connection between Tommy Bolter and this new body. The Baverstock name had cropped up at both crime scenes.

Ford frowned. Rural suicides were depressingly common. Rural murders, much rarer. Now he had two within a week of each other.

He could hear the morbid chimes of a fruit machine as the connections piled up.

Ching! Two murders.

Ching! Rural body dumps.

CHING! Lord Baverstock.

Three death's heads! *Jackpot! You win!!*

Bloody coins tumbled into the tray. This murder was linked to Tommy's. He could *feel* it.

Ford arranged to have Adlam come in to make a formal statement, then left him and returned to the corpse.

A team of four CSIs turned up on foot carrying bulging holdalls. They must have left their van on Fisher's Lane, he thought; unlike the first body dump, this one had no convenient gravelled track. He saw Hannah. She waved and walked over, her Tyveked legs rustling against each other.

'Hello, Henry. We need to get the body out of the water without damaging it any further. Do we have police divers anywhere near?'

Ford shook his head. 'We use Avon and Somerset's. They're based in Bristol. That's ninety minutes' drive away.'

'An extra ninety minutes won't make an appreciable difference to decay at this point.'

'I'll make the call.'

Ford returned to Bourne Hill, leaving the CSIs and the uniforms to establish a perimeter around the crime scene. He called the dive team sergeant in Bristol and secured a promise of 'a couple of my guys'.

His next appointment was at Salisbury Coroner's Court on Endless Street. The inquest into Tommy Bolter's death opened at 11.00 a.m. Ford rubbed his jaw. Could he avoid running into JJ? *Yeah, right!*

CHAPTER FOURTEEN

Some coroners were fortunate enough to work in modern, purpose-built surroundings. Courtrooms bristling with IT. State-of-the-art on-site mortuaries. Air conditioning. Seat cushions.

Salisbury was different. The courtroom was elegant in its way, with paintings of former coroners, antique furniture and a high, vaulted ceiling. However, being listed, it had no air conditioning. On this May day, it was sweltering.

The coroner deemed it inappropriate to have open windows that might allow passers-by to eavesdrop on the proceedings. Even though any one of them could walk in and listen for free inside.

For those attending, a slide into heat-induced drowsiness was prevented by the hard, upright benches ranged in front of the coroner's table. From his seat at the back, Ford observed the attendees, virtually all of them wearing black.

Several generations of the Bolter family had turned up, from white-haired grandparents to babies being bounced on laps. He could see the backs of the two surviving brothers in the front row. Tight shirt collars cinched their bull necks, tanned flesh bulging over crisp white cotton. JJ turned in his chair to survey the room. His eyes locked on to Ford's. His lips moved. *Tick. Tock.*

Ford held his gaze until JJ looked away. It was a minor victory, but Ford felt it all the same. If JJ was looking for answers today, though, Ford knew he was going to be disappointed.

A steady murmur of strong Salisbury accents died away as the coroner and his staff entered the courtroom. A portly figure in an old-fashioned three-piece suit complete with gold watch chain slung across his belly, he looked as much of an anachronism as the room he now dominated.

He smiled. He sat. The courtroom stilled.

'Good morning, ladies and gentlemen,' he said in a soft, cultured voice. 'My name is Raymond Beaven. I am the coroner. I hereby open this inquest. It is my job to ascertain three important things, and three things only.'

He gazed around the room, as if daring somebody to ask what this holy trinity might be. There were no takers. A baby started crying. JJ turned to the young woman on whose lap it writhed. Eyes downcast, she rose from her seat and hurried out. Silence reigned once more.

Beaven cleared his throat. 'It is my job to determine the *identity* of the deceased, the *circumstances* of their death, and the *manner* of their death. Thanks to the efforts of the police' – he glanced at Ford and offered the most minuscule of nods – 'the identity of the deceased is already known. Thomas William Bolter.'

A sob echoed through the courtroom and was just as suddenly choked off.

'The forensic pathologist has completed her post-mortem examination and has concluded that Mr Bolter was killed by a single gunshot wound. She concludes, and I agree, that the manner of his death was homicide,' he pronounced. 'At this point, no other definitive answers are available. As is usual in such cases, I hereby adjourn the inquest until such time as the police investigation is complete and a verdict is brought in the Crown Court. Thank you.'

Beaven rose and left through a side door, followed by his assistant and the court stenographer. The hubbub that Beaven had silenced with his arrival arose at twice its previous volume.

Ford knew the cause of the raised voices and complaining tones. Inquests were daunting affairs. Attendees would armour themselves in their best suits and dresses. They'd reinforce their already fragile nerves with nips from hip flasks or pints in the pub round the corner. They entered the court expecting answers there and then.

Witnesses would be called. Police officers would deliver their findings. And, at the end, the coroner would announce his verdict and give everybody a measure of closure.

To find themselves at a loose end after little more than two minutes was a bewildering experience.

Ford followed them out on to Endless Street, where they congregated in a ragged knot that spilled off the pavement and into the road. He hung back, not wanting to intrude. He also wanted to observe. It was never too early to start looking at the family in a murder case.

JJ and Rye Bolter were holding their own kind of court at the centre of the group. Ford couldn't make out what they were saying, but he could guess.

When a family like the Bolters lost one of their own, especially in the flower of youth, the word would go out that they wanted justice. He doubted they were even waiting for their own deadline before asking questions. That was to put pressure on him alone.

He crossed the road to a grand Georgian house with a recessed front door. The bright sun threw deep shade beneath the scalloped portico and he was in virtual darkness. Ideal cover from which to see the comings and goings.

Then he spotted someone on the edge of the group who he'd never in a million years have thought to see at the inquest into Tommy Bolter's death. Joe Hibberd.

Like the other people milling around at the top of Endless Street, Hibberd wore a dark suit. He kept plucking at the fabric under his arms and across his shoulders. He couldn't keep his hands still, first shoving them into the trouser pockets, then pulling them free and adjusting the waistband. His face was red and his slicked-down hair glistened with either water, like Ford's, or a great deal of gel.

But it was the young woman seemingly glued to his side who interested Ford. Hibberd was in his late thirties. His companion couldn't have been more than twenty-five. Realising he'd been taken in by her sophisticated hairdo and elaborate make-up, including heavily kohled eyes, he revised his estimate down by a couple of years.

Nothing wrong with that sort of age gap, Ford reminded himself. But they made a decidedly odd couple. Whereas Hibberd's body language gave him away – as a countryman stuffed into a suit he probably only wore once a year – she appeared an entirely urban creature.

Her dress, though modest, managed to suggest a great deal of her figure, which was slender and athletic. Though she was shorter than Hibberd by a head, a pair of staggeringly high heels elevated her closer to his level. She linked her arm through his and leaned closer to say something into his ear. He nodded, and they turned to leave the group.

A shout killed the noise outside the court as effectively as the coroner's quieter welcome had inside.

'Hey! Who are you? And what are you doing with Tommy's girlfriend? He's not even in his coffin, you bastard!'

JJ steamed through the crowd, a suited-and-booted Moses parting a black sea. Hibberd turned and manoeuvred his companion to one side, out of harm's way.

Ford tensed. He didn't know what history existed between JJ and Hibberd, but the bad blood between the latter and Tommy was enough to ensure enmity where JJ was concerned. He didn't want things to get out of hand, but he wanted to hear whatever JJ was going to say next.

JJ didn't say anything next.

He cannoned into Hibberd, arms outstretched, meaty palms landing square on his chest. Hibberd rolled around the impact and pushed JJ, who stumbled and almost went down.

The young woman with Hibberd screamed as JJ whirled round and lashed out with a bunched fist. It was a wild swing and Hibberd was already moving out of range. His own fists came up. Ford watched, amazed, as Hibberd stepped in and delivered a crisp one-two: a left jab into the side of JJ's jaw, then a right uppercut that snapped his head back and sent him staggering against the wall.

The crowd, so recently cleaved by JJ's rush, had reformed into an untidy circle around them. One or two of the men were removing their jackets. A woman in her sixties – bleached hair, leathery orange skin and a great deal of gold jewellery – took the girl with Hibberd to one side. Ford saw the flesh of the younger woman's bicep dent under the pressure of her captor's grip.

'Do 'im, JJ,' a man called out. Ford saw Rye Bolter yelling, his eyes red from weeping but now narrowed into hate-filled slits.

Ford checked for traffic, though Endless Street was quiet at this time of day, and recrossed the road. He strode towards the circle penning in the two brawlers, ID held aloft, and bellowed a command.

'Police! Step back!'

Heads turned, and he saw expressions of anger, frustration, suspicion and even regret. Nothing like a good street fight to clear the air and release a bit of pent-up emotion. Nevertheless.

He pushed through the onlookers, who didn't part for him the way they had for JJ, until he reached the centre. Hibberd had JJ in a headlock and JJ was pummelling Hibberd in the region of his kidneys. Neither man appeared to be tiring, or suffering overmuch.

Ford ascribed both symptoms to an excess of adrenaline, coupled in JJ's case with a healthy dose of alcohol. Alcohol and maybe something that came not in a glass but in a small plastic bag.

Pocketing his ID, he took a deep breath, rolled his shoulders and waded in. He grabbed Hibberd's left arm and twisted it up so he had to release JJ. Free of the headlock, JJ spun round, ready to mount a counter-attack, only to come face to face with Ford.

'Don't,' Ford said.

Panting, JJ and Hibberd both glared at him. He returned their stares. Fantastic! He'd arrived in the nick of time to save the day, and neither man wanted rescuing.

'He started it,' Hibberd said. 'You saw. He went for me.'

'He's trying it on with Tommy's girlfriend,' JJ retorted. 'My baby brother ain't even cold, and this scum's making a move.'

'I don't care who started it,' Ford said, feeling more like a yard prefect at his son's school than a detective. 'And I don't care who's going out with whom. If you want to fight, get yourselves to a gym. Don't do it in the street. And especially not on my patch.'

No sense getting into a prolonged discussion. If they didn't heed his words, he'd leave it to the on-duty response and patrol shift to sort them out. He turned and left the Bolters and their associates to find what solace they could in the nearest pub.

So Hibberd and Tommy weren't just professional rivals. They'd also been seeing the same young woman. Her relationships with the two men could have been sequential, but Ford felt that was unlikely given the circumstances of Tommy's untimely death.

Tommy could have found out and confronted Hibberd. But then what? Had a situation most people would regard as commonplace led to murder?

He couldn't see it. Or, not precisely. Fights got out of hand all the time. Any copper working in a town of any size, even one as quiet as Salisbury, would know that. As the saying went, one punch could kill.

But he couldn't see a fight over a woman escalating into a sniper-style takedown followed by a full dismemberment. What he *could* see, however, were two separate grievances between Hibberd and Tommy. One in each direction. And that was interesting.

He heard footsteps.

'Ford!'

Ford stopped. Turned. Saw JJ running towards him.

'What is it?'

'I hear you've been up at Alverchalke Manor asking questions.'

Ford kept his face neutral, hiding his shock. Someone had leaked already. 'Who from?'

'Never mind who from. I heard, that's all. Was it one of them? One of them rich bastards up at Alverchalke?'

The answer came easily to Ford's lips. 'No. It wasn't.'

He looked JJ square in the eye. Did JJ believe him? He'd bloody better. Because it *might* have been one of them. And if not them, their gamekeeper. Who had coincidentally rocked up for the inquest with Tommy's squeeze on his arm.

He wasn't about to feed JJ's thirst for revenge, though. The last thing he needed was a Bolter posse advancing on Alverchalke

Manor in the dead of night with pitchforks and flaming torches. Or, more likely, sawn-offs and pickaxe handles.

JJ turned away and stalked back to the crowd waiting for him. Ford returned to Bourne Hill, striving to think of a new angle he could follow that would yield results before Tommy's wake.

CHAPTER FIFTEEN

Midway through the next morning, Ford's PC pinged with an incoming email from George. She'd fast-tracked the PM on the second corpse. As usual, he read her covering email first.

The body was male, aged between sixty-five and seventy-five. As he'd expected, death wasn't due to drowning. No water in the lungs. But the true cause sparked an instant connection to Tommy Bolter. George had found a .22 bullet in the cranium. Plus stippling and powder burns under his chin that indicated a point-blank shot. He'd been in the water for a week to ten days. Meaning he'd been killed before Tommy. That was interesting.

As he read on, he learned why the body had sunk: the murderer had stabbed the vital organs, post-mortem. Eight accurately placed blows, neither random nor frenzied. And since suicides tended not to stab themselves after death, George – and Ford was in agreement – concluded it was a homicide. The only other premortem injury was a dog bite, from a medium to large animal, on the left buttock. The corpse bore a single tattoo: a naked green woman sitting cross-legged, cradling planet Earth in front of her breasts. George had also found two dental implants. Expensive stuff at around three grand a pop.

He finished reading and sat back. The dog bite was interesting. For one thing, Hibberd's dogs were collies, a medium breed. And what about the calibre? When he'd interviewed Joe Hibberd, he'd been shooting with a .22. Ford closed his eyes. He was already convinced by the circumstances that the two murders were linked. But *why* were they linked? What was the thread binding them together?

He had a local wannabe crime lord, into poaching and petty crime, and an older man with expensive dentistry that screamed middle-class. Similarities first. Tommy Bolter and the second victim, who Ford had mentally dubbed Pond Man, were both male. Both white. Both tattooed.

He opened the attachment and paged through until he found the image of the tattoo. The woman was indeed naked, but she wasn't sexy. If anything, she looked maternal, wrapping the planet protectively in her arms. He had a feeling it was something to do with the eco movement, and had a look online. Within seconds he'd found a page of similar images. And an explanation.

She was 'Gaia'. The personification of an idea that the whole planet was connected in a giant system of mutual respect and benefit.

Was the fact that both men had tattoos significant? Everybody had them these days. Ford had put his foot down when Sam had asked to get one, pointing out, among other things, that it was illegal. But while Sam was sixteen and Tommy, comparatively speaking, not that much older, Pond Man was around seventy.

Old soldiers like Dan had plenty of tats. So did sailors and labourers, but those tended towards the traditional: hearts with daggers through them; the names of sweethearts on banners surmounted by bluebirds. Ford couldn't see a salty old sea dog sporting a Gaia tattoo. He parked the idea.

Both men had been killed by gunshots to the head. Both dumped a couple of miles apart on farmland leased out or adjacent to that owned by Lord Baverstock.

How about the differences? The most significant concerned the shootings themselves. Tommy had been shot at a distance, Pond Man close up. Different calibres, too. That might mean two separate shooters. He'd come back to that.

More differences piled up. One old, one young. One dismembered, one not, although Pond Man had received numerous deep stab wounds. Different dump sites: earth and water. Enough differences to rule out a serial killer? He wasn't sure. Certainly, any signature was well hidden.

He returned to Pond Man's tattoo. If he was local, canvassing the city's tattoo parlours might throw up an artist who remembered inking the older guy's skin. Ford knew of half a dozen places in the city, but before putting a couple of uniforms on it, he decided to visit the oldest and biggest himself. He printed out the image and headed out.

Ten minutes later, he was showing Pond Man's tattoo to a bearded guy with full sleeves of tattoos on both arms. Ford turned the photo around on the glass counter, below which studs, hoops, spikes and chains were displayed like fine jewellery, alongside colour photos demonstrating the myriad locations on the human body where they could be inserted.

'It's nice, but it's not one of our artists' work,' the guy said, scratching his beard.

'You're sure?'

He nodded. 'I know to you one piece looks much like another, but there's a ton of difference in how two different artists work. Line, shading, depth, palette. People don't really understand how much technique goes into something like that.'

Ford sighed. 'What about that design in general? Who typically gets one like that?'

'Now, that I can tell you,' he said. He tapped the woman. 'She's Gaia, yeah? Mother Earth. Very popular with the eco brigade. We get a lot of young girls who want her.'

'Can you tell how recent it is?'

'Good question. Anyone would think you were a copper. Tattoos change, OK? All of them. Lines spread, colours fade. That's quite recent. I'd say in the last three to five years.'

Ford thanked him and walked back to Bourne Hill. George had put Pond Man's age at around seventy. He'd had his first and only tattoo at around sixty-five. An environmental design favoured by young women. Ford could see only two possible reasons. He was an old lech hoping to ingratiate himself with girls young enough to be his granddaughters. Creepy, but not unimaginable. Or he'd become some kind of eco-warrior in late middle age. Very possible.

He stopped outside Berret & Sartain and looked in at the array of shotguns on a wooden rack. The publicity photos all showed a similar type of person: posh-looking older men and a few younger and very attractive women. Wearing tweeds and long boots, they smiled widely, guns cradled in their arms or held up to their shoulders. Gun dogs – black Labs, mostly, plus a few spaniels – waited patiently at their feet. Medium breeds.

To a lot of environmental activists, these people were the enemy. Ready to kill anything that moved; hoarding land the Greens believed should belong to everyone. The feeling was mutual. To the shooting classes, environmentalists were urban keyboard warriors who didn't understand the countryside.

Had Pond Man been causing trouble for Lord Baverstock? Was that why he was found close to the Alverchalke estate? Could he and Tommy have been working together somehow? It seemed unlikely, but in his years as a detective, Ford had learned that sometimes the most unlikely things were simply a truth he hadn't come across yet. He walked on.

At the briefing, thirty minutes later, he shared his latest insights.

'So he was making a nuisance of himself and someone lost it,' Mick said, folding his arms.

'A nuisance?' Olly echoed. 'I know you find anyone with progressive views beyond redemption, Mick. But surely even you can see it's a bit of a stretch to murder someone because they're trying to save the planet?'

His face flushing, Mick leaned towards Olly and jabbed a finger at him. 'Even me? What, you mean thicko Detective *Sergeant* Mick Tanner, with his knuckles dragging on the ground? As opposed to Detective *Constable* Oliver Cable, with his degree in criminology and a broomstick up his arse?'

Ford stepped in quickly. 'That's enough! Olly, show some respect. Mick, calm down.'

Both men glared at him and then at each other. The rest had all found fascinating things to read in their notebooks.

'Do you want me to run a search on the NCA missing persons database, guv?' Jools asked.

Ford nodded. 'I saw the owner of Inkerman just now,' he said. 'He was certain it wasn't their work, but that leaves a few other places who might recognise it. Olly, visit them all and show them the picture. If we find the artist, we find Pond Man's identity.'

'Yes, guv,' Olly said sullenly.

'Mick, any news on those butchers you were tracing?'

Chest rising and falling visibly, Mick nodded and looked down at his notebook. 'We finished all the interviews. Of the original forty-three, we've got twenty-five males with their own place. Nobody got even a whiff of a wrong 'un from any of them.'

'How about alibis?'

'Still checking.'

'All right. Thanks Mick, nice work.' He turned back to the semicircle of expectant faces. 'Let's hope someone reported Pond Man as a MISPER so Jools gets a quick ID.'

◆　◆　◆

Jools watched Ford striding to his office, Mick dogging his steps, his lower jaw jutting. She turned back to her monitor and jiggled the mouse to wake her creaking PC out of its slumber. Once the monitor flickered into life, she opened the police search screen on the NCA missing persons database. If any one of the UK's forty-five police forces had reported a missing person, the National Crime Agency would have it.

She entered Pond Man's details and hit the dark blue 'Search' button, sat back and waited. A few seconds later the screen refreshed. She stared at it, unwilling to believe her luck. A single hit, for which she was sure the Gaia tattoo was responsible.

Owen Long. A white male, reported missing by his wife four days earlier. Aged seventy. With a tattoo of a female figure. The notes screen, searchable only by the police, contained the clincher: *Tattoo is of 'Gaia' – naked green female, globe/planet earth in her lap.*

The file included a full-face photo of Long. And although submersion in water had swollen the dead man's features, the resemblance was clear enough for Jools to be confident she'd come face to face with Pond Man.

She hit 'Print', then clicked away to a new screen and pulled up the reporting person's contact details.

Ford leaned back against the edge of his desk, hands beside him. 'Close the door, Mick.'

Mick complied, then came to stand in front of Ford, rubbing his hand over the bristles on his scalp. In the quiet of the office, Ford could hear them scratching under Mick's palm.

'What's going on?' Ford asked.

'What, because of that business with Olly? He's just an arsey burger-flipper. They're all the same: McDonald's on a Friday, DC by Monday. They work a single domestic homicide where the husband confesses by teatime, and suddenly they're *International Murder Detective.*'

'I agree, he can be a pain. And he was out of line. But you completely overreacted. What's up? You've been late to work a couple of times recently. And you've lost the edge off your dress sense, too.'

Mick shrugged. 'It's just work. Two murders. I just let myself go a bit.' But he couldn't maintain eye contact. And he'd folded his arms across his chest. The message blared out. *Keep off!*

Ford didn't. 'Who was that bending your ear on the phone the other day? Kirsty?'

Mick nodded. Said nothing. Ford had a flash of insight. Cop marriages had one of the worst breakdown rates.

'You two OK?' Ford asked.

Mick unfolded his arms long enough to rub his scalp again. He looked out of the window. Up at the ceiling. Down at the floor. Shifted his weight from one foot to the other.

'She wants a divorce,' he mumbled.

Ford knew better than to ask questions when people were just opening up. Silence often prompted more talk. He kept quiet.

'Eleven years we've been married,' Mick said in a complaining tone. 'And *now* she's decided to give me aggro about ignoring her. All because I forgot our wedding anniversary. She knew what I did for a living when I proposed to her.' He hesitated. 'I said we should try counselling. And if you tell anyone I said that, I'll kill you.'

Ford couldn't help smiling. Even in this moment of heightened emotion, Mick needed to preserve his macho reputation.

'What did she say?'

'She agreed. So we go along and Kirsty basically dives straight in, telling the therapist about what a shit husband I am,' Mick said. 'I try to argue and the bloody cow with the clipboard and the purple dungarees tells me to give Kirsty her *space*. Then we come out, after *I've* paid, and Kirsty goes, "There! Happy now? I've got a lawyer. I suggest you do the same."'

'Are you still at home?'

Mick shook his head. 'Renting a flat. A bloody one-bedroom flat!'

'What about Evie and Caitlin?'

'I'm seeing them on Wednesday evenings and Sunday mornings. And we've got bloody WhatsApp. But it's not the same, is it?'

'No. It's not. If you need compassionate leave, I can do that for you. Or just time off to talk to your lawyer.'

Mick nodded. 'Who's costing me a bloody fortune, by the way. The leech is bleeding me dry, and that's before I start paying Kirsty child support.'

'Look, try to stay focused, but talk to me, yes?'

'I will. I've got to go.'

Alone in his office, Ford watched Mick's progress through Major Crimes, phone clamped to his ear. Poor sod. Thoughts of his years with Lou shouldered their way into his consciousness.

Theirs had been a strong marriage. Everybody said so. She'd never lost patience with his long hours or sudden departures midway through movies or dinners out. She'd smile resignedly and kiss him on the cheek – distractedly, if she was interested in the film. Not strong enough to save her life, though, was it? And nor was he. He shoved the thought down.

Jools burst through the door, waving a couple of sheets of paper. 'I think I've got him, guv! Pond Man.' She thrust the printout into his outstretched hand.

Ford scanned the top sheet. 'I'll go and see her tomorrow. Thanks, Jools.'

He called the inter-force liaison officer at the Met to let them know a colleague from Wiltshire would be on their turf, then headed for the stairs. He reached for his phone, intending to recall

Olly from his tattoo-parlour canvass. Then he stayed his hand. Spending some time wearing out shoe leather would do Olly good.

Jools scanned the list of ammunition buyers she'd just received from the sales guy at Berret & Sartain. He'd sorted them alphabetically, for which she mentally thanked him. The list contained seventy-one names, all but one of which were men's. She realised she'd had no idea of the extent of hunting in Wiltshire.

She cut and pasted the list into a spreadsheet. Added Mick's list of meat-trade workers. Scanned down the two columns, looking for a match. Her eyes fixed on a pair at the top of the list. Virtually identical. The others faded away as her pulse ticked up a notch.

QUALIFIED BUTCHERS
AMMUNITION BUYERS

. . .   . . .

ADLAM, Thomas W.   *ADLAM, Tom*

. . .   . . .

She stood and crossed Major Crimes to the murder wall for the Tommy Bolter and Pond Man deaths. Tom Adlam had discovered Pond Man on his farm. Had to be the same man. A line from a lecture at police college came back to her: *Murderers, especially psychopaths, will often involve themselves in the subsequent investigation, partly to monitor police progress, but also for the thrill they derive from being 'seen, yet unseen'.*

Back at her desk, she scrolled through the rest of the list. Relief ran through her as she found no more matches. She closed Mick's list and pulled up the membership lists of the two Royal Colleges, of surgeons and pathologists. Neither had a match to the ammunition list.

She grabbed her car keys.

CHAPTER SIXTEEN

Jools inhaled. The farmhouse kitchen smelled wonderful. Two loaves of bread with pale ellipses slashed into their chocolate-brown tops were cooling on a wire rack beside an Aga.

Facing her across a scrubbed pine table that glowed with years of hard use sat Tom Adlam and his wife, Clare. His wiry frame contrasted with her more rounded one. The Adlams' weather-beaten faces spoke of long days outside.

Jools opened her notebook. Smiled. Looked at each partner in the marriage, and the farm, in turn.

'How are you feeling?' she asked. 'Finding a body on your land must have been a shock.'

Tom Adlam nodded. 'Can't say it didn't upset me. You see dead wildlife all the time. You get used to the smell. But not' – he looked down at the steaming surface of his tea – 'not a man.'

Jools offered him a sympathetic glance, brow furrowed to show him she took him seriously.

'What did you want to talk to Tom about?' Clare asked, covering her husband's hand with hers. 'He's incredibly busy at this time of year. He's already given a statement to a uniformed officer.'

She made 'uniformed' sound like it meant 'real'. Did Jools's plain clothes count against her? Or was it her gender? Women could be just as sexist as men. Especially in a rural county like Wiltshire. She smiled again. Harder.

'Have you always been a farmer?' she asked Tom.

'Man and boy. Why?'

'No other trade when you were younger?'

'I've been working on the farm my whole life. Left school, went to Sparsholt College to study agriculture. Then here full-time.'

Jools made a note. More for effect than to record his answer. She hadn't got to her real question yet. Now she saw a way in.

'Did you study butchery at Sparsholt?'

'Yes. Why?'

'Did you enjoy it?'

He shrugged. 'I suppose so.'

'Did you get a good grade?'

'I can't remember. I know I passed, 'cause I've got the certificate up in the farm shop.'

'But you learned all the skills?'

Jools observed him closely. Looking for a sign he was hiding something. The twitch of an eye muscle would be enough for her.

'I can handle a knife, yes. Look, what's this all about? I thought you were here about that drowned bloke.'

'Actually, he didn't drown. Someone shot him.'

'All right, that shot bloke, then.'

'Do *you* own any guns, Mr Adlam?' She made it sound so innocent. As if she were merely asking whether he owned any floor mops.

'Hang on a minute,' Clare said sharply. 'Why are you asking him if he owns any guns? And about his butchery qualification? Surely you don't think he had anything to do with that poor man being murdered? Tom *found* him, for God's sake.'

Jools smiled sweetly. *Ask questions, make proposals. Stay in control.* 'Mr Adlam?'

'I'm a farmer, aren't I?'

'Is that a yes?'

'I've got a 12-gauge shotgun, a .308 rifle and a .22 for pests.'

Jools registered the uptick in her pulse, but maintained the calm exterior of a merely curious police officer. 'And they're all licensed.'

'Do you want to see my certificate?'

'If you wouldn't mind.'

He shoved his chair back, scraping the unprotected feet across the slate tiles with a loud screech. Jools jotted a couple of notes, then took a sip of her tea. She smiled at Clare Adlam, whose own mouth had tightened into an expression of outright disgust.

'He's not a murderer, if that's what you're thinking,' she said.

Jools said nothing.

'He's the gentlest soul on God's earth,' Clare continued. 'I mean, he'll kill foxes or rats. And he enjoys the odd shoot on the Alverchalke estate when he's invited, pheasants and such. But that's animals, not people.'

'It's just routine, Mrs Adlam. There's nothing to worry about.'

Clare sniffed. 'How come I'm feeling worried, then?'

Tom Adlam's arrival let Jools off the hook. He took his seat again and thrust a folded sheet of paper at her. She unfolded it and skimmed the black and yellow certificate.

'Well, that's all how it should be,' she said. 'Thank you. Tell me, Clare mentioned you go on shoots. You take the shotgun for those, do you?'

'Of course. I'm hardly going to take a .22, am I?'

Jools smiled. 'Of course not. So, what's the .308 for? Do you hunt?'

He shook his head. 'Target-shooting. On the rare occasions I have some time off, I go down to Cranborne Gun Club.'

Jools nodded and made a note. The club headed the list the gun shop guy had given her.

'Would you mind if I borrowed your rifles?'

'Why?'

'I'd like to have them test-fired. We recovered a bullet from a second body found on your neighbour Mr Ball's farm. You may have heard about it? The bullet is a .308. And the man you found was shot with a .22.'

Clare Adlam's mouth dropped open. Jools noticed she was squeezing her husband's hand so hard her knuckles had turned pale. 'You can't possibly be serious! No,' she said, turning to him. 'Don't let her. Make her get a warrant or whatever they do. Like on the telly.'

Wincing, he freed his hand from her grip. He shook his head. 'It's fine. Knock yourself out. But I want a receipt.'

Twenty minutes later, Jools parked at Bourne Hill with Adlam's cased rifles in the boot of her A3.

◆ ◆ ◆

'Dad?' Sam said as he and Ford cleared up after their evening meal.

'What?'

'On the *Journal* website, it says there was a second body.'

Ford nodded. 'A farmer found it in a drainage pond on his land.'

'Did it float?'

'No. The farmer brought it up with a grappling hook.'

'But they do usually, right?'

'Yes. The gases produced during putrefaction fill the body cavity and make it buoyant.'

Sam pulled a face. But he ploughed on. 'So he must've, like, weighted it down?'

114

Ford was about to correct him, then held his tongue. Some details were too gruesome to share. It wasn't lying to Sam. It was protecting him. 'Something like that,' he said. 'It was a good question. We'll make a detective out of you yet.'

Sam smiled. Then Ford saw a brief expression of doubt flit across his son's features. Little more than a momentary drawing-together of the eyebrows, but he caught it just the same.

'Everything OK?'

'There's a school trip coming up. Can I go? It's three hundred and eighty-five pounds and I need a parent's signature,' Sam said, the words tumbling over themselves.

'Sure. What is it? Camping again?'

Sam shook his head, frowning. 'Not camping. But it's really important. It's for geography. Tom's going. Max, Nathan, Joe. Literally everyone.'

'I said you could go. You won't miss out. Where is it?'

'The Brecon Beacons.'

Immediately, Ford knew what the answer to his next question would be. And he felt a cold wave of fear wash over him. 'Is it climbing?'

'It's totally safe, Dad! It's supervised and there are guides and, like, only safe routes, and they've got all the best safety gear. Please can I go?'

'No, Sam. I can't let you. Not after what happened to Mum. You know that even the safest climb can go wrong in a heartbeat.'

Sam shook his head, flicking his curls left and right. 'You're wrong! I've checked the statistics. You're actually more likely to die playing table tennis than rock-climbing.'

Ford had no doubt Sam had done his research, although his assertion sounded wildly unlikely. But it didn't change the way he felt. 'It's not safe, Sam. I don't care what the statistics say.'

'You have to! I'll be, like, the only boy not going. They'll all know why, too.'

Ford saw Lou as if it were yesterday, not six years ago. Her face pale with the agony caused when the block he'd dislodged had smashed her thigh bone. Minutes before she drowned, when he left her.

He knew he ought to let Sam go. The boy was fearless. The trouble was, Ford had enough fear for two.

He shook his head. 'No. I'm sorry. That's final.'

Sam's face darkened. 'It's not fair! I *have* to go.' He clenched his fists at his sides. 'Let me, you bastard!' Then his eyes widened with shock at what he'd just said.

Ford rocked back, the final, yelled word worse than a punch. Sam spun round and stalked off, heading for the stairs.

'Sam, wait,' he called. 'Wait!'

Sam stopped mid-stride, his back to Ford. Ford closed the distance between them. He placed his hands gently on his son's shoulders and turned him round. Tears glistened in Sam's eyes, hanging off his lashes like diamonds.

'Come here,' Ford said, holding his arms wide. Sam let himself be enveloped in a hug, though he didn't return it, his arms limp at his sides.

'I'm sorry for what I just said.' Sam's voice was muffled in the crook of Ford's neck. 'Please let me go. I swear I'll do exactly what the teachers say.'

Ford sighed. Could he keep Sam wrapped in cotton wool forever? There'd come a time when he'd be free to do whatever he liked. Riding motorbikes. Parachuting. BASE jumping. And, yes, even climbing.

He knew his fear of losing him was irrational, but then chided himself. Of course it was! But what about women afraid to cross dark parks alone? Children in care afraid of what the night would bring to their bedrooms? Old people afraid to answer their own front doors? Irrational? Or a well-adjusted reaction to the threats around every corner?

He felt Sam pulling away and released him from his embrace. He looked – not down, he realised, but across – into those pleading eyes. Saw in them how badly Sam wanted to fit in. Not to be forever consigned to the role of 'boy whose mum died'. Ford felt the rope that connected them loosening. Maybe he could play this one out gently, and avoid disaster. He sighed. Prayed.

'OK.'

Sam swiped a sleeve across his eyes. 'I can go?'

Ford nodded, feeling, if it were possible, simultaneous surges of anxiety and relief. 'I'll sign the form and write the cheque.'

Now Sam did hug his dad, so tightly Ford gasped as the breath left his lungs. 'Whoa! Too tight!'

Sam ignored him and squeezed harder. 'Thanks, Dad. I'll be careful, OK? You don't need to worry.'

'I know, mate. I know. Now let me go, you big lummox. I've got a ton of paperwork to get through and those reports won't write themselves, you know.'

As an attempt at levity it flopped, but Ford's bruised psyche couldn't manage anything better. The form for the trip would be merely the first in a long list of documents he still had to deal with that evening.

CHAPTER SEVENTEEN

Knowing that Sam spent most Saturdays hanging out with his mates, Ford set off for Islington to see Ruth Long. He put *Live at the Regal*, B.B. King's finest album, on repeat and pointed the Discovery towards London. The drive up the M3 gave him ample time to think. The case loomed large, but so did a side issue. Who had told JJ about Ford interviewing the Baverstocks?

The chief suspect in Ford's mind was Martin Peterson. The PCC was well connected and loved to boast of his high-society acquaintances, even though Ford suspected half the time those acquaintances would hardly recognise him.

Could there be someone on his own team passing titbits to JJ? What would they get out of it? The answer was horribly obvious. People like JJ understood two currencies. Cash. And fear. Either he had a hold over someone, or he was paying them. Or both.

So who'd be willing to sell a little of their integrity to a man like JJ Bolter? Or, to put it another way, who needed money right now? Someone with unexpected legal bills and looming child support payments, perhaps? *Oh, Jesus, please not Mick.*

The trouble with insights like that one was that, much like genies, they were hard to stuff back into their bottle. They were out and demanding attention.

But so was the satnav: 'Turn left on to Cloudesley Street, then you have reached your destination.'

He made the turn into a wide avenue of alternating lime trees and Japanese cherries, the latter's soft pink blossom lying in drifts against the tyres of the parked cars. Every spot at the kerb was occupied and Ford had to leave the Discovery a few streets away, beneath a London plane tree with its camouflage bark of ivory, sage, khaki and rust.

Walking to the house, he admired the assorted high-end wheels. A scarlet Ferrari outside the Longs' house stood out from the mass of silver, black and grey, like a prom queen at a funeral.

The wrought-iron gate opened with a screech. Ford frowned. He'd imagined people like this would be more house-proud. Or have people who'd be house-proud for them while they went out to work in banks, social media companies or advertising agencies. The terracotta window boxes of plum-red geraniums went some way to dispelling the image of genteel shabbiness.

Ford thumbed the bell push, inhaled and exhaled. Tried to ease his neck inside the buttoned-up shirt collar. The door opened. His pulse raced. A chill flickered through him, then passed like a summer storm.

The slender figure who stood framed in the doorway did not match his expectations. He'd been picturing a woman who'd look comfortable behind the wheel of the low-slung sports car parked just a few feet away. A coiffed and Botoxed lady-who-lunches, dripping with bling and designer labels.

Ruth Long looked perfectly ordinary. A slim, narrow-hipped figure, accentuated by a beige woollen dress belted at the waist. Grey hair scraped back from an oval face devoid of make-up. Brown eyes above bruised-looking bags.

'Mrs Long?'

She nodded. 'Yes. Are you from the police? Have you found Owen?' Her voice trembled. 'Is he all right? He went down to Salisbury over a week ago now. We think he must have been taken in by students or his fellow activists.' Her lips formed into a tremulous smile. 'Owen's like that, a real shepherd to his new flock. People love him. They all do. I don't think he knows he has that effect on them. Especially the young ones—'

Seeing no possibility of a gap, Ford interrupted, showing her his ID. 'My name is Detective Inspector Ford. I'm with Wiltshire Police. I'm based in Salisbury. May I come in?'

She nodded and turned, leading him into a living room furnished comfortably with cloth-upholstered sofas. No TV, he noticed.

She gestured with a limp hand to the sofa facing the window, then sank into its companion's saggy embrace. 'Where is he? Why didn't you bring him in from your car? I assume you have a car, don't you?'

Her eyes were caffeine-bright. They ranged around the room as she spoke, as if she might find her husband perched high on one of the groaning bookshelves, or the frame of one of the modern art prints jostling for space on the walls. Her bony fingers knotted round each other.

'Mrs Long, I'm investigating a murder and we've found a body that we believe may be that of your husband,' he said. 'It's not definite, but I want you to prepare yourself for the worst. I'm here to ask you if you'd come back to Salisbury to help us make an identification.'

She frowned. Then she smiled. 'You must be mistaken. Owen isn't dead.'

Ford had seen it happen before. The brain would play all sorts of tricks to prevent the message getting through. It was a tasteless joke. A case of mistaken identity. A reality TV show prank. Anything, anything at all, but the cold, awful, blister-raising truth.

He tried again. 'We matched the body to your description of Owen on the National Crime Agency missing persons database. The photo, his Gaia tattoo. I'm afraid it does look as though it's him. That's why I need your help.'

Her head shook from side to side. 'No. You're wrong. Lots of people have Gaia tattoos nowadays. Because of the climate crisis. Owen was so committed to the planet, he . . .'

Ford waited. She'd just used the past tense to describe her husband. The ancient, emotional part of her brain might be in full-blown denial, but the rational part knew.

It always did. It started adjusting language, planning funerals, wondering where the loved one kept all their internet passwords. Figuring out the best way to explain it to Sam.

He listened to the sound of her breathing. A cat wandered into the room and performed figures of eight around her ankles. Outside, a raspy engine noise disturbed the quiet street. He looked out of the window and saw the Ferrari pulling away.

'How?' she asked, in a quiet voice.

'The man we found had been shot.'

'Shot,' she repeated. She frowned. 'You mean with a gun?'

'I'm afraid so.'

Ruth nodded. Moving slowly, her back straight, as if balancing books on her head, she stood up and left the room, telling Ford she needed to collect a few things.

Ford stood and inspected the photographs grouped on the mantelpiece. In one, Ruth stood beside a teenage girl. The girl wore a tutu and ballet pumps. Ruth wore a black wraparound cardigan and leggings. In her right hand she held a cane of some sort. A dance teacher? That would account for her posture and graceful gait.

He heard the door swing open again. He turned. Ruth stood there, a small brown leather holdall in her hand. She smiled at the photo.

'Chloe Roberts. My best pupil last year. She's headed for the Royal Ballet.'

'You teach?'

'I used to dance professionally. That's me at the end.' Ford followed her gaze and saw a younger version of the grief-stricken woman before him, onstage. In a pale pink tutu, her over-made-up face bearing a wide, strained smile, she hung in mid-air, a muscular male dancer beneath her, arms outstretched, ready to catch her.

Before leaving for Salisbury, Ford excused himself and phoned George. He apologised for calling her into work and asked her to have the body moved to the viewing room. He didn't anticipate any violence this time.

On the drive down, he asked Ruth about Owen. She explained he'd been a vicar in the Church of England for thirty-two years before deciding the planet needed him more than God did.

She told Ford that Owen had been planning some sort of solo protest, but beyond that she didn't know anything. He'd taken their car, a silver Toyota Prius, which meant Ford could set someone looking for it on CCTV.

He arrived with Ruth at the Chapel of Rest at 2.57 p.m. First he showed her photographs, just in case she gave an instant 'no, that's not him'. No sense in distressing the public with corpses if he didn't have to. But she nodded, tearfully.

Now, Ford stood beside a visibly shaking Ruth as Pete gently drew back the sheet from her husband's face. They'd done a beautiful job of restoring Owen to an approximation of normality.

Somehow, Pete and his colleagues had reduced the swelling of his facial tissues. He wore the usual peaceful expression in death that grieving families take as a sign their loved one hasn't suffered, not knowing it's simply the consequence of the muscles relaxing.

Pete had hidden the bullet hole under Owen's chin beneath a sheet. It wrapped around his neck and extended up and over his head, to cover the sutures from the incision across his forehead.

Ruth stood, looking down at her dead husband. She extended a trembling finger and stroked it down his cheek.

'Is it Owen, Mrs Long?' Ford asked.

She sniffed. 'Yes,' she whispered.

Ford led her away and nodded his thanks to Pete, who solemnly replaced the sheet over Owen Long's face.

'Would you like a cup of tea?' Ford asked Ruth as they reached the hospital's ground floor. 'They have a nice cafe here.'

'Yes, please.'

With cups in front of them, Ford explained that they would need to ask her questions, but that he could assign her an FLO to travel back to London with her.

She shook her head. 'I'll find a B&B here for a few days. I want to be close to him.'

'We'll sort that out for you. There are some nice ones in the city centre. You'll need some things. Would you like me to have someone fetch them from home for you? One of my sergeants, Jan Derwent, could do it. I'll introduce you at the police station so you can tell her what to bring.'

Ruth nodded. 'Thank you.'

Their teas finished, he drove Ruth to Bourne Hill.

He called Jan. 'Can you come to Interview Suite Three, Jan? I have Ruth Long here with me.'

Jan came in and sat beside Ruth on the two-person sofa. Ford saw the way Ruth reacted to the presence of another woman. Some of the tension left her shoulders.

Jan gave off a vibe that made people relax around her – a tool she used to devastating effect when interviewing cocky young thugs who thought they were being interviewed by their aunt, right up to the point where she allowed them, gently, to incriminate themselves. Here, it produced a calming effect.

'I'm sorry for your loss, Mrs Long,' she said.

'Please, call me Ruth.'

'Ruth, I want you to know we're all working as hard as we can to find the person who killed Owen. Now,' she said, opening her notebook, 'what can I bring you from home?'

Jan left after five minutes with a list of clothes and personal items.

Ford turned to Ruth. 'I'll get someone to walk back to your B&B with you. While Jan is collecting your things, it would be helpful if she could look around. We'd also like to collect Owen's toothbrush for a DNA sample. Would that be OK?'

Ruth nodded. 'He took a manual one with him, but we share an electric one at home. Owen's was the blue head, by the way.'

'Thank you. Tell me, did Owen have a study at home? Or a spare room he used as a home office?'

'Upstairs. The back bedroom.'

'Did he have a computer?'

'A rather flashy one.' Her mouth formed the ghost of a smile. 'He called it the Gaia Engine. He mostly used it for his vlog.'

'Did he use a password, do you know?'

She nodded, sniffing. 'He made me copy it to my phone. Hold on.' She tapped and swiped for a few seconds, then held the phone up to him.

Ford pulled a biro from his jacket pocket and copied out the password: *Gaia_Needs_Owen!*

'Thank you. I'd like to look at his vlog. What did he call it?'

'The Circle of the Earth. It's a quote from Isaiah – Owen loved it. It was his favourite book of the Bible,' she said. 'He said it combined beautiful prose with eternal truths about our relationship with the planet God created.'

Ford made a note. 'I know this is painful for you, but can you think of anyone who might've wished Owen harm?'

Her eyes flashed defiantly. 'Yes! Plenty of people. Every one of the greedy sods whose development plans he opposed. You could start with them.'

'How many people are we talking about?'

'I don't know – hundreds? Owen was very active in the movement.'

'Did he receive threats from any of them? Visits from thugs trying to warn him off? Anything like that?'

She shook her head. 'No, nothing.'

Ford left Ruth in the company of a young female PC and caught up with Jan in the car park. 'Thanks, Jan. I knew she'd take to you.'

'What do you want me to do while I'm there?'

'I want you to get into his computer. I'll text you the password. Look through his emails, see if there are any threatening ones.'

'Or I could bring it back?'

'Yes. She gave me permission to do whatever it takes. He sounds like he got bitten badly by the eco-bug. It's like Mick said. Sometimes those folk rub people up the wrong way.'

Yes, and it's a long list of people. Farmers, shooters, hunters, bankers, oil company CEOs, politicians – even ordinary people just trying to catch the Tube to their workplaces.

If Owen Long had got in somebody's face, would that have been enough of a motive for murder?

He tried to imagine a pissed-off corporate type shooting a retired vicar then dumping the body in a pond in the middle of farmland outside Salisbury. Couldn't see it. No, this crime *belonged* to its location, and there would be a local culprit. That's where he would focus the team's energies and limited resources.

The lines of enquiry were converging, turning two cases into one. Ford could see a glimmer of hope he might be able to arrest the culprit before Tommy Bolter's wake. That was if the leaker inside Bourne Hill didn't queer his pitch by alerting JJ, who'd made it plain his preferred method of justice had nothing to do with due process.

CHAPTER EIGHTEEN

On Monday morning, Jools retrieved Adlam's guns from the armoury and took them to Hannah, who looked up and smiled as she saw Jools approaching her desk.

'Hi, Jools. Did you have a good weekend?' Hannah asked.

'Not bad. I spent all of yesterday redecorating my spare room. You?'

'I was doing research.'

Jools waited for more, but Hannah didn't elaborate.

'Cute,' Jools said, pointing at a plastic giraffe at the end of a line of zoo animals arranged in order of height along the base of Hannah's workstation. 'Is he new?'

Hannah nodded. 'Did you know, a male giraffe can grow to be eighteen feet tall and weigh up to one and a half tons?'

'I did not.' Jools hefted Adlam's guns. 'Did *you* know I have here two rifles, in .22 and .308 calibre?'

Hannah grinned. 'I did not. Whose are they?'

Jools laid the cases on Hannah's desk. 'Tom Adlam's. The guy who found Owen's body.'

'This is excellent. You realise you could have found both murder weapons?'

Jools widened her eyes. 'My God, Wix. I never thought of that!'

Hannah's eyebrows drew together. 'You should have, because—'
She stopped. Smacked herself on the forehead. 'You were being
ironic, right?'

'Right. Sorry.'

'No, it's fine. It's good training for me. And you're kinder about
it than Mick.'

'He's such a dick, isn't he?'

'I couldn't say for sure. But he does exhibit a number of biases
that could impede his ability to be impartial and rational as a
detective.'

'Like I said. A dick.'

'I need to get these to the ballistics lab in Trowbridge,' Hannah
said. 'I don't suppose you could come, too?'

'Sorry, I've got a ton of paperwork to do.'

Jools saw Hannah's expectant face drop into a frown. 'No, of
course. Sorry, I just thought it would be nice to drive over to HQ
together.'

'You know what? Yes. Let me grab some reports. If you can
drive, I'll read on the way there. Who knows, if we meet some
brass we can impress them with our commitment to collaborative
teamwork, proactive investigative strategies, and best practice in
cross-disciplinary learning.'

'I think you swallowed the latest guidelines from the College
of Policing.'

◆　◆　◆

Ballistics tests normally took anywhere from two weeks to a month,
so Jools was surprised when Hannah said she'd arranged for the test
to be done while they waited.

'One of the technicians owes me a favour,' she said, when Jools
asked how she'd managed it.

They arrived back four hours later with a sheaf of colour photographs of the rounds test-fired from Adlam's rifles. Hi-res digital images were waiting on a secure shared server for Hannah to download.

Jools dragged a chair over to Hannah's desk and watched as she aligned the pairs of images. She sighed. Neither pair matched. Tom Adlam was off the hook.

'Sorry you had a wasted morning, Wix,' she said, feeling the weight of the four lost hours heavy on her shoulders.

Hannah turned to her, her face serious. 'Not wasted. We eliminated Mr Adlam. Unless—' She stopped.

'What?'

'Unless he has other guns and he didn't declare them.'

Jools nodded. 'I'd need a warrant to search his property.'

'You could ask Henry what he thinks.'

Ford was in the kitchen stirring coffee granules into a mug of boiling water when Jools appeared in the doorway.

'How's it going?' he asked.

She wrinkled her nose. 'The bullets weren't fired from Tom Adlam's guns. Hannah and I took them over to HQ to get them test-fired. No match.'

Ford shrugged. 'These things happen.'

'Yeah, but if it *is* him, he could have been trying to throw me off by offering up a couple of spare rifles,' she said. 'I thought we should apply for a search warrant for his place.'

Ford frowned, grappling with the point that had been niggling at him. 'Why two, Jools? Why not use the same one for both murders?'

She opened her mouth, and then shut it again. He watched her pondering the same question he'd been turning over in his mind while making his coffee. Why *would* someone use two such different weapons to kill two victims?

Unless it was two shooters. But that was pushing the bounds of probability. If they were in London, two murders by gunshot within five miles of each other wouldn't necessarily be treated as related killings. But here? No. The odds were against it.

'A .22's lighter than a .308,' Jools said, finally. 'Easier to handle close-in?'

He shook his head. 'That makes it sound like a deliberate choice of weapon. Tell me what you know about close-up kills.'

Her eyes widened. She'd seen what he had. 'They're usually execution-style. Something you practically never see outside terrorist situations or gang killings.'

'And then it's two pistol rounds in the back of the head, not a rifle round under the chin.' He paused. 'Can you fetch Adlam's .22 and meet me in my office?'

Jools returned ten minutes later with the wooden-stocked rifle.

'It's empty, before you ask,' she said, sliding the safety lever across to reveal a red-painted dot. 'Now what?'

'Owen was shot under the chin and at close range. I want to know how it happened. Maybe if we can figure that out, we'll see things a little clearer.' He took a few steps away from her until he was backed up against a wall. 'I'm Owen. You're the shooter. How did your gun get under my chin?'

Jools came closer, holding the gun across her body. She lowered it until the muzzle was at the level of her sternum and closed in.

Ford grabbed the barrel and pushed it aside. 'If you pull the trigger now, you're going to miss by a mile.'

Jools pulled the barrel back so that the muzzle moved under Ford's jaw.

'We fight over it,' she grunted. 'Now it could work.'

He relaxed his grip. 'Put your finger over the trigger.'

'Nuh-uh. No way.' Jools shook her head vigorously. 'First rule of using firearms. You never point a gun at something or someone you don't want to shoot. We've already broken it. I'm not touching the trigger.'

He grinned. 'Come on, Jools. I must've pissed you off at some point in the last week.'

She laughed. 'Maybe you have. But I still think—'

'Fine. Put it *near* the trigger.'

Once she'd complied, Ford pulled the muzzle up under his chin. 'We struggle. You fire. I die. Possible?'

'Possible,' she agreed, pulling the muzzle away and laying the rifle on Ford's desk. 'But I still don't see how it could have gone down this way. Why would I let you get your hands on the rifle in the first place?'

'Maybe you didn't intend to kill me. Maybe you weren't even planning on *shooting* me.'

'So I was threatening you, then? Just waving it under your nose to frighten you?'

'Exactly!'

'But why? It's hardly the MO of a murderer, is it?'

Ford saw it then. Clear as a muzzle flash. 'No! It isn't. But what if it was an accident?'

'What do you mean?'

Ford went and sat down. Jools took the visitor's chair.

'I mean,' he said, 'the shooter didn't go looking for Owen. He just happened to find him.'

'By coincidence?' Jools said with a sceptical twist of her mouth.

'Not precisely. When you said you were threatening me, do you know what I heard?'

'What?'

'Get your ghastly little feet off my land!' Ford said in a parody of an English upper-class accent.

Jools's eyes widened. 'You think it was one of the family, don't you? The Baverstocks.'

'Got to be a possibility, hasn't it? Them or one of their staff.'

'An ex-army gamekeeper, for example.'

Ford made some notes, then looked up at Jools. 'Let's say Joe Hibberd chanced on Owen filming on the estate. He gave him the old "you're trespassing" speech. Only instead of retreating, Owen doubled down on his eco-warrior thing. Told Joe the land belonged to everyone, or something like that.'

Jools nodded enthusiastically. 'Joe didn't like it. He'd already come off second best to Tommy in a fight. He marched up to Owen and they got into a scuffle.'

'Owen grabbed the gun barrel and it ended up under his chin, and that's when Joe fired,' Ford said. 'Maybe on purpose, maybe by accident.'

'If we can accept it went down like that, we still have the two-gun problem,' Jools said. 'How do you account for the switch to the .308?'

'Easily, now. Owen is a mistake. But Joe's done it once and he figures he'll clear the mess up and then do a better job on Tommy. Pay him back for the ruckus over the poaching.'

'So you don't think it was Adlam?'

'I can't see it, Jools. I'm sorry. Not as a single shooter. Not as one of a pair. He's a genuine witness, I could feel it in every word of your report,' Ford said. 'If we can narrow down the time of death for either Tommy or Owen, see if he can give you an alibi. But no search warrant. Not unless he ticks at least a couple more boxes.'

Jools nodded. 'I didn't get a killer vibe off him either, to be honest.'

He saw from her downcast expression that she knew she'd been reaching. Thought of a way to lift her spirits. 'How are you getting on with the gun clubs?'

'I'm going to start tomorrow. I've got a list of five within a thirty-mile radius of Salisbury. One more if you extend it to fifty. Adlam's a member of one of them,' she said.

'So keep him on a list of persons of interest.'

As Jools left his office, he called Hannah. 'Have you got a minute?'

'Of course.'

'Do you want to grab a coffee?'

'I would love to.'

CHAPTER NINETEEN

The Café on the Park, an independent coffee shop, occupied the lower half of a Victorian corner house facing the Greencroft, a small green space between the ring road and the police station. They had the place to themselves, which suited Ford perfectly. The conversation he had planned with Hannah was going to be difficult enough without an audience.

He carried their coffees to the table Hannah had chosen, by a picture window. It looked out over the park, where kids were running around, leaping on to swings, climbing a 'witch's hat' made of elasticated rope, and slithering through a complicated network of green plastic tunnels. Hannah sat facing the door.

'Did you want to discuss the case?' she asked.

He took a sip of coffee and shook his head. 'No. It's not about work.'

'Is it about your personal life?'

'You could say that.' He found it difficult to know how to proceed. Hannah's face displayed no emotion. He ploughed on. 'That research you were doing on mountaineering risks.' She said nothing. He realised he hadn't asked her a question. 'I saw a document on your screen about the risks of rock-climbing. What was it?'

She wouldn't meet his gaze, speaking into her coffee. 'I told you in your Discovery on the way back from the first crime scene. It was just research for a friend.'

Maybe Hannah was the official expert on lying, but Ford had years of practical experience. He pushed harder. 'Were you investigating the accident that killed Lou?'

Hannah opened her mouth, then closed it. Still avoiding eye contact, she answered, 'No. I wasn't.'

'You're sure? Because you told me once you thought I should be over it by now.'

'I didn't say you *should* be over it. I said I was *surprised* that you weren't. Because according to the data, which admittedly is American, most widowers pass through the five stages of grief quicker than you have. Many also remarry.'

He'd asked her directly now, and just like before, she'd denied it was anything to do with Lou. How would her condition affect her ability to lie? He didn't know. But that didn't matter, did it? The point was, what had happened between him and Lou was supposed to stay private. Not turned into a research project just when there was an urgent need to solve two murders.

'Look, I'm sorry for pushing you. And I have no right to ask you this, but can you at least tell me who this friend is?' As he asked her, he realised he knew the answer. 'Is it Sam?'

She looked relieved. 'Yes, that document *was* for Sam.'

Her frankness irritated him. 'Don't you think you should have discussed it with me first?'

Her forehead crinkled. Ford could imagine her trying to process the question. 'No. Sam asked me for help and I said I'd be happy to. It was easy.'

'I'm sure it was. But that's not the point, Hannah.'

'What is the point, then? And please can you use my nickname?'

'Fine. Wix. The point is, he's my son and I didn't want him to go on the climbing trip.' Ford's breath was coming in shallow gasps and he had to fight to calm himself.

'Because of Lou? Her dying in a climbing accident?'

'Yes. Because of that.' There it was again. She just couldn't leave it alone.

She frowned. 'Statistically, the chances of a mother and son both dying in climbing accidents are extremely small. About—'

'Please, I don't need the exact percentage.'

'—three hundred and twenty-eight point five million to one.'

Ford sighed. He tried again. 'What I'm trying to say is, I feel deeply uncomfortable about Sam going on a climbing trip – the same sort of activity that *did* kill his mother, my wife – and I feel that the two of you bounced me into agreeing.'

She smiled. 'That's good.'

'Good?' What the hell was she thinking? How could it possibly be good?

'That you agreed. It's important for children, especially adolescents, to test themselves. Facing risk is part of developing resilience,' she said. 'In fact, according to a clinical psychologist I follow on Twitter called Dr Hazel Harrison, lack of resilience is strongly linked to teenage anxiety and depression.'

'Which is all very interesting, but can you at least see where I'm coming from?'

She nodded, then took a careful sip of her latte. 'Hot,' she muttered. 'Yes, I *can* see. You are locked into the early stages of grief for your wife, which, as I said before, is strange.' She reached across the foot of table that separated their hands to lightly brush the backs of his fingers. 'You're compensating by trying to prevent the same fate from befalling Sam. Even though he is at far higher risk from your

136

driving him to school than from climbing a thousand mountains. But you have to let him grow up, Henry.'

He'd hoped – expected – her to be contrite, ashamed even. Apology accepted, they could move on and get back to solving murders together. Now she was besting him in an argument *and* offering parenting advice.

'Please don't tell me what I have to do to raise my son,' he said, regretting the sharp tone as soon as the words had left his mouth.

Hannah's face paled. She bit her lower lip. A blush raced up from her throat to her jawline and cheeks. 'I upset you. I can see that now. I am so sorry, Henry. Please forgive me.'

A tear welled in the inner corner of her left eye and slowly rolled down her flaming cheek before dropping off her chin on to the table. She wiped it away with the back of her hand.

He felt the steel bands round his chest loosen a little – and like a complete jerk.

'No,' he said. '*I'm* sorry . . . Wix. You're right, I know you are. It's just . . .' He sighed. 'I've tried so hard to let him have a normal childhood, even though he lost the person he loved more than anyone else in the world.'

'That's you now,' she said quietly. 'He told me. He said he wished you could forgive yourself. That's an unusually mature attitude for an adolescent boy.'

They walked back to Bourne Hill without speaking. Ford hoped he hadn't wrecked a friendship still at the stage where even a few sharp words could throw it off course.

Ford got back late that evening and Sam had already gone to bed. He'd left the letter from school on the kitchen table, scrawling across the top in untidy handwriting:

Don't forget about trip permission letter plus cheque.

Ford sighed. He signed the permission form, dug out his chequebook from a kitchen drawer, then stuck the letter and cheque into a crumpled brown envelope.

◆ ◆ ◆

At breakfast the next day, Ford handed Sam a toasted bagel with butter and Marmite, and a glass of milk. He waited while Sam consumed half the bagel and washed it down. Talking to his adolescent son before he'd eaten in the morning carried a degree of risk. More likely to lead to a tirade than anything approaching civilised conversation.

'I put your trip letter and the cheque on the hall table,' he said.

Sam nodded. 'Thanks.'

'Why didn't you tell me you'd asked Hannah to get those safety statistics for you?'

'Why d'you think?'

'I don't know. It's why I'm asking.'

'Because I thought you'd be cross. Like you are.'

'Yeah, I am cross. And you know why? Because she's the deputy chief CSI. She's supposed to be spending her time helping me solve two murders, not acting as your unpaid researcher.'

'I checked first. She said it was fine.'

'That's not the point.'

Sam pounced. 'What *is* the point?'

'The point is, my darling boy, you knew I'd be unhappy, and you went behind my back.'

The remainder of the bagel stopped halfway to Sam's mouth. 'Dad, I know that. But what about *me*? *I* would've been unhappy not going when all my friends were going. Look,' he said, softening his voice in a way that brought a lump to Ford's throat, 'I know, all right? I know it's because of Mum. You feel guilty because she' – he

138

looked down then back at Ford – 'she died and you lived. But you can't live your life trying to stop it from happening again. You'll go crazy.'

Ford took a sip of his coffee. 'When did you get so bloody mature?'

Sam smiled and took another bite of his bagel. 'You can still love me without rolling me up in bubble wrap, you know,' he mumbled.

'Are you trying to tell me you're not a little kid anymore?'

Sam grinned. 'Yeah. But don't think that means you can stop giving me an allowance. And I'll need spending money for the trip. A tenner should do it.'

'You cheeky little bleeder! How about a lift to school instead of taking your bike?'

Sam shook his head. 'It's fine. Me and Josh . . . I mean, Josh and I are going in together.'

'All right. Remember to take the letter.'

Halfway out the door, Sam turned. 'I won't. Thanks, Dad. You're cool.'

Cool was OK. Ford could live with cool. It was the idea of losing his only child to the mountains that he struggled with. He turned away from the thought and grabbed his work things.

CHAPTER TWENTY

Olly sighed. Trudging round the tattoo parlours had been a waste of time. But at least now he felt he had done a proper bit of detective work. He'd hit Mick with it if he tried his 'experienced copper' act again.

He sat at his desk, ready to review the CCTV footage for Owen Long's silver Prius.

Olly found him entering the city at 11.04 a.m., thirteen days earlier. The last image was timestamped 8.43 a.m. the following day, leaving the city on the Coombe Road heading towards Blandford.

He stared at the image and tried to force himself to think like an experienced detective. To think like Ford. He knew he could come across as a know-all, and he hated the way Mick never missed an opportunity to make fun of his fast-track status. But Olly dreaded failure. Why couldn't Mick see he was just trying to catch up with everyone else?

Half an hour later, using the time-of-death estimate from the PM report and the time Adlam had found the body, he had something he felt sure Ford would want to know straight away. Straightening his tie, he went to find his boss.

◆ ◆ ◆

Ford signalled for Olly to sit down while he finished his call with Sandy. He smiled at him. Was that a new tie? Olly did love his designer gear.

'Yes, Olly. What've you got for me?'

'I found Owen on the CCTV. Guv, we got Dr Eustace's report on Friday, right? Well, she said Owen had been dead for a week to ten days. If her estimate for time of death is accurate, even allowing for the range, then I calculate that Owen was murdered not in a three-day window but a twenty-four-hour window.'

'Good work. What's the window?'

'I think Owen was killed between Thursday the twenty-ninth of April after 9.00 a.m. and Friday the thirtieth of April at, say, the same time.'

'Let's add on a few hours as a safety margin, but that's good work. Well done.'

He caught the corners of Olly's mouth twitching upwards as he stood to leave. Maybe the boy had the makings of a decent detective after all.

Ford looked down to see his hand clamped across his stomach. His stomach had been churning all morning. He knew why. It was the day of the wake. And Ford was nowhere near making an arrest. Even if he did have Joe Hibberd in his sights.

He went to find Jools.

'How are you doing with the gun clubs?'

'I've already been to one. Salisbury and District Shooting Club.'

'Any joy?'

'No. The membership secretary showed me their list. No matches to the Royal Colleges lists. No butchers, either. A couple had bought .308 rounds in the last month, but they were full metal jackets not ballistic tips.'

'Where's the next one on your list?'

'New Forest Shooting Centre in Nomansland.'

'Let's go, then.'

Her eyes widened. 'You're coming?'

'I need to get out and do something.'

On the way out, Ford stopped by Olly's desk. 'Can you check whether Hibberd has a record?'

'On it,' he said, mimicking – whether consciously or not, Ford didn't know – Jools's favourite response to a request.

Thirty minutes later, Ford buzzed his window down as Jools drove along the bumpy track to the gun club. He could smell plenty of spring growth and – a sour counterpoint to the natural scent of trees in leaf or bud – the sharp tang of burned propellant.

Distant reports grew louder as Jools rolled up to a pine-clad single-storey building with a large 'Welcome' sign above the front door. Ford led the way inside. A Gaggia espresso machine hissed behind a heavily varnished pine counter, the nearest thing to a reception desk.

A cluster of round tables filled the far end of the room. At one of them, a couple of men dressed in olive drab shirts under sleeveless shooting jackets were drinking coffee.

Wooden plaques on the wall behind them bore columns of names and dates in gold lettering. Club trophy winners, Ford assumed. A glass cabinet beneath the plaques groaned with silverware, reinforcing the impression.

'Need some help?' one of the men asked with a smile.

Ford turned. 'Yes, we're looking for someone who runs the club. The secretary?'

'That'll be Jim. He's out on the rifle range at the moment.'

'Which way is that?'

The man shook his head. 'You can't go walking around, son, sorry. It's a members-only club. If you're thinking of joining I can give you a leaflet.'

Ford showed his ID. 'Can you take us to him?'

The man peered at the warrant card. Then he nodded. 'Of course. I didn't mean to be rude.'

'It's fine. You weren't to know.'

Ford and Jools followed their guide from the clubhouse down a wide path covered in bark chips, freshly laid judging by the smell of creosote emanating from the bright orange scraps of wood.

The reports of the firearms grew louder. Ford thought he could detect at least three different types. Deep-throated barks he imagined to be shotguns. Louder, sharper cracks he thought were rifles. And a third that eluded him.

A volley of the latter echoed through the woods surrounding them.

'What type of weapon is that?' he asked.

'Long-barrelled revolver. We've got a separate range for them. They're legal,' he added in an anxious tone.

'I'm sure they are. Don't worry, we're not here to inspect licences.'

'It wouldn't matter if you were. Jim's a monster for paperwork. You could go through the office with a team of sniffer dogs and you wouldn't find a comma in the wrong place.'

They emerged from the cover of a stand of birches into a wide-open grassy area about a hundred yards by thirty. A tall sandbank capped off the far end. Thick shrubs and tree cover demarcated the left and right edges. A row of targets marked by fluttering orange flags stood in front of the sandbank.

The man led them to the shooters' stations, a row of tables protected by a sloping wooden roof. Beside individual tables laden with ammunition, gloves and notepads, men and a lone woman stood, kneeled or lay, a rifle in their hands or by their side as they checked their latest shots with binoculars. The volleys of shots made conversation impossible.

Ford caught Jools's eye. 'Loud, isn't it?' he yelled.

She grimaced. 'Should have brought earplugs.'

Their guide walked down the row and tapped one of the shooters on the shoulder. The latter removed a pair of olive-green ear defenders and turned round.

'There's a couple of police want to talk to you.'

The man got to his feet. A beer belly bulged from beneath a green jumper with leather shoulder pads. He flicked on the safety and laid his rifle carefully on the ground, then backed out of his station and came over to Ford and Jools.

He pointed back the way they'd come, then cupped his hands around his mouth.

'Let's talk in the clubhouse,' he bawled.

They sat at a corner table, well away from the other patrons. Jim fetched three coffees, and once they were seated, he looked first at Jools, then at Ford.

'How can I help?'

'We'd like to see a list of your members,' Jools said.

Jim swivelled in his chair to look at her. 'Can I ask why?'

'We're investigating two murders. Both victims were shot. We're talking to local gun owners.'

'Oh, right. Is paper OK or do you want it as a digital file?'

'Digital would be better,' Jools said. 'Would it have records of what guns your members own?'

Jim shook his head. 'Only contact details, that sort of thing. But I know all the members personally. If there's somebody you're interested in specifically, I could tell you what they usually shoot.'

'Just the list for now, please.' She handed him her card. 'My email's on there.'

He got to his feet. 'Won't be a minute.'

While they waited, Ford wandered over to the wall-mounted plaques. One bore the heading, in ornate black and gold Gothic lettering:

Columns of names and dates marched across the rest of the polished surface. Ford scanned the list. Clearly, this club had its crack shots: people who won several years in a row, then dropped a couple before returning, triumphant, to claim another trophy.

One name in particular cropped up with amazing regularity: P. Martival. Seven times in the last fifteen years, with a recent run of three consecutive years and another of two. Ford made a note of the name.

'Here you are, Inspector!'

Ford turned to see Jim waving a sheaf of stapled sheets, and rejoined the table.

'I did email them to you as well,' Jim said to Jools. 'But I thought it would be helpful to have a hard copy.'

She tucked it into her bag. 'Thanks. Tell me,' she said, 'what sort of ammunition do your members use on the ranges? The ones who shoot rifles.'

Jim leaned back and clasped his hands over his belly. 'All the modern calibres from .22 up to .450. The only calibre we prohibit is .50 BMG. The bloody things are like artillery shells. Far too destructive for leisure shooting. Did you know, the army use them against vehicles? Buildings, even!'

'Is there a favourite calibre?' Jools persisted.

Ford noticed approvingly the way Jools didn't let Jim sidetrack her.

Jim smiled. 'Every calibre has its fans. It's mainly youth members who shoot .22.'

Jools made a note.

'Do you have a club shop?' Ford asked.

'Of course! We stock all those calibres, plus a few more besides. Then there's shotgun cartridges—'

'Records of sales?'

Jim frowned at having been cut off. Clearly he enjoyed talking gun stuff, but Ford didn't have time.

'Absolutely. Member's name plus date and amount of ammunition purchased.'

'We might come back to you and ask for your last six months' receipts,' Ford said.

'No problem. As I said, we're happy to help the police. You said two murders. Were they the ones in the paper?'

'That's right.'

Jim nodded. 'Terrible business. But I can assure you, it wouldn't have been one of our members.'

'How can you be so sure?' Jools asked.

'They come here to shoot for fun. It's their hobby. A passion for some of them. But they're not murderers. They're all responsible members of society!'

Ford forbore from telling Jim that at least half the people he'd ever arrested for murder fitted that description.

'Do they ever shoot with expanding bullets?' he asked instead.

'Oh, yes,' Jim said, warming to his theme as he faced increasingly technical questions. 'A lot of our members use tipped rounds. They're more accurate, you see, on account of—'

'Do they bring their guns with them or store them here?' Jools asked quickly.

'Most bring them in their cars. Cased, of course. We do have a few guns available for hire for day guests and the like. But that's a tiny fraction,' he said. 'I'd say ninety-nine point nine per cent of people shooting here bring their own guns with them.'

Ford pointed at the wooden plaques he'd inspected earlier. 'I see you have a few real sharpshooters.'

Jim twisted in his seat to follow the line of Ford's finger. He grinned. 'It's worse than tennis clubs. You know, the same chaps every year coming up to collect their cup at the end of the day. People don't mind. I think it just spurs them on to get better.'

'I saw that there's a P. Martival who does pretty well. Is that a man or a woman?' Ford asked.

'Oh, that's definitely a man. Phil Martival. Bloody nice chap. Especially given his background.'

'Background?' Ford asked, envisioning some likely lad who'd nevertheless managed to insinuate himself into this genteel club of shooting enthusiasts.

'Him being a lord and all.'

From the corner of his eye, Ford caught Jools stiffening. 'A lord?' he echoed.

'That's right. The Right Honourable Viscount Baverstock's his proper title, but he insists we all call him Phil. Just as well, because I doubt we'd have room for all that lot, now would we!'

Ford laughed along. 'You're gonna need a bigger plaque,' he said in an American accent.

'What? Oh, yes. Bigger plaque.' Jim chuckled. 'No, seriously, Phil's a lovely chap. Brings his kids along from time to time. They're not bad shots, either of them. Especially Lucy. She's won a few competitions in her time, as well.'

'Does Lady Baverstock ever come?'

Jim chuckled again. 'Once. Very accurate, she was. Hit the trees every single time. Nice lady, though. Made fun of herself for being such a bad shot.'

'You said you know what all your members shoot. Does that include Phil?' Jools asked.

'Well, now, that's another intelligent question.' Jim winked at her. 'Anyone would think you do this for a living.'

Jools regarded him with a stony look.

147

'Yes, er, well. He mostly brings along his Springfield .30-06. But for club competitions he uses a lovely old Parker-Hale in .308.' Ford nodded. Said nothing. Joe Hibberd had lied.

The visits to the other four clubs followed a similar pattern. By the end of the day, they'd secured promises of emailed membership lists from each of the secretaries, who'd been just as eager to help as Jim at the New Forest Shooting Centre.

'Joe Hibberd lied about Lord Baverstock owning a .308,' Ford said as Jools drove up to the tail end of a long queue of traffic waiting to get into Salisbury from the A36. 'He's also the only person we've talked to with a motive to kill Tommy. He told me he looks after the family's guns. That translates as "has access to", and it now includes a weapon in the calibre used to shoot Owen Long.'

Ford allowed himself to visualise Hibberd's arrest for murder. If only he could get to that point quicker. Tommy's wake was probably in full swing, and he had no idea how he was going to prevent JJ from launching his own, very different, murder investigation. As for his threats to ruin Ford's career, let him try.

CHAPTER TWENTY-ONE

When Ford arrived back at Bourne Hill, Mick came looking for him. He wore a wrinkle-free charcoal-grey suit and a navy tie in what Ford took to be silk. Cufflinks of some semi-precious purple gemstone sparkled at his wrists, and his shoes gleamed with polish. Ford caught a whiff of freshly applied aftershave.

'Looking sharp, Mick,' Ford said. 'Glad to see you took my words to heart.'

'Yeah, right. The wake's at The White Lion. It started at lunch-time. I thought I'd go and pay my respects. Want to join me?'

Ford consulted his watch. 'I can for a little while. Then I need to get home to see Sam.'

'OK. I just thought it'd be easier if there were two of us. We can show them we're taking it seriously.'

Ford doubted that was how JJ would see things. 'Fair point. Although if JJ and Rye have been boozing since lunch they'll be – what shall we say – volatile?'

Mick nodded. 'Talkative, too. People tell you more when they're pissed.'

Before leaving for the pub, Ford stopped by Olly's desk. 'Does Hibberd have a record?'

'No, guv. Sorry.'

'Not to worry. Thanks, Olly.'

◆ ◆ ◆

Ford could hear the racket from The White Lion from halfway down Pennyfarthing Street. Mick reached for the highly polished brass door handle and looked at Ford.

'Ready?'

Ford nodded, steeling himself for the inevitable confrontation with JJ. To their left, a couple of young blokes smoking looked them over.

'You filth?' one asked with a sneer.

Mick turned round, slowly. 'What did you say?'

The speaker shrugged. 'Nothing.'

Mick took a couple of steps closer until he was toe to toe with the guy. His mate sidled off, leaving him offering Mick a placatory smile.

'No. I definitely heard you say something,' Mick said in a dangerous, low tone.

'It's nothing. A joke, yeah? I didn't mean nothing by it. Sorry.'

Mick leaned forward, squaring his shoulders and crowding the young guy against the wall. 'Do you want to know who the real filth are? It's the perverts who rape old ladies and kids. The lowlifes who mug people to buy drugs. And shitheads like you' – he poked a finger into the guy's chest – 'who've got all the balls in the world until they need some help. And then who do you call? Your mate over there? Someone in your *crew*? No. You call us, don't you. So watch your fucking lip or I might just give it a new shape.'

Mick's violent reaction startled Ford. But he knew the source. Mick's marriage was crumbling before his eyes, and he was facing a very different future to the one he'd imagined.

Ford touched him on the elbow. 'Let's go in.'

He led the way, hoping that the stress of the divorce wasn't going to push Mick over the line. A line he constantly flirted with, like a kid balancing on a tall brick wall. Or had he jumped down already – on the wrong side? He'd complained about the cost of his 'leech' of a lawyer. Was he getting help paying her fees?

Ford didn't have time to start investigating. And strictly speaking, if he did have genuine suspicions, he ought to report them to the Independent Office for Police Conduct.

He left it. No way was he involving that lot. Not yet, anyway.

Inside, fifty or sixty people, from small children to men and women in their eighties or beyond, thronged the low-ceilinged space. Ford recognised faces from the inquest hearing.

The guests chatted, laughed, wept, shouted. Johnny Cash sang about pain and loss from speakers screwed to the blackened beams at each end of the bar. The bar staff, four of them, moved around one another in a choreographed dance born of many shifts working together in a confined space.

The outfits on display tended towards the celebratory rather than the solemn. The men mostly wore suits, in a range of patterns and exotic colours that would have had Salisbury's funeral directors sighing into their top hats. Ford saw a gold waistcoat talking to a bottle-green window-pane-checked suit, arms waving animatedly in the limited space between them.

Ford thought Tommy would have enjoyed the acres of exposed female flesh, as displayed by plunging necklines, swooping backs and slit skirts.

The smell of alcohol dominated. He imagined liquor-strength vapour being sweated out of pores to mingle with the combined aromas of dozens of different perfumes and aftershaves.

Mick nudged him and jerked his head towards a door to the left of the bar. 'JJ and Rye are through there. I'm going to go and pay my respects.'

Ford leaned closer. 'Be careful,' he said into Mick's ear. 'I know you went to school with them, but they're pissed and they're grieving.'

Mick nodded, then threaded his way through the crowd. Ford wondered if Hibberd would be at the wake, then dismissed the idea. Whatever had drawn him to the inquest would surely be overridden by a sense of self-preservation.

As he turned to place his mineral water on the bar, someone tapped him on the shoulder. He found himself facing the young woman he'd seen on Joe Hibberd's arm at the inquest. In contrast to the sober black number she'd worn then, today she was dressed to kill in a strappy coral dress. Her eyes were unfocused and she swayed on her high heels. Her hair had come unpinned, and blonde tresses looped down to brush her bare shoulders.

In her right hand, she held a pint glass three-quarters full of something pink and fizzy. Clamped between her fingers and the sweating side of the glass, a photo of the dead man bore on its white border the words 'Tommy Bolter RIP: Heaven gained a new angel'.

'Are you a copper?' she asked, brushing at a stray lock of hair that had stuck across her kohl-rimmed left eye. 'You *look* like a copper.'

'I'm a detective,' Ford replied.

'So, like, that's a yes?'

He nodded. 'Were you a friend of Tommy's?'

Her eyes filled with tears. 'Poor little Tommy. He never did nobody no harm, did he? I mean, who'd want to shoot him?'

'That's what we're trying to find out. How well did you know him?'

She sniffed. 'Me and him went to school together, didn't we? St Jude's over Laverstock way.'

'Tell me . . .'

'Gwyneth. Like the actress. My mates call me Gwynnie, but I hate that.'

'Tell me, Gwyneth, do you know of anybody who wanted to hurt Tommy?'

Her eyes widened. 'You mean, like, enemies and that?'

Ford shrugged. 'Not necessarily enemies. But somebody he got on the wrong side of. Something like that.'

She shook her head then took a gulp of her drink. She belched loudly. 'Oh, God! Sorry. It's this cider. Forest fruits. It's really gassy.'

'Tommy?' he said gently.

'Oh, yeah. Look, if I tell you something, I won't get into trouble, will I?'

'Have you done something wrong?'

'Me? No! Definitely not.'

'Then you should be fine. What did you want to tell me, Gwyneth?'

She leaned forward, then overbalanced as someone barged past her, and slopped some of her sweet-smelling cider over the front of his suit.

'Oh, no! Your lovely jacket. I've ruined it.' She started to cry again.

Ford shook his head, thinking that his decision to buy only black suits from Marks & Spencer was a sound career move. 'Don't worry. It's washable. Now, take a deep breath and then tell me whatever it is you wanted to tell me. I'm sure you'll feel better if you get it off your chest.'

She took a breath. 'Well, Tommy, right? He was a lovely bloke. But, you know, some of what he did wasn't exactly, like, legal.'

'What kind of things are we talking about? Drugs?'

She shook her head violently. 'No! Not drugs. I mean, he smoked a bit of blow now and again, but, like, who doesn't?'

'I don't.'

She grinned drunkenly. 'Yes, but you' – she poked him in the centre of his chest – 'are a p'liceman, aren't you. A dee' – poke – 'teck' – poke – 'tive.'

Gently, Ford removed her fingertip from his chest. 'What else was Tommy involved in? Look, we can't touch him now, so you can tell me, whatever it was. You're just helping me catch the person who murdered him.'

She nodded and took another swig of her drink. Ford began to wonder if she'd pass out before divesting herself of whatever insider knowledge she had on Tommy Bolter.

'He had a, like, *scheme*,' she hissed. 'You know, to make some money.' She glanced at the back room again, just as a gust of male laughter boomed out. She flinched. 'I need my bag. I wanna smoke. Wait for me?'

He watched her disappear into the crowd. While he waited for her to return, he peered through the side door, looking for Mick. He caught sight of his shaved head, one among many, nodding as JJ Bolter held court. The image disturbed him. If JJ was holding court, was Mick one of his courtiers? Eager to please?

The young woman arrived back at his side, clutching a gold-sequinned handbag.

Outside, the noise dropped away, although the louder voices were still clear through the glass-panelled door. She offered him her cigarettes, raising her dramatic brown eyebrows in enquiry. Ford shook his head.

She lit her cigarette and drew on it luxuriously, blowing out a stream of blue smoke into the warm early-evening air. She smiled at him. The expression transformed her face. He saw a pretty, young girl who, for whatever reason, had got mixed up with a crowd her parents had almost certainly warned her about when she was growing up.

'Me and Tommy, right? What we had was special. He, like, trusted me. And I trusted him. We weren't exclusive or nothing. But it was OK, you know?'

Ford nodded. Was there a point to all this, or had she just wanted some company while she smoked?

'I saw you at the inquest with Joe Hibberd. What's the story there?'

'We're sort of together.'

'Bit soon after Tommy, isn't it?'

She sipped her drink. 'Like I said. We weren't exclusive. Anyway, Joe's helping me grieve.'

'Tell me about this scheme of Tommy's.'

'Scheme?'

Had she forgotten already? He improvised. 'You know. The thing he had going on to make a little cash.'

'Oh, yeah. You know JJ and Rye?' she murmured, standing close, holding her cigarette out to one side. 'They never let Tommy do anything for himself. Said he had to keep his nose clean while they, you know, made the money.'

Ford saw at once how the relationships between the Bolter brothers played out. 'He wanted to prove himself to them.'

She nodded and took a sip of cider. 'Yeah. So, he told me he was going to do something for himself. Make some money and then they'd have to take him seriously.'

'What was this thing he was going to do?'

'Hare-coursing. He wasn't doing any harm. Not really. He said loads of hares get, like, killed by foxes. It's nature's way.'

'I'm not worried about that, Gwyneth. I'm a murder detective, OK? I investigate murders. Like Tommy's. Did he tell you where he was going to do the coursing?'

'Not exactly. But he sent me a picture. D'you wanna see it?'

'Yes, please.'

She brought out her phone, spent a few moments tapping and swiping, then rotated the screen to show him a photo of Tommy grinning into the camera, countryside stretching away behind him.

Ford saw a grassy field, white-flowered hedgerows and, in the distance, the cathedral spire. Puffy clouds decorated a clear blue sky. A long, branching shadow stretched away from him across the grass. A tree. A big tree, at that. Tommy must been standing facing it, so the selfie revealed the shadow but not the tree itself.

He got her to send him a copy.

'So you didn't go with him, then?'

She shook her head, then staggered and grabbed his arm to steady herself. 'Sorry 'bout that,' she said, releasing him. 'No, I did go with him. But I stayed in his truck while he went off to the actual, you know, *secret location*.' She giggled.

'Where in his truck?'

'Like, the passenger seat?'

He sighed. 'I meant, where did Tommy park the truck?'

'Oh. Just off the lane.'

'Which lane?'

She looked at Ford as if he were stupid. 'The one up to the place! Opposite Pentridge Down. It's sort of part of a private estate. You know' – she adopted an upper-class accent, which sounded comical with its underpinning of broad Wiltshire – '*Trespassers will be prosecuted.*'

Ford had studied the maps long enough to know instantly which private estate she was talking about. Alverchalke. Where all roads in the case seemed to lead.

'What was his state of mind when he got back?'

'He was buzzing, like after doing a line. I asked him if he'd found the right place and he's like, "I found something much better than that, babes. I just found the golden effing ticket." Only, he didn't say "effing", he said, you know, the actual f-word.'

'What else?'

'He said he'd seen this old bloke up on the hill making this film, yeah?'

Ford nodded, feeling the link between the two murders crystallising right in front of his eyes.

'Then there's this other, you know, *person*, comes up and starts shouting and it all kicks off and they, like, have this massive row or whatever, loads of pushing and shoving, anyway, and then this gun goes off and the old bloke falls down dead.'

Ford picked up on her use of the word 'person'. It sounded wrong on her lips, let alone Tommy's. But inside, he was rejoicing. She'd just confirmed his own intuition that the two deaths were linked, and strongly at that. Tommy had witnessed Owen Long's murder. And he'd planned to blackmail the perpetrator. Which meant Tommy had known the murderer's identity.

'Did Tommy tell you the name of the person with the gun?'

Gwyneth shook her head, sending his hopes flying away. 'I asked him, but he's, like, "I knew 'em, that's all you need to know."'

'And he definitely said he *knew* them, not he recognised them?'

She shrugged. 'It's the same, isn't it?'

'No, it isn't. Think hard. It's important.'

'He said he *knew* them.' She dropped her cigarette and ground it out beneath her stiletto. 'Have you finished? Can I go now, please?'

'In a moment. Why didn't you come forward sooner?'

'It's JJ and Rye. They frighten me.'

'But they wouldn't hurt you, would they?'

She laughed, and it sounded bitter to Ford. 'Wouldn't they? Look, JJ spoke to me after the inquest. He said if I heard anything about Tommy I was to go to him, not the cops – sorry, I mean the police – or he'd make my life *uncomfortable*.' She made air quotes round the final word. They both knew what that word would mean coming from JJ Bolter's lips.

It made a kind of sense. JJ may well have given Ford until the wake to find Tommy's killer, but he could have changed his mind and decided to go for his own brand of justice.

Ford reached for something reassuring to say. 'JJ's all talk. He'd never hurt you. He just likes to frighten people.'

'Promise?' she asked him with pleading eyes, reddened by crying.

'Promise.'

She nodded, then turned away, wandering over to a group of women in high heels and higher spirits. They embraced her, and soon all five were laughing at some shared joke.

She'd said Tommy claimed he 'knew' the shooter. Who would Tommy have known on Alverchalke land? The answer leaped out at him: Joe Hibberd. He might have been gentle with Gwyneth, but he had a hot temper bubbling just below the surface. Ford had seen that up by the rearing field.

A minute later, the pub's front door flew open and JJ burst out on to the pavement. Weeping or drink, or both, had made his face puffy.

He turned his red-rimmed eyes on Ford and grabbed his lapels. 'My little brother's dead, chopped into pieces like Frankenstein's monster, and I see you hanging round his wake boozing when you should be out catching his murderer. I told you what would happen if you didn't catch the bastard who did it.'

Ford was too slow. JJ's fist smashed into the side of his face, spinning him round and making him stagger into a couple leaning against a windowsill stacked with empty glasses. They shattered as Ford stuck his hands out to stop himself falling.

His face blaring with pain, Ford turned and saw JJ's meaty right fist heading towards his eyes. He ducked and drove forwards, jamming both hands into JJ's left shoulder and spinning him in a half-circle.

JJ bent forward, then kicked out backwards with his right heel. But Ford had already sidestepped, thus avoiding having his knee broken or the ligaments sheared.

The kick glanced off the side of his leg. Ford punched hard, aiming for a spot at the base of JJ's neck where nerves ran close to the surface. JJ yelled out as Ford's knuckles crushed the fragile fibres.

In that moment, Ford grabbed JJ's right wrist, yanked it up behind his back, then pushed him against the wall beside the front door. He punched JJ in the side, over his kidney, drawing forth a low moan.

Ford felt able to ease off the pressure. He leaned closer and spoke into JJ's left ear, between panting breaths. 'If that's your idea of fucking up my career, then I'll give it to you. Call it a Get Out of Jail Free card. But don't try it again.'

JJ offered a grunted laugh in response. 'You have no fucking idea, Ford. I had a chat with Rye. We thought of something much better. Your boy. Sam, isn't it?'

Ford's heart stuttered. He felt a wave of pure fear crash over him. 'Don't even think about it,' he growled.

'He goes to the grammar school, doesn't he?' JJ twisted his head round to look straight at Ford. He dropped his voice. 'Schools can be dangerous places. Chemistry labs full of acid. All those sharp edges in the workshops. *Bullies*. Anything could happen.'

Ford yanked JJ's arm back up, drawing forth a hiss of pain. 'If I hear you've even looked at Sam, I'll come for you,' he muttered. 'And your brother. And I will finish you.'

JJ laughed. 'Finish us? What, with some underpaid CPS brief and a half-baked case my lawyers'll destroy before the tea break? I don't think so.'

'I'm not talking about lawyers, Bolter.' Ford pushed JJ once more against the wall, then took his hands off his shoulders. But he was fully ready for a counter-attack.

Instead, JJ headed for the pub door. Then he stopped and turned back. 'Carry on with your investigation, Ford. But all bets are off. Me and Rye are doing our own digging,' he said. 'Keep an eye on Sam,' he added with a wink, then went back into the pub.

Mick emerged a minute later.

'Christ, H! What happened to you?'

'Ah, the cavalry,' Ford said ruefully, rubbing his cheek. 'JJ happened. I could have done with some backup.'

'Sorry. I was in the toilet.'

Ford grimaced. 'Next time, eh? I'm leaving now, Mick. Take care, yes?'

Jaw throbbing, Ford pulled on the handbrake and climbed out of the Discovery on to his own drive. He glanced in the wing mirror to see a purplish bruise spreading over his cheekbone. He limped up to the front door and let himself in.

He called out to Sam, who came hurtling down the stairs, his face creased with concern.

'Are you OK, Dad? I saw on Twitter there was a fight at the pub for Tommy Bolter's wake. It said a policeman was involved.'

Ford accepted his son's fierce, brief hug. 'Watch the face,' he said with a lopsided grin. 'I'm fine. Mick and I went to the wake. Tommy's brother, JJ, had too much to drink. He lost his temper and hit me.'

Sam looked outraged. 'You should have arrested him.'

'I *could* have arrested him. But it wouldn't have served any purpose. He's just lost his little brother. I let it go.'

'You shouldn't have,' Sam said, gently prodding Ford's bruise and making him flinch. 'Mick's a big bloke. You should have got him to beat JJ up.'

'We need JJ and Rye on our side.'

'And assaulting a detective inspector is part of that, is it?'

Sam rarely used Ford's title, so he knew how seriously his son was taking it. Then he saw why. Beneath the adolescent bravado, Sam was down to one parent. He could be as wilful, stroppy and uncooperative as any teenager, but he had a vulnerable side he only occasionally let Ford see.

He realised that Sam's insistence on going on the climbing trip with school was him forcing himself to face his fears. Even as Ford tried to avoid facing his own.

'I'll be fine. Call it an occupational hazard. How about we go out for tea tonight?'

Sam's face relaxed and he smiled. 'Burgers?'

'Biggest they have.'

'Cool.'

As Sam climbed into the passenger seat beside him, already running through the menu on his phone, Ford's feelings of anxiety redoubled. What if JJ wasn't just making idle threats? Ford doubted he'd actually hurt a teenage boy just to get at a cop who'd failed to catch his brother's killer. But what if . . . what if . . . what if . . .

CHAPTER TWENTY-TWO

Ford settled down to review the last few videos on Owen Long's vlog. Just as he'd pressed 'Play' on the first one, Jan entered his office carrying a mug of coffee and a plastic box. She unsnapped the lid and placed two flapjacks beside his elbow on a paper plate.

'Here you go, Henry,' she said, putting the mug beside them. 'Cranberry and chocolate chip. You have to eat.'

'Thanks, Jan. Have you seen Mick this morning?'

She shook her head. 'You know Kirsty wants a divorce?'

'Yes.'

'Maybe it's to do with that.'

Ford nodded, wondering if it was Kirsty keeping Mick from his duties, or JJ Bolter. He bit into the flapjack. Delicious. Chewy and sweet with a sharp tang from the cranberries.

The videos were a bit samey, and after a while he tired of Owen's arm-waving histrionics about Gaia and the planet. The man's passion shone through, but Ford wished he'd taken a chill pill occasionally.

He turned to the written posts and began reading. Most of them had either no comments or just a few breathless compliments from followers.

You are a modern-day prophet, Owen! I could watch you all day (and I actually have!!) Gaia is blessed to have you as her saviour. Your love is so inspiring and powerful. Namaste!

EcoGirl999

Keep speaking truth to power. The church's loss is the planet's gain. I stand with you.

RosieTheRioter

I literally CRIED after reading this. Why is nobody LISTENING to us? The CLIMATE APOCALYPSE is here and the FAT CATS and LANDOWNERS just laugh in our faces. This is OUR WORLD and they have set it on FIRE!!!

ExtinctlyRebelliousPete

After forty minutes of more of the same, he sat back. The flapjacks had set off a sharp pain in one of his back teeth and he probed it with his tongue, thinking he needed to visit the dentist and wondering when he'd find the time.

As for the vlog, Owen might have put a great deal of effort into making his films, but he was preaching to the choir.

Ford didn't see the fans as the type to commit murder. But the people against whom Owen railed in his videos – now they were a different story.

He decided to watch one more video. He clicked the 'Next' button for a new page of titles and scrolled down. One caught his eye.

Avarice at Alverchalke

He pressed 'Play' and leaned forward to watch. In this video Owen sat at his desk, a bookshelf in the background. The intimate surroundings and his closeness to the camera made Ford feel a personal connection to the dead man.

For much of the first five minutes, Owen ranted against landed families in general, and what he called 'their unfeeling rapacity, egotistical contempt for the environment and hubristic disregard for natural justice and the fundamental well-being of all living things'.

Bloody hell! Were they sure cause of death wasn't swallowing a dictionary?

Then Owen said something that jerked Ford into full alertness.

'That is why I intend to make a special video on Lord Baverstock's own land. I have done my research. He plans to build one hundred and thirty new houses on pristine countryside. His motive? Pure and unalloyed greed. And he employs an armed gamekeeper to protect him. But please don't worry for my safety. Gaia will keep me safe, as she always does.' He placed his hands together in front of his forehead. 'Namaste.'

Ford hit 'Pause'. Bingo! This was the video they needed: the one that would prove he'd been trespassing on Lord Baverstock's land when he was killed. But Owen had been murdered before he could upload it, and they didn't have his camera.

A question occurred to him. He called Ruth Long.

'Do you know what sort of camera Owen used to make his videos?' he asked her.

'He used to use his phone, but I bought him a GoPro last Christmas.'

Ford went online. A few minutes later he had his answer. The latest models had a feature that allowed users to upload their footage automatically to the Cloud. Had Owen's caution extended to keeping a Cloud backup of his raw footage?

He checked his emails. Just one, from Hannah.

The meta-data from the photo Gwyneth Pearce gave you tells us Tommy took it at 11.12 a.m. on Thursday 29th April.

I intend to try enhancing the image. Tommy had an eight-megapixel camera in his phone and there was plenty of light.

He took a mouthful of coffee and grimaced. Cold. He finished it anyway and dabbed up the last remaining crumbs of the flapjacks. Questions were arriving faster than he could process them. Had the killer moved the body to deflect suspicion away from Lord Baverstock and on to Adlam?

That's what it looked like. And that meant the two murders were definitely linked to the Baverstock family. And Owen had mentioned 'an armed gamekeeper' – Joe Hibberd.

After the last CCTV picture, Owen's car had vanished. Had the killer shot him, realised that this far from the city he must have come in a car, found it, and driven it away? It must be parked somewhere well hidden. Ford wanted it badly: it would have the killer's DNA all over it. He made a note to get Jan searching farms and outbuildings. *What if he burned it out?* He added lay-bys and known dump sites for joyriders.

Mick popped his head round the door, breaking his concentration. 'Morning.'

'Morning,' Ford said. 'What time did you leave last night?'

'Late,' Mick said, then took a huge slurp of coffee. 'Nice shiner you've got there.'

Ford sighed. 'Mick, I can't have you waltzing in late when the rest are burning the candle at both ends.'

Mick shook his head, then winced. 'It's not what it looks like. I had a few drinks with Rye and JJ, sure, then a few more with some of the others. And,' he said, then paused dramatically, 'I found something out, didn't I?'

'What?'

'I got talking to one of Tommy's mates last night after you left. Tommy boasted to him about some money-making scheme that was going to make his hare-coursing exploits look like a Saturday job. Said it was going to make him rich.'

'I heard the same story from his girlfriend. Did he have any idea at all what Tommy meant?'

Mick put the tip of his index finger on his chin. 'I never thought to ask him,' he said in a goofy voice. 'Of *course* I bloody asked him! I may not be a DI like you, but I can, just about, do the job. Despite what Olly thinks.'

'And?'

'He wouldn't say. I got the feeling he was angling for some cash, or a favour.'

Wondering how much Mick had had to drink before he questioned his informant, Ford pushed on. 'Did you get a name?'

'Connor Dowdell.'

'Let's have a chat with him, then.'

Mick threw back the last of his coffee. He pressed his free hand to his temple. 'You haven't got any paracetamol, have you? Or a Nurofen Express?'

Shaking his head, Ford reached into a drawer, rummaged among the busted staplers and rubber bands and found a squashed packet of painkillers. He tossed it over to Mick.

'Thanks,' Mick said, pressing three tablets out of their blisters and swallowing them with a grimace. 'This one's a bastard.'

'How are things at home?' Ford asked before he could escape.

Mick rubbed a hand over his scalp. 'Kirsty's trying to clean me out. She wants the house outright, plus a car and child support for the girls. Which I don't begrudge, by the way,' he said. 'But she's got a job, Henry! At the council. It pays better than mine, for God's sake.'

'That's why you've got a lawyer,' Ford said. 'Listen, I meant what I said the other day. If you need time off, you can have it. But if you're here, I need you to bring your A game. You did well, finding this Dowdell guy. But spending half the night in The White Lion boozing with the Bolter clan and their hangers-on?' He shrugged. 'It's not a great look.'

'What's that supposed to mean?' An edge crept into Mick's voice. It sounded aggressive, but with Mick, as with so many people, it often masked its opposite.

'Sit down.'

Mick dragged out a chair and slumped into it, massaging his temples. 'What, you going to give me the headmaster's talk about the demon drink?'

'I think somebody on the team's giving JJ information about the investigation.'

Mick reared back, bloodshot eyes wide. 'And you think it's me? Just because I was at that dump of a school with him? Christ, H, what the fuck?'

'Is it?'

'No! No, it isn't. Why would you think that?'

167

Ford leaned forward, putting both elbows on the desk. Had he gone too far? He didn't want to alienate his most experienced DS over an unfounded suspicion. But was it unfounded? Really?

One more try.

'Look, Kirsty's after you for money and she's using the girls to get to you. I understand you're desperate to hold on to them.' He paused and inhaled. 'So desperate you might need additional funds for your lawyer—'

Mick jumped to his feet. His eyes were blazing. 'And you think I'm taking brown envelopes from JJ Bolter? Is that it? You think I'm bent?'

The last thing Ford wanted was a shouting match in earshot of the rest of the team. He stayed sitting. Trying to keep the stakes low enough to manage.

'I didn't say that.'

'No, but you implied it.'

'Sit down, Mick. Please. I'm sorry, OK? I shouldn't have said it.'

Mick folded himself into the chair again, but he looked ready to leave at any moment, back straight, hands gripping the armrests.

'I do need money,' he said, his voice an urgent murmur. 'But I've borrowed it from my dad, OK? So what if I'm closer than most to JJ? That's my superpower. I know all the local villains and they know me. Doesn't mean I'm in their pocket.'

Ford spread his hands wide. 'I had to ask.'

Mick huffed out a breath. 'Why don't you look at the one man we know loves to poke his nose into our investigations? Martin bloody Peterson. He's much more likely to be taking money from a lowlife like JJ Bolter than one of our own.'

'I will. And thanks. I'll let you go.'

With his office to himself once more, Ford stared at the ceiling. Mick's act was impressive. Nobody did wounded outrage better.

But the attempt to deflect suspicion on to Peterson at this stage of the investigation was weak. Ford had dismissed the possibility early on. Peterson only bothered with people he regarded as his superiors. People with influence in what he no doubt thought of as the 'right circles'. He'd no more take cash from JJ than he'd keep an opinion about policing strategy to himself.

Ford's phone rang.

'Hi, George, what have you got for me?'

'I wanted to narrow down the time of death, so I sent some of the pupae and maggots from Tommy Bolter's body parts to a colleague at University College London. He's the best forensic entomologist in the country.'

'A bug man, eh?' Ford said, enjoying the chance for a minor piece of banter.

'Yes, Henry. A bug man,' she said patiently. 'But not just any bug man. Duncan is in great demand. If it's not the Met, it's as likely to be the NCA or the security services.'

'And what did he deduce, your King of the Chrysalises, your Pope of the Pupae, your—'

'You, DI Ford, are incorrigible!' she said, though he could hear the humour behind the mock outrage. 'However, I shall forgive you. This time. By analysing the species, number, instar stage and condition of the pupae and maggots, Duncan could estimate time of death for Tommy Bolter. Ready?'

Ford grabbed a pen. 'Ready.'

'First, two assumptions. One, the killer didn't freeze the body. My analysis of tissue samples supports that conclusion. Two, the insects found the body within an hour of death. Which, given assumption one, is well within the bounds of known behaviours of Calliphoridae.' A beat. 'That's blowflies to you.'

'Thanks,' he said drily. 'The time of death, George?'

'I'm getting to that. All things being equal, not that one would ever use such a *sloppy* phrase in one's report, you're looking at sometime between noon on the thirtieth of April and midnight on May the second.'

'George, you're a star! I'd like to show my appreciation by buying you a drink at your earliest convenience.'

'Now *that* is what I call a proper thank you. I'll email you.'

When George hung up, Ford grabbed a piece of paper and started noting down dates, times and locations. He stared at what he'd written. According to Gwyneth, Tommy had witnessed Owen's murder on the Alverchalke estate. And within three days, he too was dead – on the same estate. That level of coincidence was more than Ford could entertain.

His phone rang, and his suspicions increased still further.

'I've got a Graham Cox on the line, sir,' the receptionist said when he answered. 'Says he's got information about the Alverchalke murders.'

The line clicked. Ford breathed out. 'Yes, Mr Cox?'

'Are you the one who's in charge? Ford? I saw your name in the *Journal*.'

'Yes, that's me. How can I help you?'

'I'm the deputy estate manager up at Alverchalke. It said in the paper you found some poor sod dumped down a badger sett.'

'That's right.'

'Yeah, well, I didn't call before because I didn't think it mattered. But the wife said I ought to,' he said, with a note of complaint. 'Sunday before last, Lord Baverstock told me to fill in this sett. Damn big one, it was. He said he was worried someone'd fall in and break their leg or whatever.'

'Can you remember the location of this sett?' Ford asked, feeling a rush of adrenaline.

'It's on Mark Ball's place. Just south of the Ebble, about half-way between Homington and Nunton.'

'It didn't look filled in when I went down it, Mr Cox.'

'No, well, it wouldn't, would it? I didn't bother.'

'Can I ask why not?'

'No point, is there? Bloody-minded little buggers would've just dug it all back out again, wouldn't they? I wasn't about to waste a morning on it.'

'But you didn't tell Lord Baverstock.'

'No, I didn't. He's a good boss, don't get me wrong. But he doesn't always know as much as he thinks he does about the countryside.'

Ford thanked Cox and ended the call. He added the information to the murder book. Just like the Ebble, the clues in this case were flowing through Alverchalke land.

CHAPTER TWENTY-THREE

Ford received a summons from Sandy. She used her Python tone of voice, so he went in vowing to tread carefully.

'Tell me about the case,' she said. Then added, 'Or is it *cases*?'

'Case,' he said. 'The murders are connected, I'm sure of it. There's a good chance Tommy actually witnessed Owen being killed. And both men were shot by rifles in calibres we can place in the possession of Lord Baverstock, who, by the way, is aka Philip Martival, and something of a crack shot himself.'

'You're not telling me you suspect him of two murders? On his own land? Henry, have you truly lost it? Do you *want* to push Martin "Cheers Now" Peterson's on button?'

'I just heard from a witness who claims Lord Baverstock told him to fill in a badger sett on Mark Ball's land. Which looks decidedly odd, don't you think? But to keep you sweet, let's just call him a person of interest.'

'Good. Because unless you can bring me compelling *evidence* of his involvement, I would prefer you to keep your distance. What other leads are you working?'

'Let's assume, for the moment, it's not Lord Baverstock we want. I still believe the motive is tied up with the land where the murders happened. I spoke to a young woman who was with Tommy just after he witnessed Owen's murder.' He consulted his notebook. 'Tommy told her another "person" appeared while he was scoping out land for hare-coursing. They started arguing, there was some kind of struggle, a gun went off and Owen dropped dead.'

'Leaving aside the technicality that what you've got is hearsay, what did she mean by "person"?'

'Tommy was cagey. But whoever it was, they were armed, on Alverchalke land and clearly proprietorial. I'm looking at the game-keeper, Joe Hibberd. He's ex-army and had an axe to grind with Tommy.'

Sandy made notes in a small red leather-covered notebook with a gold propelling pencil. She looked up at him. She'd lost the fear-some glare in those pale blue eyes. He felt a small measure of relief.

'Good. Well, focus your energy on Hibberd for now,' she said. 'Unless or until you have something concrete on Lord Baverstock, I want you to leave him alone. That's an order.'

'Yes, ma'am.'

Sandy's eyes flashed at Ford's gentle teasing. He thought she could handle it.

'Have you spoken to Owen's wife?' she asked.

'Yes.'

'Could she have done it?'

He shook his head. 'CCTV from the Met puts her in London throughout the relevant time period for both murders.'

'I had to ask. But I don't see her as the type. She's a ballet teacher, right?'

'Yes. But even if she *could* handle a rifle, I can't see her slinging her dead husband's body in a river after stabbing it multiple times to prevent it floating. That feels like more of a man's MO.'

'What's your gut feel?'

Ford counted off points on his fingers. 'It's one – or less likely, two shooters. But if it's two, they're connected. We know Tommy witnessed Owen getting shot and was planning to blackmail the shooter. I think he made his threat and, instead of getting rich, he got killed. That motive is simple. The killer decided to put a stop to the blackmail once and for all.'

'Which you can understand. Tommy could easily have gone back for more. But what about Owen? Why was *he* killed?'

'Well, my working hypothesis, based on what Tommy's girlfriend told me and the unusual shot positioning, is that the shooting itself was an accident. OK, following a scuffle, but still not deliberate.'

'Why not report it, then?'

'Come on, Sandy. We all know that people don't always do what's sensible. Plus, this *person* was arguing, struggling really, with Owen. They might not have felt it was an accident in the heat of the moment. I think they panicked. One thing led to another and they ended up dumping an elderly ex-vicar in the river.'

Sandy screwed her face up. 'It holds water, no pun intended. Keep on it.'

As he left her office, he was thinking about what might link two killers on Alverchalke land. The answer had been staring him in the face all along. Family! Everyone who lived or worked on that land was linked to the Martival family. And the strongest links of all were between its members.

Mick caught his eye as he walked through Major Crimes. Connor Dowdell was waiting for them in the Greencroft.

They found him leaning against a climbing frame, smoking. The meeting was short and fruitless. Dowdell only confirmed what they already knew. For form's sake, Ford gave him a card and invited him to call if he remembered anything else.

◆ ◆ ◆

Hannah put on her noise-cancelling headphones and stared at the image the girl in the pub had shared with Ford. Tommy Bolter's selfie.

Above her head, the incandescent bulbs cast a soft yellow light over her workspace. Elsewhere, fluorescent tubes painted the room a horrible flickery blue-white that drove her crazy.

She'd spent the first part of the morning consumed with the tool marks on Tommy Bolter's bones. The photos Dr Eustace's photographer had taken in the post-mortem would come in useful when they had a suspect in custody, and knives or saws recovered in a search, but the image on her screen now could help them *find* that suspect.

Humming to herself a tune Ford had played for her once on his red electric guitar, she imported the image into Photoshop. It was actually rather beautiful.

'You had a good eye for composition, Tommy,' she said, hearing her own words as fluffy buzzes through the bones of her skull. She recited their names mentally, a calming mantra as she worked: *temporal, occipital, parietal, sphenoid, ethmoid, frontal.* But then other, less calming, thoughts intruded: memories of conversations in other departments, other forces, other countries.

. . . *multiple blunt force trauma to occipital bone . . . entry wound through right temporal bone, massive exit wound destroying left parietal bone . . . blade entered through left orbit, penetrating optic canal into frontal lobe . . .*

Anxiety swelled in her chest. Her breath came in short gasps. She squeezed her eyes shut. Hummed louder.

The memories receded. The horrific images faded. Her pulse slowly returned to normal.

She'd noticed the way Henry looked at her whenever they were talking about America and the memories came back. He'd ask if something was the matter. She'd shut down, tell him she didn't want to share that. And he would back off. So far, it had worked. She hoped he wouldn't keep probing.

She opened her eyes again and returned to the photo. Her right index finger trembled on the shiny surface of the mouse. She shook her hand out and tried again. Better.

The cursor skated around the control interface of the image-editing software. She felt her breathing slow and deepen. Permitted herself a small smile. She had friends who scoffed at TV crime shows where, with a few mouse clicks, CSIs turned blurry pictures into magazine-quality artwork. But they were starting with a poor-quality image. Tommy's had been excellent. She just had to fine-tune the information already present in the pixels.

She saved the image as a new file: *Bolter_image_1_hi-res_HF_edit-1*, then maximised the window until it took up the entire screen.

First, as she'd been trained, she looked at the image as a layperson would, making notes as she went. She saw rough grass in front of her. A sharp-edged shadow spread its fingers across the ground.

On the left, she could see a deep-green hedge speckled with white blossom. 'Hawthorn,' she said. Then, 'Ne'er cast a clout till May be out. Because May is a month and also a common name for hawthorn, whose scientific name is *Crataegus.*'

To the right, a hedge and a tree with spreading branches. From its shape, she identified it as an oak – *Quercus robur.* The land sloped away towards the city in the distance. The cathedral spire glistened on the horizon. Above its needle-tip, clouds that looked like those painted by young children – limbless sheep – dotted the sky.

She placed a grid of fine yellow rules over the image and took a second look, this time working methodically from left to right and top to bottom. 'Because you can walk the grid on a photo as well as on the ground,' she said.

In the middle of the meadow, she saw two small brown shapes. Now she *did* start to enlarge the photo.

'Control-Plus,' she murmured, 'Control-Plus, Control-Plus.'

With each tap, the image jumped in size. She kept going until the shapes resolved into a pair of hares, up on their long hind legs, forepaws raised in pugilistic poses. '*Lepus europaeus*,' she said with a smile.

She returned the image to its normal size and kept scanning. Just above the hawthorn hedge she found a hovering kestrel – '*Falco tinnunculus*!' – its wingtips blurred.

And then, in the second to last of the gridded squares, at the bottom-right corner of the image, she saw a figure. Heart racing, she clicked the mouse in a series of stuttering movements, enlarging the figure so that it grew in jerky increments, from a few millimetres until it – he – occupied a quarter of the screen.

'Who are you, then?' she asked the blurry figure.

Because at this level of magnification, and despite her Photoshop skills, the face had dissolved into a simple trio of dark splotches. A greyish scrim covered the lower half of his face.

Frowning, she opened the post-mortem report on Owen Long. The attached photo showed he wore a neatly trimmed beard. A neatly trimmed *grey* beard.

The man in the photo wore blue trousers that might have been jeans, and a maroon short-sleeved shirt. A mark on his left arm caught her eye. Even though she knew it would reduce the clarity still further, she zoomed in on the area of skin between the wrist and the inside of his elbow.

She could make out a general shape and colour. An organic form wider at the base than the top, in shades of green. She clicked away, back to the PM report, and paged through to the section she wanted.

Her breath caught in her throat as she looked at the distinguishing marks.

Tattoos: Naked green female sitting cross-legged, cradling planet earth in front of breasts.

'Hello, Owen Long,' she whispered.

A shadow crossed her desk. She looked up from her pad to see Ford waving.

She took off her headphones. 'Look.' She pointed at the figure on her screen.

Ford screwed up his eyes. 'Is that Owen Long?'

She nodded, pleased he'd reached the same conclusion she had. 'I think it is.'

'Can I?' Ford asked, coming to stand beside her and staring at the screen.

She moved her chair back to let him squat in front of her workstation. 'Press "Control" and "Plus" and zoom in on his left arm,' she said. 'I think it's his Gaia tattoo.'

Ford did as she instructed. 'I think you're right. He's got a beard, too. Where did Tommy take this? Any idea?'

'That's my next task. We know *when* he took it. The time and the date. And if you look at the cathedral, you can just tell it's the west front. The shadow extends straight out down the midline of the photograph. If we extend it, it will eventually reach the spire.'

'Go on, I'm still just about keeping up.'

She smiled. She liked the way he listened closely, not butting in with his own ideas or mocking her abilities. 'I calculated the height and position of the sun in the sky for the time and date of the photo. We can draw a straight line extending out from the cathedral at a 225-degree angle and be reasonably sure that Tommy was somewhere on that line when he took the photo.'

Ford rubbed his jaw, pleased with where this was going. They were zeroing in on the exact spot where Tommy had witnessed Owen being shot. With a bit of luck, they might find evidence that would identify Gwyneth's mysterious 'person'.

'Gwyneth told me they parked at the start of a lane opposite Pentridge Down,' Ford said. He straightened, patting his pocket for his car keys. 'Let's go and find the scene of the crime.'

'What, now?'

'Yes, now. This is a two-person job and you're available, which the others aren't.'

She felt a squirm of nerves in her stomach. And she labelled it as excitement. *Not anxiety, Wix. Excitement.* Before she left, she called Ruth Long's FLO and asked her to confirm whether Owen owned a maroon short-sleeved shirt. She timed the wait using the stopwatch function on her Casio. Two minutes, eleven seconds.

'Yes.'

CHAPTER TWENTY-FOUR

Ford drove out of Salisbury, heading for the Chalke Valley. Beside him, a map open on her knees, Hannah traced her finger along a straight red line she'd drawn just before they left.

The Discovery entered a long tunnel of trees, through which sunlight speared down in flickering bands of bright and dark.

'Sorry, Henry,' Hannah said, 'I have to close my eyes until we're through these trees.'

'Not good for your Asperger's?'

'Not good at all. It feels like a swarm of bees in my head.'

He put his foot down and cleared the final arch of overhead branches, doing eighty.

'You can open them again,' he said.

She sighed. 'Sorry about that.'

'Don't worry about it. It's fine. I think Owen's GoPro may have had an automatic upload to the Cloud. If we could find his account, could you try getting in?'

'I can try. But I've seen his password. A man who takes that much trouble over it won't have used anything simple to guess. We might be better off approaching GoPro themselves for help.'

'I'll put Olly on it.' Ford pointed ahead. 'Here we go.'

A road sign pointed left to Pentridge Down and right to Woodyates. Ford indicated right and turned into the side road. It led past some chocolate-box thatched cottages with roses growing round their ancient timbered porticos, and began climbing and narrowing at the same time.

'How are we doing on the red line?' Ford asked.

'We were veering south of it but we're going to cross it in about half a mile.'

Slowing down as the hedges on each side of the narrow lane reduced visibility to fifty yards or less, Ford came round a bend to find a rudimentary crossroads. To the left, a track led into a wheat field. To the right, a metalled road would take them back to Salisbury. Straight ahead, past a white house with a grey slate roof, the lane carried on northwards.

Hannah looked up from her map. She pointed straight ahead through the windscreen.

'Up there,' she said.

Ford motored on, and after a few more minutes they emerged on to a grassy plain offering an uninterrupted view all the way to Salisbury, and the spire.

In the absence of a lay-by, he simply pulled off the road and parked on a wide grass verge, the Discovery canted at an angle so he had to climb out over the sill. Hannah had to grab the door pillar to avoid falling out.

'Which way?' he asked.

Hannah consulted the map, then, shielding her eyes with the folded sheet, pointed off to the right. 'Thataway!'

Ford saw a gate, secured with a heavy chain and a padlock. The sign screwed to the bars bore an unequivocal message:

ALVERCHALKE ESTATE – PRIVATE LAND
NO PUBLIC RIGHT OF WAY
TRESPASSERS WILL BE PROSECUTED

Ford climbed over the gate and waited for Hannah to join him. They set off across a stretch of grassland, pockmarked here and there with cones of crumbly soil.

'What are they?' Hannah asked.

'Molehills,' Ford said.

'Are you a nature expert, then?'

He smiled. 'I wouldn't say expert. But we used to take Sam on nature rambles. He used to love finding feathers, birds' eggs, owl pellets. Anything he could take home and display on a table in the garden.'

'Look over there,' she said. 'That dead tree.'

'What about it?'

'The branches remind me of the shadow in Tommy's photo.'

Ford looked again. He could see what Hannah meant. They spread out like grasping arms. At some point, lightning had struck the tree and killed it, splitting the massive trunk. It had burned the bark away, too, turning the once-magnificent tree into a bleached skeleton.

'Where are we in relation to the red line?'

'We're close. The scale's not large enough and the margin for error in my calculations means this is as precise as we're going to get. But if we can find the right spot and look back towards the cathedral, we'll know.'

'It'll look right?'

'A tree behind us, a hawthorn hedge to our left. A single oak tree in leaf. A hedge falling away on the right.'

'And the spire in the distance.'

By the time they reached the blasted tree, Ford's shirt was soaked with sweat. He took off his suit jacket and folded it over his arm. A breeze from the west brought a sweet, sappy smell. He flapped the front of his shirt in and out, enjoying the cool sensation.

Overhead, on a thermal rising off the hillside, a buzzard wheeled in circles, keening.

Standing side by side, they faced the tree and looked over their shoulders. The shadow stretched away from them on the grass. In the distance, the spire gleamed in the sun, the same golden hue as in Tommy's photo. Sheep and cows grazed in the neighbouring fields. For a moment, Ford allowed himself to enjoy the freedom of being out here, away from the forms and the admin and the paperwork.

Hannah pointed. 'Look, a hawthorn hedge.'

'Lone oak,' Ford said, nodding towards a broad-branched tree.

Ford looked towards the spire. Beside him, he could hear Hannah's breathing.

'This is it,' she said. 'I was right.'

'Were you in any doubt?' he asked, unused to her expressing anything other than total confidence in her ability to solve problems.

She shrugged. 'I had to make more assumptions than I would normally feel comfortable with, but I had no alternative.'

Ford turned to the tree. 'I wonder,' he said.

He peered inside the hollow trunk. Insects or fungi had eaten the wood and transformed what they hadn't digested into a thick layer of soft powder resembling ground cinnamon. He saw two footprints of regular diamonds, dots and chevrons. Half-buried in the sawdust, he noticed a couple of cigarette butts.

Ford saw how it had unfolded. Tommy taking the selfie to send to Gwyneth waiting in the truck. Unknowingly, capturing Owen striding up the hill in the distance. Then clambering into the hollow tree to hide while he scanned the landscape, imagining people betting on which lurcher would catch the unfortunate hare.

'Come and look,' Ford said. 'I think Tommy sat in here.'

Hannah joined him and peered in, then started taking photos with her phone. When she'd finished, she took a clear plastic evidence bag and a pair of tweezers out of her pocket and collected the butts.

'Why bother hiding?' she asked. 'We're in the middle of nowhere.'

'You saw the sign. This is private land, and he had hare-coursing in mind. Trespass is a civil tort. But coursing's a criminal offence. He wanted cover for his recce.' Ford frowned. 'Do we know where Lord Baverstock plans to build that housing development?'

Hannah nodded. She pointed back the way they'd come. 'You know that white house we passed?'

'Yes.'

'If you'd turned right at the crossroads and gone on for another mile, you'd have arrived in the centre of the plan.'

'I wonder why Owen didn't make his film there, then. Why come up here?'

'Better backdrop? Or he filmed it there and came on up here to get some footage of the unspoiled version. It doesn't matter, though, does it? The point is, the evidence puts Tommy and Owen within feet of each other at the exact same time.'

Ford nodded. He'd leaped beyond the evidence, where Hannah felt most comfortable, and into the realm of the imagination, where he knew she struggled. Because they could also put the shooter there, couldn't they? Tommy watched Owen get shot by someone he knew. He waited until the coast was clear and then he went back – ran, probably – to his truck and told Gwyneth about the golden 'effing' ticket.

Ford pictured a confrontation. Owen ranting against Lord Baverstock's 'unbridled rapacity' or some such high-flown phrase. Hibberd turning up, outraged at the trespass. Telling Owen to clear off. Owen refusing, probably asserting that he was following a higher calling, or obeying a greater authority. Hibberd unshouldering the .22 and threatening Owen, maybe at that point not intending to shoot.

He closed his eyes and the scene became real. After watching so many of Owen's videos, he could hear the man's accent and distinctive phrasing.

Owen is unfazed by the gun. He laughs at Hibberd. 'What are you going to do, shoot me?'

'I could. You're trespassing. Who's to say you didn't attack me?'

Owen spreads his arms wide. 'You're right. Nobody here but us chickens. But our sins find us out, you know. My life is as nothing compared to the great interconnected world that is Gaia.'

Then he surprises Hibberd by going for the gun. Probably planning some dramatic move like throwing it as far as he can, into the hedge. Or over it, with a bit of luck.

The two men tussle over the rifle.

Hibberd is by far the stronger of the two. He's an ex-soldier up against an ex-vicar. He yanks it back. The gun goes off with the muzzle jammed under Owen's chin. He falls dead at Hibberd's feet. Hibberd panics, but only for a second. He runs back and fetches his Land Rover. Drags the body into the load bay and hurtles away. Under cover of night he dumps the corpse into a deep part of the Ebble, not knowing the storm surge will ruin his plan.

Hannah's voice broke into the vision. Ford opened his eyes to see her looking at him, not with impatience, merely curiosity, as if studying a new species of rural wildlife.

'Should we get back to Bourne Hill now?' she asked. 'I have a lot of work to do. And I think we should put a rush on DNA profiles from those cigarette butts.'

'Agreed,' Ford said.

On the walk back to the car he reminded himself not to get fixated on Hibberd. Plenty of other people on the estate had access to firearms. Not least the aristocratic family with the silly boarding-school nicknames. Maybe it was time to pay them another visit. He could talk to Stephen. He'd probably been the least visible of the quartet.

Ford's first mentor on the force, a whip-thin DS with a mind as sharp as his features, had told him on his first day as a DC, 'People don't like the idea of it, but being a good copper is all about being nosey. Never be afraid to stick yours in where it isn't wanted.'

He dropped Hannah off at Bourne Hill, then turned the Discovery round again and drove out to Alverchalke.

CHAPTER TWENTY-FIVE

On arrival, Ford was told that Stephen was out shooting. The maid gave him directions and, ten minutes later, heart pounding from the climb through woodland, he emerged on to a wide grassy avenue flanked by towering oaks, elms and cedars.

He heard a shot. Loud in the silence of the countryside, it sounded more like the large-calibre rifles being fired at the gun club than the little pops a .22 would make. The shot came from his left. He walked towards it, then realised he was heading into a live-firing area where the shooter had no idea of his presence. Not wanting to be mistaken for a deer, or whatever Stephen was shooting, he put his hands to his mouth and called out.

'Hello? Stephen? It's DI Ford. Hold your fire!'

Is that what he was supposed to shout? Hold your fire? *Really?* It sounded ridiculous, as though he was in a war film. Nevertheless, he was relieved when he heard an answering call.

'This way, Ford.' Stephen dropped into a parodic London gangster accent. 'Don't worry, I've put me shooter up!' A laugh followed, braying, self-satisfied.

Ford found Stephen dressed head to toe in a very convincing woodland camouflage outfit, leaning against a tree trunk, a rifle resting in the crook of his elbow.

'Come to do a spot of hunting?' Stephen asked.

'You're a good shot?' Ford asked, pointing at the rifle.

Stephen shrugged. 'Not bad. And Dad's Parker-Hale is a beauty. But he and Loopy are the real sharpshooters. She can shoot the balls off a fly with it on a good day.'

'It's a .308, isn't it?'

Stephen nodded, smiling. 'You know your guns.'

'Did you ever come across Tommy Bolter out here?' Ford asked, mentally adding a tick to a checklist.

'Me? Why would I?'

'He used to trespass on your land. Poaching, creating mischief. Did you?'

Stephen looked away, shading his eyes as a shaft of sunlight broke through the canopy and hit him full in the face. 'No. I let Joe deal with the riff-raff. Shh! Look,' he whispered. 'Over there. A roe. Nice buck.'

Ford watched as Stephen Martival settled the fleshy part of his jaw against the rifle's polished stock and looked through the telescopic sight. He was smiling. Odd. Or was he just screwing his face up as he sighted on the deer?

'Let's see you eat our fruit trees after this,' Stephen muttered.

He squeezed the trigger. Ford flinched at the huge bang as the bullet left the muzzle. Pigeons clattered from a tree behind them, adding the rattle of wings to the echo of the gunshot.

'Did you hit it?' Ford asked.

Stephen smiled broadly, nodding. 'Amidships! Just like Dad taught us. Got to hit them cleanly in the heart or they wander off hurt and you have to spend all bloody afternoon tracking them down and finishing them off. Cruel to leave them to die in pain.'

He picked up a coil of rope at his feet and strode off, crashing through the bracken, and beckoned Ford over his shoulder without looking back.

Standing beside Stephen, Ford looked down into the dead deer's sightless right eye. It wore the same film he'd seen so many times before, in the eyes of dead people. The shine gone, along with the life that had so recently animated it.

Stephen drew a knife from a leather sheath on his belt and squatted. As he bent to his task, Ford heard rapid hoofbeats. He looked round to see Lucy galloping up on Woodstock.

She arrived and slid from the saddle in a single flowing movement. Holding Woodstock by the reins, she led the horse to a tree some thirty feet away and tethered it. The horse flared its nostrils and whinnied.

Stephen looked over, then turned to Ford. 'Horses don't like the smell. Makes them twitchy. Can't say I blame them,' he grunted, heaving out a pile of stinking intestines. 'Absolutely bloody rank.'

Lucy joined Ford and Stephen and nodded to Ford.

'Hello again, Inspector.' If she was surprised to see him, she gave no sign.

'Calmed down, have you?' Stephen asked her, grinning.

She kicked him – none too gently, Ford saw – in the thigh. 'I came to tell you I forgive you.'

'Thanks, Loops. The old man didn't mean anything by it.'

'Easy for you to say, when you're the one he took hunting the other day.'

'Whatevs.'

Turning back to the carcass, Stephen finished gutting the deer and roped the hind legs together, fashioning the free end of the rope into a short leash.

'I parked the Subaru over there,' he said to Lucy, pointing to a copse fifty yards away. 'Bring Woody over and we'll tie this on. Get him to do some proper work for a change.'

Lucy's eyebrows lifted. 'Woodstock is a thoroughbred, not some bloody dray horse.'

'Come on, sis, don't make me drag it all the way myself.'

She stuck her hands on her hips. '*You* shot it.'

'I know. And now I'm asking for a bit of help. Go on. For your big bro. Be a sport. Pretty please?'

She grinned. To Ford their banter looked genuine enough – born of long association, like that of any other pair of siblings. Did the Bolters chaff each other like this, he wondered? Not anymore.

'Oh, God, fine! Hold on while I get him. But bring it away from those,' she said, jerking her chin towards the gut-pile. 'There's no way he'll stand still long enough over here.'

'Thanks, you're a brick.'

Ford shook his head. These two young aristocrats seemed to have completely forgotten he was there. Which suited him. It gave him an opportunity to see how they behaved together. And around firearms.

Both seemed more than comfortable. And Stephen had used his hunting knife on the carcass with practised ease. Was it really such a big step up from a dead deer to a dead man? Ford found he could quite easily imagine Stephen shooting Tommy, butchering his corpse and then jollying Lucy along to help him 'chuck the bloody stuff down this 'ere 'ole'.

He watched Stephen drag the deer away from the discarded viscera, which were already attracting flies. With Lucy holding Woodstock by the bridle, and keeping the horse's head turned away, Stephen tied the other end of the rope around the saddle's pommel.

Lucy mounted Woodstock and, at a slow, steady walk, the stallion dragged the deer to Stephen's dented olive-green pickup. With the carcass in the load bay, he closed and latched the tailgate.

'Thanks, Loops. See you back at the house,' he said.

She nodded, wheeled Woodstock round and kicked the horse into a trot, then a canter. Ford watched her go, nodding to himself as she reached the wide grassy avenue and shot off at full tilt, clods of earth flying up from Woodstock's hooves.

With Lucy gone, Stephen seemed to lose interest in hunting. He shouldered the rifle and stuck his hands on his hips. 'Did you actually want something,' he asked, 'or do the police just enjoy watching other people having fun?'

Ford ignored the provocation. He hit Stephen with the simple, direct question that had unhorsed men a lot more arrogant than him. 'Where were you between nine a.m. on Thursday April the twenty-ninth and the same time the following day?'

Stephen pulled his head back. 'You're not asking me for a bloody alibi, are you?'

'Can you remember?'

Stephen stared up at the tree canopy. 'God, I mean, I suppose so. Let me think. It's not as if I keep a bloody journal like a teenage girl. *Dear Diary, today I murdered a bloke and dumped his body.*' Grinning, he looked back at Ford. Who didn't smile. Some of the cockiness left Stephen's eyes. 'Yes! I do remember. I spent Thursday with a couple of mates, and in the evening I had dinner with Coco.'

'I'll need names and contact numbers for your friends. Where did you have dinner?'

'The Beckford Arms in Tisbury. They'll have details of my reservation.'

'Thanks. As soon as you can, please. How about between midday on Friday the thirtieth and midnight on May the first?'

'OK, yah. Well, let me see, I had a bit of a hangover. I hit the brandy pretty hard when we got back from the Beckford. Got up late, about half eleven, had a spot of lunch, then I went up to town. I had a business meeting and stayed over.'

That was interesting. Somehow, Ford hadn't pictured Stephen working. Or Lucy for that matter. He decided to switch tack for a little while, let Stephen relax before pushing him on his second alibi.

'What kind of work do you do?'

'I'm a valuer for Selman's – the auctioneers?'

Ford smiled encouragingly. He'd heard the firm mentioned on the news once or twice when a big sale came up. And they'd recently handled the sale of a famous rock musician's guitar collection. A Stratocaster not dissimilar to Ford's own had gone for over two million pounds.

'What's your speciality?'

'Chinese ceramics. Why do you ask?'

Ford shrugged. 'I'm just interested. You do vintage instruments from time to time.'

'That an interest of yours, then?'

'I have a sixty-two Stratocaster.'

'Very nice. Colour?'

'Fiesta red.'

'Well, if you ever decide to sell it, let me know. We could get you a very good price.'

Ford smiled. 'I'll bear that in mind. I'll also need contact details for your colleagues. And anything else you can think of that might help us determine your movements that day. Train tickets, credit card receipts, that sort of thing.'

'Yah, sure. I get it now. OK, it'll take a little while. Is it all right if I email it?'

Ford handed him a card. 'As I said, soon as you can, please.'

He accepted Stephen's offer of a lift back to the manor house but refused his offer of tea. He had work to do.

◆ ◆ ◆

Sam nodded along to the beat of the music playing through his wireless earbuds. Normally he walked home with Josh and they'd be chatting or showing each other videos on their phones. But Josh had got an after-school detention, so Sam was alone.

He walked down Exeter Street, trailing his fingers along the rough stonework of the wall to his right that surrounded the Cathedral Close.

One of his earbuds wasn't sitting right. He frowned with irritation and reached up to adjust it. It fell out just as his finger reached it, and dropped to the ground. He stooped to retrieve it and noticed a bloke stopped about ten metres back.

Something about the guy sent a shiver of tension through him. He was staring at Sam. He looked fucking evil. Sam glared back, put his earbud back in and started off again.

But he could sense the bloke behind him now. Didn't like the feeling. He glanced back over his shoulder. He was still there.

The bloke was bulky. Fat, really. With slitty eyes in a weird, doughy sort of face. Really big forehead that made him look like a caveman. Sam turned away and walked on. He passed a couple of sixth-formers coming back from rugby in their kit, laughing loudly and shoulder-barging each other.

He wanted to say something about the bloke but couldn't think what. Then they were gone, and it was too late. He took a right, heading towards Harnham and the woods he cut through on the way home.

On the corner, he flicked another glance behind him. The bloke was right there.

Sam wasn't massive, like some of the sports guys. He didn't get into fights. *Much*, he corrected himself. Only when absolutely necessary. But he wasn't a coward, either.

The bloke was smirking like he knew some dirty secret he couldn't wait to share.

Sam stopped dead. Turned. Pulled his earbuds out and stuffed them deep into a pocket. He waited until the guy was only about a metre away.

'What's your problem? Are you following me or something?' Sam asked. His heart was pounding, but he was determined not to show any fear.

'Your dad's a cop, isn't he?' the guy said, leaning close. Really getting into Sam's face. His breath stank like a dead dog.

'Yeah. And?'

The bloke pointed a stubby finger. 'Tell him he better get a fucking move on, finding my brother's killer. Or you're going to suffer.'

Sam squared his shoulders. No way was he taking shit from anyone over his dad's work. Especially not some Neanderthal. 'Tell him yourself. Who are you, anyway – one of the famous Bolter brothers, I suppose?'

The man's pale, sparse eyebrows lifted. 'Yeah, I am, actually. Tell him Rye Bolter knows which way you go home from school. I'll be watching you, Sammy.'

Then he turned round and shambled off.

Sam's mouth was dry and his pulse was really bumping in his throat. But he dragged out his phone quickly and shot a video of the bloke as he disappeared round the bend in the road.

CHAPTER TWENTY-SIX

Hannah signed Owen's PC out from the exhibits room. She carted it up to Forensics and assembled the tower unit, monitor, keyboard, mouse and speakers on a spare desk. She pressed the power button and went to make herself a cup of tea. When she arrived back at her desk, the screen was asking for the password. She entered the characters using one finger.

Gaia_Needs_Owen!

She read what she'd typed. 'Gaia needs Owen. Well, that's not even slightly egotistical.'

The screen popped into life: a neat grid of all Owen's programs and apps. Hannah double-clicked on the set called 'VLOG'. Here were Owen's tools for his one-man video campaign: shortcuts to the blogging platform, Google docs, a video editing package and a sound recorder. But not the program she'd been hoping to see: the management software for Owen's GoPro.

She began delving into the hard drive's file structures, reasoning that Owen might have hidden it among the PC's management folders. It had to be here somewhere.

She eventually found the program buried three layers down, in a folder innocuously labelled 'Microsoft Application Library', itself hidden in part of the PC's operating system.

'You *were* a cautious man, Mr Long,' she said.

She double-clicked the icon. A second dialog box popped up, requesting a password. Her finger hovered over the keyboard.

Most people of Owen's generation, having managed to find a password one company would accept as 'Strong', often stuck with it for everything, from banking to shopping. Not sensible. But understandable. Had Owen followed the herd? It was worth a try.

She typed it again.

Gaia_Needs_Owen!

The computer responded instantly.

Some of your security details are incorrect.

She hit the 'Reset Password' button. It asked her to enter her email address. She checked Owen's email program and entered the address from his profile.

We do not recognise that email address.

That was interesting. Owen must have been using a Cloud-based email account for his GoPro. Ten minutes later, having failed to find anything that worked, she reached a conclusion. Owen had been so security-conscious, he'd used one of the many cloaked email services that provided users with anonymous email accounts.

She smiled to herself. A challenge. Hannah enjoyed challenges. Abandoning the reset idea, she went back to the password dialog box.

She put a finger to the point of her chin and stared at the winking cursor. It seemed to be daring her to enter enough incorrect passwords that it could shut her out. Surely Owen hadn't created different but equally obscure passwords for all his accounts? She herself had memorised over thirty separate passwords. All strong. But she knew she was different.

She tried a new strategy. He might have kept the main password as the root and added on account-specific codes for all his apps.

Gaia_Needs_Owen!_gopro

Some of your security details are incorrect.

Gaia_Needs_Owen!_GoPro

Some of your security details are incorrect. You have two more attempts.

Gaia_Needs_Owen!_G0Pr0

Some of your security details are incorrect. You have one more attempt.

Gaia_Needs_Owen!_GoPrO

You may not attempt any more passwords for 24 hours.

Hannah inhaled deeply, then exhaled, shutting her eyes. How frustrating. She hated the thought of having to tell Henry she'd failed.

◆ ◆ ◆

After work, Ford had driven the long way home to clear his head. He cooked lamb chops and roasted baby potatoes in olive oil with sea salt and rosemary for him and Sam.

Sam polished his off and looked straight at Ford. 'Hey, guess what?'

'What?'

'I was on my way home from school, right? And this bloke was, like, following me. All the way down Exeter Street and then up to the Old Bridge. So, I turned round, OK? And I was, like, who the fuck are you and why are you following me?'

Ford's stomach flipped over. He knew who it had to be. 'Sam, you shouldn't—'

Sam shook his head. 'No, wait. I haven't finished. He's like, tell your dad to hurry up and find who killed my brother. Then he said his name. But I already guessed most of it. Rye Bolter. But I totally owned him. And I got him on video in case you want to arrest him for, like, verbal assault or whatever.' Sam sat back, smiling.

'Show me.'

Sam fiddled with his phone for a few seconds then held it out to Ford. Even from the back, there was no mistaking Rye's distinctive build and gait. Ford felt anger boiling up inside him. He needed to stop this before it got any worse. But first he needed to make Sam understand a bit more about how the world worked.

'Right, number one, that was really stupid. You don't confront anyone who follows you in the street. Run if you have to, or shout for help. Go into a shop or something. But especially not Rye bloody Bolter. He's unstable and a total thug, Sam. What if he'd hit you? You'd be in hospital by now.'

'But he didn't, did he? I faced him down. I owned him! Don't worry, Dad. I'm fine.'

'Never mind that! And number two, I'm going to sort out some protection. *Discreet* protection,' Ford added as Sam's mouth opened to complain. 'Just for a day or two while I sort it out. He won't bother you again. I promise. OK?'

Sam smiled. 'OK, fine. But I think you're overreacting.'

Ford bit back his response. Because explaining why he wasn't overreacting would only frighten Sam.

Once they'd cleared away from dinner, they both headed for the small sitting room at the back of the house. Ford did his best to behave calmly, but inside he was planning an action that would stop Rye Bolter in his tracks. Or so he prayed.

He leaned back in his usual spot on the worn leather sofa and looked at Sam, who was poring over a magazine, his long legs folded beneath him.

'What yer readin'?' Ford asked.

Sam looked up, then held the magazine out towards him. The cover shot showed a woman in neon pink and green Lycra traversing a rock face.

'*Climber*,' Sam said. 'There's an article all about your first ascent.'

'Learning much?' Ford managed.

Sam nodded. 'I'm reading about knots at the moment.'

'That'll be handy for your trip,' Ford said, grateful Sam hadn't asked him to show him how to tie any.

'I want to be safe, Dad. I'm doing a ton of research before we go.'

'I'm pleased.'

'You know I'm going to be fine, right? You don't need to worry.'

'Yeah, I know. It's just . . .'

'I understand. I do. But I think this will be good for me. For both of us.'

Ford felt such a flood of love for his son it threatened to overwhelm him. Who was parenting whom? And when had the little boy who'd stood silently, shocked into tear-free immobility at his mother's funeral, turned into the young man reassuring him that all would be well and all manner of things would be well?

'I know it will, Sam,' he said, swallowing down his fears and trying not to picture his son suspended above the void on nothing more substantial than a length of nylon rope.

'Really?' Sam asked with a smile.

'Really.'

Sam turned back to his climbing magazine. Ford checked his watch. Just before eight. Plenty of time.

'I'm going out,' he said. 'Don't answer the door to anyone.'

Sam held up his right hand, thumb and forefinger in a circle.

◆ ◆ ◆

Ford drove back to Bourne Hill. The traffic was light and the trip only took ten minutes. Instead of heading upstairs, he made his way to the response and patrol shift sergeant's office. The woman in uniform behind the desk looked up and smiled.

'Evening, sir. Don't often see you in R&P. Everything OK?'

'Hi, Nat. Listen, Rye Bolter threatened Sam this afternoon on his way home from school.'

Her eyes popped wide. 'Oh my God, is he all right?'

'Yeah, he's fine. Too fine, actually. Giving it the whole "I showed no fear" bit. Listen, I need a favour. Can you put a body on him for a day or two? Nothing obvious. Just on his way to and from school?'

'Of course. Are you going to arrest Rye?'

Ford looked at her levelly. 'Something like that.'

She nodded. 'I'll sort out a little roster. Off the books.'

'Thanks, Nat. I owe you one.'

Next, Ford stopped off in the training suite. The sergeant in charge of the Method of Entry team had been running through the equipment with a couple of trainees. Ford collected two items, and five minutes later was stowing them in the back of the Discovery.

◆ ◆ ◆

It was 8.31 p.m. The sun had just set, and the Bolters' hacienda was glowing in the last remains of the orange light.

Ford stopped the Discovery just in front of the gates. He retrieved the first item he'd borrowed from the training room: a hydraulic spreader. He inserted its jaws between two of the bars and started pumping the lever.

As if they were made of soft plastic, the steel bars bowed outwards until they hit their neighbours. As soon as he had a wide enough gap, Ford put the tool back in the Discovery.

He returned to the gate and squeezed through, gripping the second item from the training suite, a stubby object made of bright yellow plastic that sent twin red dots playing over the front of the hacienda.

He approached the front door and rang the bell. Stepping back, he waited. Breathing slowly. Rolling his shoulders.

Rye opened the door, holding a baseball bat by his side.

Ford squeezed the taser's trigger. The two barbs shot out on their fine wires and embedded themselves in Rye's hoodie. As it delivered the charge, Rye went down like a stunned animal, convulsing.

'JJ Bolter,' Ford roared. 'Get out here now!'

Seconds later, JJ emerged into the wide hallway, face dark with fury. Ford saw with pleasure the way his expression changed as he clocked his brother, supine and unconscious on the floor.

'What the fuck is this, Ford?'

'Your brother followed and then threatened my son this afternoon,' Ford said in a voice that was level but still quivering with rage. 'If it happens again, or if I even *think* it's happened again, I will come back and I will kill you both. I will make your bodies disappear like dust in the wind. And when I've finished misdirecting the investigation, nobody will ever find you. Nobody will connect anything to me. And you and your pathetic little criminal empire will be history.'

JJ held his hands out towards Ford. 'Listen, I had no idea Rye was going to pull something like that, OK? I would've told him not to if he'd come to me first. You have to believe me.'

At that moment, Rye raised himself on his elbows. 'Fuck just happened?' he mumbled.

Ford squeezed the trigger again. He hadn't taken his eyes off JJ the whole time. He heard Rye's head hit the parquet flooring.

'You'll kill him!' JJ shouted.

'Not today. And not with this. It's like I said. You leave my son alone and everything's fine. You touch him or go near him, and yes, I will. Rye first. And then you.' Ford gestured at Rye with the taser. 'Take the barbs out of his clothing and hand them to me.'

JJ bent down by his brother and unhooked the little metal darts. He passed them to Ford, who backed up and out through the open front door.

'Sam got him on video,' he said from the porch. 'My story is, I came to arrest him and the two of you attacked me. I tasered Rye and staged a tactical retreat. Complain if you want. At worst, I'll get a rap on the knuckles. And you'll spend the rest of your life looking over your shoulder.'

JJ nodded, looking up at Ford. 'Don't worry. We don't make complaints. What about Tommy?'

'I'm close. Goodbye, JJ. By the way, I fucked up your gate. I'm sorry.'

CHAPTER TWENTY-SEVEN

Ford reached home at 9.10 p.m. Sam had disappeared.

Ford called out, 'Sam?'

'In my room!' came an answering yell.

Smiling, Ford went to the fridge and collected a bottle of beer. He took a long pull, and felt the alcohol ease the edges off the tension he'd felt since leaving to confront Rye and JJ.

Needing a change of scene, and a distraction, he headed upstairs to the room where he kept his guitar and amplifier.

Shit! He'd just crossed a line. A line wound round with crime scene tape and flashing blue lights. But JJ wouldn't make a complaint, would he? It wasn't his style. Ford had known that before JJ admitted it. This was a private matter between the two of them. Rye had acted without his older brother's say-so. And Ford had shown his teeth. Honours even.

Pushing the thought aside, Ford focused on his playing, concentrating on getting the phrasing just right. And gradually, he lost himself in the blues music he'd loved since childhood, his focus shifting from the crimes of today to the heartbreaks, losses and betrayals of the past.

Thoughts of Tommy's blackmail plot led him to an old Delta blues song: 'I Seen Just What You Done'. He'd heard it once on a scratchy seventy-eight on a visit to his grandparents' house. It had stayed with him ever since. On the brittle black disc of shellac, a male singer with a high-pitched, wailing voice had sung the same lines Ford sang now:

> 'Oh, baby, I seen just what you done.
> Yeah, baby, I seen just what you done.
> I'm a witness to your crime
> and I'm tellin' you it's time
> for you to run.'

As the last line left his lips and the notes rang on the strings of his guitar, he let his hand drop away.

Time to return to the problem, which he now saw more clearly.

Assume one shooter.

The charge for Owen's death would be either murder or manslaughter, depending on what evidence Ford and his team could produce. Even if it had been an accidental shooting, that would still make it involuntary manslaughter. The shooter had been at best grossly negligent and at worst dangerous or unlawful in getting the gun so close to Owen that an accidental discharge had killed him.

Fearing the consequences of going to the police, they'd panicked and dumped the body. Then Tommy turned up with his blackmail threat.

This time there was no heat-of-the-moment scuffle or panicked disposal of the corpse. Tommy had been murdered in cold blood, coolly dismembered and disposed of down a deep hole in the ground. The shift in attitude to killing didn't feel right.

So, assume two shooters.

Given the two deaths were linked, the two shooters also had to be linked. Shooter one killed Owen and, on being blackmailed, told shooter two. Shooter two took over and murdered and disposed of

Tommy. Given the differences in MO, this felt like the most likely scenario.

If it were true, it would resolve a secondary niggle Ford had been uncomfortable about. The sort of person who could accidentally kill someone close up with a rifle didn't feel like the sort of person who could kill someone with a sniper shot. One sounded like a leisure shooter out of their depth. The other, something altogether more professional.

Assassins being short on the ground in Wiltshire, he leaned towards the idea that shooter two was a soldier. Either serving. Or former.

Like Joe Hibberd.

Or Lord Baverstock.

The switch from .22 to .308 had to be about effective range. A .22 was a vermin gun. Useful at close range. On small targets. The irony was, if Owen had been shot at long range, he could well have survived.

Tommy's killer had used a .308 ballistic tip. A long-range round, as George had confirmed at Tommy's PM. A round you'd choose to take down a deer, or a man.

Ford did a quick internet search. British soldiers in Afghanistan had used sniper rifles chambered for the 7.62mm round, which was effectively the same as the .308. The maximum effective range was around the thousand-metre mark. He performed a rapid calculation and discovered to his horror it yielded a circle of 3.14 square kilometres.

No. Combing that much ground looking for a sniper nest would swallow up too many people on a search. And they'd probably never find it. Even if they did, the chances of it yielding anything useful in the way of forensics were slim.

Forget forensics for now. This was about pursuing the family he was increasingly sure lay behind both murders.

◆ ◆ ◆

First thing the next morning, Ford called Alverchalke Manor. He wanted Lord Baverstock to feel a little heat. And to confirm the possibility that one of his offspring could have shot and killed Owen Long.

Because that was where Ford had got to overnight. No way would an experienced former soldier allow himself to be bested in a tussle over a rifle and end up accidentally shooting his opponent. It would have been deliberate or not at all.

Lord Baverstock himself answered. 'Alverchalke.'

'Good morning, Lord Baverstock, it's Inspector Ford here. I hope you can help. I need to identify anybody who was out and about on the land you own opposite Pentridge Down nature reserve on the morning of Thursday, the twenty-ninth of April.'

'That's close by the rearing field. Joe would have been the only chap up there. It's strictly private. Can I ask what this is all about?'

'And when you say "Joe", you're talking about Joe Hibberd, your gamekeeper?'

'Yes. But I fail to see—'

'Nobody else? Stephen? Or Lucy?'

He could hear Lord Baverstock's breathing. Pictured the man struggling to remain calm. Either from suppressed anger at what he no doubt thought of as an unwarranted intrusion, or because he was guilty.

'Not as far as I'm aware. Why do you ask?'

'Do your children have access to your gun safe?'

'Of course they bloody do! Have done since they were in their teens. Again, why?'

'Is it possible either Lucy or Stephen was up near the rearing field shooting between nine a.m. on Thursday April the twenty-ninth and the same time the following day? With or without your knowledge?'

The silence stretched out to five seconds.

'Lord Baverstock?'

'It's possible. As it is that almost anybody else in my employ was out there. Was there anything else, Inspector?'

This was the first of Lord Baverstock's questions Ford answered. His lips curved as he spoke. 'Not at the moment. Thank you. You've been most helpful.'

Ford ended the call just as Jan placed a mug of tea and a home-made chocolate muffin on the desk in front of him.

'Eat that,' she said. 'You're wasting away.'

Ford bit into the muffin and smiled. A great detective *and* a superb baker.

Olly came into his office.

'Stephen Martival sent through all the stuff about his movements. It all checks out. I've got CCTV from The Beckford Arms, copies of the bill, statements from waiters. He was there with his mum till about eleven thirty.'

'What about his trip to London?'

'Got CCTV and statements from his colleagues. But it's not complete, is it, guv? He could still have done it. Just at night.'

Ford shook his head. 'No, it's not completely out of the question. The man acts like a bloody psychopath, but I just didn't get a killer vibe off him.'

Olly was still standing in front of the desk, shifting his weight from foot to foot.

'What is it?' Ford asked, impatient to be on to the next stage of his pursuit of Lord Baverstock.

'I spoke to the GoPro people, too, guv. Got the runaround. They bounced me from marketing to corporate communications, then HR, finance and finally, guess where?'

'Legal?'

Olly screwed up his face. 'In very helpful language they informed me they couldn't help. They have a strict data privacy policy and can't do anything without written authorisation from the account holder.'

'But he's dead!'

'I know. And I did explain. They said in that case they'd need written authorisation from the executors of his will.'

Ford sighed. *Lawyers*. 'Get on to Ruth Long. And be tactful, yes?'

'Of course,' Olly said, looking affronted.

Ford went down to Forensics. Hannah was at her desk, sitting in a pool of yellowish light cast by the incandescent bulbs she'd used to replace the neon tubes overhead.

'Any joy with cracking Owen's GoPro password?' he asked her.

'No. No joy at all. Not even a little moment of bliss. But I'll keep trying.'

Had it been anyone else, Ford would have asked if they'd tried permutations of the elements from the PC's main password. As it was Hannah, he didn't. He knew better. She'd have gone through everything, methodically, obsessively – until the small hours, probably.

CHAPTER TWENTY-EIGHT

Ford had photographic evidence that placed Tommy and Owen within feet of each other when Owen was killed. He had a pool of potential suspects, topped by Joe Hibberd, hot on whose boot-shod heels galloped Lucy, Philip and Stephen Martival.

He also had the nagging threat posed by JJ Bolter. The deadline had passed, and he was nowhere near making an arrest.

What would give Ford reasonable grounds to arrest Hibberd for Tommy's murder? Or Owen's, come to that? The photo was good, but still just strong circumstantial evidence. He'd no doubt the sort of barrister Lord Baverstock would line up to defend his gamekeeper would scoff at it.

What he really wanted was a bullet from the gun Joe Hibberd had been shooting when he went out to the rearing field to interview him. No wonder the man had reacted so violently when Ford had gone to retrieve the rabbit he'd just shot. He knew it would link him to the murder.

If only he'd insisted. Then he'd have a bullet Hannah could compare to the one George had dug out of Owen's skull. He could go back now, but he had a feeling Lord Baverstock would send him packing. Unless he had a warrant. Which he felt sure Sandy would block. For now.

He needed another approach. Something creative.

And then he gasped and laughed out loud. 'Idiot!'

He wanted a bullet from Joe Hibberd's gun. He'd had one all along. In his own freezer. 'Stodgy' Stephen had given him a rabbit as they were leaving Alverchalke Manor. What had he said? The self-assured young nobleman's words floated back to him. *Joe bagged them this morning with a .22.*

Ten minutes later he climbed out of the Discovery, ran round to the garage and let himself in at the side door. Gleaming in the blue-white light of the fluorescent tubes sat a silver E-Type Jaguar. IOPC investigators might see such a vehicle and wonder, 'Where does someone on an inspector's salary get the funds to buy a car worth the thick end of a hundred grand?'

On asking DI Ford, they would be respectfully directed to a photograph in said officer's wedding album. Father of the bride posing beside groom, both grinning into the camera with the E-type in the background. Successful bankers did that kind of thing for their newly married offspring. They'd named it – well, Lou had allowed Ford to name it – Izabella, the name Jimi Hendrix had given one of his guitars.

Ford skirted the car and yanked up the lid of the freezer. He pulled out the carrier bag containing the rabbit he'd dumped there eight days earlier.

In the kitchen, he put the rabbit on a chopping board. The fur was stiff to the touch, rimed with frost. He probed the left-hand side, finding the tiny bullet hole with the tip of his finger. Somewhere inside the insignificant, freezing carcass was a bullet that might be enough to arrest Joe Hibberd.

He considered taking it back to the garage and having a go at dissecting it with a jigsaw. Then he dismissed the idea. He could afford to wait for it to defrost. Should he do it himself, even then? Or would he damage the bullet with an ill-judged cut? He had a better idea, and called George.

◆ ◆ ◆

George had been amused at Ford's request that she perform an autopsy on a rabbit. Once he'd persuaded her it wasn't a joke, she'd agreed readily. 'A bit different to my normal work. It could be fun,' she'd said.

She was waiting for him in the dissection room, gowned and masked, her instruments resting on a wheeled tray.

'Thanks for doing this, George. It's going to break the case.'

'Let's hope so, eh?' She pointed at the bag swinging by his side. 'Is that the deceased?'

Ford laid the defrosted rabbit on the dissection table.

George peered at the bullet hole. She rolled the soft little body over.

'No exit wound. Right, let's see what we can find, shall we?'

She took a pair of long thin forceps from the tray and gently inserted them into the entry wound. Ford found he was holding his breath, and let it out in a controlled sigh.

After a few more seconds, George nodded. 'Got it,' she said.

In a slow, deliberate movement, she withdrew the forceps. Gripped in their serrated tips was a small, dark grey bullet. She dropped it into a stainless-steel kidney bowl with a tinny clink.

'Looks like a .22. I'll just clean that up for you,' she said.

Having run it under a tap for a few seconds, she handed Ford the bullet. He held it up to the light. The tip had deformed on impact, but not by much. The real result for him was the shaft, which was intact. He dropped it into an evidence bag, thanked George, who reminded him of his offer of a drink, and was on his way to Bourne Hill five minutes later.

Once there, he took the stairs up to the third floor and ran down the corridor to Forensics to see Hannah.

He gave her the bagged bullet. 'Can you photograph this for me and run it against the .22 from Owen Long? It's urgent.'

She smiled. 'Yes, of course. Where'd it come from?'

'The rabbit Stephen Martival gave me.'

Hannah nodded. 'Give me an hour.'

CHAPTER TWENTY-NINE

While he waited for Hannah to report back on the bullet from Joe Hibberd's .22, Ford went to see what Olly was up to.

The DC swivelled round in his chair. 'Guv, you should see this.'

'What is it?'

Olly pointed at the screen. 'Lord Baverstock's service record. He was a major in the Grenadier Guards. He served in Afghanistan and got the Military Cross for exemplary gallantry.'

'Brave man.'

'Yeah, but look, guv. The details are totally relevant to our case.'

Ford dragged over a chair and sat to read the narrative entry.

In an action against the Taliban, Major Philip Martival's sniper was killed and his spotter badly wounded by a dug-in enemy fighter using a heavy machine gun. With no concern for his own safety, only that of his men, Major Martival advanced single-handedly under heavy fire and killed the enemy machine gunner with the fallen sniper's rifle. He then carried the wounded spotter back to their own lines.

Ford read on. The spotter's name was Hibberd. Sergeant Joseph Hibberd.

'Nice work, Olly. Now, can you pull His Lordship's firearms certificate for me?'

'Yes, guv. Oh, and I spoke to Ruth Long. She's the executor of Owen's will. She's getting in touch with GoPro for us.'

Back at his own desk, Ford closed the door.

He'd been keeping a close eye on Sam, looking for changes in his mood or his routine, anything that might indicate Rye had tried anything again. But it looked as though his own threat had done the trick.

Would he carry it out? The answer came fast.

Yes. In a heartbeat. If they hurt Sam he'd press the nuclear button. It would put him forever on the wrong side of the law he'd pledged to uphold, but there were things he valued far more highly.

He needed to arrest someone, fast. He needed to prove to JJ he'd got there before him, so he'd call the dogs off.

Hannah burst into his office. Her eyes were shining and her cheeks were flushed.

'You're going to be pleased. Look.'

She crossed the office to the meeting table and gathered all the papers into a rough pile before placing them on the carpet. In their place she laid out a sheet of A3 paper, on which he saw the characteristic split-screen image of a ballistics comparison.

Ford already knew what he was going to see, but was excited to have it confirmed. Hannah's enthusiasm was contagious. She pointed to the left-hand half of the composite image. 'Exhibit A: a .22 bullet recovered from Owen Long's skull.' She pointed to the right. 'Exhibit B: a .22 bullet recovered from Mr Flopsy.'

He looked and found he didn't even have to squint. The striations on the bullets lined up perfectly.

'They're identical, Henry. You've got the murder weapon.'

Ford smiled. 'Not quite. But I know where to find it.'

He waited until Hannah had gone before opening a blank arrest template on his PC. Was he convinced it was Hibberd? No. He was not. Lucy and Stephen Martival, and their father, hovered on the periphery of his thoughts. But protecting Sam meant making a dramatic move now.

He had more than enough circumstantial evidence to arrest Joe. It would have to do. He had to keep JJ and Rye away from Sam. Nothing mattered more to him than that.

He now had definitive ballistics evidence that the bullet George had recovered from Owen Long's skull matched the one recovered from the body of a rabbit shot by the suspect.

And unless Joe had got rid of the .22 rifle, it had to be on the Alverchalke estate – either in the gun cabinet at Alverchalke Manor, at Joe Hibberd's cottage or in another building.

So, there it was. More than just circumstantial evidence. He had ballistics, too.

He rewrote his reasons for the arrest. The means hardly needed spelling out. Hibberd had handled the rifle forensically proven to be the weapon used to kill Owen Long. As the murders were inextricably linked, that also made him the prime suspect in Tommy's murder.

He'd shot Owen in an altercation over trespassing. How about the motive for Tommy? Joe had two, both powerful: revenge and sexual jealousy. The two men had history, and most recently they'd been involved in an altercation, in the course of which Tommy gave Joe a bloody nose. And both were romantically involved with Gwyneth Pearce.

He'd also had ample opportunity. Ford pictured Joe agreeing to meet Tommy somewhere remote on the Alverchalke estate. But instead of handing over the cash, he hid some distance away and shot him with Lord Baverstock's .308 Parker-Hale rifle. He then chopped up the body and – alone, or with help – disposed of the parts down a badger sett on land farmed by Mark Ball.

Those were the entries on the credit side. The debit side was daunting and Ford took extra care over the risk assessment. Hibberd was a former British army sniper. That meant he was intimately acquainted, and extremely deadly, with firearms of all kinds.

And the man was a combat veteran, for God's sake. Ford thought it entirely possible that Joe was suffering from PTSD. He'd personally witnessed his volatile temper, hadn't he? That added the possibility that things could go sideways during the arrest. In his report he used the more official-sounding phrase, 'significant risk of escalation in violence'. They both came down to the same thing. Bullets flying.

He concluded that with the suspect presenting a high risk of fight or flight, especially fight, his recommendation was for a firearms deployment.

He went to see Sandy.

'You look like a dog with two dicks,' she said.

'One and a half, maybe. I want to arrest Joe Hibberd for Owen's murder. I have ballistics that put the murder weapon in his hands.'

Sandy went into business mode. 'What do you need?'

'It has to be a firearms deployment, just in case things turn nasty.'

'Are you expecting them to?'

'No. But we'll do it by the book, which contains my risk assessment, by the way. I put my maverick hat down when there's the chance of bullets flying.'

Sandy offered him a wry smile, then jotted a few words in her red notebook. 'I'll put the call in to Gordon Richen at HQ after this, tell him to get his firearms team on standby. Anything else?'

'Yes. I want to talk to Lord Baverstock again. It looks like a member of his staff may have murdered one or possibly two men on his land. One of them was making a protest film about his development plans. If it had gone viral, or been picked up by the mainstream media, protests could have meant planning permission being withheld, which would have cost him a lot of money.'

'OK, go and talk to him. But Henry . . .'

'Yes?'

'Be nice. The gamekeeper looks good for it, but you've nothing on Lord B. I don't want you getting a reputation as some sort of officially sanctioned class warrior.'

'Yes, ma'am,' he said, tugging his forelock. 'Absolutely, Your Grace. Ever so 'umble I'll be, oh my goodness, yes. What wiv me bein' a lowly DI and 'im wot lives in that there big 'ouse being a lord an' ev'ryfing.'

She grinned. 'Get out of my sight, you horrible little wretch, and bring me results!'

Ford went to find Hannah, who was hunched over her keyboard.

'Can I drag you away from your desk for a while?' he asked. 'I'm going out to see Lord Baverstock and I'd like you to do your FBI voodoo.' Seeing the beginnings of a frown, he anticipated her question. 'By which I mean, just size him up. I think he may have been involved in one or both of the murders.'

'How exactly?'

Ford hesitated. How could he tell Hannah he needed to arrest Hibberd fast to fend off JJ and Rye Bolter, even though he had his doubts about the man's guilt? He told himself it didn't matter. If Hibberd was innocent, Ford would find evidence pointing to the true killer. If he wasn't, the problem disappeared.

'I'm not sure. Call it a feeling,' he said. 'I've got a little surprise up my sleeve that might unsettle him. If it works, and he loses his temper, stay calm and just listen more carefully, OK?'

She nodded. 'Stay calm. Listen carefully. Sacrifice a black cockerel and sprinkle its blood over a photograph of Lord B.'

Ford grinned. 'Was that a joke, Wix?'

She smiled broadly. 'It was. Was it any good?'

'Not bad.'

On the drive over, they discussed other possibilities that would explain the ballistics while letting Hibberd off the hook.

'What if, for some reason, Hibberd didn't use his own rifle to shoot the rabbit?' Hannah asked.

'Then it must have been an Alverchalke gun.'

'Which means anyone with access could be the murderer.'

'Let's hope it's a small list, then,' Ford said.

He pointed to the sign ahead. It bore the simple phrase:

Alverchalke Manor ½ mile

CHAPTER THIRTY

At the manor house, a maid directed them to the rose garden, where Lord Baverstock was tending to his blooms. The garden was a five-minute walk from the main building, behind a wall of old red bricks punctuated halfway along by a wrought-iron gate. Ford pushed the gate open and walked into a sun-drenched square of colour: reds, pinks, oranges, deep plums and creamy whites.

Some ancestor of Lord Baverstock had laid out formal beds in a geometric pattern, divided by raked gravel paths. Pervading the whole garden was the heady scent of ripe peaches and a zingy smell that reminded Ford of lemon sherbet. The air vibrated with the low hum of thousands of bees going about their business.

Lord Baverstock stood beside a galvanised zinc wheelbarrow, about fifty feet away, a pair of secateurs in his right hand. A battered Panama hat shaded his eyes from the bright sunlight, casting the upper half of his face in deep shadow. As Ford and Hannah crunched towards him down the path, the sound alerted him and he looked up.

Seeing them, his face broke into a smile. 'Inspector! And Wix! Come to help me deadhead the roses?'

'They're beautiful,' Ford said. 'Mine are only just coming into flower.'

Lord Baverstock pointed at the brickwork behind Ford and Hannah.

'Walled gardens create their own microclimate. That, and the early spring created perfect conditions this year. But I assume you didn't come all the way out here to discuss horticulture, Inspector.'

'I'd like to ask you a few more questions, if that's all right?'

'Do you mind if I keep working?' Lord Baverstock indicated the spread of roses with an extended arm. He wore tan leather gardening gloves.

'Not at all.'

'Good. Ask away, then,' he said, resuming his clipping and snipping, and dropping the spent blossoms into the barrow.

'Can you tell me what sort of firearms you have in your gun safe?'

'Oh, the usual. Shotguns, rifles.'

'Can you be more specific?'

'Of course. Shotguns first, eh? Four Beretta 12-gauges. Two Purdey 20-gauges. Rifles: couple of Remington .22s, a Sako .243 and my old Springfield Arms .30-06.'

'That's it?'

Lord Baverstock stopped pruning and looked upwards for a moment. 'Yes, of course. I have a couple of little four-tens from when the children were little. Little more than popguns, really. Stephen and Lucy had one each. Brownings.'

'No others?'

Ford watched Lord Baverstock. If he didn't own up to the Parker-Hale, Ford would take great pleasure in reminding him.

Lord Baverstock sucked air in over his teeth. 'Yes, I did forget one. A .308.'

'That's a rifle, isn't it?' Ford asked in an innocent tone.

Lord Baverstock smiled indulgently. 'Last time I checked, yes.'

'What make would that be?'

'A Parker-Hale Safari Deluxe.'

'Accurate?'

'Very. It's a fine gun.'

'You said the other day that Lucy and Stephen have had access to the gun safe since they were young. Who else has access?'

'Well, this might be where I get a little lecture from you, Inspector.'

'Why?'

'I keep the key in a box in the main house. Obviously, the rest of my family know where it is and use it whenever they like. Apart from Coco. Poor thing couldn't hit a barn door with a blunderbuss. Then there's Joe, of course,' he said. 'And my estate manager and his deputy. I'm afraid so many people want a shotgun or a vermin rifle that it's easier just to make sure they all know where the key is.'

Ford smiled, though he could see his carefully constructed theory fraying. 'It's not my place to lecture responsible members of the public about their gun safety. Though that does sound a little risky.'

'Life is full of risks. I feel that's one I can manage.'

'Roughly how many people have access to the gun safe, would you say?'

Lord Baverstock looked upwards and Ford watched his lips moving. Jesus! How long a list was it?

He looked back at Ford. 'In total, I should say somewhere between ten and fifteen.'

Ford made a note. Even if Hibberd turned out to be innocent, that wasn't such a huge pool to get through.

'Joe Hibberd served under you in the army, I believe,' he said. 'As a sniper?'

Lord Baverstock frowned. Clipped off another brown-edged bloom. 'Yes, he did. Bloody good sergeant, too.'

'He owes you his life.'

'I don't know about that.'

'The people who dish out gallantry medals seem to think so.'

'Have you been researching my past?'

'It's a matter of public record.'

Lord Baverstock sighed. 'In the heat of battle, Inspector, you do what you have to. A couple of my lads were in trouble. I did what I could. It's the training.'

'He'd go a long way to protect you, wouldn't he?'

'You'd have to ask him that.'

'Owen Long was trying to halt the development on your land.' He paused. 'That would have cost you a small fortune.'

Frowning, Lord Baverstock laid the secateurs on top of the short thorny lengths of rose stems piled in the wheelbarrow. He removed the gloves and mopped his forehead with a spotless white handkerchief he drew from a pocket. He folded it into squares and replaced it.

'I rather resent your insinuation, Inspector,' he said in a quiet, level voice. 'But I understand you have a job to do. I think it would be better for both of us if you were to confine your questions to these dreadful murders.'

Ford nodded, readying himself. He planned to ask Lord Baverstock if he'd asked Joe to murder Tommy Bolter. That was conspiracy to murder. He'd be admitting to a crime carrying a life sentence.

It wasn't so much the answer that interested Ford. It would be a no, he knew that. It was the manner in which it was delivered. He hoped Hannah was paying close attention. Then he admonished himself. Of course she would be! It was the only kind of attention she knew how to pay.

Ford registered his increased pulse and sweating palms. He fought down the urge to wipe them on his thighs.

He inhaled. 'Just one more question. Did you ever talk to Joe Hibberd about wanting Tommy Bolter dead?'

Lord Baverstock's face changed in an instant. Gone was the smile. In its place a wild-eyed look of utter astonishment. 'Sorry. Say again?'

'Did you ask Joe Hibberd to shoot Tommy Bolter for you? You've ordered him to kill in the past; why not now?'

Lord Baverstock took a step towards Ford. His face had paled and he'd clenched his fists. Ford fought the urge to back away.

'Have you ever served your country, Inspector?' Lord Baverstock asked, in a quiet voice. Ford saw a muscle firing in his cheek.

'It's what I'm doing right now.'

'We could debate that. I *meant* in the armed forces.'

'No.'

'If by ordering people to kill, you mean have I led men into battle, then I plead guilty. I have closed with the enemy with rifle, bayonet and grenade. The infantry's mission. Did you know that?'

'No,' Ford said.

'I have zipped men, or what was left of them, into body bags. I have held the hands of boys barely out of their teens while they cried for their mothers. Legs missing, half their faces shot off, guts spilling out,' he said, maintaining a level tone, which was all the more disturbing for its lack of emotion.

'None of which—'

'Hold! I haven't finished. I ordered *nobody* to kill *anybody*,' Lord Baverstock hissed through gritted teeth. 'I am *done* with death, do you hear? Done with it!' The muscle in his cheek was firing twice a second. 'I saw enough death in the army to last me a lifetime. I thought I'd left it behind when I received my honourable discharge. Then Sasha contracted that vile, disgusting disease. Tell me, do you know what MND does to a body?'

Ford hadn't expected this turn in the conversation. He shook his head. 'I don't.'

'It's a cruel thing, Ford. All Sasha had in front of her was years of unremitting, worsening and incurable pain. She didn't want that. She asked me to take her to Libertas. I take it you've heard of that?'

Ford felt a sudden flash of hostility and no way of reining it in.

'One of those death clinics the Swiss are so hot on,' he said.

Lord Baverstock sneered at him. 'Put it like that if you wish. I don't care. I begged Sasha to reconsider. But she was as strong-willed as she was beautiful. I accompanied her because I loved her,' he said. 'It was a risk, but one I was willing to take for her.'

'You were willing to take her to her death, you mean.'

Lord Baverstock's face darkened. 'I *beg* your pardon?'

Ford could feel his heart hammering in his chest. Beside him, he sensed Hannah stiffening. He wasn't sure whose buttons were being pressed anymore. 'How long did the doctors give her?'

'I don't see how that's any of your damn business. I thought we were discussing Joe Hibberd's role in Bolter's murder.'

Ford couldn't help himself. He felt tears pricking at his eyes. 'Five years? Ten?'

Lord Baverstock stared at Ford. Finally, he spoke with what seemed to Ford like genuine compassion. 'I'm sorry, but I have no interest in prolonging this conversation. I assume you are suffering from some sort of work-related stress,' he said. 'PTSD, most likely. They tell me it's common among police officers nowadays. My advice to you is to get yourself to the MO, or police surgeon, or whatever you chaps have these days. Get yourself signed off for a couple of weeks. See somebody about it. No shame in it.'

He picked up the secateurs, turned away and, with a trembling hand, resumed dead-heading the roses.

◆ ◆ ◆

As they drove away, Ford put his phone on speaker and called a friendly magistrate he knew. He really wanted the .22 rifles from Lord Baverstock's gun safe. With them in his possession he could get Hannah running forensic ballistics tests – the works. After he'd explained, the magistrate readily agreed to provide a search warrant. Ford picked it up on the way back to Bourne Hill.

'What did you think about Lord Baverstock this afternoon?' he asked Hannah after she'd seated herself opposite him in his office.

'I think he was telling the truth about Owen. Your last question unsettled him severely. I saw many signs of emotional distress,' she said, consulting a notebook. 'Under that degree of pressure, it's virtually impossible for anyone to maintain a lie without giving something away.'

'He had nothing to do with Tommy's murder?'

'I don't think so. Not with its commission, anyway.' Hannah looked as if she needed to say something.

'Was there something else?' he asked.

Hannah frowned and bit her lip. 'No. Nothing. Thanks, Henry.'

She stood and left, closing the door behind her. She'd looked tense. Had she been about to confront him with something about the accident? He pushed the idea away. He thought back to the conversation with Lord Baverstock.

If he'd wanted to let Joe off the hook, admitting to lax control of the gun safe was a master stroke. Ford started wondering. Had he just been played?

The sound of Sandy's bustling gait interrupted his thoughts. He looked up and saw her striding through the main office, nodding at the various *ma'am*s coming her way, offering a quick word here and a pat on the back there.

'Henry, got a minute?' she called.

'What's up?'

'I've got Gordon Richen here. He wants to discuss the Hibberd arrest plan with you.'

Looking forward to seeing the tactical firearms commander, Ford followed Sandy into her office, resolving not to mention the new intel about just how many people had access to the murder weapon. Nor his suspicions about who might really have pulled the trigger.

He bumped into her back as she stopped dead just over the threshold. Once she'd moved to her desk, he saw why. Martin Peterson sat beside Gordon Richen. Not for the first time, Ford wished Peterson's office was somewhere less convenient than the top floor of Bourne Hill. The South Pole would be a start.

Richen stood and shook hands with Ford. At well over six foot, he towered over the other three people in the room. Like a lot of the firearms team, he'd moved straight from the army into the police and continued to wear his hair cropped to his skull.

'Can I help you, Martin?' Sandy asked. 'Only, we're about to run through a highly sensitive arrest plan.'

Peterson beamed. 'Yes, Gordon just told me. I saw him arriving and, well, it's not every day we have a senior firearms officer at Bourne Hill. So I thought I'd just drop in and see what's' – he pointed a finger at her like a pistol and adopted a terrible American accent – '*goin' down.*'

Ford caught Richen wincing. Sandy's neutral expression didn't flicker, though Ford could see the way the muscles tightened at the angle of her jaw.

'Fine, but this is confidential. Lives are at stake.'

Peterson nodded vigorously and smiled again. 'Understood. You carry on and don't mind me. I'm just here in—'

'—an overwatch role?' Sandy asked.

He beamed. 'Exactly.'

'What about the murder weapon? Will it be in the house?' Richen asked.

'It could well be,' Ford said. 'Or else he returned it to the gun safe. If he needed it, or another firearm, he's got the key.'

'What about his own firearms?'

'He's got a shotgun.'

Sandy interrupted, turning to Ford. 'If you don't find the .22 at Hibberd's place, you're saying it's at Alverchalke Manor?'

'In all likelihood, yes.'

Sandy frowned at him. 'Let's cross that bridge when we come to it, eh?'

Ford nodded, thinking now wasn't the time to fess up about the search warrant. He wanted to lubricate that particular conversation with alcohol.

Richen asked a few more questions, and the meeting broke up with an agreement to make the arrest at 6.00 a.m. the following morning.

◆ ◆ ◆

Back in Major Crimes, Ford reviewed the plan with the team. Each element sounded logical, precise, thoroughly worked out. If only he didn't have a niggling doubt that, despite the evidence, they were looking at the wrong man. Was he hammering a square peg to make it fit a round hole drilled by JJ Bolter? Cutting corners to protect Sam?

Lord Baverstock himself had, unwittingly, put his finger on it. Joe didn't have exclusive use of the .22. So even if he had shot a rabbit with it, that didn't mean he'd used it to kill Owen. They had the murder weapon, but not necessarily the murderer.

Next he phoned Sandy. 'Fancy a quick drink at The Wyndham?'

'Oh, go on, then. I've got a mountain of budget forecasts to get through, but I can spare thirty minutes for my favourite DI.'

They walked up to the pub together and found a table in a quiet corner.

'How did it go with Lord B today?' Sandy asked when Ford returned from the bar with a large vodka and tonic for her and a low-alcohol lager for himself.

'Fine.'

She regarded him steadily over the rim of her glass. 'Please tell me you didn't accuse him of murder?'

Ford returned her stare. 'I didn't.'

He hadn't just lied to his boss, had he? No. He was in the clear. He hadn't accused Lord Baverstock of murder. He'd just asked him if he'd been involved in a *conspiracy* to murder. Not the same at all.

'Good. Because the last thing I need is a disgruntled aristocrat barging into my office complaining about rough handling.'

'How about a competent DI who's just bought you a lovely drink telling you he's already applied for a search warrant for Alverchalke Manor and associated properties?'

Sandy put her drink down, frowning. 'And you've done that because?'

'We've identified the murder weapon. I can prove Joe used it. But I don't believe he still has it. I think it's in the gun safe at Alverchalke Manor. I need it, Sandy! Without it, we've got bugger all that would stand up in court and get a conviction.'

Sandy took a long pull on her drink. 'Fine. I know you think I've become too much the politician, but police work is still in my blood. If you tell me it's up there, I want you to go and find it.'

He nodded. That was what he intended to do. And he needed to do it fast. The Bolters were sniffing around where they had no business sniffing, and despite his threat to JJ, he was sure they'd be keeping up their own private investigation into Tommy's murder.

◆ ◆ ◆

Lord Baverstock hated the public who traipsed around his grounds from April to September. Worse still, because they required his grinning, suited presence, were the tedious fundraisers to whom Coco devoted so much of her time. Away from both, he preferred his own name to the burdensome title that came with the stately home he struggled to keep afloat.

He'd tried to get the staff to call him Philip, but the looks they gave him on receipt of his suggestion ranged from puzzlement to outright horror. Had he asked them to call him Your Most Evil Satanic Majesty, he couldn't imagine shocking them more.

At least Joe didn't call him 'Your Lordship' or 'My Lord'. He stuck to 'Major Martival'. Joe sat before him now, in the library, a cut-glass tumbler of single malt in his right hand. With his left, he scratched the top of a black Lab's glossy head. The Lab's tongue lolled from its mouth, and when Joe's fingers found a particularly pleasurable spot, it emitted a low rumble of satisfaction.

Late-afternoon sunlight illuminated the leather spines of the books, picking out the gold-tooled lettering. The grandfather clock in the corner struck five.

Martival took a deep breath. 'We've been through some times together, Joe, haven't we?'

'Yes, Major, we have.'

'I want you to know that since you came to work for me at Alverchalke, I've seen you change. For the better,' he added, in case Joe didn't get the compliment.

'I love the work, Major, you know that. And I want you to know that I'll never forget what you did for me in Helmand. Ever.'

Martival nodded. He knew that. Save a chap's life, he owed you. He closed his eyes. Heard the whine of bullets and the screams of his wounded sergeant thousands of miles and many years distant, but as fresh as yesterday's new blooms in the rose garden. He sipped his whisky, enjoying the burn as the spirit hit his throat.

'The police are getting close, Joe. I don't think I can hold them off much longer. I had Inspector Ford up here earlier, grilling me about you.'

'That's all right. When they talked to me, I knew what I'd have to do. It was just a matter of time before we put your plan into action.'

'Good man. Now, a little bird at Bourne Hill tells me they're coming for you tomorrow morning at oh-six-hundred. I want you to go quietly, Joe. No fuss.'

Joe frowned. Took a pull on his drink. He stopped scratching the dog and, in response, it butted its blocky head against his thigh. He ignored it.

'You're sure this is the only way, Major?'

Martival looked at his gamekeeper. He liked Joe. Respected him, even. But a good commander knew when sacrifices had to be made, however unpleasant.

'No other option. It's for the best.'

Joe sighed and resumed scratching the dog's head. 'I understand, Major. What shall I tell Ford?'

'You found Long trespassing. He acted aggressively towards you. Then he grabbed your gun and in the struggle it went off. Tragic accident. Self-defence, even.'

'What about Bolter? They know we had a fight.'

Martival thought back to his earlier conversation with the detective. 'We'll talk to the lawyer, but my feeling is we go for the PTSD angle. Say the accident with Long disturbed the balance of your mind. Bolter tried to blackmail you and the stress caused a blackout.'

'Will that work?'

'Honestly, Joe? I don't know. I never went in for that barrack-room lawyer nonsense. But if it does all go to shit, I will fight for you tooth and nail, like I did in Afghanistan,' Martival said, leaning on the last word. 'I will get you the best lawyers money can buy, starting with my own solicitor. Coco knows a few QCs up in town. We'll ask around. If it comes to trial, you'll plead not guilty. If they convict anyway, we'll try and get you into a decent prison. And when you get out, you'll come straight back here to your old job.'

Joe finished his drink and set the glass down. 'Thanks, Major. I won't let you down. Just like you didn't let me down.'

'Least I can do, Joe. Now, you'll have to forgive me, but I need to go and put some stuff together. I'm going up to London tonight. I'll be gone for a couple of days. You'll be all right, yes?'

'Yes, Major. Right as rain.'

The Lab began whining, a thready, high-pitched sound that for the first time ever set Martival's teeth on edge. They said dogs were adept at picking up on their owners' emotions. He made an effort to calm himself and smiled at his gamekeeper.

'Probably best if we don't have any more contact till they arrest you,' he said. 'One never knows who's listening in on one's calls.'

◆ ◆ ◆

JJ pointed to a chair opposite him at the long, polished table in the hacienda's meeting room. He pushed the bottle across to Rye.

'Sit down. We need to talk.'

Rye dropped into the chair, poured brandy into the heavy tumbler and drank off half in a single gulp. 'What about?'

'What do you think, you muppet? Ford.'

Rye's voice took on a complaining tone. 'I gave the kid a warning and look what happened.'

JJ took a pull on his own drink, then shook his head. 'I told you not to do anything and you ignored me.'

'He tasered me. We should make a complaint.'

'For fuck's sake, are you really that stupid? You threatened his kid in broad fucking daylight. And he got you on video. Ford's right. He could say he came to arrest you and it went south. Forget the kid, I've got something much better. Much more clever.'

'Don't drag it out then. What?'

'I've been doing a little digging into Ford's past. Did you know he left his wife to drown?'

Rye sat up straighter. His eyes flashed and a grin stole across his face. 'What? You serious?'

'It was a climbing thing in Wales. On the coast. She broke her leg and he *apparently* went off to get help. When the coastguard got there, she was dead. Drowned.'

'Fuckin' 'ell!'

'Yeah, well, don't get too excited. It all got written off as an accident. They had an inquest like they did for Tommy.'

Rye's face closed in on itself. He finished his brandy and poured another.

'Why tell me then?' he asked sulkily.

'I didn't think that was the whole story. I went over to the land of the sheep-shaggers. Spoke to this guy at Milford Haven Coastguard. Persuaded him to talk,' JJ said, rubbing thumb and forefinger together.

Rye grinned as he swallowed another enormous mouthful of brandy. 'What did he say?'

'He gave me this internal report. They had their suspicions it wasn't all kosher but nothing ever got done about it.'

'So we're going to blackmail him with it?'

'No, you arsehole! Look where blackmail got Tommy. We're going to be much more subtle. You're going to put it in the hands of someone who'll take over digging where I left off.'

'Who's that?'

'Her name is Dr Hannah Fellowes. She's the second in command of the Forensics department at Bourne Hill.'

'Cool,' Rye said, drawing out the word. 'D'you get this from your source, then, did you?'

JJ nodded. Grinned. 'We're not the only ones with family troubles.'

CHAPTER THIRTY-ONE

The terms of the search warrant in Ford's jacket pocket were clear. Under Section 8 of PACE, the Police and Criminal Evidence Act, he was permitted to search Alverchalke Manor and all buildings within a one-mile radius.

The magistrate had been more than happy to sign it, on the basis that Ford believed that he would find one or more murder weapons on the property. It wasn't perfect, but they didn't have the manpower for a bigger area.

He'd managed to scare up sixteen uniformed search officers to work under Jan as the supervisor. They were parcelled out between four marked cars currently following Ford and Jan in his Discovery. He turned into the private road that led to Alverchalke Manor.

'I suspect we'll be here for two days, at least,' he said. 'We'll get a couple of people in a car at the gate there overnight.'

'Got it,' Jan said, making a note.

Ford pulled up in the large semicircle of gravel outside the manor house.

'Ready?' he asked her.

'Ready,' she replied, with a brief smile.

Ford walked up to the front door and rang the bell.

'This is a copy of a warrant to search this property,' he said, handing it to the maid who opened the door. 'Please stand aside.' He turned to Jan. 'In you go.'

Jan beckoned half a dozen officers to follow her in. A second team headed to the stables. In his office, Ford and Jan had plotted the house and outbuildings. They'd outlined them in red or blue, as hot or cold zones, according to their importance. The stable block and the house, where they expected to find the firearms, were hot.

Still clutching the copy of the search warrant, the maid ran towards a door and disappeared. Ford waited. He knew what was coming. Rich or poor, people reacted the same way to police intrusion into their property.

The hallway smelled pleasantly of furniture polish and the scent of roses, a couple of dozen of which – of the palest pink – stood in a huge glass vase on a table.

He heard the clack of heels on tiled floor. Straightened up and turned to meet – who? Lady Baverstock? Yes. In a navy dress, buttoned at the front, and matching suede stilettos. He took in the fierce gaze and tight mouth. She looked furious.

No 'Coco' for you today then, Ford.

Arriving in front of him, she brandished the search warrant in his face.

'Inspector, what is the meaning of this? Why are all these police officers in my house?'

'That is a copy of a search warrant, Lady Baverstock. I obtained it yesterday from a magistrate. It entitles me to search this property and those allied to it.'

She flushed. 'This is preposterous! We've done nothing wrong.'

'I'm not saying you have. The warrant is to search for material we believe may have a significant bearing on a murder investigation. I am drawing no conclusions about anyone in particular,' he said. 'Is there somewhere you could go while we work? A friend's house, perhaps?'

Her nostrils flared. 'You must be bloody joking! I'm not leaving here and letting those people with their great big boots wreck my home. I'm staying.'

'That's your right. But you can only observe, and please stand well out of the way. If you try to interfere with my officers, I will have no option but to arrest you for obstruction.'

Breathing heavily, she turned on her heel and stalked off.

'Lady Baverstock?' he called after her.

She stopped. Turned to face him, still glaring. 'What?'

'I need the key to the gun safe. Could you fetch it for me, please?'

'Fetch it yourself. It's in a key box on the wall outside my husband's office. First door on the right over there,' she said, pointing to a corridor.

Following her instructions, Ford found a wooden box screwed to the wall. Inside, six sets of keys hung on little hooks. Each bore a label except one, linked by a short chain to a tiny brass shotgun.

He pocketed it and went outside, heading for the stable block and the workshop containing the gun safe. He met a uniform coming the other way.

'Found the safe, sir. We just need the key to the padlock.'

Ford held it out to him. 'Here you go.'

'Thanks, sir,' said the officer before trotting off back to the stables.

Ford followed him. Inside the workshop, a single-storey brick building with a pitched slate roof, a couple of gloved search officers were standing in front of a six-foot-wide grey-painted steel cabinet. One by one they were removing long guns and laying them on a long wooden trestle table.

The guns varied in size and appointments. Some had ornate engraving on their metal parts, and gleaming, richly figured wood. Others were more serviceable-looking weapons, with stocks of camouflage-painted plastic or plain wood.

One of the larger rifles had a telescopic sight. Was he looking at the rifle used to murder Tommy Bolter? He peered at it but couldn't see a manufacturer's stamp. One for Hannah. The ballistics tests might take a while, but she'd still be able to start processing it for forensics.

He left them to it and went to find Jan. She was outside the front door with an aerial photo of Alverchalke Manor spread out on the bonnet of a marked car.

'Hi, guv,' she said. 'All right?'

'It's going well. Your team in the workshop are bagging up all the weapons from the gun cabinet.'

'Yeah, what if there are more? Hidden, maybe? They're supposed to keep them secure, but on a spread this size, who knows?'

'You'll find them, Jan,' he said with a smile. 'I have to go. I suggest you clear one wing of the house, then confine the family and staff there. According to the plans we looked at earlier, the east wing is accessible via a single corridor.'

She nodded. 'We'll clear it, get them down there, then station a single uniform at the end. I'll put a team at each corner of the house when we leave. Maybe a dog-handler on roving patrol?'

'Yes. Good idea.'

◆　◆　◆

Ford's phone pinged twice as he pulled up outside his home that evening. Two texts from Sam:

Staying with Josh for tea
And sleepover

Smiling, he let himself in, made a cup of coffee and took it upstairs to his music room. He sipped the coffee, and while he waited for the amp to warm up he thought about Joe Hibberd.

Everyone was focused on Joe, and rightly so, because Ford had directed them to. But Ford was now looking beyond the arrest.

What if Joe hadn't fired the fatal shot that killed Owen? Or what if he had, but then enlisted someone else to help him murder Tommy? He'd served under Lord Baverstock. Wouldn't he be the natural one to ask if Joe had found himself in trouble?

Ford shook his head. Would someone in Lord Baverstock's position *really* engage in a conspiracy to murder just to save his gamekeeper's skin?

If not to save Joe, how about to save someone else? That would point the finger at either his wife or his children. He shook his head. Bumble, Coco, Loopy and Stodge. They sounded like the cast of one of the screechy TV shows he and Lou had sat watching with a very young Sam.

Lord Baverstock had said ten to fifteen people knew where to find the key to the gun safe, including Joe. So it could just as easily have been another member of staff Joe had gone to. If Hibberd wouldn't talk, Ford would start profiling all the estate workers. And he would look first for any who'd served with either Joe or Lord Baverstock in the army.

But it wasn't just the Martival family occupying his thoughts. He also had the Bolters to contend with.

Ford saw, clearer than before, what would happen if the Bolters decided to act on the information they'd gleaned about him investigating the Martivals. He pictured a tooled-up gang of black-clad hard men, JJ and Rye at their head, storming Alverchalke Manor blaring defiance and demanding justice. Heard the rattle of small arms as Lord Baverstock and his family returned fire using a cache of unlicensed weapons.

Martin Petersen would shit himself at the damage that would do to 'the brand'. The image made Ford smile, despite the pressure, and he picked up his guitar. Now he'd externalised his thoughts, he felt ready to play. The music flowed. He turned the volume up.

◆ ◆ ◆

Hannah pulled her chair closer to her iMac in her softly lit home office. She opened the document she'd been working on every night for several weeks:

Eleven Reasons Why 'Henry' Ford Should Stop Blaming Himself For Louisa Ford's Death

She'd felt bad, lying to Ford in the cafe. But then, it wasn't *really* lying, because the document he'd seen on her PC *was* for Sam. It was just that she had another one at home that *did* focus on Lou's death. If he'd asked her the right question, she would have had to tell him the truth. And that would have been a disaster. But he hadn't. So it was fine. For now.

The research had been easy. She'd been hoping for more of a challenge, but the case had made quite a splash in the Welsh papers, and even one or two of the nationals had picked it up briefly. And the *Salisbury Journal*, of course, but it had concentrated more on the human angle.

The prize for her had been a feature in a climbing magazine. It had analysed the risks and rewards of climbing ten sea crags around the British coast, including Pen-y-Holt. Where there had been fatalities, it had examined them and offered dispassionate analysis on how, or if, they could have been avoided.

'Yes, Uta Frith,' she said, stroking the cat, who had jumped up on to her lap and was purring loudly. 'That is watertight. When the time is right, and I show Henry, he'll see I'm correct.'

Then she frowned. But would he? Or would he give her one of those searching looks she'd seen him bestow on subjects in the horrid-smelling Interview Suite Four? The look that said, to her, *You think you're so clever, but there are realms of understanding in which I roam freely and into which you are simply unequipped to enter.*

The doorbell rang. She frowned. Nobody rang her doorbell at night unless she had invited them. And she hadn't invited anyone this evening. She *never* invited anyone. So nobody should have been there, ringing her doorbell at night.

She pushed Uta Frith off her lap and went downstairs, feeling a squirm of anxiety in her stomach. She could see a dark shape through the frosted glass panels in the upper half of the door. Her heart beating rapidly, she put the safety chain on and then peered through the spyhole.

A man stood there, looking around. Early thirties. She forced herself to be more precise. Thirty-one- to thirty-three-year-old male IC1. Height between five-eight and five-ten. Stocky, bordering on fat. Short light-brown hair swept back from a high, oddly bulging forehead. Narrow eyes. Clean-shaven.

She opened the door and looked through the narrow gap the chain permitted.

'Can I help you?'

'You Hannah Fellowes?' His accent was local, his voice rough.

'Yes. Who are you?'

'This is for you,' he said, and thrust a padded envelope through the gap before turning and leaving, shaking his head.

She didn't like people turning up at her front door uninvited and ringing her doorbell. Especially not when they pushed unmarked packages into her hands. But he'd gone, and that was good.

Her pulse calming, she closed the door and took the envelope upstairs. At her desk, she examined the exterior of the envelope. It was new. No previous labels stuck over with paper or scribbled out with black marker. She pressed it experimentally. No lumps, bumps or protrusions.

She turned the package over in her hands, wanting to open it but frightened of what might happen. Might the flap conceal a trigger of some kind?

She told herself off. This was Salisbury. People didn't drop off bombs in Jiffy bags at eight in the evening.

Then she had an idea. She took a modelling knife out of her desk drawer and used its razor-sharp blade to slit the side of the envelope. Grey fluff spilled from the gaping cut and she tutted as it tumbled to the floor. That would have to be vacuumed up immediately after she'd seen what was inside the package.

She lifted the top of the envelope using the point of the knife. She saw the edges of sheets of paper. Breathing more easily, she slid out a stapled report of some kind. No images, just a lot of text, set in long, dense paragraphs. The headline intrigued her.

ACCIDENT REPORT: CONFIDENTIAL –
INTERNAL USE ONLY

The spilled fluff forgotten, and with Uta Frith reinstalled on her lap, she began reading. It was a report into the death by drowning of Louisa Kathryn Ford, written by the Maritime Operations Controller at Milford Haven Coastguard Operations Centre.

Half an hour later, she put it down. In many respects, it echoed and reinforced the findings of the coroner's inquest. She spent another half an hour cross-checking it against her own research.

But when she'd finished, she had underlined a few sentences in the final paragraph of the coastguard report that weren't anywhere in the other documentation she'd unearthed online.

> My only concern is, why did Mr Ford leave his wife in the first place? He says he dislodged the rock that broke her leg. And we confirmed it wasn't securely bedded into the stack. But surely the sensible course was to stay with her? He could have roped them both on higher up, and either kept trying to get a signal or simply ridden out the tide.

Frowning, Hannah put the report aside and looked at her own summary of the death of Ford's wife.

> Although not attempting one of the nine (9) established routes, Henry and Louisa were experienced climbers.

> Any new route likely to have been within their capabilities.

> Climbing is a leisure activity. No coercion or pressure involved, unlike, for example, military training.

> Accident investigation revealed dislodged block (underlying fissure result of natural wear) broke LF's right femur (compound fracture), causing severe blood loss and limiting her mobility, making a climb out impossible.

Unusually high tide caused by 'once in a century' freak alteration to Gulf Stream.

HF roped LF to rock <u>to prevent her being washed off platform</u>.

HF soloed out <u>in order to effect rescue of LF</u>. HF called coastguard <u>as soon as mobile signal restored</u>.

Weakened by injury, shock and blood loss, LF drowned as tide rose.

No arrest of HF by police: <u>no criminal charges brought</u>.

Coroner's inquest verdict: death by misadventure, i.e. death caused by accident while taking known and voluntarily accepted risks. <u>No negligence</u>.

Point Four worried her. She could see a different version of events now. One where Henry didn't dislodge the rock by accident. Had he kicked it down on to Lou on purpose? Or wrenched it free and aimed it down on to her? Maybe he wasn't even going for her leg. He might have tried to kill her outright.

'No!' she said, startling Uta Frith, who mewed plaintively and jumped down, scattering envelope padding as she left.

She ignored the cat. Henry wouldn't do that. She knew him. OK, so she didn't have the same easy emotional insights as people like Jools did. Or Henry himself. But she had analysed him. She had thought hard about everything he'd told her. And she'd done all that research herself. It couldn't be true. It *wouldn't* be true. She had found a family at Bourne Hill. Now somebody was trying to take that security away from her. This was malice at work.

She wouldn't talk to Henry about it. Not in the middle of a case. She could wait. She wanted, needed, him as a friend. She wanted to help him heal. To move on. To unstick. Was that the right word? It would do.

She had a brainwave. She knew that inviting someone for dinner was a good way to open up the conversation. She could do that, present her research findings and then show him the coastguard report and tell him about the man who'd delivered it by hand. They could discuss it together. She resolved to ask him to dinner after the case was closed.

CHAPTER THIRTY-TWO

At 5.50 a.m. the next day, Ford raised the binoculars Richen had passed him and focused on the kitchen window of Hibberd's cottage.

He could see Hibberd's head and shoulders. He was sitting perfectly still, looking at something in front of him. The window-sill cut off the view, so Ford couldn't tell what was occupying his attention.

Behind him he heard muttered conversation and metallic snaps and scrapes as the AFOs readied their weapons. He'd also brought a canine unit and could hear the handler murmuring to his dog.

Inside the cottage that had been his home since the major had rescued him, sat former Grenadier Guards sergeant Joe Hibberd. Molly and Bess, his border collies, padded round the kitchen, their claws clicking on the slate floor tiles. He sat at a table pitted and scarred from many decades of use, but otherwise spotlessly clean.

Joe had risen early. And, as usual, he'd made a pot of tea. Strong, like the brews they had in Helmand. He'd eaten a hearty breakfast: sausages, fried eggs, fried bread, bacon and baked beans. Two thick slices of toast and marmalade. He hadn't moved since, spending the time flicking through a photo album of his time in the army and fingering the set of medals he kept on his dressing table. The props weren't in the plan: they'd been his own idea. He hadn't troubled the major with them. Nor with his additional piece of drama.

In front of him sat his Willow pattern plate, smeared with brown sauce and a few slowly congealing streaks of bacon fat. He placed the plate on the floor and the dogs padded over to share the unusual bounty.

He reread the note he'd written before going to bed. Nodded. It would do the job.

His shotgun lay on the table. Its wooden stock shone in the early-morning sunlight coming through the leaded window. He inhaled its smell: gun oil, cleaner and polish. Beside it, a half-empty box of shells waited.

Through the open window, he could hear the chatter of rotor blades. Altitude 5,000–8,000 feet, he estimated. It would be a Wiltshire Police Eurocopter EC135 in navy and yellow livery. He saw them from time to time, overflying the estate. Nothing like as loud as the Apaches, Merlins and Chinooks they'd had in Afghanistan. Decent birds, all the same.

Joe put his knife, fork, plate and mug in the dishwasher. He added a tablet to the compartment, set it to a short cycle and clicked the door closed.

He placed the photo album and medals on the kitchen counter, dampened a cloth to wipe the table, then folded it and hung it over the swan-necked tap. A place for everything, and everything in its place. The dogs were lying down, watching him move around the kitchen. Their eyes were bright, expectant. They thought they'd be going out soon, accompanying him to some part of the estate or another. Molly's tail thumped lazily against the padded edge of her bed.

'Not today, girls,' he said, sadly. 'I think Major Martival will be taking care of you from now on.'

He reached for the Browning, thumbed the latch and broke it. He took two red cartridges from a box, inspected their brass caps and inserted them into the breech. With a snap, loud in the silent kitchen, he closed the gun.

The action had disturbed his note, which shifted off-square by a few degrees. Tutting, he realigned it with the edge of the table, beside his phone.

Even though he'd been expecting it, the call startled him. He looked back at the dogs and lifted his phone to his ear. 'Hello?'

'Joe, this is Inspector Ford. I'd like you to come to the front door with your hands on top of your head, please. Then follow the instructions given to you.'

'You going to arrest me, Inspector?'

'Afraid so, Joe. Now, don't do anything silly, OK? I want this to go smoothly so we can all get home in one piece. You included.'

'Don't worry. I won't cause any trouble.'

Joe ended the call and realigned the phone with the note. He picked up the shotgun. With a final scratch of the dogs' heads, he walked to the front door.

As agreed with Gordon Richen, Ford stood thirty feet back from the cottage door and off to one side, giving the AFOs a clear field of fire. As the door swung inwards he had to fight down the urge to throw himself flat in the dirt.

Joe Hibberd stood there, holding a shotgun loosely across his body, barrels pointing down at the ground.

'Hello, Inspector,' Joe said.

Behind him, Ford heard heavy boots thundering up.

'Armed police! Put the gun down! Armed police! Drop your weapon!'

Gordon Richen rushed past Ford, pistol gripped in both hands and pointing at Joe. Two more AFOs took up kneeling positions, their black assault rifles aimed at his head.

In the slowed-down time that descended on him, Ford noticed Joe's freshly shaven cheeks and the greyish circles under his eyes. He watched as, with infinite care, Joe bent his knees and laid the shotgun on the ground.

The two AFOs rushed him. One forced him to the ground at gunpoint. The other snapped on rigid cuffs, pinioning his wrists behind his back in the stacked formation for maximum restraint. A third ran up and retrieved the shotgun.

Letting out the breath he'd been holding, Ford walked over to the prone figure. Joe twisted his head round to look up at him.

'That was a good decision, Joe. Thank you.'

With Hibberd on his way back to Bourne Hill, Ford went inside. He walked down the hall to the kitchen and opened the door to be confronted by the two black and white border collies he'd seen with Hibberd before. They were barking furiously. Stiff ruffs of hair stood up on their necks. They came to a stop a few feet from Ford, long yellow teeth bared. He fought down a primal terror. He had time to think, *This is what cavemen felt when they met wolves.*

He kneeled down and extended a hand, closed into a downward-pointing fist. He remembered Joe telling him their names: female, though right now he couldn't recall them precisely.

'Hey, girl,' he crooned to the closer of the two growling dogs. 'Don't worry about your master. He's just coming for a chat at Bourne Hill.'

The nearer dog – the alpha, he assumed – cast an appraising glance at him. Her ears, which had flattened against her head on seeing Ford, pricked up again. He stayed motionless, avoiding eye contact. The other dog remained still, though Ford felt relieved she had stopped growling.

The lead dog inched forward and bent her snout to his hand. She sniffed loudly, twice.

'There, that's all right, then, isn't it, eh?' Ford said. He curled his hand under the dog's jaw and scratched at the loose skin there. The second dog, sensing the threat had passed, whined a little before shouldering her way in for Ford to scratch her behind the ears. Slowly he stood. He turned round and called for someone to take the dogs outside to the canine unit.

Alone, Ford stood in the doorway, taking in the scene. Getting a feel for Hibberd's life. Had he not already known of Hibberd's military service, the cleanliness and order all around him would have been a strong clue. The only jarring note was the open box of shells on the table.

He saw zero evidence of cooking or any kind of food preparation. No crumbs in front of the bread bin, no smears on the work surfaces, no splashes on the stainless-steel stove top. He looked into the corners. Unlike his own kitchen, he saw no cobwebs freighted with tiny white shrouds. He noted the medals and the photograph album on the countertop.

He walked in, pulling on a pair of blue nitrile gloves, then picked up the sheet of notepaper sitting dead square in the centre of the pine table.

To whom it may concern,
I, Joe Hibberd, confess to the murders of Owen Long and Tommy Bolter.
    Long attacked me when I challenged him on Lord Baverstock's land. I shot him with a .22 I took from Lord Baverstock's gun safe.

I acted in self-defence, not that I expect a court to believe that. They are prejudiced against veterans, always persecuting us for things we did in the heat of battle years ago.

I also shot Tommy Bolter. I used a .308 hunting rifle also belonging to Lord Baverstock. Bolter saw me kill Long and demanded fifty thousand pounds to keep quiet. It triggered my PTSD. I don't know what happened except I came to beside his dismembered body.

I do not wish to bring disgrace on Lord Baverstock and his family. They have always been good to me and know nothing about what I did. This is one hundred per cent on me.

As I do not expect a fair trial, I am taking the only other way out.

I leave my entire estate to the Royal British Legion.

Yours faithfully,

Joseph Hibberd, CGC (Conspicuous Gallantry Cross)

Ford wrinkled his nose. Something didn't feel right. He folded the note and placed it in a paper evidence bag he took from his inside pocket. He went outside.

At the side of the house, Ford saw a battered Land Rover Defender – the basic utility vehicle rather than the more upmarket Discovery he drove. This one had been built as a pickup, with an open load bay behind the stubby two-person cab. Whatever shine the sage-green paint had once enjoyed had long been weathered away, leaving it virtually matte.

He looked over the slab-sided load bay. Dust and grit covered the ridged steel floor. He peered into the corners, searching for the darker colouration of blood spots. Seeing none, he turned and called over to a uniform unrolling crime scene tape.

'Over here, please.'

When the PC arrived, he recognised her. 'Hello, Lisa, how's it going?'

She smiled. 'Ace, sir, thanks. I'm so grateful to you for getting me in to Bourne Hill as a proper copper.'

'I said I would. I try to keep my promises.'

'What can I do?'

'I want you to put a cordon round this vehicle and get a sheet – or, better yet, a tent – over the load bay in case it rains. Then get it recovered to HQ.'

She cupped her hand and leaned towards the driver's-side window. About to warn her against touching the glass, he realised he didn't need to. She stopped a few inches short as she looked inside.

'You think he used it to transport the bodies, sir?'

'It's a hypothesis.'

He left PC Moore calling for a flatbed on to which they could load the Land Rover.

Ford turned and surveyed the scene. Hannah had arrived with a team of CSIs. Once they had what they wanted, he'd send Jan in. He jogged over.

'Hello, Henry,' Hannah said, pulling down her face mask as he arrived. 'Do you think it's him?'

'I'm not sure, Wix. We had to arrest him, but I'm not feeling it.'

'Ah, the famous Ford gut. I think I'll stick with the evidence, if that's all right?'

He frowned. More offbeat humour? He pushed on. 'On that subject, I've got Hibberd's Land Rover protected over there,' he said, gesturing to the Landie with PC Moore standing guard. 'I thought it might have blood or DNA in the back.'

She nodded briskly. 'I'll get right on it. What about firearms?'

'Joe told me his .22 is at the gun shop,' Ford said. 'Gordon's guys have the shotgun.'

'On that subject, I put Ellen and George on the firearms from Alverchalke Manor. They're doing the .22s and the .308 first.'

'Thanks. Let me know as soon as you have anything.'

Heading back to Bourne Hill with Mick Tanner beside him, Ford thought about Hibberd's suicide note. Or what he realised he had started thinking of as his 'suicide note'.

He'd read other examples of the genre. They were often so packed with emotion that reading them evoked tears even in hardened cops. Hibberd's lacked feeling, apart from that single reference to veterans being persecuted by the courts. And even that felt contrived, somehow.

The note felt like it had been not so much written as constructed. Each sentence, each paragraph, calculated to provide a piece of the puzzle. Joe had shouldered the entire burden of guilt. He'd absolved Lord Baverstock and his family. And he'd forestalled any further police enquiries.

Ford thought the PTSD angle was a nice touch. It tapped into a strand of thinking that had moved in recent decades from the world of psychiatry to everyday conversation, TV shows and social media. Hell, Lord Baverstock had even suggested Ford had it.

Against that, he had to weigh the evidence. That's why they'd arrested Hibberd in the first place, after all. In prime position, the bullet George had retrieved from Owen Long's skull matched the one used by Hibberd to shoot a rabbit. Juries liked facts like that.

Then there was the circumstantial evidence. And Hibberd's experience. Strike that. *Combat* experience. As a *sniper*. Add in a grudge against at least one of the victims.

Something else was bugging Ford, but he couldn't drag it out of the dark long enough to scrutinise it. It would come. If he let it.

'Penny for 'em?' Mick asked.

'Huh?'

'You've been on autopilot for the last five minutes. Have you even registered a single thing I've said?'

'Sorry, Mick, I was thinking about Hibberd's note.'

'Yeah. Result! CPS won't give us any grief over this one.'

Ford had his doubts, but kept them to himself. 'How're things with you?' he asked.

'Me? Oh, just bloody peachy! She's trying to turn the girls against me. Yesterday, I'm on the phone to Caitlin and she says, "Oh, Dad, Mum says you're trying to wriggle out of child support." Which is a complete lie! Not by Caitlin, she's just repeating what bloody Kirsty told her.'

'At least they're still talking to you.'

'Yeah, yeah. But it's killing me. I mean, they weren't at the cuddling stage anymore but, still, they used to give me a hug. Now Kirsty is pouring this, this *poison* into their ears. Drip, drip, drip! What if they start to believe her? I can't lose my girls!'

Ford looked sideways. Mick's eyes were glistening. He swiped a hand across them and then rubbed furiously at the stubble on his scalp. Ford spotted a lay-by coming up and braked hard, swerving off the road and bringing the Discovery to a scuffing halt.

'Jesus! What did I say?' Mick asked, removing his hands from the dashboard, where he'd been bracing himself.

'Nothing. I mean, lots, but nothing bad. You said you wanted to keep working. I respect that. God knows, I need you. But if you feel things getting on top of you, come and see me. That's an order.'

Mick sniffed, then cleared his throat. Without looking at Ford, he nodded. 'Thanks. Means a lot.'

Ford knew Mick wouldn't want to prolong the conversation. The DS wore his heart where it belonged, not on his sleeve. He'd built a persona as the hard man of Major Crimes, if not Bourne Hill, and it wouldn't do to let people see his fragility. And Ford felt he needed to build bridges after practically accusing Mick of taking money from the Bolters.

And what of Ford himself? God only knew what would happen if people saw the sometimes precarious state of his own sanity.

He pushed the thought aside. *Later. I've a murder suspect to interview.*

CHAPTER THIRTY-THREE

The chatter in Major Crimes stilled as Ford and Mick walked in together. Olly and Jools hurried over.

'Are you all right, guv?' Jools asked, looking into Ford's eyes with concern.

'I'm fine, Jools.'

'I listened in on the radio from here. They said he pointed a shotgun in your face.'

Ford smiled. 'Not even close. I think the AFOs were disappointed they didn't get to use their toys.'

'When are you interviewing Hibberd, guv?' Olly asked.

Ford checked his watch. 'It's ten past eight now. We booked him in at six thirty-five. The PACE clock started ticking then, so we've still got plenty of time, but I want to move fast, so as soon as his brief gets here.'

'I just thought, with my degree in criminology, I could help you formulate the interview strategy.'

Out of Olly's eyeline, Jools smirked. Ford caught the expression and frowned at her.

'What did you have in mind, Olly?' he asked.

'I've prepared a dossier for you with some thoughts about profitable avenues for questioning to get him to open up. It's on your desk.'

'Thanks. I'll read it now. And you know what?'

'What, guv?' Olly asked, the pleasure evident on his face.

Ford smiled. 'I'd have more time for reading if I didn't have to make myself a coffee.'

Jools grinned. 'I'll have white, no sugar, as you're making, Ols.'

Ford left them to their bickering and retreated to his office to read Olly's report.

It made for interesting reading. After receiving an honourable discharge from the army, Hibberd had found work in London as a nightclub bouncer – 'door staff crew member', his online CV read.

But after a fracas that ended with him cold-cocking a clubber, he'd moved up to Scotland, where he'd found work on a shooting estate owned by a Saudi billionaire. That had lasted for a year until he'd been caught stealing from guests and fired, though not prosecuted.

Hibberd had returned south and fetched up as his former commander's gamekeeper, where he'd been ever since.

Ford finished the report, the rest of which concentrated on Hibberd's background, and turned to Olly's observations, all of which were couched in the sort of academic language that had Ford reaching for an imaginary red pen.

He mentally turned Olly's highfalutin phrases into plain English. His least favourite was 'Childhood spent in benefit-dependent community characterised by intersecting antisocial vectors.' Ford translated that one as: 'Grew up in a poor neighbourhood with lots of crime.'

Ford sighed, and shut the folder. Once you cut the fat, some decent stuff remained. But it showed merely that Olly had found out from lectures and books what it had taken Ford a couple of decades to figure out on the job. No more, no less.

Actually – yes, less. Because Olly hadn't the life experience Ford had. Then a wicked voice in Ford's head interrupted his train of thought. *No, and isn't he lucky!*

Locking the thought away, he went to see Olly. The days were passing and still they hadn't got access to Owen's GoPro account.

'Have you got that bloody GoPro password yet?'

Olly's face fell. 'I spoke to them again this morning.'

'And?'

'They said even with Mrs Long's permission, their legal department would take at least a week. Due diligence, apparently. They're very nervous of fraud.'

'A week? For God's sake! Did you tell them we were investigating a murder?'

'I did. I'm sorry, guv.'

Ford sighed, taking in the DC's crestfallen expression. 'This isn't on you. Bloody corporate risk aversion. I'd like to show them a few of our crime scene photos. Maybe that would gee them up a bit.'

He checked his watch again. Called the front desk. 'Has Joe Hibberd's brief arrived yet?'

'No, sir.'

'When they do, have someone take them to Interview Suite Four, please. And call me.'

While he waited, he thought back to the moment he'd walked into Hibberd's kitchen. Something then hadn't felt right. He stilled his mind. Went back to the gamekeeper's cottage. What the hell was it? Just out of reach yet screaming for attention?

He closed his eyes. Opened the front door and walked down the hallway to the kitchen. Opened *that* door. Heard, then saw, the dogs. Calmed them and had them taken away.

He walked to the centre of the immaculate kitchen and looked around. Moved himself outside and looked in again through the window.

The closed doors. The dogs. The locked window.

He'd seen the flaw in the suicide scene.

Hibberd's kitchen matched George's dissection room for cleanliness and order. He'd produced a neatly typed and formatted suicide note and aligned it with the corner of the table. He'd even folded the cleaning cloth and hung it over the tap.

But if they'd arrived a couple of minutes later, Hibberd would apparently have redecorated his kitchen with his own brains. Would he have cared? A man about to kill himself, worried over what mess he left behind?

Maybe not. But he cared about his dogs. He'd said they were like family. He wouldn't have blown his brains out in front of them. And he'd never have left them locked in with his corpse. They'd have got hungry. And they'd have turned to the only available food source. Ford had seen it happen before.

Smiling, he scribbled a few notes, then went down to the canteen to grab a sandwich and a bar of chocolate.

Munching his way through the fluffy, tasteless bread and watery tuna mayo, he consulted his notebook. In the rose garden, Lord Baverstock had said up to fourteen people apart from him had access to the Alverchalke gun safe. Ford was still convinced the murderer lived on the estate. And was equally convinced it wasn't Joe.

Olly appeared, out of breath, by his side. 'Hibberd's medical records came in just after you left. I've summarised them for you and added a couple of other pointers.'

He handed Ford a single sheet of paper.

'Thanks, Olly. Nice work. And even better timing.'

Ford scanned Olly's summary:

Medical records
– Army: No mention of mental health issues. Only injury prior to attack on machine-gun nest: fractured little finger on left hand.
– Civilian: No sleeping pills, anti-anxiety medication, antidepressants, therapy or referrals to anger-management courses.

Police
– No complaints of domestic abuse. No charges of public order offences or brawling in bars.

Veterans' charities
– No Joe or Joseph Hibberd has ever contacted them.

Financial
– Shops at Tesco using credit card. Clubcard account shows just 30 cans of Heineken and a bottle of Scotch in last five weeks' shopping.

It didn't look like Joe was self-medicating with alcohol. Ford suspected most members of his team – hell, the whole of Bourne Hill – drank more than Hibberd did.

Of course, Hibberd might be suffering from PTSD without seeking help. Ford just didn't believe he was. But if he challenged him over it, he could simply agree to the contents of Olly's report and claim he was battling it alone.

His phone rang.

'Front desk, sir. Joe Hibberd's brief has arrived.'

Ford scoffed the rest of his sandwich and half the chocolate. He stood and brushed the crumbs off his suit trousers, grabbed his file on Hibberd and went to collect Jools. On the way to the interview suite he suggested a tactic for probing Joe's claims about his PTSD.

He'd been expecting one of the duty solicitors – Gillian Kenney or another overtired, overworked, publicly funded lawyer who'd read the client's file two minutes before accompanying them into the interview. The sight of Jacob Rowbotham's cadaverous form surprised him. Today, Salisbury's leading criminal solicitor wore an immaculate pinstriped suit made of soft-looking fabric that absorbed light like a black hole.

The surprise didn't last long. *The faithful retainer's in trouble, and his aristocratic boss and former commander puts on a good show by sending his own lawyer.*

Time and date stated, and introductions made 'for the tape', Ford began.

'I read your letter, Joe.'

'Then why am I here? Open-and-shut case. I'm just sorry you got me before I went through with it.'

'Let's leave the letter for now. I want to ask you about the murders you say you committed.'

'I don't *say* I committed them,' Hibberd said, leaning forward. 'I *did* commit them.'

'Tell me how you killed Owen Long.'

'I found him up near the rearing field, making some sort of video, ranting about Lord Baverstock. Bloody class warrior. I went over to him with the dogs and told him he was trespassing.'

'And you had a rifle with you at this point?'

'Yeah. Always take something out with me. I had a .22. It's nothing much, just thought I'd get a rabbit for the pot like when you met me up there,' he said.

'And then?'

'He went bloody berserk, didn't he? Grabbed the rifle and started yelling in my face, swearing, calling me a lackey. I tried to hold him off 'cause I was genuinely in fear. Then bang!' Hibberd clapped his hands, making his lawyer jump. 'The muzzle jammed under his chin and he died on the spot.'

'Which gun did you use to kill Owen?' Jools asked.

'Like I said, the Remington .22 from Maj— Lord Baverstock's gun safe.'

'Why not use your own?'

'Like I told your mate here the first time we met, it's at Berret & Sartain. Needs the trigger looking at.'

'How long have they had it?'

'Since the twenty-eighth of April.'

Ford kept his face neutral. If Joe was telling the truth, and it would be easy enough to check, he was offering Ford concrete proof that he hadn't used his own gun. Owen had been shot on the twenty-ninth.

'Where's the rifle you used now?'

'Back in the gun safe up at the main house.'

Ford nodded. Clearly Hibberd had no idea they'd searched the manor house and seized the rifles.

'You didn't think to get rid of it?'

Hibberd shook his head. 'Not mine, is it?'

'And you weren't worried about potentially incriminating Lord Baverstock or a member of his family? Or another member of staff?'

Hibberd's eyes slid sideways then locked back on to Ford's. 'Like I said, I did it. And I confessed, too. No need to worry. Anyway, it doesn't prove anything if their fingerprints are on it, does it? It'd be weirder if they weren't, seeing as how it's their gun.'

Ford switched to the present tense to put Hibberd right into the centre of the scene the man claimed he was describing from memory. 'You've just shot Owen. He's lying dead at your feet. The dogs – what are they doing?'

'Molly's lying flat. Bess is a bit nervy. She's gone up to him and she's, you know, licking it.'

'The blood, you mean?'

'Yeah. I shooed her away and got her to lie down.'

Ford nodded, made a note. The detail about the blood was a nice touch. He looked up at Hibberd and smiled.

'How did you get him from there to the Ebble, Joe?'

'Back of the Land Rover, wrapped up in a tarp. I chucked him into a nice deep bit. If we hadn't had those heavy rains, he would've stayed where I put him till the eels and the crayfish ate everything but the bones. You'd never have found him in a thousand years.'

Ford nodded sympathetically. 'Just your hard luck.' He doodled a small tick on the pad in front of him. A sign for Jools to take over.

'Did you see Tommy at any point?' she asked.

'No. But he must have been hiding somewhere. The next day, he calls me up, right? He says he saw me kill Long and he wants fifty grand or he'll tell you lot.'

'Have you got that kind of money?'

Hibberd's eyes widened with what looked like genuine surprise. 'Do I look like the sort of bloke with fifty grand in savings?'

'I don't know. I try not to judge by appearances.'

'Well, I don't. The cottage is tied to the job. I've got a small army pension and what Lord Baverstock pays me. That's it.'

'So you decided to kill him.'

'That's right. I told him to meet me on Alverchalke land. Said we'd be guaranteed privacy. Bolter turned up expecting his big payday but I'd got myself nicely tucked under a camo net about a hundred yards away, in case he brought his brothers.'

'Describe what happened next.'

'He just stood there, bold as brass.' Hibberd ran his tongue over his lip. It looked like nerves to Ford. 'And I shot him.'

'What with?'

'Lord Baverstock's Parker-Hale.'

'Why didn't you use the .22 again?'

'No good for a long-range shot. And I didn't want to be any-where near Bolter.'

'Shot placement?' Jools asked. A flicker of doubt crossed Hibberd's face at her use of a military term. She smiled at him. 'I'm ex-army, too. MPs.'

'Huh. A monkey, eh?'

She shrugged. 'Somebody had to eat all the bananas.'

That won her a brief smile. 'Left ear.'

'Must have made a mess.'

He shook his head. 'Ballistic tip. Expanded in his head. No exit wound, no mess.'

'Did you clean that gun, too?'

'Yes.'

'Wouldn't it have helped your cause if you'd left your prints on both rifles?'

'I didn't think I *had* a cause, did I? Plus, I'm an old soldier. You always clean your weapons after use. I had it drilled into me by my gunnery instructors. I like to keep things clean and tidy. Once you learn that in the army, it stays with you for life.'

'How did you dispose of Tommy's body? The Ebble again?' Ford asked.

'No.'

'Why not?'

'I tried to be more rational about it.'

'Rational?'

'Yes. I reckoned putting two bodies in the same place doubled the risk one might float or something.'

'Yeah, I can see that,' Ford said casually, but made a note. 'Instead of using the Ebble again, you did what?'

'I cut him up and dumped the pieces down a badger sett.'

Ford retrieved Joe's suicide note from the folder in front of him. He made a show of reading it.

'That's odd. It says here you had some kind of blackout. But now you recall chopping him up. Which is it, Joe? You do remember or you don't remember?'

Hibberd rubbed the back of his neck. Glanced at his solicitor. Then looked back at Ford. 'I remember the first bit.'

'OK. How many?'

'What?'

'Sorry, Joe. I know it's a gruesome question, but how many pieces did you cut Tommy into?'

Hibberd blinked. His mouth opened and then closed again.

'Joe?' Ford asked again.

Having remained utterly immobile until now, Rowbotham leaned over and spoke to Hibberd behind his hand.

Hibberd nodded. 'I can't remember. That's what I meant in my letter. I was having some sort of flashback. Like you said, I basically blacked out, and when I came round I was at mine in the shower.'

Ford shook his head, gratified his ploy with the letter had worked. 'Sorry, Joe, I was paraphrasing. What you actually wrote was, "I don't know what happened except I came to beside his dismembered body." Clear it up for me,' he said with a smile. 'When you came out of this apparent blackout, were you beside the body or in the shower?'

'Body,' Joe muttered.

Ford nodded and made a note. 'Thanks for that, Joe. Now, you said you didn't want to double the risk that one of the men you murdered would float if you put them both into the water,' Ford said.

'That's right.'

'How did you stop Owen from floating, Joe?'

'What?'

'When the farmer found him, he was at the bottom.'

'Not following you.'

'Let me try again. Bodies do sink to begin with. But then they float. Owen didn't. How did you ensure he stayed down?'

'Like I said, I'm in this flashback. It's all a blur.'

Ford frowned, made a show of consulting his notebook. 'Sorry, Joe – that's what you said when you killed Tommy.'

Rowbotham leaned over again and offered Hibberd more murmured advice.

'It affects my memory. My PTSD. When Long went for my gun, it brought it all back.'

'So you're saying you had a blackout then, as well?'

'Yes.'

Jools leaned forward. Ford caught the movement and let her take over.

'You know, I met quite a few people in the army who had PTSD. Some after I left, too.'

'And?' Hibberd said, crossing his arms.

'I think you're lying. You see, real sufferers of PTSD, they do have memory problems. But they're the opposite of the ones you're describing,' she said. 'They can't help reliving the traumatic episode. Every single detail. The memories don't fade with time like normal ones do. They stay as fresh as if they were happening right then. I'm surprised you're saying it caused blackouts and memory lapses for fresher events.'

Ford knew that it was perfectly possible for PTSD to work like that. But as a non-sufferer, Joe might not. How would he react?

Joe looked at Rowbotham, who went through his murmuring routine a third time. He stared at the table as he listened, nodding.

Then he looked back at Jools. 'You are not a qualified person to pronounce on my medical history or the particular symptoms of my condition.'

Ford thought Rowbotham could have a career as a stage ventriloquist if he ever tired of the law. He didn't believe a word of what Joe had said. It was obvious the two of them had cooked up the PTSD line between them. Maybe at Martival's suggestion. Had they discussed how to use it in Hibberd's defence?

'Let's go through the sequence of events again,' he said. 'After shooting Owen Long dead in self-defence and dumping his body in the River Ebble, you murdered Tommy Bolter in cold blood while in some kind of trauma-induced fugue state. Then you chopped his body up into an unspecified number of pieces and dumped them in a badger sett. That about it?'

'Yes. As I said.'

'Where did you chop him up and what did you use to do it? Your place?'

'I can't remember, can I?'

'I thought you said you *could* remember.'

Joe looked panicky. His eyes flitted round the interview room as if he might find an answer scrawled on the grimy paintwork.

'Let me help you, Joe,' Ford said. 'Did you do it at the manor house? An outbuilding?'

'I can't remember!'

'Well, where then? It must have made a hell of a mess.'

Hibberd folded his arms. 'I. Can't. Remember.'

Ford decided on a change of direction.

'Did Tommy know you were in a relationship with Gwyneth Pearce?'

'Who told you that?'

'Gwyneth.'

Hibberd groaned and shook his head. 'I'm not in a *relationship* with her.'

'I saw you together at the inquest.'

Hibberd shook his head. 'I've been seeing her sister, Tess, if you must know. She's more my age. And my type. Sensible head on her shoulders. She's ill, though, so she asked me to go with Gwynnie to the inquest to look after her.'

'Why did Gwyneth tell me you and she were involved?'

'Why don't you ask her? She'll make up some lie, but do you want the truth?'

'Go on.'

'Gwynnie hates it if Tess has something she doesn't. She probably hoped word would get back to Tess to make her jealous. The girl's a fantasist.'

Inwardly questioning Gwyneth's reliability as a witness, but not his own conviction that Hibberd wasn't the killer, Ford smiled and closed his notebook. Jools did the same, following his lead.

Ford closed the interview, saying Hibberd would remain in custody and he would see him again 'before too long'.

He left Hibberd with Rowbotham.

CHAPTER THIRTY-FOUR

Hannah came to see Ford in his office immediately after the interview.

'I think you're right about Joe. I watched the interview on the monitor. He's lying.'

'I could tell he was lying, but I didn't hear him avoiding contractions in his speech. You said to watch for that as a possible tell.'

She pointed to a chair. 'May I?'

'Go ahead.'

'That is only one of a number of tells. He also switched between extremely detailed explanations for parts of his behaviour and then falling back on his claim of PTSD-induced amnesia.'

'Didn't ring true to you?'

'No. It did not. In fact I saw a man willing to agree to scenarios suggested by the interviewer, i.e. you, without being able to supply details that should have been burned into his cerebral cortex.'

'Like cutting a man up but not being able to say how, where or into how many pieces until I helped him out?'

She smiled. 'Yes, exactly.'

'What about when he mentioned dating Gwyneth's older sister? Was that a lie?'

Hannah looked away from him on the final word. A pink tinge had crept into her cheeks. Odd. He waited until she faced him again, though he noticed she was having trouble meeting his eye.

She shook her head. 'No. You were—' She blushed furiously. 'I mean, *he* was telling the truth. I'm sure of it. When you resume the interview, concentrate on the PTSD. Ask him about his symptoms. What are they? When did they start? How does he feel before, during and after an episode? What does he think triggered it?'

She continued speaking and Ford frantically scribbled notes. When she'd finished, he looked up. 'Thanks. That's about a million times more useful than Olly's half-baked amateur psychology.'

She nodded and got up to leave. 'More than anything else, Olly wants to impress you,' she said at the door. 'But he *is* an amateur. I am a professional.'

He watched her go. Something had spooked her about Hibberd. But Ford didn't have time to ponder the question. He stared at the copy of Hibberd's suicide note. It read more like preparation for a temporary insanity defence in court.

He called the team together and filled them in on his current thinking, and allocated tasks designed to prove Hibberd *wasn't* their man, from checking local CCTV to tracing any card payments he might have made at the relevant times.

Before she left for Trowbridge to examine Joe's Land Rover at HQ, Hannah confirmed that the CSIs had recovered every knife from Hibberd's cottage with a blade longer than three inches. And they'd found no traces of blood on any of them. Nor of bleach, which forensically aware killers often used to clean their weapons. No saws with the right type of teeth anywhere on the property. Nothing that would match the tool marks George had found on Tommy's skeleton.

Ford leaned back in his chair and stared at the ceiling. He had too many questions and not enough answers. A JJ Bolter-shaped shadow hanging over the investigation wasn't helping either. He got up and grabbed his suit jacket from the back of his chair.

Crossing Major Crimes, he called out to Jools, 'I'm going for a walk. I need to think. Call me if you need me. And can you track down Gwyneth Pearce's sister? Ask her to confirm Joe's story about them being in a relationship.'

As Ford walked through the Cathedral Close, a broad area of landscaped lawns swarming with tourists, his phone rang. Unknown caller.

'Who is this?'

'It's Connor Dowdell. You said if I remembered something helpful to call you, right?'

'*Do* you have something?'

'I might.'

Ford had no difficulty decoding the verbal signal. Dowdell had information. And he wanted something in exchange.

'And what *might* you remember, exactly?'

'Something about one of Tommy's *associates*.'

'Such as?'

'There's something I want to ask you first.'

'Go on.'

'I've got a court case coming up. I thought maybe you could put in a good word for me 'cause I helped you in a murder investigation.'

'Send me the details. I'll see what I can do. No promises, mind.'

'Fair play.'

'Tell me.'

'You know Gwynnie? I said she was one of Tommy's girls, didn't I? What do them sheikhs have?'

'A harem?'

'Yeah, that. Well, one of the girls Tommy had in his little *har-reem* was that posh bit who lives on the Alverchalke estate.'

270

Ford's eyebrows shot up. 'You mean Lucy Martival?'

'Likes a bit of rough, that's what I heard. Plus, Tommy weren't a bad-looking lad.'

'And when you say you "heard", who told you?'

'Tommy, of course! Who else? Girls used to love his curly hair. He told me she used to like pulling it when they were doing it.'

His mind processing this startling piece of intelligence at high speed, Ford thanked Dowdell and repeated his promise to look at the upcoming court case.

Could it be true? Could a high-born woman like Lucy Martival – correction, the *Honourable* Lucy Martival – see anything in a little scrote like Tommy Bolter? No. Never. Not in a million years. Tommy had been boasting. Fantasising. And then Ford's brain switched gears. *No? Never? A million years? Come on, Ford, think the unthinkable!*

He called Jools. 'I need to ask you about what women find sexy.'

'Okaay. Is this going to be weird?'

He smiled. 'Do you think Lucy Martival could fancy Tommy Bolter?'

'I don't know. Maybe.'

'Enough to shag him? Is it conceivable?'

'Anything's conceivable. Lady Chatterley had a thing for her gardener, didn't she? But Tommy Bolter? Even if Lucy did fancy a bit of rough, there's rough and then there's the Bolters.'

'OK, thanks, Jools. I'll let you get on with Gwyneth.'

◆ ◆ ◆

Ford got back to Bourne Hill and a virtually empty Major Crimes. Jools emerged from the kitchen with two mugs of coffee. She saw Ford.

'You want one, guv? Kettle's just boiled.'

'Please, Jools. Then bring it into my office, would you?'

'I spoke to Tess Pearce while you were out,' Jools said as she sat and gave Ford his coffee. 'She confirmed she's been going out with Joe Hibberd for three months. Looks like Gwyneth was telling porkies.'

'Actually, I think Gwyneth holds the key.'

'To what?'

He pushed his doubts aside. The news that he'd arrested Joe Hibberd would find its way back to JJ, then hopefully he'd relent in his threats to harm Sam. 'To bringing in Lord Baverstock. I want to arrest His bloody Lordship, but Sandy will have a fit if I don't have bulletproof grounds. Never mind the PCC, she'll have my arse in a sling all on her own.'

'How does Gwyneth fit in?'

'She was waiting for Tommy in his pickup when he witnessed Owen get shot,' Ford said. 'I pushed her about whether Tommy said he *recognised* or *knew* the killer. She insisted he said "knew". Originally, I thought it would have been Hibberd, because of their run-ins. Now I'm not so sure.'

'You think with the right handling, she could tell us more?' Jools asked.

'She said Tommy wouldn't tell her the killer's name. But what if he let some other detail slip? Something we could use to identify him?'

'You want us to ask her to come in?'

Ford shook his head. He'd already dismissed this option. 'I get the feeling Bourne Hill would make Gwyneth nervous. Can you track her down and find somewhere neutral to talk? And she's worried about JJ and Rye. Do what you can to reassure her that we'll keep her name out of it.'

With Jools off to talk to Gwyneth, Ford returned, reluctantly, to updating his policy book. A necessary piece of arse-covering every lead investigator and SIO had to contend with, but one that took up a huge amount of time he would have preferred to spend pursuing suspects.

He pulled up Tommy's record. And looked at the mugshot. Although Tommy didn't look his best in the photo – who did? – he had a twinkle in his eye and a crooked grin Ford supposed women could easily find attractive.

If Dowdell was telling the truth, the case had just taken on a new dimension. If.

He decided to solicit another female opinion.

Twenty minutes later, he crunched across the gravel in front of Alverchalke Manor, straightening his tie and buttoning his suit jacket.

Directed to the stables, Ford found Lucy in a paved courtyard, brushing the gleaming ebony flanks of the big horse he'd seen her with before. What was its name? Woodstock. That was it.

Above chocolate-brown jodhpurs and gleaming black riding boots, she wore a sleeveless top. She glanced up as his own boots scuffed in a patch of grit.

'Hello,' Ford said.

She looked up, but didn't stop grooming the stallion. 'Were you just checking me out, Inspector?'

'Just the horse,' he said with a smile.

She grinned back at him. 'Liar!'

'I wanted to ask you a few questions, if that's all right?'

She pulled the stallion's nose down to her face. 'We don't mind, do we, Woody?' she asked, maintaining long steady strokes with the brush.

'He's a magnificent animal,' Ford said, aiming to establish a rapport before hitting her with the big question.

'Thank you. We have this special bond, don't we?' she said as she nuzzled the horse's neck.

'Do you ever ride out towards Pentridge Down?'

'No. It's too far from here.'

'Ever go up there shooting?'

She looked back at the horse and resumed vigorously brushing its coat. 'I've never been one for shooting, Inspector.'

He thought back to his chat with the gun club secretary. He could remember Jim's words exactly. *They're not bad shots, either of them. Especially Lucy. She's won a few competitions in her time, as well.* Registered the lie.

'Of course, I understand. Only, we're looking for people who were out there on the day Owen Long was killed.'

She turned and flashed a crooked smile at him. 'It weren't me, guv!'

Time to move a step closer.

'Tell me, did you ever see Tommy Bolter on the estate?'

'Nope. But I know Joe had a couple of run-ins with him.'

And closer.

'How would you describe your relationship?'

'With Joe?'

'With Tommy.'

The brush caught a tangle in the horse's mane and made it whinny. She frowned. 'Sorry, darling, Mummy wasn't concentrating.' She continued, though speaking to the horse, not Ford. 'Well, he used to poach on our land, but I'd hardly call that a relationship.'

And close enough to smell a second lie . . .

'You weren't sleeping with him, then?'

She straightened and turned to face Ford.

'*What* did you say?' she demanded, hands on hips.

'Were you in a sexual relationship with Tommy Bolter?'

'My God, you've got a bloody nerve, haven't you?' she asked, raising her voice. 'Do my parents know you're here interrogating me like this?' Her face flushed and her chest heaved.

'You haven't answered my question,' Ford said.

She rubbed the back of her neck. 'No, and I'm not bloody going to, either.'

'You know, it's nothing to be ashamed of,' Ford said, committed to his line of questioning no matter what the blowback. 'Not nowadays. I certainly wouldn't judge you for sleeping with Bolter. I took a quick peek at his mugshots. Lovely curly hair!' He offered her a leer as he spoke. Surely that would push one or two of her buttons?

Her cheeks were blazing as she glared at him. 'Inspector, do I *look* like the sort of woman who'd shag a lowlife like Tommy?'

That was interesting. Under stress, she'd called him 'Tommy'. Not 'Bolter'. Had she just told him lie number two?

'Honestly, I don't know. What do those women look like?'

'Well, not like me, for a start,' she said, her breath still shallow and catching in her throat as she spoke. She spread her arms wide. 'I mean, he had a tattoo of a porn model, for God's sake!'

Ford took a couple of steps back. 'Sorry. My mistake. I'll let you get on with your grooming.'

He turned and walked back to the Discovery. Smiling. Yes. She *had* delivered a second lie. Because Tommy *did* have a tattoo of a nude woman. But on his chest. And the *Journal* had refused to publish it on grounds of taste. Only someone who'd seen him with his shirt off would have known about it. And Ford hardly thought Lucy had found him sunbathing on Alverchalke land.

What if Tommy had seen *Lucy* shoot Owen? Tommy tried to blackmail her – a person he definitely 'knew' – and she told her father, who then murdered Tommy? It worked. Better than that, it felt right. JJ and Rye were ready to kill to avenge the murder of their baby brother. Ford could quite imagine Lord Baverstock – a man who had willingly flown his first wife to her own death – doing the same to keep his daughter out of trouble.

He checked himself. Because if Tommy was a regular poacher on the Alverchalke estate, there was every chance he 'knew' Stephen, too. Who, as Ford had seen for himself, was a good enough marksman to bring down a deer with a clean shot through the heart.

He started the engine. 'Well, it was one of you,' he said to the empty cabin.

CHAPTER THIRTY-FIVE

Ford parked the Discovery and walked towards the station. JJ emerged from between two parked cars and strode across the tarmac towards him. Ford looked him in the eye. Had he been waiting? Patiently staking out the car park until Ford's blue Discovery reappeared? He wouldn't put it past him.

'What do you want, JJ?'

'Just came to tell you something. You better get a move on, because we're getting close to knowing who killed Tommy.'

'Really? Because we've arrested a suspect. So you can lay off the threats.'

'But it's not Joe Hibberd, is it, Ford? We both know that.'

Ford didn't want to think how JJ knew so much about the case. 'Do we?'

JJ smiled. An expression utterly devoid of good humour. 'Yeah, we do. And if we find the real killer before you do, they're going to regret the day they ever saw my little brother.'

Ford took a step closer to JJ. Squared his shoulders. They were about the same height, and though JJ was broader, Ford had bested him physically once already, outside The White Lion. Not to mention the standoff at the hacienda with Rye out cold between them. Maybe his confidence showed. JJ backed up a little.

'Don't take the law into your own hands,' Ford said. 'You'll regret it.'

JJ sneered. 'I've never regretted anything I've done in my entire life, Ford. I'm not about to start now.'

'Friendly warning, JJ. Your last,' Ford said, walking away.

'How's Sam?' JJ called after him. 'Still happy at Chequers?'

Ford strode on, fighting an impulse to turn back.

As soon as he walked into Major Crimes, Mick came over. 'Hannah's looking for you.'

Ford nodded and headed to Forensics, noting that Mick tended to avoid using Hannah's nickname.

'Hi, Wix,' he said when he arrived. 'You called?'

She frowned and shook her head. 'No, I didn't. I asked Mick to tell you I need to see you.'

Ford smiled. 'Figure of speech. What did you want to tell me?'

'We've analysed the prints from the rifles seized at Alverchalke. No prints match Joe's, which I'd expect because he said it was his habit to clean guns after using them. We did find prints and partials from at least two other users on each gun, probably family members. But these would have been left after Joe cleaned them. Therefore, also after the murders. The prints don't match each other or IDENT1.'

Ford sighed. 'Joe cleaned off the murderer's fingerprints along with his own. Everything after that is useless.'

Hannah nodded. 'We also found blood in the barrel of the .22,' Hannah said. 'It's a match to Owen Long's blood group and we've sent it off for DNA analysis. We should have the results back mid-morning tomorrow.'

'Brilliant. We'll have a chat about them later. Right now, I'm going back for round two with Hibberd.'

Ford didn't need anyone else for the second round of questioning. The evidence was mounting that it wasn't him, although he clearly knew the killer's identity.

Ford suspected the interview would be short. No lead-up questions this time. Straight into the middle of it. He glanced at Rowbotham, composed and immaculate. Then fixed Hibberd with a stare.

'When you decided to kill yourself, how did you plan to do it?'

Hibberd blinked twice, and wetted his lips with his tongue. The first proper chink in his armour. 'What?'

'Your shot placement. Head? Heart? You can't have been going to shoot yourself in the foot.'

'Head.'

'Really?'

Hibberd recovered. He leaned back. 'Why not? Guaranteed to work. Don't know if you've seen what a shotgun round does to a human head at point-blank range.'

'Actually, I have. Nasty business a couple of years back. One of the local farmers went into a deep depression when the bank wouldn't extend his overdraft. Poor sod blew his brains out in his barn.'

'Yeah, well, you know, then.'

'But that's the thing, Joe. The barn where this poor bloke took his own life? It looked like an abattoir. In the end, his widow burned it to the ground. Couldn't bear to be reminded of her husband's suicide, I suppose.'

'Inspector, do you have a question?' Rowbotham intoned gravely.

'Yes, Mr Rowbotham, I do. Joe, you told us in our first interview that' – he consulted his notes –. '"I like to keep things clean and tidy." Now, if we accept that the balance of your mind was disturbed, I can just about understand you leaving your pristine kitchen looking like the inside of a slaughterhouse. But what about your dogs?'

Hibberd's eyes flashed fear. 'What about them?'

'You told me on the first day we spoke that the girls were like family to you. "Better than kids," you said. Are you seriously telling me you planned, coolly, calmly and deliberately, to put a shotgun barrel into your mouth and pull the trigger while your children looked on?'

Hibberd's eyes were darting all over the place. 'I—'

'And then what? You've just unloaded a shotgun into the roof of your mouth. Your head has basically exploded. There's blood and whatnot all over the place. You've closed the front and back doors, and the door to the kitchen itself,' Ford said. 'You've locked the kitchen window. The dogs would have been terrified at first. But eventually they'd have got hungry. They would have started on what was left of you. Like Bess did when you murdered Owen. Do you remember? You said she licked the blood. Wouldn't you have sent them outside first?'

'I don't know, do I? Like I said, my PTSD affects my memory.'

'But not your ability to be rational about disposing of Tommy's body. You remember where you put it and that you cut it up, even if not in how many pieces.'

'It's unpredictable.'

'Is that what your doctors told you?'

'What doctors?'

'Whoever diagnosed your PTSD.'

'I . . . I never went to the MO about it.'

'What about after leaving the army? Did you go to see your GP? Or a psychotherapist? A charity?'

Hibberd closed down. His eyes dropped and his mouth drew into a thin line.

'It's quite acceptable to talk about PTSD these days. Were you ashamed?'

'No!'

'So why, then, Joe? Why didn't you go to the doctor about what is, by all accounts, a pretty terrible illness?'

Hibberd's breathing had become shallow. Sweat had broken out on his forehead and the bridge of his nose. 'I thought I'd be all right just working through it. Lord Baverstock's very understanding.'

Ford nodded. Time for a change of tack. One that would bring him closer to the endgame.

'He saved your life in Helmand, didn't he?'

'Yes.'

'It placed you in his debt.'

'You could put it that way. I wouldn't.'

'No? OK, but how about when he gave you a place to live and a secure job after you were fired for stealing in Scotland?'

Hibberd's face changed. His mouth tightened. His eyes flicked to the solicitor. Ford knew why. He'd been assuming that in the absence of a criminal record, that detail would have remained a secret.

'So, what if he did?'

'Joe, listen to me. It's clear to me you staged your suicide. I don't think you had any intention of going through with it,' Ford said. He leaned forward and clasped his hands together on the tabletop. 'It was just a piece of set dressing that allowed you to present your confession as a dying declaration. A man about to kill himself would have no reason to lie about being a murderer. But you're not a murderer, Joe, I can tell. I think you were covering for someone. Who was it? Lord Baverstock? The man who saved you twice over? Once from death, once from ruin? Or was it someone else in the family? Stephen, perhaps.' He paused for a couple of seconds. 'Or Lucy?'

Ford watched Hibberd's chest rise and fall. A drop of sweat rolled from the bridge of his nose to the tip, hung there for a couple of seconds, then fell on to the table. Hibberd didn't so much as twitch.

Finally, without taking his eyes off Ford, he uttered two words that Ford knew would be his last. 'No comment.'

Ford nodded. Hibberd wouldn't yield. He wouldn't incriminate Lord Baverstock or anyone else in the family. Here was a man who knew how to keep his mouth shut. Had Lord Baverstock ordered him to take the fall? Calling in the debt owed since Helmand? It seemed possible.

He closed his folder of notes. 'Joseph Hibberd, under caution, you have confessed to murdering Owen Long and Tommy Bolter. And to disposing of their bodies. But owing to your self-diagnosed PTSD, you can't remember certain details of either crime. Is that correct?'

Hibberd's head jerked up and down twice.

'For the recording, the suspect nodded, indicating acceptance of my summary. Interview suspended at 2.05 p.m.'

Ford remained in the smelly little room after Hibberd, Rowbotham and the uniform in silent attendance had left for the custody suite.

The suicidal farmer had been Ford's own invention. A composite. Becky Gaisford, the rural crimes officer, had told him that, nationally, farmers killed themselves at a rate of one a week. He doubted a single farming family in Wiltshire had been unaffected by suicide, one way or another.

But Joe wasn't suicidal. Nor a murderer. However, after their chats, Ford now thought he had a shrewd idea who was.

CHAPTER THIRTY-SIX

Hannah drove over to Trowbridge in her Mini, looking forward to spending some time with machines. She liked machines. They were logical and you didn't need to empathise with them, which she could do with people but found tiring. On arrival, she signed in, then made her way to the garage.

The vast concrete-floored space smelled of motor oil. The heaviness of it didn't bother her the way strong aftershave or perfume did. When Juno – her private nickname for Sandy, after a Roman goddess renowned for her strength, vigour and statuesque beauty – wore her Chanel N°5, it made conversation with the big boss difficult.

In a protective visor, navy boiler suit, leather gauntlets and steel-toed boots, Hannah brought the blades of a large pair of hydraulic cutters to bear on the load bay of Hibberd's Land Rover.

The motor-pool manager had introduced himself as Robbie Harris, but said that she should call him Tweed. She'd got it at once and felt inordinately pleased with herself. 'Because of Harris Tweed,' she'd said, to a nod from Robbie. She'd explained to him about her aversion to loud noise and he'd found her some ear defenders, which she'd gratefully settled over her ears.

Just as well, she thought, wincing at the muffled screech as the blades sliced through the steel as if it were cheese.

With two cuts through the side wall of the load bay, she placed the hissing cutters on the ground and signalled to Tweed for help. Together, they pulled on the metal flap, and with barely a protest it folded down like the side of a cardboard box.

Now she could get at the layer of dirt she'd seen when peering into the corners on her preliminary inspection. Kneeling, she brought her face closer to the channel in the pressed steel.

She pushed up her visor so she could look even closer, and there! She saw it. A dark patch in the dry, gritty earth. Something stuck to it caught the light.

Sliding the gauntlets off first, she fished out the magnifier from the boiler suit's pocket. What she saw made her smile. From the other pocket she fetched out an evidence bag and a pair of tweezers, picked up the hair and deposited it into the bag.

She scraped some of the stained earth into a debris pot and screwed the lid on tight.

Over the next two hours, she and Tweed reduced the Land Rover's rear half to so many bright-edged pieces of otherwise grimy steel. She found further traces of what, with ninety-five per cent certainty, she'd identified on sight as blood. But no more hairs.

It didn't matter. Ninety-five per cent was enough. Once she was back at her workstation at Bourne Hill, she'd spend some pleasurable time on her own, delivering the other five per cent.

CHAPTER THIRTY-SEVEN

The entire case against Hibberd rested on a single bullet fired from a gun not bearing his fingerprints, and his written confession. Ford suspected neither would last five minutes under the scrutiny of a skilful defence barrister. Not that he had any intention of letting things progress that far.

Everything else pointed away from Hibberd, from the staged suicide to the medically improbable PTSD. As far as Ford was concerned, Hibberd was off the hook for murder. But he knew who he'd caught on its sharp point instead. The gamekeeper was protecting his boss: the man who'd saved his life in Afghanistan. Or, just possibly, his daughter. Maybe Ford could yet forestall JJ's taking the law into his own hands.

Jools came into his office. Her eyes were bright.

'I spoke to Gwyneth Pearce this afternoon. She remembered something Tommy said after he witnessed Owen's murder. Tommy overheard the killer saying . . .' Jools consulted her notebook. 'Hold on, here it is. "This land's been in my family for a thousand years." You know what that means, don't you, guv? *My family*. It's His toffee-nosed Lordship himself. You were right!'

Ford nodded, offered her a smile and some well-earned praise. But once she'd gone, he returned to the snag he'd been worrying at like it was a shred of loose skin on the side of a nail. The 'Lucy Problem', he'd started calling it.

The lying about Tommy didn't help her case. But he could imagine plenty of upper-class women feeling acute embarrassment or shame at having enjoyed a sexual relationship with someone so far below them on the social scale. She'd lied about not liking shooting, too. Add the unresolved question – why two guns? – and the Lucy Problem got worse from there. And 'my family' could have been spoken by any of the Martivals.

On the plus side, Gwyneth's jogged memory – although as hearsay, virtually worthless in court – gave him reasonable grounds to arrest Lord Baverstock.

With him in custody, Ford would be free to conduct a second search of his house, his outbuildings, the whole bloody estate if he wanted to, including Lucy's quarters. They'd get his phone and his computer. They wouldn't even need Gwyneth's testimony. And they'd have his DNA. And Lucy's. Nothing to compare it with yet, but Hannah might return from HQ with good news.

Jan's search of Hibberd's place had come up with nothing. He hadn't even password-protected his computer. But that spurred Ford on, rather than depressing him, because it reinforced his feeling that Hibberd had nothing, or very little, to do with either murder. Jan had also confirmed with Berret & Sartain that Joe had taken in his .22 on the twenty-eighth.

He wrote 'The Lucy Problem' at the top of a sheet of paper, and tapped the pencil against his front teeth. He tried to bring the problem into sharp focus.

He was ready to arrest Lord Baverstock. But now, Ford wondered whether Lucy had shot Owen, even if by accident. The trouble was, he didn't have a shred of evidence linking her to either death.

Well, an internal voice said, *why don't you go back over the case documents and see if you've missed anything? And don't forget, Hannah's over at HQ taking Hibberd's Land Rover to pieces. Maybe she'll come up with something.*

He had other priorities, though, and one of these needed sorting. He straightened his tie and went to see Sandy.

'You're a star,' she said, smelling the coffee in front of her. 'That's not the usual muck.'

'It's from CID's secret stash,' he said, taking the chair facing her across her paper-strewn desk. He pointed at the documents slithering every which way. 'Having fun?'

She glared at him over the rim of the coffee mug. 'It's lucky you just pinched a decent cup of coffee for me, DI Ford, or I would have torn you a new one for that little question. But to answer it honestly, no, I am not having fun. Having fun would be enduring a root canal without anaesthetic. Having fun would be . . . would be . . .'

'A romantic dinner with Martin Peterson?'

Her eyes flashed. 'Let's not get carried away! What did you bring me?'

'A suspect. You're not going to like it, but I do have strong and compelling grounds for suspicion. Plus a ton of high-quality circumstantial evidence we can build on once we start the search.'

'Why do I get the feeling I know who it is?'

'Because you haven't lost your razor-sharp copper's instinct for a wrong 'un?'

She shook her head. 'Flattery will get you nowhere. Plus I leave all that gut-feel bullshit to you. I don't know how you do it, but it works.'

Ford looked at Sandy calmly.

'It's Lord Baverstock, isn't it?' she asked at last.

'It is.'

'Jesus, Henry! You do like to go after the rich and powerful, don't you? I thought his gamekeeper wrote out his confession in a suicide note?'

'He did. But it's so flimsy you could poke holes in it with a feather. I think he's protecting someone, probably his boss.' *No need to mention Lucy. Not yet.* 'Remember, this is the man who saved his life. That's a big debt to carry.'

Sandy sighed. 'How do you want to handle the arrest?'

'I believe he committed murder with a firearm. He's got access to an arsenal of weapons. He's ex-army, and from an infantry regiment, which means he's used to fighting. On the fight-or-flight matrix, he scores maximum on likelihood to fight,' Ford said. 'It has to be a firearms arrest.'

'Agreed.'

'This is a full-fat firearms deployment. No softly-softly to catch this monkey. We take him at home: contain and call-out. It's a big house. We'll need a dozen AFOs, attack-dog handler, negotiator, the works. Plus we've only got Joe's word the guns were all locked up in the stable block.'

'Fine. Write up the risk assessment and get it in your policy book. But in principle, that's agreed. I'll be gold commander and I'll talk to HQ and the firearms guys. It'll be Gordon again as tactical firearms commander.'

'Thanks.'

'Anything else?'

'I want you to help set up the arrest. Do a bit of honest police work for a change instead of playing with spreadsheets.'

Her mouth dropped open. 'You cheeky sod! Right, come on, then. Brief me.'

'I rubbed him up the wrong way when we first met. And when I went out to see him last time, I pissed him off further.'

'So?'

'So, we use it. Call him and lay it on thick about how disappointed you were in my actions. Say we've got compelling evidence beyond the suicide note that points to Joe's guilt in both murders,' Ford said. 'That will relax him and nudge him into dropping his guard. Ask him if you can personally come to see him at home because you have some questions for him about Joe's background in the army. Say we suspect Joe has PTSD and we need to get a read on how seriously it affected him after the time Lord Baverstock saved his life.'

'Then instead of me, he gets the full "come out with your hands up" treatment. You're a devious man, did you know that, Henry?' she said, grinning.

'I like to say "creative". You're a detective superintendent. That plays to his sense of self-importance,' Ford said. 'Tell him he's got better insights into Joe's character than anyone else alive. He'll love the idea he's been handed an opportunity to weaken the prosecution case by fleshing out Joe's PTSD defence. And being the kind of man he is, I suspect he won't credit you with the smarts to see that's what he's doing.'

'Did I just call you devious?'

'Yes, ma'am.'

'Scratch that. It's not even close. You're the Machiavelli of Major Crimes.'

Ford grinned. 'Now there's a nickname I could get to like!'

'Last question. When?'

'I thought tomorrow. If he's around. Say ten a.m.'

'Agreed.' She rubbed her hands together. 'I'm getting quite excited now. I'll call him this evening.'

'Thanks.'

'Right. Get going. And let's hope we can achieve all this without shots being fired. The last thing I want to have to explain to the

PCC, the chief con and *News at* bloody *Ten* is how we created the Gunfight at the O.K. Corral in rural bloody Wiltshire.'

'Not good for the brand?'

She glared at him. 'Not even slightly.'

Back in his office, Ford started drawing up the risk assessment matrix on Lord Baverstock's arrest.

Finishing it after half an hour, he looked at the chewed end of his pencil. The Lucy Problem wouldn't leave him be.

◆ ◆ ◆

Ford looked up to see Sandy in his doorway. He checked the time reflexively – 7.03 p.m. – good to see the brass putting in the hours.

'Come in, boss. Take the weight off.'

She sat down and leaned towards his desk. 'Your plan needs tweaking. I just spoke to Baverstock. He's not at home. He's in London, staying at his club. Bigwood's. I arranged to meet him tomorrow afternoon at three to talk about Joe Hibberd's supposed PTSD.'

'Right. Actually, that works,' Ford said, running through a couple of scenarios in his head. 'We've got two more options for the arrest. One, we could plot up outside the club with a couple of Met AFOs and jump him when he comes out.'

'Huge potential risk to the public if he's got a firearm. I can't see him with a shotgun, but if he's ex-army he might have a nine mil,' she said. 'He may not be expecting to be picked up, but he's got to be on his guard. Plus we'd have to work with the Met and you know how leaky they are.'

'Or two, we do a hard stop on the route between London and home. Take him on a quiet bit of road.'

'Better. You could get him secure without a shootout in central London.'

'It's the less risky of the two,' Ford said. 'We get the Met to pick him up on ANPR on the M3, then we send a firearms commander plus four AFO units up to intercept him on the A303. Or the A30 if he decides to come via Stockbridge.'

'What do you want to do with Hibberd?'

'Keep him here until the arrest's out of the way. He's been charged with an indictable offence, so can you authorise another twelve hours?'

'Authorised. Next?'

'Nothing else.'

Hannah appeared in the doorway holding a folder. Five minutes later she'd briefed them on her findings from the Land Rover. Traces of blood whose type matched Tommy Bolter's. And a hair stuck to the blood, implying the blood was still wet when the hair was shed. DNA tests were being fast-tracked with results expected the following day.

Ford asked what kind of hair, hoping she'd say long and blonde. Her answer set him back a step.

'Short and brown.'

Ford felt the Lucy Problem wrap itself in another layer. Hannah explained the hair had its root attached and had also been fast-tracked.

Once under arrest, Lord Baverstock would have to provide a DNA sample. They'd compare it to the DNA from the hair, and then would that be that? Or would Ford find himself still tugging at one more loose end?

Hannah stood. 'I have to leave now. It's been an exhausting day and tomorrow's going to be busier. Good night.'

'Night, Hannah,' Ford and Sandy said in unison.

Sandy smiled once Hannah had gone.

'I like her,' she said.

'Me too.'

'I suggest you do the same as Wix,' Sandy said, getting to her feet. 'Get some sleep tonight. Like the lady said, tomorrow's going to be a big day.'

Ford did as he was told, deciding after a quick mental struggle not to reveal to Sandy his suspicions about Lucy Martival. Or his concerns about the Bolters.

◆　◆　◆

After Ford and Sam had cleared up from supper, Sam disappeared off to his room. Smiling at his son's thunderous ascent of the stairs, Ford opened a beer and took it through to the sitting room. He took a long pull and looked out at the lawn, where a pair of collared doves were waddling along together like an old married couple.

Sam reappeared, holding a length of lime-green climbing rope. He waggled it at Ford.

'Look. I got it off eBay. Five pounds. It's great for practising. Plus a carabiner.'

Ford's insides fluttered. He ignored the sensation and smiled. 'Go on then. Tie me a double figure-eight.'

Sam grinned. 'Too easy!'

Ford watched as Sam's slender fingers doubled, twisted and threaded the rope into a perfectly good knot.

'What next?' Sam asked.

'Bowline.'

This one took longer, but within twenty seconds, Sam flourished a decent bowline with a biggish loop. 'Another?'

Ford smiled. 'Right. Let's see how well you've been doing. Tie me a clove hitch.'

Sam furrowed his brow, but the knot he tied round the dull grey carabiner was on the money. Ford was impressed, though below the pride he felt welling fear.

'That's good, Sam. Really good. Keep it up.'

'I'm going to. Don't worry. How was your day?'

'Busy.'

'OK. That was brief,' Sam said with a frown.

'Sorry, mate. Can't say more. Hopefully tomorrow evening, though.' He took a deep breath and let it out quietly before speaking again. 'Listen, have you seen any more of Rye Bolter?'

Sam shook his head. 'No.' Then he grinned. 'I think that gorilla in a blue suit might have scared him away.'

'You saw him, did you?'

'You might want to send him on a covert surveillance course.'

'Cheeky.'

Sam shrugged. 'Yeah, yeah.'

He slumped into an armchair and began tying and untying a series of increasingly complex knots. Ford watched, telling himself, *It* will *be fine. He'll* be fine. *Don't worry about Sam. Focus on the case. Leave the trip till it's here.*

CHAPTER THIRTY-EIGHT

At 8.00 a.m. the next day, Ford called the Met's control room and introduced himself.

'We need to do a hard stop on a suspect. He'll be leaving Mayfair today. Can you get your traffic guys to put his index number on to ANPR and call me when he pops up?'

Then he called a police staff investigator who he knew had a fast motorbike. He sent her up to London to wait outside Bigwood's and watch for Lord Baverstock.

He also popped down to see Natalie Hewitt in R&P and told her she could pull Mark off his protection duties with Sam.

Ford looked at the pile of paperwork on his desk, and decided it could wait. He'd reread about half the documents and hadn't found anything he could take to Sandy that pointed to Lucy Martival.

There might be nothing concrete, but worrying at it overnight he'd become even more confident that she'd played a role – how big, he didn't know yet – in one or both of the men's deaths. Because if the gossips – and his gut – had it right, then Tommy absolutely 'knew' Owen's killer.

Gossip! He rang Connor Dowdell.

'When Tommy told you he was having sex with Lucy Martival, did he give you any details?'

Dowdell's voice took on an incredulous tone. 'What? Like positions and that?'

'More like anything personal about Lucy.' Ford thought back to the Martival family's fondness for silly nicknames. 'For example, did he have a pet name for her?'

The line went silent except for the noise of Dowdell breathing. 'Yeah. Yeah! He told me she wanted him to call her Loopy. Don't know why, though. Makes her sound like she's got a screw loose.'

And there it was. More proof that she'd been lying. How would Tommy Bolter know about Lucy's nickname unless they'd met?

Ford wanted to act. He needed to. JJ and Rye Bolter were circling Alverchalke, pack dogs closing in on a kill. Who knew who might get caught in the crossfire between these two murderous families? And he could feel the pressure from Sandy and every level above her, right up to the chief con. That was before the PPC, the press and all the many people on social media chipped in. All of whom felt they knew more about solving murders than someone as lowly as a mere DI.

He needed a break. The slow grind of police work had drawn him closer to the murderer, but he still hadn't located the killer clue that would smash the case open and allow him to penetrate its secrets.

Using the stairs to avoid meeting anyone who'd thrust even more paper into his hands, he reached the car park unseen. Ten minutes later he climbed out of the Discovery at Old Sarum, the Iron Age hill fort that had been the original site of the city.

Walking anticlockwise on the inner rampart, he let his thoughts drift. The sun warmed his back. The leaves of the beeches towering over him shifted in the breeze, adding a soft rattle to the sound of the wind through the higher branches. To his right, on a gently sloping field, a tractor trundled left to right, spraying the vivid green crop with a whitish haze of insecticide.

A small dog ran up to him and barked, twice, before being called back by its owner.

'Sorry,' she called.

Ford waved her apology away. 'No problem.' *Except for the bloody big one occupying my every waking hour: the Lucy Problem.*

He called the two victims to mind. *Come for a walk with me.* He placed Tommy on his left, Owen on his right. Walked with them companionably. They were both murdered on a landscape just like the one surrounding Old Sarum. Owen while trying to protect it; Tommy while trying to make a bit of money from it.

Neither man should have been there. But neither deserved to die at the hands of the people who owned it.

'If you had his Cloud footage, you'd see what I saw,' Tommy's voice intoned from somewhere inside Ford's head. *Yes, but I haven't, have I? That's the point. Because Owen was too bloody cautious with his password. And GoPro's lawyers make the CPS look like bloody ambulance-chasers.*

Mentally, he turned to Owen. The former vicar smiled at him, water dripping from his hairline. *'What do you know about me, Inspector?'*

Ford stopped. The two men faded. Because he'd had an idea. Owen's main PC password was complex, but it was anything but random. It said 'Gaia needs Owen', didn't it? So he used memorable phrases as clues to help him remember his password. Gaia represented what Ford thought of as 'new' Owen: the eco-warrior. But before that, he'd been a vicar. And Ruth, bless her, had given him a clue on the day he'd travelled up to Islington to deliver the death knock.

He cast his mind back to their conversation at Bourne Hill. What had she said about Owen's favourite book of the Bible? It related to the title of his blog.

The Circle of the Earth. It's a quote from . . . Dammit! The memory wouldn't hold still long enough for him to grab the next word. What was it? Jeremiah? Isaac?

He pulled out his phone. He tapped in the quote and then saw to his dismay that, despite his elevation above the city – with the spire, as always, visible in the centre – he had no signal.

'Shit!' he yelled, startling a couple of tourists, before turning and running back to the car park, narrowly avoiding tripping over a little dog gambolling in the lush grass.

Back at Bourne Hill he rushed up to Forensics, taking the stairs two at a time. He saw no sign of Hannah. He asked the nearest CSI where Owen's PC was, and she pointed to a desk shoved against a wall in one corner of the room.

Ford pulled up a chair and sat before the 'Gaia Engine'. He joggled the mouse. Hannah had left the GoPro software open on the screen. He left it where it was and opened a browser. Typed in his search query:

Circle of the Earth Bible book

And, oh Lord, thank you, there it was. The first result contained the clue he'd thought of on the windy crown of Old Sarum's ancient earthworks:

The Circle of the Earth: meaning and interpretation, Isaiah 40:22

He switched back to the GoPro software. He was about to type in the Bible reference when he stopped. That space after 'Isaiah' wouldn't work. It needed to be a symbol. Or deleted altogether. *Let's start there.*

297

Isaiah40:22

Some of your security details are incorrect.

He sighed. He realised he'd put all his faith in his intuition. Now he realised he was back in Wix's territory. Detail. Method. Focus.

Fine. He could do that. He tried again. *Let's try a hyphen.*

Isaiah-40:22

Some of your security details are incorrect.

OK. An em dash, then.

Isaiah—40:22

Some of your security details are incorrect. You have two more attempts.

Ford felt his patience slipping. He began to fear that he'd got ninety-nine per cent of the way there, but someone higher up the food chain had decided that was as far as he was going to get.

He couldn't waste any more attempts on guesses. What would Hannah do? *She'd think*, came the obvious answer. She'd be logical. She'd look for patterns. Ford closed his eyes. *Yes, Hannah, but which patterns?*

The answer, when it came to him, was obvious. The patterns visible in Owen's own actions. He'd separated the words in his main password with underscores. That would surely be it. He typed once more.

Holding his breath, he hit the 'Return' key. The screen blanked, then refreshed.

He sighed. And smiled. He was in.

Ford clicked the icon for Cloud storage. The screen displayed a list of alphabetically arranged folders. And, topping the list, he saw it:

Alverchalke

He opened the folder. It contained a single file.

Baverstock_Protest_OL_1

The file data confirmed that Owen had stopped recording the video at 11.53 a.m. on the day of his murder. Pulse racing, Ford opened the file, then clicked the white 'Play' triangle in the centre of the still image.

In the distance, across twelve miles of rolling countryside, the spire glowed white in the hazy sunshine. Owen, dressed in jeans and a crumpled maroon shirt, grey hair blown into a wild halo, addressed the camera. Where had he put the GoPro? On a stand? Clipped to a fence or a tree branch?

'Behind me, you see an ancient landscape, unchanged for millennia. The landowner is the Right Honourable Viscount Baverstock, known also as Lord Baverstock and, given that all men are equal before Gaia, Philip Martival. Owing to a toxic combination of greed, hubris and disdain, he plans to desecrate it by building one hundred and thirty houses.'

Owen turned away and swept his right arm in a half-circle.

'Philip Martival professes to care about the environment. But his actions speak much, much louder than his words. I urge you, who are watching this, to protest with me. Visit this beautiful part of the country. Camp. Bring your children. Sing. Pray. Together we can—'

A second voice intruded on the soundtrack. 'Hey! You there! What the bloody hell do you think you're doing?'

Ford had heard it before. With a grim smile, he nodded. He'd solved the Lucy Problem.

CHAPTER THIRTY-NINE

Ford leaned closer as Lucy Martival strode into shot. She wore an outfit typical of a certain class of rural dweller. Blue and white gingham shirt beneath a navy-blue sleeveless jumper. Tight-fitting moss-green trousers. Knee-high boots of tan suede interrupted by bands of polished brown leather.

Two black Labs trotted beside her. In her right hand she carried a rifle. She stopped a few feet away from Owen. A scowl transformed the face Ford had thought pretty into one harsh and unforgiving.

'Who the hell are you?' she demanded.

'My name is Owen Long.'

'You're not local, are you? Not with that accent.'

'I live in London. But my calling brought me here.'

She tossed her head. 'Oh, it did, did it? Well, *I'm* calling you to get the hell off this land.'

'I am offering a testament to Philip Martival's rapacity.' Owen spread his hands wide. 'He would destroy this beautiful—'

'What *Viscount Baverstock* does with his land is nothing to do with you. Now clear off!'

Ford watched, transfixed. He knew what was coming, but still hoped Owen would heed Lucy's warning and get the hell away. Instead he doubled down on his attack. 'I should have thought someone of his obvious wealth would have little need of such a tawdry moneymaking scheme as this.'

'Oh, would you? Not that it's any of your business, but appearances can be misleading. Anyway, this is private land. It's been in my family for a thousand years.'

There it was. The phrase Jools had somehow dragged out of Gwyneth Pearce. Further proof, if more were needed.

Lucy was still speaking. 'You must have ignored half a dozen signs to get here. You're trespassing!'

'We are *all* mere trespassers on this planet. I am serving a higher cause. No less than Gaia. To her, a thousand years is as the life of a mayfly.' Owen's voice had taken on a preaching quality, and Ford heard the cadences of the pulpit as the former vicar hit his stride.

Lucy snorted. 'Gaia? Now I get it. You're one of those bloody climate people, aren't you?'

Beside Lucy, the dogs were staring at Owen, breaking off only to cast glances up at their mistress. Ford heard their low growling.

'If you have children, or plan to, you'd do well to join me,' Owen said, raising his voice. 'Nurturing a new life while all around you it is being extinguished is a wasted existence.'

The dogs' growling intensified. Lucy worked the bolt on the rifle. The metal parts emitted a sharp *snick-snack*.

'I said, clear off,' Lucy said, in a low, threatening tone that Owen must surely have detected.

But still he stood his ground. 'Why? What are you going to do? Shoot me? I bear you no ill will.'

Jesus, the old boy had balls the size of grapefruit to keep answering back to a clearly angry landowner with a loaded gun.

'No? Well, that's just as well, isn't it? I'm going to tell you one last time. Get. Off. This. Land.'

With each of the final four words, Lucy prodded Owen in the sternum with the rifle's muzzle. Where any sane person would have backed away, hands out in surrender or supplication, Owen went forward. He grabbed the barrel and tried to wrench it from Lucy's grip. They scuffled, and Ford watched, mesmerised, as the rifle swung wildly from left to right, and jerked up and down as Owen and Lucy fought for control.

The dogs were barking properly now. Owen screamed as one sank its teeth into his left buttock.

The report as the rifle went off surprised Ford. Little more than the crack of a cheap firework. He rewound the video and slowed it down. He saw, in agonising detail, the final few seconds of Owen Long's life.

The rifle, swinging about between the two combatants, dropped by six inches as Lucy tried to pull it down and out of Owen's hands. Ford could see Lucy's right index finger on the trigger.

Owen yanked the gun upwards. The slow motion changed the sharp crack to a drawn-out boom as the .22 went off, then Owen's head snapped back and he toppled sideways, blood flowing from a neat black hole under his jaw.

Lucy stood, looking at him, eyes wide, her left hand clamped over her mouth.

Ford reset the playback to normal speed. The dogs were running in circles, barking, darting over to Owen's body then back again.

She turned and ran, crying 'Heel!' as she fled.

Ford wiped a hand across his lips and took a few deep breaths. The video spooled on, a still image accompanied by the rustle of wind blowing across the mic. Owen lay partially in shot, the edge of the screen cutting him off at the knees.

And then, supplying the final piece of the puzzle, Tommy strolled into shot and looked down at Owen.

'Silly old bugger!' he said with a hint of a smirk. Then he turned and ran, exiting from the left side of the screen.

Ford went to stop the video, then took his finger off the mouse, wanting more.

Sure enough, after five minutes, he heard the roar of a diesel engine. A familiar sage-green Land Rover raced up the field then lurched to a stop. Lucy jumped out, slamming the door to keep the dogs inside.

Ford rolled his neck to ease the tension that had built as he watched. Lucy squatted down and got her hands under Owen's armpits before dragging him to the vehicle and manoeuvring him up and into the load bay.

She closed the tailgate, then glanced straight at Ford with a frown. His pulse bumped in his throat and then he understood: she'd spotted the GoPro for the first time, and realised it was still filming.

She marched over until she filled the screen. Her right arm shot out, so close Ford could see the individual checks of her shirt. Then the screen went black. He asked one of the CSIs for a flash drive and copied the file over.

In Major Crimes, he called Jan and told her to bring the entire search team back from Alverchalke Manor. 'Tell them we've got everything we need. And be especially polite to Lady B,' he added. 'Apologise for causing any distress.'

Next he sent a group text to the team.

Get back to BH now. URGENT

Sandy looked up as he entered her office. She frowned.

'What's up?'

'Lucy Martival killed Owen. It's on video.'

Her eyes popped wide. 'What?'

'Owen's GoPro had an automatic upload to the Cloud. I cracked the password. I just watched the footage he shot at Alverchalke. We have to redo the arrest strategy.'

'Too bloody right. What's your take on Lucy?'

'Even if she killed Owen by accident, she won't want to spend the rest of her life in prison.'

'High flight risk, even if not a high fight risk?'

'Yup. Although, from a risk-assessment point of view, she also has access to weapons. And she's already killed once with a firearm.'

'I thought you impounded the family's guns?'

'The ones in the gun safe, yes. There could be others. In the house, outbuildings, stashed in a horse trough, who knows?'

'Good point. So, simultaneous on father and daughter?'

'Exactly. We take Lucy at home with a contain and call-out, and her father in a hard stop.'

'He told me he's leaving London at midday.'

Ford performed a quick calculation. 'He told you he's leaving his club at noon, right?'

Sandy nodded.

'Right. Say forty-five minutes from his club to the M3, then he leaves for the A303 around thirty minutes after that. Allowing fifteen minutes to select the best place for the stop, we could do it at 1.30 p.m.'

'Right, get going. I'll call Gordon and update him. We'll need a second firearms team.'

Ford played the video for the team in the sugar cube. They watched in silence, apart from a collective gasp at eleven minutes and seventeen seconds. Ford let the film play out until Lucy reached out towards them all and stopped the GoPro from recording.

He put Mick in with Sandy in the control centre, and Jan and Olly with the AFOs on the hard stop. Jools would accompany him to Alverchalke Manor on the Lucy arrest.

Over the next thirty minutes, Ford sent a covert team into action at Alverchalke Manor to establish that Lucy was at home. He called the Met control room again.

He felt excitement in the pit of his stomach – like playing live for the first time. But he also had every senior investigator's fear whenever firearms were involved. Guns meant bullets. And bullets meant the potential for an almighty screw-up. Best case, dead suspects. Worst case, dead members of the public.

Not on my watch.

Ford's phone rang: the head of the covert team at Alverchalke Manor.

'Confirmed sighting of Lucy Martival, sir. Indoors. She's in a downstairs room, working on a PC.'

Ford's phone rang again five minutes later. The investigator he'd sent to plot up outside Bigwood's told him Lord Baverstock had just come out of the club, visited a shop, then gone back inside.

The rest of the morning passed in a flurry of briefings. Firearms teams, additional CID and uniforms for the two arrests; the media team at Bourne Hill; even the PCC. How Martin Peterson had got wind of the arrests, Ford didn't want to think about.

'You're serious,' he said, when Ford told him the identity of the suspects.

'As I can be.'

Peterson puffed his cheeks out. 'All I can say is, I hope to God you're right, Ford. Because if you're not, the optics on this are going to be terrible. Absolutely bloody terrible.'

Ford stared at Peterson. How things looked to the outside world were about ninety-ninth on Ford's list of priorities.

'We have the media team for the *optics*,' he said in as calm a voice as he could manage. 'My main concern is preventing anyone being hurt. You know. For the *brand*.'

'Oh, yes, well, of course,' Peterson blustered. 'I understand that, of course I do.'

'Then we're on the same page.'

'And you really need all the firearms guys? Surely you have all the family's guns now?'

Sighing, Ford repeated the point he'd made earlier to Sandy about there being the possibility of further, concealed weapons.

Peterson nodded. 'Yes, yes, I see. What can I do to be helpful? Shall I call Lady Baverstock and tell her and Stephen to leave the house – you know, give your firearms guys a clear line of fire?'

'Absolutely not! No!' Ford took a calming breath. 'The best thing you can do is' – a phrase of Peterson's that Sandy had mimicked earlier came to him – 'maintain an overwatch role here at Bourne Hill.'

Peterson nodded enthusiastically. 'I'll go and speak to Sandy.' With that, he hurried off.

Two hours later, Ford's phone rang in the middle of a briefing with Sandy and the senior firearms officers.

'Sir, it's Met traffic control. Just picked up your suspect vehicle, black Bentley Continental GT, index number Charlie One Seven Seven Papa Romeo Foxtrot. M3 westbound, Junction One.'

Ford checked his watch: 12.45 p.m. – right on schedule. Traffic permitting, Lord Baverstock would be leaving the motorway on the A303 at 1.15 p.m.

He called Jan to update her. Yes, she was qualified as a POLSA, but she was also an experienced DS and had taken part in plenty of dynamic arrests. She was his link to the team on Baverstock.

Ten minutes later, at the wheel of the Discovery, he waited for the firearms team to climb into their unmarked BMW X5 SUVs.

Behind him, the other members of the arrest teams sat in pool cars, all in anonymous shades of grey, blue and silver, plus marked Skodas and a couple of transit vans.

With a roaring of a dozen or more high-performance engines, the convoy peeled out from Bourne Hill car park, headed north towards Stockbridge and west towards Alverchalke Manor.

CHAPTER FORTY

Gordon Richen had designated colours to each side of the house to avoid confusion regarding different directions. Nobody wanted to be running right instead of left. And colours were easier to remember than compass points in a 'kinetic' situation.

Ford watched him give orders in crisp language shorn of all ornamentation: 'Cover the four sides: yellow, blue, red, white. Radio when you're in position and eyes on. Go.'

In crouching runs, black rifles held diagonally across their bodies, the AFOs took up positions around the perimeter of Alverchalke Manor, their dun-coloured rural camouflage blending into the background vegetation of shrubs and trees.

Minutes later, Richen's radio crackled into life.

'Yellow team. Eyes on.'

'Red. Eyes on.'

'White. Eyes on.'

'Blue. Eyes on.'

Richen lowered his binoculars and turned to Ford. 'We're on. I've got the other four covering the access road to the south and the main drive. If she rabbits, they'll go for the tyres. Failing that, we've got roadblocks set up at the gates. It could get messy, though.'

'Let's hope it doesn't get that far, then.'

'Copy that.'

Ford walked over to the firearms team's dog handler. Shorter than Ford by six inches, what he lacked in height he made up for in bulk. Muscle, mostly, though his flak jacket looked snug around his midriff.

A large, mostly black German shepherd stood erect at the other end of a short length of thick navy webbing. It quivered with excitement, drool spotting the dry earth beneath its jaws.

As Ford approached, the dog turned its head and growled deep in its throat.

'Quiet, Kessler!' its handler said sharply.

The dog stared malevolently at Ford, but the growling ceased.

'Morning, sir,' the handler said.

'Morning, Johnno. Been a while.'

Johnno smiled. 'That business over in Swindon, wasn't it?'

'Yeah. New dog?' he said, nodding at the slavering beast by Johnno's side.

'Sheba retired. Kessler's a right bastard.'

'In a good way?'

Johnno grinned. 'For us, yes. Not for the bad guys.'

Ford had seen Johnno's previous charge earn her role as a firearms attack dog. Three men tooled up with sawn-offs had attempted to knock over a cash transport van. Two dropped their weapons, the third made a run for it. He got ten yards, thirty stitches and fifteen years.

'Sir, we're ready to go,' Richen said from behind him. 'If you wouldn't mind, I'll take over from here. Could you wait by your car, please?'

Ford nodded and returned to his Discovery. Opening the driver's door, he took up position behind it, a hand over his eyes to shade them from the sun.

Richen marched to a position fifty feet from the grand front door of the manor house. He held a pistol in his right hand and a loudhailer in his left, which he now brought up to his mouth.

'Lucy Martival! This is the police. Come to the front door and exit the building with your hands on your head. Follow instructions.'

Ford stared at the front door. Although the grounds immediately surrounding the house were crawling with police, all he could hear was a solitary blackbird warbling its fast-beating heart out.

Richen tried again. 'Lucy Martival! Armed police! Come to the front door with your hands on your head. Armed police!'

◆ ◆ ◆

Jan was sitting beside a male AFO in a BMW 5 Series. All four teams had plotted up in a lay-by just east of the Junction 3 slip road on the M3. The car reeked of the guy's aftershave. She'd already sneezed twice and had to explain it away as hay fever.

The tactical firearms commander – Zulu Control – had parked on the flyover directly above the motorway. He was monitoring the traffic below, ready to give the signal when the black Bentley passed underneath.

Beside Jan, the black-clad AFO flexed his gloved hands on the steering wheel. Looking at his stubbled cheeks and shaved head, she wondered whether they issued all new members of the firearms teams with a cut-out-and-keep guide to male grooming. In all her years of service, she'd never seen anyone deviate from 'the look'.

He turned to her and caught her staring.

'OK?' he asked.

'Yup.'

Nine minutes later, the radio crackled. 'Zulu commander, all units. Target just passed us. Go!'

Jan gripped the armrest as the driver put his foot down. With a screech from the rear tyres, the car leaped forward. She glimpsed the speedometer as they joined the traffic. They were already doing eighty.

Twenty minutes later, as they were nearing the exit for the A303 and Salisbury, the radio buzzed into life again. She took her eyes off the rear end of Lord Baverstock's black Bentley to glance at the screen.

'Zulu Control, all units. Target is indicating left, left, left, confirm.'

'One.'

'Two.'

'Three.'

'Zulu Four.'

Jan held tight as the unmarked silver BMW swung off the motorway behind the Bentley. She glanced sideways into the door mirror. She saw the other three cars in tight formation, plus the commander's.

'What do you think?' Jan asked the driver.

'Skip said he wants to take him on the A303, about five miles further on. If he takes the A30 and heads for Stockbridge, so much the better: it's a quieter road.'

She nodded. It made sense. They needed four cars for the hard stop and one to hang back and set its flashers going, to hold up the traffic till they'd completed the arrest. The fewer cars driven by the general public in the vicinity, the lower the risk of something going wrong.

◆　◆　◆

Lord Baverstock enjoyed driving. The Bentley had been an extravagance when he'd bought her, but that was fifteen years ago and the old girl had more than done her duty. He let the softly padded leather seat cosset him as he headed back to Alverchalke.

He hummed along to the opera he'd been listening to obsessively for the last week or so, smiling as the soprano created the most unimaginably beautiful sounds. How could a human voice do that? The aria reached its crescendo, and Lord Baverstock felt the pricking of a tear at the unearthly sound.

He remembered he wanted to ask Coco if she'd managed to get the opera tickets he wanted, and glanced at the touchscreen. He frowned. No signal. Not even one bar! The mobile company called it – with irritating flippancy, he thought – the 'Wiltshire Banana'. A broad, sweeping crescent where mobile reception was as patchy as the food at his club.

He yawned. Meeting lawyers, as he had been doing for much of the previous couple of days, always left him tired and bad-tempered. Seized with a need for a coffee, he indicated left for the services.

◆ ◆ ◆

Jan prepared herself for the action just minutes away. Then, in an instant, the plan changed.

'Zulu commander, all units. He's signalling left, left, left for the services. Do not let him enter! Go now. Go, go!'

Jan's pulse accelerated, though not as hard as the car, which lurched forward as the other cars raced up. One overtook; one moved in on the Bentley's right side.

In perfect synchrony, the three high-performance cars slowed from sixty to fifty, forty, thirty, then twenty. They boxed in the Bentley, forcing Lord Baverstock to match their speed or hit the car in front.

Ten.

Five.

Stop.

At the last minute, the fourth pursuit car shot up on the inside of the Bentley and stopped so close the passenger door couldn't open. Blue smoke from the screeching tyres drifted past them.

Barely had the BMW's wheels stopped turning than the two AFOs in the back seat were out of the car. They raced forward, one to the left and one to the right. Up went their rifles. Aimed straight in at Lord Baverstock. She could see pistols and rifles aimed from the stationary cars to left and right.

Jan watched the AFOs yell their commands in through the glass. She found she could lip-read quite easily. 'Armed police! Exit the car now! Hands above your head!'

The AFO aiming in through the driver's-side window took a step back. Lord Baverstock, white-faced, emerged with his hands clasped on top of his head. A third officer darted in and yanked his hands behind his back before snapping on a pair of Quik-Cuffs.

As the AFOs frog-marched him to one of the pursuit cars, Lord Baverstock cast a look back at Jan. She saw a look of passivity on his face. No scowling or bared teeth, no rage distorting his features.

Ford sighed out a breath he'd been holding while Richen called Lucy Martival through the loudhailer. What the hell was she doing? Loading a rifle? Please God, not that. Richen brought the loudhailer to his lips for a third time.

Then a shout went up from the side of the house designated blue.

Ford didn't hear shots, so she'd not left by a side door and opened fire. He only had to wait a few more seconds for an answer.

With a clatter of hooves, Woodstock burst through the shrubs at the side of the house and galloped across the stone terrace straight towards Ford, Lucy clinging to the reins.

He just had time to take in the fact that she was riding bareback. With a hoarse yelp, Kessler lurched forward. Johnno took a long step to keep his balance, but as Kessler's weight snapped the leash tight, he came up on to his hind legs so he was taller than his handler. The dog's ragged barks echoed off the front of the house.

The stallion swerved and reared, front hooves pawing the air.

Ford watched, horrified, as Lucy flew up and back, arms windmilling. Screaming, she sailed through the air, a clear ten feet from the ground, before landing on the flagstones with a sickening thump.

She came to rest on her back with her arms flung wide and one leg bent under her. Ford thought he'd heard the sharp snap of a bone breaking. Richen spoke into his radio, standing down the AFOs.

Ford ran over to where Lucy lay and pressed two fingers into the soft flesh below her jaw.

'Get an ambulance!' he yelled.

Richen jerked his chin at Lucy. 'Why do they run, Ford? They must know it's hopeless.'

'I don't know. A woman like her, facing life behind bars? Losing her reputation, her friends, her status? I've seen people run for less.'

Richen sighed. 'Me too. Silly cow. I've got to go. See you back at Bourne Hill for the debrief?'

'Yeah, see you, Gordon. And thanks.'

After the ambulance had left, Ford called Sandy and filled her in.

Her parting words were reassuring. 'You did it by the book. The accident isn't on you. There'll have to be an enquiry but I'll make sure that's how my report reads.'

His phone rang. It was Jan.

'We just arrested him, guv. No shots fired. They're searching the car now. How did it go your end?'

Ford told her.

'Bloody hell, guv. I'm sorry. Are you all right?'

'I'm OK. Look, when you get him here, do a Route One.'

He knew she'd think his order odd. Normally, only violent prisoners were whisked straight from the Black Maria along the intake corridor and into a cell, bypassing the usual custody procedures until they were safely locked up.

'He's not violent, guv. If anything, he looked resigned to his fate.'

'I'm sure he is, but I want him where I can control who he talks to. I don't want him hearing the news about Lucy from anyone except me.'

'Got it. Anything else? I can see the van pulling in.'

'Are *you* all right, Jan?'

'Me? I'm fine. You know what these hard stops are like,' she said. 'Apart from nearly choking to death on testosterone and Aramis, I just sat in my seat like a good girl while the boys and their toys did what they do.'

'Funny. Got to go. Let me know when you're five minutes out.'

CHAPTER FORTY-ONE

The hospital consultant led Ford to a private room off a corridor.

'I'll leave you here, then,' he said. 'She took a nasty knock to the head and cracked a couple of ribs, and she broke her collarbone, but she's going to be fine. Not even a concussion. Luck of the devil, I'd say. We've given her light sedation, so don't expect her to make much sense.'

Ford closed the door behind him. Lucy lay hooked up to drips, monitors and an oxygen line clipped to her nostrils. The light was low, throwing the bright greens and reds of the digital monitoring devices into sharp relief. Ford smelled disinfectant.

Sitting at the bedside was Coco. She held her stepdaughter's left hand in hers, patting and stroking it rhythmically. She turned tear-streaked eyes towards Ford. They flared with hatred.

'What are you doing here?' she hissed.

'I came to see how she was doing.'

'Lucy is extremely poorly. The consultant said she could have died.'

'I'm very sorry.'

'So you should be! What on earth were you thinking, arriving with all those armed men? If you really felt you had to arrest her, you could have asked to her – oh, what do they say – *attend* the police station.'

Ford decided this wasn't the time to explain the finer points of his arrest strategy. He backed away. 'As soon as Lucy's well enough to leave hospital, I'll be arresting her for murder. In the meantime, I'll be stationing an officer outside her room.'

Coco shook her head. She frowned, then half-smiled. To Ford it seemed as though her features couldn't agree on what sort of expression would fit best.

'Sorry? Murder? Lucy hasn't killed anyone. And why do you need a guard outside? You don't think she's in danger, do you?'

Ford thought of JJ, and of Rye. Danger was *exactly* what he thought Lucy was in. 'Just a precaution.'

'And where is my husband? I've been trying to reach him but it just goes to voicemail.'

'We arrested Lord Baverstock this afternoon. Also on suspicion of murder.'

Her eyes widened until Ford saw white all the way round the irises. 'You're insane! You've made a terrible mistake. Bumble hasn't murdered anyone. And neither has Lucy.'

'Coco?'

Coco turned away from Ford and leaned close to Lucy.

'Oh, my darling, you're awake! I'm here, Lucy. I'm right here.'

'It's true. I—'

'No, darling. Don't try to speak. You're confused. They gave you some strong painkillers and a sedative. The consultant explained it to me. I'm sure—'

'Please,' Lucy murmured. Even at the reduced volume, her voice carried a sense of urgency that silenced her stepmother's pleading.

Coco got up from her chair and advanced on Ford. She closed the distance between them to a foot. No more.

'Anything she says to you in here won't be admissible in court, you know that. She's confused.'

'Just let me talk to her, please.'

'Just go,' Lucy said, her voice stronger now. 'I need to talk to him alone.'

Coco's lips twitched, and Ford could see her instinct to protect the injured young woman warring with her desire not to upset her. He would have done the same. But in the end, Lucy's force of personality wore her down. Coco turned on her heel and left, shooting Ford a glance of the purest venom as she closed the door behind her.

Ford took the chair and drew it closer to the bedside. He took out his phone, started the voice recorder, then placed it on the nightstand.

Wincing, Lucy rolled her head over so she could look at him.

'I'm sorry you hurt yourself,' Ford said.

'Silly of me to ride Woody without a saddle. He's far too headstrong. Then that dog . . .'

Ford looked into her eyes. He felt an upwelling of pity. If only she'd called the police when she'd shot Owen, instead of her father.

'I've seen Owen Long's video from the day you shot him,' he said quietly.

'I didn't mean to. It was an accident.'

'Then what happened?'

'I went and told Daddy. He said to leave everything to him. Then Tommy called me and said he wanted money.'

'What did you do then?'

'I told Daddy again. He was furious. But he said he'd deal with Tommy. I thought he was going to pay him off.'

'But he didn't, did he?'

'No,' she said, and a tear rolled from her left eye. 'He made me meet Tommy and he, he . . .' Ford held his breath. He needed her to complete the sentence. 'He shot him,' she finished.

'Then what?'

'He and Joe took him away. They put him in the badger sett.'

There it was! The leverage he needed to get to Lord Baverstock. Admissible or not – and that was one for the lawyers – she'd just confessed *and* implicated her father.

'Lucy, why did you run?'

'Tommy's brother called me.'

'Which one?'

'JJ. He said he knew the police were coming to arrest me and he was going to get to me first. He said they were going to punish me for Tommy. I thought it was them.'

It made sense to Ford, and once again he found himself facing the uncomfortable truth that someone was tipping off the Bolters.

'How did you ever meet Tommy?'

She smiled weakly. 'Not exactly my type, was he? We met in a club. He asked if I wanted to do a line with him. We got talking and I liked him. He was different. It just went from there.' Her eyes fluttered. 'I'm sorry. I'm so tired. I need to sleep.'

'Sleep,' Ford said. 'I'll come and see you again.'

He stepped out of the room and turned left, heading back towards the exit. And his heart stopped.

Filling the narrow space between the green-painted walls, JJ Bolter was striding towards him.

He stopped a pace away from Ford. His dark eyes were black.

'She down there, is she?' he asked.

'Turn around, JJ,' Ford said.

'Let me through, or you'll regret it.'

'I can't. I know you've got one of my team in your pocket, but this ends now. She's unconscious. When she comes to, I'm arresting her for murder.'

JJ shook his head. 'Murder's right. That's why I'm here. She's going to pay.'

'She's not the one you want. She didn't kill Tommy.'

'Then who did?'

'I can't tell you that.'

'Fuck you!' JJ said. He pushed Ford hard in the chest and went to move past him.

This time, Ford wasn't prepared to give JJ any slack. At the wake he'd been drowning in grief and vodka. Now he was bent on murder.

Ford staggered as if the shove had unbalanced him, then drove an elbow up into JJ's solar plexus. The bigger man's breath left him, in a convulsive gasp. As JJ doubled over, Ford pushed down hard on the back of his head, sending him sprawling to the floor. Ford straddled his prone form, and grabbed his wrists. He yanked them round and slapped on a pair of cuffs.

Two nurses came round the corner and saw them struggling.

'Hey! What are you doing?' one shouted.

'Police!' Ford yelled. 'Get security.'

They ran off. Ford turned back to JJ, who was writhing and bucking beneath him.

He bunched his right fist and pushed a knuckle into the pressure point inside the angle of JJ's jaw, on the right side.

'That's enough!' he barked.

Whether from the pain or the realisation he'd lost, JJ lay still. Ford climbed off him and stood. JJ managed to get himself to his feet, at which point Ford turned him to face the wall.

'Bastard!' JJ grunted, pushing back against Ford's restraining hands. 'I'll get you for this.'

'Shut up,' Ford said. 'You used your Get Out of Jail Free card at Tommy's wake. Double when Rye threatened my boy. I *ought* to arrest you for assaulting a police officer. But frankly, I've got better things to do with my time. So I'm going to have you escorted off the premises. I'll personally keep you informed of what happens as

far as Tommy's murder goes. But stay clear of me and my officers.'
He paused. 'And my family. Clear?'

JJ said nothing.

'I said, are we clear?' Ford shouted, just as a pair of burly security guards ran up to him.

'Fine,' JJ muttered. 'But you better make sure they get what's coming to them, Ford. Or me and Rye will.'

'I'll do my job,' Ford said. 'If you'll let me. How did you get up here?'

'Drove, didn't I?'

'Where's your car?'

'Lay-by near the entrance.'

Ford turned to the two security guards. 'Take him out to the main road. He won't be coming back.'

Ford called Bourne Hill, then stayed outside Lucy's door until two tall, broad-shouldered uniformed constables arrived.

Ford made his wishes known in plain, unvarnished language. 'Anyone comes to this door who isn't wearing an NHS badge, you turn them round. If they won't go, show them your taser and tell them again. If that doesn't work, you immobilise them, cuff them and call me. Use force as appropriate to restrain and/or subdue them.'

'What if they're family, sir?' Mark asked.

'No exceptions. No, wait. Lady Baverstock's OK. But get photo ID.'

◆ ◆ ◆

Later that day, Hannah brought Ford a raft of good news. The DNA results from the blood and hair found in Joe Hibberd's Land Rover had come back. The profile from the blood sample matched Tommy Bolter's, so they could place his remains inside the vehicle.

NDNAD had no match for the hair, but Ford was sure it would match Lord Baverstock's.

The lab had also confirmed that the blood in the barrel of the Remington .22 belonged to Owen.

According to Lucy, JJ had warned her the police were coming. That meant his source was very close to the investigation. Ford's suspicions, which had been quiet recently, flared up again.

The firearms team? No way an AFO would want to give a suspect the chance to arm themselves. Had Mick been lying to him all along? Or was it that little toad, Peterson? It would all have to wait. He had a murder suspect to interview.

CHAPTER FORTY-TWO

Ford stared at the man he now knew had murdered Tommy Bolter in cold blood. The lawyer, Rowbotham, looked composed and elegant in another understated but clearly expensive suit.

Lucy Martival had confirmed his suspicions, but Coco had been right: what her stepdaughter had told Ford while under sedation would never make it into court; his recording would be inadmissible.

A lawyer would simply argue she'd been under the influence of a powerful narcotic, possessing neither the capacity to consent to the interview nor the ability to distinguish fact from drug-induced fantasy.

He needed to find a way to get Philip Martival himself to admit it.

Ford nodded to Jools, who switched on the tape recorder.

'Philip Martival, you have been arrested on suspicion of murder,' Ford said, looking straight at him. 'You do not have to say anything but it may harm your defence if you do not mention when questioned something which you later rely on in court. Anything you do say may be given in evidence. Do you understand?'

Martival nodded.

'For the tape, please?' Ford said.

Martival lifted a hand and spoke behind it to his lawyer, who listened while keeping his gaze fixed on Ford. Rowbotham nodded.

'My client will be exercising the right of which you have just reminded him. He will not be saying anything.' A beat. 'At all.'

'For the tape, the suspect, Philip Martival, also known as Lord Baverstock, nodded,' Ford said, 'indicating that he understood the caution delivered to him.'

Ford had suspected Martival would pull precisely this trick. He'd rely on his solicitor to keep the interview as short as possible, preferring to take his chances in court with, no doubt, an even more expensive barrister to argue his case.

But Ford had one, devastating card in his hand. He knew Lucy had nearly died trying to evade arrest. And that she'd confessed in the hospital. Her father did not. Ford felt the moral weight of it as he tried to decide when and how to play it. He consulted his conscience, then his detective's brain.

He felt for the father sitting before him. But he also had a job to do: securing justice for the two murdered men. But which option would yield the confession he wanted? Playing the card now, or waiting? He decided to wait. There was plenty of other evidence he could lay before Martival.

'We found a human hair stuck to some blood in the load bay of Joe Hibberd's Land Rover,' he said. 'The blood belonged to Tommy Bolter. When we compare the DNA from the hair to the sample you provided on being booked in, I think they'll be a perfect match. Do you want to tell me how your hair got stuck to Tommy Bolter's blood?'

Martival folded his arms across his chest and stared at Ford.

'My client has asserted his right to silence, Detective Inspector,' Rowbotham said. 'I do not believe he intends to answer any of your questions. If you have any hard evidence against my client, I suggest you present it now or release him under investigation.'

Ford shook his head. 'There is other evidence that leads straight back to you, Philip. Wouldn't it be better to talk now and make a clean breast of it? Judges tend to look favourably on people who admit their wrongdoing.'

Martival's mouth stayed shut, his bloodless lips a rebuke to Ford.

'You have Joe Hibberd in custody, yes?' Rowbotham asked.

'Yes.'

'He has already confessed to both murders,' the lawyer said with a wintry smile.

Ford ignored him.

'Philip, have you got money worries? Is that why you applied for planning permission to develop your land? Lucy asked me if I was a banker the first time I came to see you. Is that what you were doing in London? Begging for money to keep your estate afloat?'

Ford saw instantly that he'd found his way through Martival's armour. The man's left eye twitched and his lips tightened still further. Ford could see he desperately wanted to rebut the charges or at least answer the insinuation Ford had just made.

'No comment.'

Ford nodded as if in sympathetic understanding. But with 'no comment', Martival had broken his vow of silence. Time to turn up the temperature.

'Owen Long was murdered while making a video on your land. In it, he poured scorn on your development plans and the greed he says lies behind them. We have that video.' He saw Martival's eyes widen fractionally. It was a satisfying moment. He'd caught the man out, wrongfooted him. 'You destroyed his GoPro. But you forgot about the Cloud. I didn't. His camera uploaded everything automatically. I watched your daughter, Lucy Martival, shoot Owen Long dead. Did she come to you for help? Did you dispose of the body?'

Martival's lips twitched.

Ford tried again. 'Did you shoot Tommy Bolter with your Parker-Hale Safari Deluxe rifle because he was blackmailing Lucy?'

Martival maintained his silence. Ford sighed. Rowbotham obviously took it as an indication that Ford had no further questions, because he began gathering his papers.

'Wait!' Ford said sharply.

Rowbotham stopped, eyebrows raised. 'We've established that my client has no intention of answering any of your questions.'

Ford laid his card down.

'I'm afraid I have some bad news for you, Philip,' he said, ignoring the lawyer. 'I went out with a team to arrest Lucy while you were driving home. She tried to escape on a horse and it threw her. She suffered a head injury and is currently in a private room at Salisbury District Hospital.'

The lawyer's mouth tightened and his eyes slid sideways to his client, then resumed their steady gaze at Ford. Jesus, the man was a cold one! And what of Martival? The man who had so far maintained the haughty air of someone far above the concerns of ordinary folk? How would he react?

While he waited for Martival to respond, Ford analysed his features, his muscle tone, his skin colour and his posture. He hid the shock well, but not completely. The pink drained from his cheeks. The tiny muscles around his eyes tightened, drawing back the skin and revealing more of the whites. A tremor passed across his face from lips to forehead, like wind rippling wheat in a field. His Adam's apple bobbed in his throat.

He leaned forward. 'Say again?' he croaked.

'Your daughter tried to evade arrest. She mounted a horse, the black one called Woodstock, I believe. It threw her and she landed awkwardly. We called an ambulance and she was taken directly to

A&E. She's not in any danger now, but I believe it was touch-and-go for a while.'

Martival gripped the edges of his chair, whitening his knuckles. Ford saw his chest heaving.

'Threw her, how?' he asked.

That was interesting. No demand to be taken to see her or horrified enquiries as to her injuries. Shock? Or a need to keep a lid on his emotions lest he reveal more than he ought to?

'The horse had no saddle, just a bridle. It reared up at a police dog. Lucy just fell off.'

'Lucy is an accomplished horsewoman,' Martival said, frowning. 'She's ridden for her country, goddammit! Has my wife been informed?'

'She's with Lucy now.' Ford thought of something that might prise open Martival's oyster shell of a conscience. A sharp little knife with a wicked edge. 'I've also assigned two men to guard her room.'

'Two men? What on earth for? Is she in some sort of danger?'

Ford readied his blade. 'She may be, I'm afraid.' Slid it home. 'The brothers of the man you shot are bent on revenge. They threatened Lucy's life.'

'You've got to have her moved then, Ford! Get her home where we can protect her!'

Ford withdrew his knife. It had done its job.

'You're admitting it, then?'

'What?' Martival sat back.

His lawyer leaned over and whispered in his ear. Ford watched the way Martival's eyes changed. Resignation replaced surprise. He slumped and exhaled slowly.

Ford recognised the signs. He'd seen them before. The moment when the weight of an interviewee's lies became too much and the flimsy structure collapsed in on itself.

'I just told you that the brothers of the man you shot are trying to hurt Lucy. You didn't deny you'd killed him.'

Philip sighed heavily and ran a hand over his face, from forehead to chin. Ford waited. Once a suspect had made the internal decision to confess, the interviewer's best weapon was silence.

'Do you know your Marcus Aurelius, Inspector?' he asked, finally.

'Can't say I do. We didn't study Latin at my school.'

'I memorised some of his words as a young officer. "Here is a rule to remember in future, when anything tempts you to feel bitter: not 'This is misfortune', but 'To bear this worthily is good fortune'."'

'Is that you telling me you're ready to confess?'

'Lucy told me she'd shot a man dead and had him in the back of Joe's Land Rover. I don't think she meant to kill him. Just to frighten him. She said it was an accident.'

'Did Joe know she had his vehicle?'

'No. He leaves the keys in the ignition. The children have always borrowed it for driving on the estate. He has access to other vehicles so it wasn't a problem for his work. They've always rather liked it. Call it "the Camel".'

'What happened next?' Ford asked.

'Well, I asked her who, obviously. And she said an out-of-towner making a nuisance of himself with a camera. I've looked him up, you know,' he said. 'One of those bloody environmentalists who live in the city but think they know all about the countryside. Self-appointed guardians of the land, as ignorant of rural life as I am of what they serve at fashionable Islington dinner parties.'

'That doesn't make him fair game, though, does it? It doesn't give you and your family the right to take the law into your own hands?'

Martival glared at him. 'You talk a lot about the law, Inspector. But there are things that run deeper than the law. Since the twelfth century, the Martival family has stewarded Alverchalke. *Stewarded*, do you hear? I am merely the latest in a long line of servants.'

'Servants,' Ford repeated, not believing what he was hearing.

'Yes, servants. And do you know whom I serve? I serve my family. I serve my forebears,' he said. 'I serve the generations to come. I serve the very many people who depend for their livelihoods on the estate I look after. And I do all this uncomplainingly while fools like Long pontificate in front of their *stupid* little video cameras about Gaia.'

Martival sat back, breathing heavily. Ford caught Rowbotham's disapproving glance at his client.

'You're forgetting something,' Ford said. 'In your mind, you were acting as a servant when you and your daughter committed murder. But then you practically ordered Joe Hibberd to take the blame. Hardly the act of a servant, was it?'

'Joe owed me.'

'Because of Helmand.'

Martival nodded. 'And afterwards. He struggled with life on civvy street. I'm sure you've met men like him. Straight out of one uniform and into another. I dare say those chaps pointing Heckler & Kochs at me in my car were ex-army.'

'Who dumped the body?'

'I did, with Joe's help.'

'Where are his things now? The GoPro, his phone, wallet?'

'Burned, ground into powder and buried. Along with Bolter's.'

'Did you do anything before you threw him in the Ebble?'

'Clever question. You're testing me. Yes. Before I dumped him in the water, I used a knife to puncture his lungs and vital organs to prevent the body floating.'

'Where is Owen's car? And Tommy's truck?'

'Old barn about five miles due west of the manor house. Corrugated iron roof. Double doors at the rear. The vehicles are inside, under tarpaulins.'

'What happened when Tommy Bolter made his blackmail threat?' Ford asked.

'Lucy came and told me. I had no choice but to kill him.'

'You didn't even consider paying him off?'

'No. I did not. He'd only come back for more. And as you seem to have surmised, I don't happen to have a great deal of spare cash at the moment.'

'What happened next?'

'Lucy drove out to the woods in her little BMW 4x4. Parked at the meeting place. Then that greedy little bastard arrived. Cocky as all get-out, strolling up to Lucy as if they were at a garden party. She should never have become' – Martival shuddered – '*intimate* with him. But that's Lucy. She's always been a wild one, from the moment she entered this world. Screamed her little lungs out.'

'And then?' Ford prompted.

Martival closed his eyes and pinched the bridge of his nose. 'As we agreed, she put the holdall on the ground between them. Told Bolter she'd padlocked it and gave him the combination. She stepped back out of harm's way and I shot him through his ear.'

'Did you get her to help you dispose of the body?'

'Only as far as getting it into the Land Rover. She returned to her BMW and I went to the woodshed I'd prepared. Joe helped me butcher the body – then, alone, I drove out to the badger sett and dumped him down. I told my deputy estate manager, chap called Cox, to fill it in. I said it was a risk to walkers.'

'Why not use the river again?' Ford asked, silently thanking Cox's country-sense for having led him to disobey his master's orders.

Martival opened his eyes. 'I didn't want to push my luck. Thought I'd lessen the risk of discovery by using different methods and locations. Might even have suggested two killers to you lot, eh?'

'You're being unusually candid, Philip, for which I thank you. Just to be perfectly clear, do you admit that you murdered Tommy Bolter and disposed both of his body and that of Owen Long?'

'I think I just said that, didn't I? But if you need it stating in plain language, yes, I do admit that. I would also like it to go on the record that neither my wife nor my son knew anything of what transpired between Lucy and me and Tommy Bolter and Owen Long,' he said, dragging a hand across his face. 'And now, if you don't mind, I should like to rest. I have just confessed to murder and learned that my daughter nearly died. I believe I'm within my rights to request a break.'

Ford checked his watch. 'Interview suspended at 4.21 p.m.' He nodded to Jools, who turned off the recorder.

'Inspector?' Martival said. 'Before you go?'

'Yes?'

'I did it to protect her, you know? She's my flesh and blood. My child. Do you have children of your own?'

'A son, yes.'

Martival nodded. 'Then you know. A father will do anything for his children. Even murder.'

Ford swallowed. Of course he did. Hadn't he threatened JJ with just that? 'And it doesn't bother you? That you murdered a man in cold blood?'

'The men of my family have served their country in war, all the way back to Waterloo and beyond. Some died in battle, but they did so with grace, fighting for an ideal in which they believed,' Martival said. 'Bolter and his kind embody the absolute opposite of that spirit. They steal, they poach, they brawl, they run dog fights and course hares: they give nothing and take everything.'

'Lucy didn't seem to think so.'

Martival sat back in his chair and his arms flopped down by his sides. He blinked rapidly three or four times.

Ford glanced at Jools. She was staring at him. Even Rowbotham, the master of the impassive stare, had registered his words with an expression of shock.

'I'm sorry,' Ford muttered. 'I shouldn't have said that.'

Then he stood and left the room.

Ford nodded towards his office. Jools followed him in, disapproval written all over her face. He knew why. The crack about Lucy was unworthy of a senior detective. Yet he'd been unable to hold it back in the face of Martival's arrogance.

'I want Hibberd charged with preventing a lawful burial and wasting police time,' he said. 'The CPS will throw out anything else so don't bother asking. And if you're thinking of saying anything about what just happened, don't.'

She nodded, and left him alone.

Ford spent the rest of the day completing his policy book, filing a separate report on Lucy Martival's injuries during arrest, and dozens of other necessary pieces of documentation. His last calls of the day were to JJ Bolter and Ruth Long, informing them he'd arrested the murderers of their loved ones. In JJ's case, he reiterated his warnings about interfering with the legal process.

◆ ◆ ◆

In his cell, Philip thought about his family. Not as he imagined Ford would think of his own family. Dad, mum, children. Couple of uncles and aunts, maybe a grandparent or two.

No. Philip was thinking of *the* family. The Martivals. A thousand years on the land gifted to an ancestor by William the Conqueror. There when the cathedral was just a plan and some shallow trenches in the ground. There as the new city grew up around it. There when wars were fought and invasions repulsed.

The family was more than any single member. So much more.

In that, if in nothing else, he could see how the Bolters and the Martivals obeyed a deeper code of justice than that pursued at all costs by Ford.

Philip had screwed up. He knew that. But he was insignificant compared to the Martival name. His confession would preserve the family, he hoped, from too much lip-licking interest. But either way, it would endure long after he had joined Long and Bolter in the ground. Another thousand years at least, God willing.

◆　◆　◆

JJ stared at his phone. So it was the lord of the manor who'd killed Tommy. Not the gamekeeper. Not the posh-totty daughter. Lord Baverstock. From what Ford had said, it was a cold-blooded execution. He'd get life, with hopefully a nice long tariff to go with it. Ford had asked if JJ was satisfied. If he'd pull back from his threat to deliver his own brand of justice.

JJ had said yes. JJ had lied. JJ could wait.

He called his source.

'What do you want? I thought we were done. I fed you all that intel about the case and we got the guy – and his daughter. I'm free and clear.'

'That's what you think. You're mine until I say you're not. From now on, my operation is free from police interference, understand? Any raids, any plans to put the squeeze on me, I want to know. In advance. Don't worry, this is a commercial arrangement. I'll keep paying you.'

'I can't! It's too risky!'

JJ smiled at the sound of panic in the copper's voice. 'No, no, no. *I'll* tell you what's too risky. Not doing what you're told. Because then I'd have to have a word with your boss. And I can just imagine how he'd take *that* little piece of news. One of his team, as bent as a nine-pound note?'

'Fine. But just the small stuff, OK? Drugs, nicking, even the dog fights I can help you with. But you get into anything serious and I can't.'

JJ smiled. He had him right where he wanted him. 'Let's see how we go, shall we, Mick?'

He ended the call.

CHAPTER FORTY-THREE

Home, Ford grabbed a beer from the fridge and yelled out for Sam. No reply. Recently, he'd taken to sitting in the driver's seat of the Jag watching climbing videos on YouTube.

Ford opened the door that led directly from the kitchen into the garage. He found Sam slumped in Izabella's worn red leather driver's seat, head down over his phone. Ford opened the passenger door and sat next to his son.

'Hello,' Sam said, freezing a man halfway through a roped descent.

'Hi. What yer watchin'?'

'Abseiling. It's so cool. I think we're going to be doing it.'

Ford nodded. 'It's fun. Scary, but fun. How was your day?'

'Fine. Out with Josh. How was *your* day?'

'I found a video in the Cloud that showed Lord Baverstock's daughter, Lucy, shooting Owen Long. Then we arrested Lord Baverstock and he confessed to murdering Tommy Bolter, because Tommy was blackmailing Lucy.'

Sam turned in his seat. 'Result!'

'Yeah. Although when we went out to Alverchalke Manor to arrest Lucy, she tried to escape on a horse. It threw her off and now she's in hospital.'

Sam's eyes widened. 'Is she going to be all right?'

Ford nodded. 'Once the doctors say she's well enough, I'll go up there and arrest her for Owen Long's murder.'

Ford found he didn't want to dwell on the day. There'd be an enquiry into Lucy's arrest and no doubt unpleasant questions from Professional Standards. He pushed the thought away. 'Fancy a road trip?'

◆ ◆ ◆

Izabella's straight six howling, and Sam grinning beside him, Ford smiled as they tore along the Coombe Road that ran south-west from Salisbury. After twenty minutes, they reached a viewpoint. Ford signalled, decelerated and pulled off the road into the gravel semicircle, bringing the car to a stop at the fence.

Ford stood side by side with Sam before an etched steel map of the surrounding countryside. He gestured at the rolling hills on the horizon. 'Not bad, is it?'

'It's cool. I like it. I'm going to take some photos. We're doing town and country in art.'

Ford watched his son snap away with his phone. He remembered days when he and Lou had walked down the narrow path from here, picnic blanket under Ford's arm, the infant Sam in his mother's.

His phone rang. It was Hannah.

'Hi, Wix,' he said, watching Sam lying on his belly to take more photos. 'What's up?'

'Now the case is closed and congratulations by the way would you like to come to dinner at mine because I think it would be nice.'

Ford blinked at this rush of words. He sensed how much it had cost Hannah to invite him to her house.

'That would be lovely. Just let me know when.'

'OK, I will. We'll have something to eat and some nice wine and we'll have a cocktail to start and then there's something I want to show you that I think you'll find interesting. Oh! No, I didn't mean—'

She hung up.

Ford frowned as he pocketed the phone. Didn't mean what? Didn't mean to say that? What could she have to show him that couldn't be done at work? The report about the risks of mountaineering on her PC flashed before his eyes.

Now he saw it. Maybe the document he'd seen on her PC really was for Sam. But there must be a second one. This was about Ford. And Lou. Oh Jesus, what was she doing, digging into the past like that? Was she going to show Sam, too?

Sam ran back to him, holding up his phone. 'What do you think? I used an unusual angle to make the landscape look like a model.'

Ford looked at the image on the screen. 'It's good. Great. Weird, but great.' He placed all thoughts of Hannah and her report into a folder and slammed it into a steel drawer. 'Listen, I'm going to take some proper time off. You want to go and buy some climbing gear next weekend?'

Sam's face lit up. 'You're serious?'

'Yes. What do you say? Find you a decent helmet, some boots, a rucksack, whatever you need.'

'That would be awesome. Thanks, Dad. I love you.'

Ford risked tousling Sam's curls. 'I love you, too, Sam. A lot.'

He saw Lou's smile on his son's lips. He thought she would have approved of him letting Sam go climbing. Despite his fear. Because Philip Martival was right.

A father would do anything for his children.

Anything.

ACKNOWLEDGMENTS

I want to thank *you* for buying this book. I hope you enjoyed it. As an author is only part of the team of people who make a book the best it can be, this is my chance to thank the people on *my* team.

For being my first readers, Sarah Hunt and Jo Maslen.

For sharing their knowledge and experience of The Job, former and current police officers Andy Booth, Ross Coombs, Jen Gibbons, Neil Lancaster, Sean Memory, Trevor Morgan, Olly Royston, Chris Saunby, Ty Tapper, Sarah Warner and Sam Yeo.

For sharing his knowledge of the gamekeeper's life and calendar, Tim Weston of the National Gamekeepers' Organisation.

For helping me stay reasonably close to medical reality as I devise gruesome ways of killing people, Martin Cook, Melissa Davies, Arvind Nagra and Katie Peace.

For sharing their insights into autistic spectrum disorder, Amanda J. Harrington; and childhood anxiety and resilience, Dr Hazel Harrison.

For lending Hannah's cat her name, Uta Frith, Emeritus Professor of Cognitive Development at UCL Institute of Cognitive Neuroscience.

For her advice on strategies for detecting lies, Professor Dawn Archer, Research and Knowledge Exchange Coordinator for Languages, Information and Communications, Manchester Metropolitan University.

For their patience, professionalism and friendship, the fabulous publishing team at Thomas & Mercer: Jack Butler, Gill Harvey, Russel McLean and Gemma Wain. For his fantastic, evocative cover, Dominic Forbes.

And for being a daily inspiration and source of love and laughter, and making it all worthwhile, my family: Jo, Rory and Jacob.

The responsibility for any and all mistakes in this book remains mine. I assure you, they were unintentional.

Andy Maslen, Salisbury, 2021

ABOUT THE AUTHOR

Photo © 2020 Kin Ho http://kinho.com/

Andy Maslen was born in Nottingham, England. After leaving university with a degree in psychology, he worked in business for thirty years as a copywriter. In his spare time, he plays blues guitar. He lives in Wiltshire.